HOUSE BY AN AFRICAN PATH

Evelyn Evans

BROADMAN PRESS
Nashville, Tennessee

Dedicated

to

My Fellow Missionaries
who
live by many paths
around the world

4263–16

ISBN: 0–8054–6316–x

Dewey Decimal Classification: F
Subject headings: MISSIONS / AFRICA, WEST / FICTION

Library of Congress Catalog Card Number: 78–67998
Printed in the United States of America

Contents

Acknowledgments

I want to express my gratitude to my husband, Orlynn, who read the early manuscripts and the later ones, and was an honest and discerning sounding board; to Virginia Wallace and Carolyn Stone who typed parts of the first manuscripts; to Jesse Fletcher who believes in humility for authors and made valuable suggestions when the book was in its beginning stages in 1974; and to Dr. Cornell Goerner who obtained Foreign Mission Board approval for publication.

Finally, I thank the missionary kids and missionaries of Liberia who unknowingly were living stories.

1

House in West Africa

Maggie stared into the dawn, not quite knowing where she was. Her mind seemed on a far-off adventure all its own as she tried to focus on the almost empty bedroom. The sound that had awakened her came again. What was it? Her eyes darted to the window and she leaped out of bed and went over there. Africa! The steamy air hit her.

The soft tinkling sound came again. Bells. Huh, bells from the back of the house. Maggie turned and gave a final puzzled look at the fruit which hung from a tree right at the bedroom window. It was yellow and bigger than a grapefruit, but what was it? The ringing of the bells came again before Maggie reached the living room window.

Lights began to come on in a building which she guessed was three hundred yards away. Nice building. Large. The first girls came down the stairway and out into the half light. They wore blue dresses and after a few minutes Maggie could tell that the dresses were identical. Uniforms. School uniforms. Maggie remembered a letter about Gbolupa which had mentioned blue uniforms, but seeing them was a surprise, after years of teaching students who wore all types of clothes in United States schools.

A loud bell way off bonged. Maggie walked through the dining area to the kitchen and looked toward the other side of the campus. Her brief tour in the darkness at 10 P.M. hadn't left many details in her mind. Maggie suddenly remembered the map one of the missionaries had sent. She went to the bedroom and found her purse among the suitcases.

The map showed dormitories, a clinic, a dining hall, and a classroom-administration building. So, the girls' dormitory was behind the house and the dining hall was at the far end of the campus, where the big bell continued to bong. Now what was in front of the house? Maggie rubbed her eyes again as the muddy water feeling clouded her thinking. Why couldn't she wake up? There was so much to see. Her excitement grew as she checked the view from the front windows.

Palm trees, green grass, big birds that walked on stilt-like legs on a path, and beyond that the bush. Beautiful. Maggie drew closer to the window. Wow! The tropical bush was dark and lush. It was a silhouette where a few trees rose like periscopes above the surface. And below steam rose from the vegetation. Maggie wiped her wet arm and thought of the houses she had seen dimly in the dark on the road last night—the tall houses. Now they would catch the breeze if there were any.

Missouri was greening when she left with dew in the morning, heat at noon, and toward sunset a brief, refreshing shower that promised the next day a shoot of corn would come through the moist, black soil.

But this atmosphere was like the Fourth of July right before a cloudburst—hot, close, and stifling. Maggie breathed deeply but wasn't refreshed. It was too humid!

Maggie tried to see into the bush but it was too far away and too closed. A bird could scarcely fly through the tiny spaces between shrubs and trees. Monkeys? There must be monkeys. What else? Maggie had heard the hooting of an owl several times in the night. Now other sounds of waking animals began to drift over the campus. Birds—mostly birds. What a world! A new, different sphere.

Maggie's attention was drawn to several women in long skirts who came down the footpath which was only fifty yards away. Where had they come from? Bananas! A whole stalk of bananas and on one woman's head? Good grief! How could she manage that? The woman's feet moved like they were wheels and her head and body seemed to glide along on a steady, level suspension system. The bananas didn't bounce or slip.

There was a kinky head sticking out of a tightly wrapped piece of material on the other woman's back. A baby. His head hung back almost at a right angle while his body and limbs were secured to his mother's back. On this woman's head was a huge basket, but Maggie couldn't guess what it held.

As the women passed, the large birds on the path flew away. In the air, the first rays of sun turned their white feathers to silver. Maggie watched, fascinated, as they glided gracefully over the tall bush.

Her eyes still held the spot where the birds had been when a voice from behind startled her. Maggie turned quickly to see her husband coming from the bedroom. "Did the bells wake you?" John Blake asked.

"Yes and no. I was awake half the night. Did you hear the birds?"

"No, I slept," John said, with a yawn.

"You would. You could sleep anywhere, anytime. My sheets were damp with perspiration and finally I got tired of turning over. The view is worth getting up to see, though. Feel the breeze that just came from nowhere?" Maggie said.

John raised his arms as the breeze passed and Maggie bubbled on. "The palm trees in the front yard were quiet. Now hear them clap in

appreciation for the cool! And did you see those purple blooming trees in the backyard?"

"No, but I noticed the papaya tree right by our window," John replied.

Maggie was glad that John had told her the name of the yellow fruit, but she was too preoccupied to say so. "OK, OK. Go look out back. The trees are something else," Maggie emphasized by giving John a push in their direction.

John yawned again as he walked to the back windows and tried to focus on the amazing trees. They were pretty, indeed. What huge, delicate blooms. Maybe like an apple tree in bloom. John came back to Maggie and put his arm around her waist. "Your new house—what do you think of it?"

"Wonderful, what I've seen of it, but I've been too busy this morning looking outside to think about the house. Everything is so lovely. . . ." Maggie paused, unable to put her feelings into words.

"It is pretty, isn't it?" John said, and pointed to the right. "I didn't see that house last night. Who lives there?"

Maggie searched the map that was still in her hands. There were three houses on that side of the road. The first one. Ah, there was a name. "The Wilsons. Yes, the Wilsons live there and the second mission house is the Pearces'."

Interest in the map faded as the sound of laughter reached the two new missionaries. They strained to see a group of boys and girls come onto the campus. As the group walked they pushed each other and laughed, but that was not what amazed Maggie. "I don't believe it. Look at those books!"

John, who was accustomed to seeing books enter the classroom in students' hands, couldn't for an instant even locate any books. "On their heads?" As the group passed John watched in amazement. "The books don't shake. They don't fall. They just glide along." John grinned, and kissed Maggie on the neck, as another idea came. "I bet our kids will be trying that by nighttime!"

"Probably." Maggie frowned at the thought of torn pages and bruised toes. "I wonder what else our kids will see and imitate?" Apprehension began to creep over Maggie as she realized there would be many other things that she had not expected. "They didn't tell us *everything* during orientation, did they?"

John was too intent on discovering how the students could carry a stack of books on their heads without using their hands to give attention to Maggie's question. "That's a good balance act. Their necks respond with sudden movements, but the books never jar."

Maggie thought about the women who had passed earlier. "You should have seen the headloads that the women carried. Do these people have flat heads?"

John laughed, certain that that was not the explanation. "Sure they do," he said in a kidding way. "It's a national trait."

"Quit being funny," Maggie said, with some heat. "Then they have carried things on their heads for years?"

"That sounds like a better answer. This is certainly a noisy place. Do people pass all day?" John asked.

"I don't know, but I heard several people during the night. One man had a flashlight. I guess he was the night watchman. Did you hear him?"

"No," John replied. "I was really out after all those hours on the plane."

Maggie nodded in an absentminded way and continued to marvel at the headloads, the flowers, grass, and palm trees. Every picture her eye took in was exciting. This was not quite the barren, solitary place that she had envisioned seventeen years earlier, when with fear and doubt she had responded to God's call to mission service.

Even the house was not what she expected. There was a living room, kitchen, pantry, and a dining area large enough for a mahogany Ping-Pong table, which had been made by the former occupant. It was too much. This wasn't quite like missionary biographies, where food was cooked over outdoor fires after snakes were shaken out of the cooking pots. No safari-type setting with wild animals and restless natives. Praise the Lord! Maggie decided to write to her parents today. They would be eager to know about their arrival and the modern, large house would reassure them.

Yes, the realities looked better than the fears of the years before. God in action. He held a million surprises and this one was pleasant. Africa! Impossible! But his call was no longer a goal, a dream. This was reality. Life was going to be interesting here.

John broke into Maggie's thoughts with, "Last night was a night to remember. The welcome. The familiar faces. I'm glad the Bakers were there. The ride here. The lightning bugs in Karen's room."

Maggie chuckled and added to the list. "And Mark's tiger-outside-my-window fears. The Bakers weren't the first to welcome us. It was the steam. The minute the plane door opened I felt damp and engulfed with thick air."

The rerun of last night's arrival was quickly ended as a wheelbarrow full of paint cans squeaked across the yard, not twenty feet from the house. The man behind it bent at the waist as if to speed the motion of his sneaker-clad feet. His baseball-sized muscles knotted up where sleeves should have been, but they had worn off his holey T-shirt, leaving ragged edges. The knee-length shorts he wore were splashed with many colors of dried paint. They looked like hand-me-downs, two sizes too large, for the excess at the waist was drawn into folds by a wide belt.

The painter stopped, went to the side of the wheelbarrow, and pushed the long ladder, which balanced on the cans, back onto the center of the load. Maggie took a second, closer look at him. Short. Skinny. What was that on his head? "Good grief. A red, white, and blue wool stocking hat! In this heat!"

John let out a low whistle. "You'd better believe it." He recovered quickly from the surprise and turned with a wide grin. "And do you know why he is wearing it?"

John paused for effect, and Maggie searched through fifteen years of marriage for what John would say next. She answered with sarcasm, "No, I can't guess."

But she did guess and when John said, "To cover his flat head," she turned with a I-knew-it look. John pretended he didn't notice and went on. "You never did appreciate jokes in the morning!"

"Sometimes not at night, either." Maggie flicked John's ear in a playful way. "So give up."

"So why does he have on a wool, stocking hat? Your turn."

Maggie tried. 'Well, huh, that looks like something a teenager would wear to get attention, but that man doesn't look young." Maggie looked for gray hair, but saw none. A moment's speculation showed her that she could not even estimate the man's age. "You know what?" she asked, as she turned toward John.

"No, but you're going to tell me," John answered with another grin, as he touched Maggie's hand. "You're clicking your fingernails like you always do when something important is brewing down deep."

"Well, I've been awake—half awake—for about an hour, I guess, and I have already seen at least a dozen things I don't understand and a lot of things I can't name. I'm confused."

"Sweetheart, you've been confused ever since I married you." John gave Maggie another squeeze and added. "Don't change. I like you that way!"

Maggie realized that John had not caught the chill that had suddenly come over her. She tried to explain. "But I never felt like this before—so bold and yet frightened. Expecting a lot, but with no idea where to begin. We have no experience at all with boarding schools. I wonder what we've gotten ourselves into!"

A baby's cry caught the missionaries' attention. The puzzles that John could not have solved at that time were left hanging. Maggie reluctantly left the window view to hurry to Sam.

"Hi, big boy. How do you like your new room? Lay down so I can change your diapers. Then I'll get you up to see your new home."

Where was the powder? Oh, yes, in the other bedroom. Maggie hollered down the hallway. "John, bring the diaper bag from our room."

Soon John came empty-handed. "I can't find it."

"That's our first job today—to make order out of those nine suitcases. Try the other bedroom," Maggie suggested.

In a few minutes John reappeared with a bag and a cheerful, "Found it." Then turning to Sam, who was wiggling out of Maggie's reach, he said. "Lie still."

When the job was completed, Sam bounced to his feet and held his arms out to his father, who quickly drew the small boy close. John whispered in Sam's ear and he giggled and rubbed his nose against John's cheek. John quieted him temporarily by saying, "Now I want to show you some big birds. They're right in our yard."

As Maggie carried the wet diapers to the bathroom, her thoughts quickly returned to last night's arrival. Yes, there was something special about last night. The arrival was an end to a dream and the beginning of a mission. The arrival had been a happy time and the joy had erased part of the lostness of being six thousand miles from home. The good-byes had been sad. Sad. Glad. Two sides of the same experience. How could Maggie feel so great and yet so miserable? She chuckled as a new thought came. The sad-glads—that's what she had. Quickly she decided it was better to concentrate on the glads.

Maggie went on down the hallway to the last bedroom where Karen and Mark still slept. Her footsteps woke Mark and while his eyes were only slits, he saw a small, gray lizard on the wall beside his bed. "There's my pet dragon!" he cried. "See, Mom, that's the lizard I saw last night. He's still here. I'm going to catch him."

Mark leaped to his feet and the lizard disappeared behind the curtain.

Karen, who was pretending to be asleep, shouted, "Don't catch that thing. He'll bite you, Dummy!"

Mark kidded. "So who's afraid? These lizards are small and cool. Cool, Man, cool." Mark pulled the curtain out and the lizard scurried to safety on the ceiling.

Maggie ruffled Mark's curly hair. "Come on kids. There are other things to see on your first day in Africa. Leave the pet dragon! Get dressed and let's go."

2
New Friends

Prince sat in the classroom. Why didn't that bell ring? It was past 1:30. It had to be. At least his stomach said so! Besides he had other things to do today. This morning there had been lights in the house next door. Maybe the new missionaries had come. Ring bell! Ring!

Prince had heard that the new missionaries had a boy. He liked that. He was tired of girls. There were girls everywhere. Besides his two sisters, all the missionaries on campus had girls. This boy had to be his size.

When the bell finally rang, Prince walked as rapidly as the rules allowed from the large classroom building. When his feet hit the last step, he picked up speed. He flew past the Baker's house, past the new family's house, and into his own door, where he slung his books on the table. He was about to dash out when his mother came across the yard from school. Why was she home so early? Teachers were supposed to wait after school. Prince knew what her first question would be and tried to think of a way to answer that would be true but not inconvenient.

"Do you have homework?"

Prince thought hard. No answer seemed good.

"Did you hear me, Prince?" his mother inquired in a louder voice. "Do you have homework?"

"Yes," seemed the only answer Prince could give. But then he had another thought. "But I have only small-small homework! I can do it later!"

Prince looked hopefully at his mother, but he knew the cause was lost when she turned with a hard look. He pleaded, "But, Ma, I wanted to go see the boy next door. He came, didn't he?"

"Yes, the principal said this morning that the Blakes came in late last night."

"Cool, Man, cool, and their boy is my size, isn't he?"

Mary Jones laughed and slapped her thigh. "You are excited, aren't you, Prince?" She went carefully through what the principal had said, but could remember no details about the children. "I don't know—you finish and you can go see."

Prince sat down at the table and combined the work he liked—eating Jallah rice—with the job his mother insisted on—homework. When the rice was gone, he began the spelling list with lightning speed. In eight minutes he had finished. He waited, though, until his mother was in the other room, and then sneaked toward the door. If he could only get out before she came back, there would be no check to see if the homework were neatly done.

Prince closed the door softly and tiptoed down the steps. Two steps off the porch he reached freedom and he fairly flew to his neighbor's carport.

Many people were gathered around to see what was in the crates that had set unopened for two weeks. Prince had watched when they had been delivered from the port. Mr. Baker said they had come by ship and every day as Prince passed he wondered what toys would be inside. Now he would find out for there was a tall man with a crowbar. The man's muscles bulged as he pried a supporting plank loose. Prince thought the man looked like a football player he had seen on TV when he lived in the United States, and suddenly he became shy and stepped behind a post of the carport.

Prince watched from his half-hidden position until a boy came from inside the house. Prince could hardly believe it—the boy was about as tall as he was, but slimmer. Prince's attention stayed on the boy until he shouted, "Here it is, Dad! It's in this crate. There's my new bike! Can you get it? I just want to touch it again!"

This was too much for Prince and he sprang forward. No one noticed him until he leaned over the crate and then Mr. Baker turned. "Hey, Prince, I didn't see you. Did you come to help?"

Prince nodded affirmatively as the man with the crowbar came to the boy's side. "OK, Son," he said. "We'll have to move these small boxes. You help carry them inside and then we can reach the bike."

The boy Prince's size grabbed a box and the man that had to be Mr. Blake pushed another box in Prince's direction. "Here, do you want this one?"

"Sure," Prince exclaimed, as he carefully carried the box up the three steps, through the kitchen, and into the living-dining room. There he saw a tall lady bending over a playpen, soothing a boy who was a lot smaller than Prince. "Sam, Sam," she said in a strained voice. "Who took you out of your playpen again? You'll get stepped on. You've got to stay put. Play with your new truck or something—please, please!"

Then the lady turned and noticed Prince and her face became sunny. "I'm Aunt Maggie. Who are you?"

Prince was caught off guard. "Ah, I'm—I'm Prince. Prince Jones." He backed toward the door and almost ran into the boy his size, who was carrying a box much too large.

Maggie pointed to the boy and made quick introductions. "That's Mark and the baby is Sam and outside somewhere is Uncle John and we have a girl—but you wouldn't be interested in girls!"

A sly grin crossed Prince's face, as Mark yelled. "I thought you were going to help. Come on—quit talking. We're almost to the bike!"

Outside the boys found John had climbed into the crate and only his curly, black head showed over the top. As he struggled to raise a huge box that was stuck at the bottom of the crate, Prince noticed the man's T-shirt was wet. John stopped straining for a moment and removed his black-framed glasses and wiped his forehead. But the workout wasn't finished and John quickly turned back toward the troublesome box. "This time, I'll get you," he said, with determination. "OK, everybody get ready to grab this one—it's heavy."

With one giant heave the box came over the side of the crate and two workmen grabbed it before it could fall. They struggled and shoved and finally got the box through the kitchen door.

John raised up again, wiped his forehead, and said, "OK, boys. Now for the bike."

Up, up, and over and there it was—a shiny, new bicycle. When the bike finally was lowered to the cement floor, Prince touched it. "Wow, blue and silver! Neat!"

Mark rubbed off the dirt that he imagined had collected during the eight months the bicycle had been in the crate, while Prince inspected the banana seat and sissy bar. Another exclamation rose, "Wow! This is the neatest bicycle I ever saw. It's fineo!"

Mark looked around and said, "It is fineo!" He did not realize until later that he had had his first lesson in African English. Soon, the "O" addition to words would come naturally and the superlatives *much* and *more* would be dropped. "Small-small and plentyo" would become the terms he and Prince would use to describe what they saw and ate.

Mark pushed the bicycle out into the yard before he turned his attention toward getting acquainted. "I'm new here. I came on a plane last night. I flew clear across the ocean and over the desert and I wasn't scared at all!"

"I came here on a plane, too," Prince said. "This is my mom's home and she came back when I was a small boy." Then Prince added, boastfully, "I was born in the United States, too."

"Really?" Mark was obviously impressed. "You were?"

"Yeah, my dad's still there."

"Then you know all about TV and cowboys and all that stuff?"

"Sure," Prince replied. "In America I watched cartoons every Saturday."

The bicycle was temporarily forgotten as the two boys began to talk about cowboy movies they had seen. Soon they hurried to Mark's bedroom for a look at the toy pistols Mark's grandma had given him as a going away present. When they came back outside, each boy carried a pistol. As they passed John and Mr. Baker, Mark went "Bang! Bang!"

Prince faked a turn to the left and then threw himself to the right and behind a palm tree.

The bang-banging continued for an hour while Maggie decided where to set the large pieces of furniture that John and the men carried into the rooms at an amazing speed.

Finally she pleaded. "Can't you stop now? I'm hot and my head feels full of muddy water. I don't know where anything should go."

John replied over his shoulder as he hurried back outside. "Not now. Once a crate is opened you have to get things inside. We've got three finished and one to go."

Mr. Baker, who had been standing by, finished the explanation. "It's the rainy season and things get wet and you see all those people outside, don't you? You can't leave anything where someone can pick it up."

It was almost dark when the last boxes were carried into the house, which looked like a disaster area. There was one empty chair in the living room and Maggie slumped into it to survey the situation. What should she do next? Before her gaze covered half of the room, she gave up. No way. What a mess! Then her eyes rested on Sam, who was reaching through the mesh of his playpen trying to open a box. He seemed to be content at the moment. Where was his baby food? Maggie decided to try to find it just as John and Mr. Baker came into the kitchen. John looked in Maggie's direction. "I'm pooped, but we have beds made."

Maggie looked toward the bedrooms where the mission's beds were still up. "Yes, and we have cold water!" She turned and opened the wrong refrigerator door. This one was the Blake's and still held toilet tissue and sofa pillows. She laughed, "Who ever heard of side-by-side refrigerators? Now which twin has the water?" Maggie opened the mission's refrigerator, found a couple of glasses, and poured some water for John and Mr. Baker, who had become Dennis by this time.

"Dennis," John said, as he looked toward his fellow missionary, who was much shorter than he, but just as hot, "I thank you. It was great of you to help us. By the way, I don't think I thanked you for the other work all of you missionaries did on the house before we came. Thanks a lot. It was great to arrive and have food in the refrigerator and sheets on the beds." John thought about the other six moves he and Maggie had made since their marriage, where there had been no preparation for their arrival. "Yes, we felt welcome." Suddenly his throat tightened with emotion. "It's good to finally be here—unbelievable, in fact."

Dennis looked up quickly and read John's feeling. "I know how you feel. I remember when we came. We need you, and the students are very excited." Dennis looked toward his own house, which was across the road. "I have to run. My wife, Ruth, in case you've forgotten, is expecting you for supper. I was supposed to get home early to take care of the baby so she could cook. I didn't quite make it. Come as soon as you can get ready."

Before anyone could answer, Dennis was out the door and into his own yard. Maggie turned to John. "Do you know where the aspirin are? I have a terrific headache."

"Me, too," John answered. "But I'd rather have it than look in all that mess for aspirin, unless they are still in your purse where they were when we needed them in Spain."

"Spain seems a million years back. Were we actually there?"

A ten-minute search produced no aspirin and Maggie decided to bathe Sam instead. It took all the energy Maggie could call up to get everyone dressed, but finally they walked toward the Baker's door.

Inside, Maggie noticed the living room was orderly and attractive, not quite like hers. She fell into a chair in front of a fan as Dennis said to John, "Did you know the principal wants you to begin teaching Monday?"

Maggie looked up with some alarm and John answered, "So soon? That gives me only eight days to get settled!"

As soon as Maggie got quiet she was suddenly possessed with the need to sleep. Far away, John and Dennis began to discuss the seven-hour time difference between the United States and Africa and how it affected the sleeping and eating habits. Just how well, Maggie knew.

Maggie couldn't remember later what she ate that night. She roused herself only long enough to say good-bye and when she got home, she let the children sleep in their clothes.

John, who was also having a jet-lag problem, forced himself to check each door. Yes, they were all locked. The outside light was on so the watchman wouldn't stumble around in the dark. What else was to be done? John's tired brain would reach no further. He pulled aside the curtain beside his bed and noticed a breeze was blowing in the window. Rain was on the way. What a day—his first in Africa. John fell asleep before the rains reached the house.

3

Hand-Me-Down Roles

"But you can't mow with the blades in the air!"

The newly hired yardboy looked up at Maggie in confusion. Then he looked back at the hand mower which he had pushed across the yard, just as Missy had instructed. Hadn't he mowed in a straight line rather than in a circle? What more could be expected?

Maggie groaned. So this was the yardboy the Lord had sent! He was as inexperienced as the first four yardboys she had chosen without asking for special guidance. Somehow Maggie felt tricked. Why, she couldn't have done worse if she had picked any of the twelve or so men who had asked to mow the yard. This whole unfamiliar business of dealing with workers was getting to her.

Maggie stepped toward Alfred with little enthusiasm and began in the best local English she could muster. "Alfred, you're not mowing—you're just walking. The blades. . . ." Maggie banged on the blades. "These knives, see! They like grass cutter. They cut the grass, no? They not cutting anything. They in the air!"

Alfred looked from the blades to the grass and back at Maggie without comprehending. He stood there for what, to Maggie, seemed an hour. Then he pushed the mower a few steps forward and he pulled the mower backwards. The blades turned. A light came into Alfred's black eyes. He grasped the handle tightly and turned it slowly over. The rest of the mower followed. The blades were down. Alfred pushed cautiously, as if the whole thing might blow up in his hands. The blades struck grass and the pushing got hard. Alfred mowed a few yards and stopped to look at where he had been.

"Ah," Maggie encouraged. "Now you see—the blades cut the grass!"

"Yah, Missy," Alfred said with a look that revealed he had made a tremendous discovery. He began to mow faster. On the second round, the tall, muscular young man began to perspire, but he sang as he worked.

Maggie turned to go in. How about that? No wonder John said he had never tackled anything harder than teaching science to village students.

Alfred mowed the yard twice with the push mower before the power mower was repaired. Maggie clenched her teeth every time she thought of the scene in her yard when the first yardboy took the mower apart piece by piece without any previous mechanical experience. When he was finished, a part was broken and he kept insisting the mower would work, "Fineo, fineo," as soon as he figured out how to put it back together.

A month and a half later, when the repair shop finally had the mower running again, John gave Alfred detailed instructions on its use. Somehow he always got back to, "Don't touch the motor. Don't use my tools!" Even when Alfred touched only the handle, John almost shouted, "If anything happens to that motor, I'll sack you. It cost me $60 to get that mower fixed! You hear!"

Alfred was properly frightened. Although he mowed the grass, which responded in leaps of growth to the daily rains, every week, he scarcely touched the engine except to add gas.

With the yard work taken care of, Maggie decided to concentrate on a new tile floor for her bedroom. She had quickly grown tired of stumping her toe on broken pieces of tile and the black adhesive which showed in a dozen places was an eyesore. At first Maggie thought of doing the work herself, but her fellow missionaries instructed, "Oh, no, you can't deprive the workmen on the campus of a job. They need the money. Hire them."

Maggie purchased the tile, contracted the workmen, and waited. A month later she was still waiting and decided to go see the workmen again. The following week they showed up for what they explained was a two-day job—one day to take up the old tile; the next to lay the new floor.

The first day the men didn't warm to any suggestion that Maggie made so she decided to ignore them until closing time the second day. With anticipation she peeped into the bedroom. Her eyes flew from tile to tile. Great. No more black adhesive. No more hurt toes. Wonderful!

Then Maggie looked where the men were laying the last row of tile. All the tile in this row had to be cut in order to fit. One man was estimating the size and then, while holding a tile in the air, was cutting it with a pocket knife, whittler's fashion. The result was a jagged edge. Maggie watched in dismay as the man laid the jagged edge against the last row of tiles and the even, uncut edge where the baseboard would cover it. Maggie stepped into the room for a closer look. All the tiles in the last row were laid that way. Adhesive was oozing through in a dozen places. Maggie almost cried as she tried to imagine how this could happen. Her new floor—what a horrible, sickening mess! How could she mop and wax a floor that had that black glue all over it?

Maggie couldn't stand it when the workman cut another tile and laid it in the same fashion. Older missionaries' warnings or not, she had to say something! "You lay the tile so the adhesive comes through the uneven edge—see!" She pointed to the spot.

The workman looked up as if to say, "Go away." The others paid no attention.

Maggie tried again in a louder voice. "I say, can't you put the cut edge under the baseboard where it won't show?"

The workman looked up. "Laying tile hard work." Then he whittled on the tile which was to go in the corner.

"I know. I know. I have laid tile!" Anger crept all over Maggie as she rejected his reason for poor workmanship.

Slowly all heads turned toward Maggie. She looked hesitantly from face to face and easily read the looks. They didn't believe her! Why would a woman who drove a car and lived in a fine house lay tile? Why would anyone work who didn't have to?

Maggie thought of the students who had come into the yard one day when John was chopping out a palm tree. They had been upset that a man of John's position would do yard work. Maggie remembered how many times back home she had heard her dad say, "He's a hard worker," when he wanted to pay someone a high compliment.

But the day the students saw John working there had been no compliments. In fact, Dennis had come later to tell John about a talk he had with the same students. Dennis had said, "You really made an impression. The students asked if you were too stingy to hire a workman to chop out your tree!"

There it was—missionaries weren't supposed to do manual labor.

As Maggie looked from workman to workman a sorrow came over her. These men knew nothing about dignity in labor. They had no rights as workmen, no illness compensation, no Social Security, no pensions. Any one of them would gladly trade places with any big shot he knew. No wonder they didn't care how the tile floor looked. How could Maggie show concern for these men and still expect a good job?

She tried again. "It is hot. It is quitting time. I know you want to finish and be paid, but the last row of tile is not laid right!"

The boss rose and began a five-minute oration and concluded "The floor is fineo. It looks fineo."

It did look better than the dirt floors in the houses where most of the workmen lived, but these men had worked on the campus for years. They had laid tile in every building several times.

When the boss told the men to clean up to be ready to leave, Maggie became desperate. "You must take up the last row of tile and turn it. I won't pay for a job that looks like that!"

The word "pay" caught some attention, for several men looked at Maggie as if she were some insect that insisted on buzzing when it should just go away. The boss was decidedly annoyed, but said in a patient voice, "The floor is fineo! We finish." All heads nodded in agreement.

John took this appropriate moment to come from school. Maggie glared at him with a "do something" look as she backed out of the door and said softly, "Look at the last row of tile!"

Maggie's feet carried her quickly outside. Why couldn't she handle situations here like she did in the United States? Why was everything so complicated? She walked past the shrubbery where the weaver ants were sewing leaves together to make nests. She stopped at the bird of paradise plant that had been transplanted a week before. It had taken root.

Maggie remembered the first time she had seen the plant in Dennis and Ruth's yard. The orange and blue blossom had looked like a bird in flight. When Dennis had said, "Take any plants you want," Maggie had been overjoyed. She had transplanted some shrubbery, but the bird of paradise and the poinsettia tree were the things that fascinated her the most. She thought forward to the time when she would have a ten-foot poinsettia tree in her own side yard. It would be quite a contrast to the foot-tall poinsettia plants that grew in pots in the United States. In the tropics all plants were oversized—quite a feat when the soil was so poor. But the minerals were locked in the vegetation, rather than the soil, and were circulated and recycled continually.

The beauty of what was around her renewed Maggie, as it always did. She turned back toward the house. The workmen had gone and Maggie glanced questioningly at John.

Reading her doubts, John said, "They turned the last row of tile!"

"They did?" Maggie went for a reassuring look and quickly returned with a puzzled, "How did you do it?"

"I told them."

"They didn't palaver or ignore? They just did what you said? Just like that?"

"Yes, we talked about it and they took up the tile."

Maggie's temper soared, "What kind of deal is that? They ignore me and then do what I said because you say so!"

"Don't get ruffled. Everybody told you workmen won't listen to women. You're a woman," John said, with a twinkle in his eyes.

Maggie, who had thought her discomfort was caused by the tile floor, now realized there was more. "But I'm not stupid! I know some things and I know how to lay tile!"

"But they don't know that and they wouldn't recognize your ability in that area if you laid tile in every building on the campus. That is not woman's territory!" John chuckled. "Some of these men have three wives—do you think they could survive if they listened to women!"

Maggie considered for a moment. John did have a point, but she wasn't just a woman—she had some rights as a human being.

"Sweetheart, don't get upset," John said as he pulled her close and kissed her on the mouth. "To me, you're one special, pretty woman but to them you're a female and too skinny for a fourth wife. They like their women short and chubby."

Maggie pulled away. She wasn't in the mood for affection and comfort. "So I'm beginning to feel like a stick here. Nothing works right. I don't do anything right and nobody listens to me!"

John decided to kid Maggie out of her bad temper. "Even to these men you're something—you're economics. A good woman is worth about as much as a cow!"

Maggie wondered if this was what was called, "Culture shock." Whether it was or not, she was rapidly losing her self-confidence. She worked on this knotty problem through dishwashing every night that week, but the next few months brought no success in handling new situations.

Maggie's next dilemma came when she needed help in the house. In fact, it was the floor again which finally caused Maggie to go to Ruth, next door, with an exasperated, "I need a houseboy. MK's, students, and villagers keep that twenty-four-by fourteen-foot living-dining room of mine in a mess. I can't mop the floor for answering the door."

Ruth laughed, "You probably don't remember, but I told you the first night you ate here that we kept a houseboy just to answer the door and do the floors. Now you know why."

Maggie ran through all the advice she had been given. It would fill ten volumes if she could catalog it all. "I don't remember. My head was so full of muddy water the first week, I don't remember a thing. The second week I had my head in a packing box all the time. Now I'm spending all my time trying to sort out people's needs. Do you know I have not yet been farther into the bush than the end of this campus. I've got to get organized so I won't have to spend every minute in the house!"

Ruth didn't know how to answer so she went into the kitchen and poured Maggie a cup of hot tea. When she returned, she asked, "Do you like sugar and cream, the way everyone here does?"

Maggie looked up startled—cream in tea? So that was why the students wouldn't drink the tea she offered and they didn't even say anything.

Maggie added another item to the growing list, "Don't do that again!"

She watched as Ruth put three spoonfuls of sugar and a lot of cream in her hot tea. Then she returned to the reason for the visit. "I want to know about hiring a houseboy."

"Remember, you asked for this," Ruth said with a chuckle, as she began a lengthy dialogue on the do's and don'ts concerning houseboys, which were actually men of any age.

The next day about all Maggie could remember was Ruth's warning, "Be cautious. Don't hire a rogue!"

Rogue? Ruth had meant a thief. What did Maggie know about thieves? The kids had never locked up their toys when John was in Purdue. Married student housing had been secure. Maggie's dad didn't even know if he had a key to his farmhouse door.

Maggie looked around the living room, which had begun to have personality. A rogue might like the ivory statue she had just bought. There was her grandma's walnut mirror—it reminded her of home and the people she loved. Would a rogue take that?

Maggie thought about the ten or so men who had come asking to be her houseboy. She didn't know anything about them. Who did she know?

Alfred, the yardboy—well, he seemed OK. Somehow she was drawn to him. She had taken time to know his background. No parents. He had been on the campus for ten years. The church had given him a scholarship. He lived with an uncle and walked eight miles each day to school.

Maggie decided to take the chance. After all, she had prayed for a yardboy and Alfred had appeared. Why not make him a houseboy? He had asked for the job several times.

The next day a salary was agreed on and mopping the kitchen floor became Alfred's first task. To all of Maggie's questions about whether he knew how to mop a floor or not, Alfred showed great confidence. After all he had been a houseboy for missionaries before!

Maggie had been out of the kitchen only five minutes when she heard Sam scream. She ran through the dining room door, into the kitchen, and slid in the inch of water which covered the floor. Sam was in the middle of the floor and each time he struggled to get up on his toddler legs, he fell again.

"Oh, no!" Maggie said, with a startled look at Alfred. "What did you do?"

"I mop the floor."

"With a whole bucketful of water?"

"Yah, Missy, it be plenty clean!"

This was the houseboy who knew how to do everything! Maggie shuddered. God could find Alfred another job!

Sometime between the time Maggie picked up Sam and then got back to the kitchen after bathing him, a small voice spoke. "Alfred needs work. I sent him to you for help."

Maggie argued. "But, Lord, that's backwards, I asked for help not for someone else to help. I'm carrying more people now than my back will hold!"

This fact didn't solve anything and Maggie looked toward Alfred with, "OK, let me explain what I want you to do."

A lengthy demonstration followed and Alfred repeated each step. The next day, when Alfred did a fine job on the floor, Maggie was pleased. No wonder he was an honor student! She sent up a, "Thanks, Lord, at least he learns fast!"

Soon Alfred was proving to be a blessing. He could mow the yard and wax the floors and clean the bathrooms without using one half of a can of cleanser for each. But he could not put the sheets properly on the beds. For four weeks Maggie pleaded. Then she demonstrated. Still Alfred tucked the top sheet tightly around the mattress as if it were a bottom sheet and put the small hem at the top.

Maggie knew by this time when Alfred was thinking about lessons or his girlfriend. These were not the reason for his lack of ability to put the sheets on the bed. Alfred had decided to see if Missy meant what she said. Other missionaries had been easy. Would this Missy insist or give in? Alfred had a list of things a mile long he intended to ask for if he saw any sign of weakness.

Maggie seized the opportunity. "This is the day, Alfred, that you learn to make the beds the way I say."

Alfred snickered. Obviously, he wasn't too experienced as a houseboy for houseboys never laughed at Missy—that is until they were safely back in their own village!

Maggie continued. "I'm going to show you once more and then you know what will happen?"

Alfred looked up and responded, "Nah, Missy," in an offhanded way.

"It will cost you one half of an hour's pay, if you do it wrong again!"

Maggie knew she had been right—Alfred was pushing—for when she came back into the bedroom the sheet was on wrong and Alfred was reading a magazine. She had been wise to choose payday for this important lesson.

Alfred did little during the rest of the afternoon and when he was ready to go, Maggie counted out his monthly salary. She laid it on the table out of his reach and noticed the gleam in his eyes when every penny was there.

Slowly Maggie reached up to a pile of coins and counted some into her own hand. "This is for me. I do your work—I get the money!" She dropped the coins one at a time into her pocket.

Alfred looked up bewildered. Then a dark cloud passed over his face. Finally he grinned, "I hear you, Missy."

As he left, Maggie knew they were ready for a more honest relationship. Some of the masks had come off.

For several weeks Maggie held to the employer-employee relationship. Then, one day Alfred came asking for something personal. Maggie decided it would probably be safe now to help him so she asked June, a missionary nurse, to go the next morning to Alfred's village with her, where his small cousin was very ill.

The two women and small Sam left the campus early. When Maggie turned the mission car onto the dirt road which led to Alfred's village, she saw that the road was nothing but deep ruts and muddy holes. The pigs on her dad's farm would have found it heaven.

Maggie looked at June. "Alfred said the road was fineo!"

June laughed. "It is if you always walk in like he does! Don't stop or slow down or we're stuck!"

Maggie considered. From feet to wheels. From dirt floor to cleaning a modern house. Yes, those were big changes. Out loud she ventured, "No wonder Alfred and I don't see things alike. I'll have to be more patient."

June added another thought. "Alfred has gone from tribal dialects to English, also. Having tried that switch, I can appreciate the fact that he never wastes words. His English isn't good enough for that extravagance!"

Maggie's attention was forced back to the road as it got worse. June continued. "I think Alfred hears three dialects and they're as different as English, Spanish, and French."

Maggie wondered, but didn't ask, how June knew so much about her houseboy. Maggie tried to steer but found herself barely hanging onto a wheel which responded to chuckholes that were the largest she had seen. Even spring thaws at home didn't produce holes like this!

About a mile from Alfred's village, Walker Town, the car slid down a hill through a creek, and started up the next incline. Maggie saw three deep holes side by side in the road. It was too late to stop and Maggie steered toward what appeared to be the smaller two holes. The front wheels hit with a bang, but went over. June and Sam flew forward and Sam screamed. Seconds later the back wheels dropped. The car bounced straight into the air and came down with a crunching sound in the same place. It bounced another time before it set still, the motor still racing. Maggie clutched and shifted to reverse. Reverse to first gear and back again. The car didn't even rock.

Maggie turned off the ignition and checked her impulse to put on the emergency brake. No need for that. June got out and looked under the car. "Good grief, both wheels are off the ground. The axle is caught on a mound of dirt!"

Maggie also knelt to look under the car. Both tires were a good six inches away from traction. "Wow! No shovel—no log."

"It would take a huge log to fill one hole," June said, "and both wheels are up."

Both women fell silent. June continued to try to figure how to get the car out while Maggie calculated how long it would take to walk to Gbolupa—eight miles from Walker Town through the bush and they were still a mile away from the town. Maggie instantly thought of Alfred walking that distance twice a day to and from school. Maybe she could get him a dormitory scholarship. How had he kept up his grades and extra work all these years?

Maggie looked toward Sam and gave up the idea of walking. Sam would have to be carried all the way. The other way out was back to the road to hail a taxi, if and when one happened to come by that day. Maggie dismissed that as the thought came that the car would be stripped when they returned for it. She had seen deserted cars with no tires, no headlights, no seats, and no mirrors.

The third choice seemed best—get the car out. But how?

Soon Maggie saw a village man walking toward them. June said, "Maybe here comes God's answer!"

Maggie laughed to herself—God's answer to my plea for a yardboy got me into this mess! I should have listened when Ruth said, "When you get a houseboy, you get all his family, too."

The short, stout man approached, "How-doed" and then squatted to look under the car. Maggie explained her mission and the man shook his head knowingly. "I help," he said, and walked on toward the next village.

Maggie watched his disappearing form as four women and eight children came along the road and stopped. They would help, too. Maggie decided this was going to be another fiasco! She walked into the bush to find a log. Everything was wet and rotting. Palm tree logs weren't any good. She picked her way carefully, certain that snakes must be everywhere. They were always where there wasn't a path and there was no need for a path in the direction she was going.

Finally, away in the distance, Maggie heard the car start. What had happened? She raced back to the road unaware of where she was stepping. She was just in time to see the car, with June at the wheel, pull up to the top of the hill.

Maggie ran the thirty yards down the road and called to June, "How did you do it?"

June gestured to the man, who had come by earlier and returned after Maggie went into the bush, "God's answer!"

Maggie was still bewildered and went to where the car had been stuck. The man stood by the holes—cutlass in hand.

In very poor English, the man said, "Cutlass plenty goodo."

The full explanation of what had happened waited on June, who had parked the car and was coming back down the road. "The man got it out! He used the long-bladed knife to loosen the dirty which held the axle and then with the same blade he pushed the dirt under one wheel. Finally the hole was full of dirt and I just got in and drove out." Then with a nod in the direction of the women, June added, "They pushed!"

"Well, how about that?" Maggie said. She kept looking toward the car to reassure herself that the man had actually freed it with one cutlass. Suddenly her estimation of village ingenuity grew. She turned to the man. "That's clever. Very clever. I did not think it would work. Thank you, plenty."

Then Maggie looked toward June. "You said this man was God's answer."

The man who had been overcome with praise swelled to an extraordinary height as he contemplated what it meant to be God's answer and this nurse's helper. He knew June very well for he had seen her in the villages many times.

June turned to the women and said, "Thank you. Thank you for pushing."

The women were displeased and grumbled among themselves. June knew they wanted a dash. She walked back toward the car and they followed. Maggie's purse was in the car. June wondered what change she had as she searched her own pockets and found nothing. June opened the purse and found fifty cents.

The man had been very happy with being praised when he thought no money would change hands, but now he came with his hand out. He didn't want to miss a good thing.

June was trapped. Four women and one man and she had only one coin. "You have change?" she asked the man.

"Yah." He reached into his torn pocket and pulled out a nickel and a dime. June placed the fifty cents in his hand and said, "Give the change to the women."

The women quickly gathered and June backed off. The man placed the small change in two extended hands and the other women stood motionless with their hands still out. When no further change was produced, they began to babble in sharp tones. The man pulled his pocket linings to the outside to show he had no more change and then he strolled through the finger-pointing, screeching women. He had been God's answer and now he had fifty cents. This was a good day.

The women continued to palaver as June and Maggie pulled over the hill. In Walker Town a woman recognized June and came quickly to her. "Nurse, nurse, you come."

Maggie sat dumbfounded, but June quickly picked up her nurse's bag and followed the woman into a hut.

Inside June found a baby with burned hands. He screamed when he saw June and ran behind his ma's lapa skirt. June guessed what had happened and asked, "He crawl in the cooking fire?"

"Yah."

June had seen many babies like this and quickly decided she must first get the sand and dirt out of the burns.

As Maggie came into the hut, holding Sam, June approached the child. Again he screamed and June backed off. She sat down across the room and looked at the mother, "You tell this baby the white woman will get him if he not good?"

The mother ducked her head and snickered. June chastened her, "Ah, Mommy, now it hard for me to help this baby. He feared of me."

When the baby saw small Sam, he was fascinated and slowly forgot to be afraid. Inch by inch he came from behind the lapa which was wrapped around his mother's waist. Finally he stood at his mother's side and Sam reached to touch his eyes. Everyone laughed and the child looked up surprised. He was almost ready to flee again when Sam started to talk. "Baby. Baby."

June waited until the infant's attention was completely on Sam and then she sneaked a closer look at the burns. Turning to the mother she said, "I not clean this baby, Mommy, because he scared of me. I would hurt him more. I will tell you what to do and you must do it.

"OK, Missy."

June gave careful instructions and waited until each step was carried out. They were ready for the salve when Maggie remembered what someone had written before she came to Africa. The letter had said something about nurses and agricultural workers building up goodwill in the villages around Gbolupa. Now Maggie knew what that meant.

Finally June got close enough to the child to help with the dressing. She looked up satisfied, "He'll be fine. They'll heal."

June finished her instructions and told the mother to bring the child to the clinic in several days. Then she noticed that the women who had helped push the car on the road had come into the hut unannounced. They were hot from the walk and grumbled again at June.

June passed Maggie and whispered, "We must sit outside and talk."

Outside the mother offered her only chairs and June and Maggie sat on them while the village women squatted in front of them. June watched the burned baby, who looked again and again at the odd gauze bandages on his hands and asked, "Mommy, what his name?"

"No name."

"Ah, Mommy," June said, realizing that children were often unnamed until three years of age, because of the fear that an evil spirit would more easily find a child who had a name. "That boy healthy. He be OK. You give him a name. Huh?"

The women made no answer and one of the children who had come with the women from the road found a piece of leftover gauze in the hut and came outside to play with it. June turned toward the child. "You pretty girl! Come."

This child did not hesitate but came within a foot of June, who gently indicated she should come closer. "I fix ribbon for your hair." June reached for the gauze and the child readily let go. June tied it in a bow and placed it at the end of one of the child's many braids. "Ah, she pretty, no?" June asked with a glance toward the women.

"Ah," they answered, and one smiled. Maggie could sense that the women were warming to June.

Maggie asked, "Where does Alfred's auntie live? I come to see her."

"Missy, she at clinic," one woman said and pointed down the road on which Maggie had traveled.

"The baby worse?" June asked.

"Yah, Missy. Baby not stay."

"You mean dead already?"

"Almost."

June looked to Maggie. "Then we must hurry."

The mother of the burned child rose. "The chief can show you." She sent a small boy to call the old chief.

Before they returned, June noticed that one of the women had a badly swollen foot. June inquired and the woman said she had stuck a broom straw in her foot. June knelt for a close look and found that the straw had broken off. She looked to the woman for approval, "You want me to take out the straw and give you shot?"

The woman looked around the circle and the other women encouraged her. "Yah. Yah." These women thought a shot was powerful medicine, which could cure any disease. Even if it couldn't remove the straw, it would heal anything else the woman might have.

June worked for ten minutes with the foot and then rose to give the shot. Then she patted the lady on her arm. "I finished. Don't walk so much on your foot and it will be OK in a week."

Then she shook the hand of each woman and gave each a small word of recognition. As they climbed into the car, Maggie knew the chill was gone. June had brought friendship to each woman.

The chief climbed into the backseat of the car and June turned to kid him. "If we get stuck again, you can push?"

He threw his head back and laughed. June knew no chief would ever push while women were along. She flexed her own muscles. "I push then!"

The chief laughed again and the women waved as the car pulled out of Walker Town.

When they got to the three holes in the road, Maggie said with seriousness, "We won't get stuck this time, we're going downhill." And she was right. The car hit hard but bounced on through.

When they reached the main road, the chief pointed the way to the clinic, where June asked for Alfred's auntie.

Maggie decided she had had enough of medicine for one day. If the baby were actually dead, she had no desire to see it. She held Sam close and gave part of the reason for why she didn't want to go into the clinic. "Sam doesn't need to be exposed."

Maggie waited outside a few minutes before Alfred's uncle appeared with outstretched hand. He had seen Maggie several times on the campus and said with a big smile, "You come. I thank you. The nurse have the right medicine. The baby will be OK."

Maggie was taken back by this sudden change in information. "You mean, the baby will recover?"

"Yah. Yah. The nurse say so."

"Well, praise the Lord!" Maggie blurted out in a burst of enthusiasm. "That's wonderful."

Alfred's uncle hesitated a minute and then rephrased Maggie's statement to fit his own religion. "It is Allah's will."

Maggie was startled. Allah? What did he have to do with it? So Alfred's relatives were Muslims. What should she say? Her ineptness was evident.

Finally she mumbled, "Jesus sent us. Jesus loves everyone. I come in Jesus' name."

The uncle felt no need to reply. She had come—that was what was important and the nurse had the right medicine.

At this moment, June appeared. She came toward Maggie with a smile. "It wasn't as bad as we thought. The child's skin is yellow—that frightened the people. He has jaundice, but with the right medicine he should recover!"

Maggie smiled faintly as Alfred's uncle indicated she should come into the clinic to see the baby. Maggie looked toward June with apprehension. "It's OK. It's not contagious. I'll watch Sam while you go in," June said.

Inside Maggie noticed the government clinic was almost bare except for a desk and one bed, where Alfred's auntie sat holding the sick child. Maggie greeted her and then watched closely as the thin, short woman, her own age, who had eleven children, came forward. The aunt extended her hand and there were tears in her eyes as she said, "Thank you. Thank you, Mommy."

Mommy? Maggie was startled. Now what did that mean? June called the women that and they called each other that, but Maggie didn't know they called missionaries by that name.

As Alfred's aunt continued to shake Maggie's hand, Maggie decided the name must be used for all women, who offered kinship or help. Did Alfred's relatives see her that way? She had given Alfred a job. The whole family had come to thank her for that.

Soon Maggie was outside and headed for home. As she drove, Maggie thought of all the surprises the day had held—the man with the cutlass, the women who now admired June, and Alfred's relatives.

With a glance toward June, Maggie found words for some of what she was thinking. "I have never seen you in action before. You do well."

June looked up, but continued to pat Sam, who was almost asleep on the seat. "I've been at village work a long time."

"Yes, that's obvious. You know the first morning in Africa I realized there was a lot I didn't know, a lot of open space. Today I didn't realize why the women who pushed the car were grumbling. It never occurred to me that they wanted money. Then when you walked into that hut, it frightened me. I guess I've read too many witch doctor stories!"

June took a sideways glance at Maggie's serious face and remembered the first hut she had ever entered. Yes, there was some apprehension. "Maggie, you'll never see a visiting professor boiled for lunch here, or a Tarzan! You know, some of those old stories ought to be replaced by something more truthful. These people are very kind, ordinarily." June contemplated, and added, "But mainly God has given me a spirit of boldness. I walk into any hut without fear." June considered telling Maggie how the courage had come, but Maggie switched to other problems her day had brought.

"When Alfred's uncle talked about Allah, I was shocked. Alfred is a Christian. I just assumed his relatives would be." Maggie searched for words. "I feel like an adult who has suddenly lost her ability to walk—to perform. I feel like a toddler! About as steady as Sam. When the old habit systems don't work, you have to center in on every act. It's exhausting and you don't get anywhere!"

Maggie sighed and dared not go on. June wouldn't understand anyway. June's job fit her. But why did three or four people come every week to Maggie for medicine? She couldn't anymore be a nurse than she could fit into June's size sixteen uniform. Maggie didn't like these hand-me-down roles which were continually being forced on her.

For several months she had felt cold inside. Today the paralysis had really set in. She had felt like an actress on center stage before a live audience who didn't know her lines and didn't like her part. When stage fright came, she had wanted to move out of the pressure and tension.

Wait! Wait? She had no order to evacuate. The voice said, "Stay. Stay."

Why? Had God cast her wrong and then left her in holding position? Why should she stay hemmed in, when it would be more comfortable to flee? She wanted to run like a wild horse in the wind to where it was quiet and beautiful, back to her own familiar terrain.

She wanted to, but there must be value in staying here. The Holy Spirit's orders weren't careless and hasty. He had spoken. Surely she had not misunderstood his call.

Then there was a step she had missed, that she had to learn. Obedience? Submission? Still a quiet panic seized her. What if she couldn't make it? She had known others who had been as certain as she was but they had gone with the explanation that the mission field was not for them.

Maggie's heart cried out. *I don't feel you, Lord. I know you must be there but I didn't feel you today in that village. I've prayed so hard lately, but I didn't have your words. I was on my own again.*

Maggie's heart warmed a little that afternoon when she told Alfred that his cousin would recover. Alfred grabbed her hand and shook it just as his uncle had. For the first time he said, "Thank you." Then Alfred repeated, adding the role he wanted Maggie to assume with him, "Thank you, Mommy."

4
Boss Man

When the principal left the campus for a week, John found himself with a new responsibility—night watchmen. Numerous checks during the first night always resulted in finding all the watchmen warm, dry, and snoring! Even an inexperienced rogue could safely enter, take a headload, and leave the campus without being noticed. For two nights, John woke the men and lectured. Then he decided something else had to be done. But what?

He brought the problem to Maggie over a late-night cup of hot tea, which Maggie was trying to drink with cream, the proper way in West Africa.

Maggie suggested, "Pray. Remember the houseboy search?"

"Do I?" John exploded. "That's how we got so involved with Alfred and lots of other students. Is there anyway to pray and not get personally involved?"

The next night, John found the first watchman asleep again. An instant plan came. John picked up the sleeping man's shoes and walked off with a crunching sound as gravel rolled hither and yon. A quick glance back showed the watchman had heard nothing.

John walked more carefully up to where the second watchman slept. He took an umbrella and a flashlight. One hundred paces later, John took a cutlass right out of the open hand of the third sleeping watchman. "Great weapon," he thought, as he felt the long steel blade. "Might be OK in the hand of an alert man!"

When John found the watchman at the gate awake, his plan changed. "I thought I heard a rogue! I come to see. You must be about! No?"

The old man yawned and replied, "Yah, Boss. I be about."

An hour later John found this man asleep, also. This time, John took the old man's plastic bag. He wondered if a watchman's job wasn't just social security for an old man who had no other income. It appeared that they felt the pay was coming regardless of whether it was earned or not.

Two nights later John called the watchmen together for an important meeting. "I saw a rogue one night. He was all over the campus. Did you see him?"

Heads began to shake in a negative reply. "You not lose anything?" John asked. The heads continued to shake.

"We awake, Boss. We go about." The men looked to the ground and continued to get the most out of these phrases by repeating them again and again.

"Huh!" John said loudly, as he brought the plastic bag which belonged to one of the men from behind his back. John turned the bag upside down and the items he had taken from the other men fell on the ground. John looked at the men and said, "The rogue brought these. Now who they for?"

Eyes opened wide. Mouths dropped. But no man reached for the items that he knew were his. John was certain as he searched each surprised face that none of the watchmen had yet figured out how he got the items.

John picked up the flashlight. "Good flashlight. Work fine." John shined the light down the path. "Well this not for you. Must be for another man." He innocently put the flashlight back into the bag.

John picked up a shoe, emptied the dirt from it, and dropped it into the bag. He picked up the other shoe and said, "This is fine shoe. Maybe fit me." He put out his foot and measured. Only a slight twitch of one man's hand indicated an impulse to reach for what was his.

John wondered how long this drama would go on but decided to play it to the end. He picked up the other items—one by one—and with appropriate comments they, too, disappeared into the bag. Still the men said nothing. John rose slowly and tucked the full bag under one arm. "That be plenty clever rogue. No one see him. No one hear him. Plenty clever!"

John turned and made a grand exit. When he was ten feet from the astonished men, he turned and threw back the watchmen's own words, "You be awake. You go about." Then in a louder voice he added, "Or the rogue will take your pants tonight."

All that night the watchmen made hourly trips around John's house. When they came to the carport they stopped to sharpen their cutlasses on the concrete. The noise sounded like instant danger to Maggie, who woke each time with a start. The first time, John said, "Well, they want me to know they are being vigilant tonight." After that the noise did not disturb his slumber.

The third time Maggie was awakened, several choice ideas came—part were directed toward John's original methods and part toward the watchmen. Maggie was determined, though, to show no sign that the watchmen were getting the best of her. She suffered with her head under the pillow for the remainder of that night.

The second night the men again made hourly grinding noises on Maggie's carport. This was too much. She crept through the dark house and watched out the peep window in the kitchen door, until a watchman squatted with his back to her and began to scrape his cutlass blade on the concrete. Silently, she opened the door and jumped out with a quieter version of the karate yell Mark and Prince used every day.

The watchman screamed and bounced up like a yo-yo on a string. Maggie leaned quietly against the side of the house as the watchman turned his head around gingerly to see who was behind him. When the outside light picked up her white face, the watchman turned full around and laughed nervously. "Oh, Missy. I feared. I think a rogue have me!"

Maggie began her lecture, "The Boss want you to stay awake. He not want me to stay awake all night. I not sleep with you making noise!"

Fifteen minutes of dialogue followed and Maggie went back into the house, uncertain what the watchmen's next move would be. The rest of the night brought only quiet, though, and Maggie slept contently.

Several nights later, John went out at 2 A.M. to unchain the dog, who had barked most of the night. There must be a new dog or a strange person on the campus. The dog put his nose to the ground, ran across campus, and disappeared for a while. Finally barking came from in the bush, but not a watchman appeared.

John knew it was time to run his routine in reverse. He took the plastic bag with the items he had stolen and left the house with, "I'll see who's awake!"

Thirty minutes later John returned with an empty bag. "Not a watchman awake. I returned all the items. I'm through with this watchman business. The principal will be back tomorrow. Let him yell at the men or withhold their pay!"

Maggie laughed. "Well that adventure turned out about like when June asked you to give the man with tuberculosis a shot while she took local leave from duty!"

John thought a moment. "Actually I had better results that time. The orange I practiced giving shots to, never got sick after that!"

Although John waited, none of the watchmen ever mentioned the items that had been stolen and then returned to them. Several weeks later John was on his way back from the school building one night when he met a watchman on the path. The watchman drew close to see which missionary was out late. When he recognized John, he stepped back startled, clutched his flashlight tightly, and almost as a reflex looked at his shoes. Assured they were still on his feet and not in John's possession again, he giggled, and relaxed enough to shake John's hand.

John, who had noticed with pleasure the watchman's check of his own things, could not resist shining his own flashlight right on the man's shoes. "Those fine shoes!" John said. "And they fit me!"

The watchman jumped away from John as if he thought some magic hand might grab his possessions right from under his watchful eyes.

John grinned, said, "Good day," and strolled on down the path.

Behind him the watchman made a hasty retreat in the opposite direction. When the old man got to the place, ten yards up the path, where another watchman was asleep, John heard him say in a loud voice, "Hear ya. The rogue out tonight. You be awake. Hear ya. You be about. The rogue take your pants tonighto!"

A few nights after that Maggie found her sleep disturbed again. This time by singing in front of the house. She got up, fuming. What were the watchmen up to this time? Why had she been assigned to such a noisy campus? Didn't the Lord know she was a light sleeper? How many nights had she been up lately? And there was no time for an afternoon nap with the constant "Bock-Bocks" at the door. Suddenly Maggie envied the missionaries who had air-conditioned bedrooms. They didn't have to hear the night noises. But $60 a month to run one air conditioner was a lot. Tranquilizers would be cheaper!

But Maggie wasn't inclined toward escape. She could surely handle this problem someway. She peered out the window, over the palm trees, and in the direction of the noise. Finally she saw a lone figure making an unsteady advance on campus. Three steps forward and one back. What was wrong with him?

Maggie watched a few minutes and decided the man wasn't a watchman. He couldn't be a rogue. After he almost fell, she diagnosed his condition—he was drunk; staggering drunk!

After ten more minutes of three steps forward and one back, the man had gained a few yards. At that rate his passing would take all night. And each step brought that loud, repeated song. If alcohol could dull the brain, why hadn't it silenced the vocal chords?

Maggie got a wicked thought. Why not unchain the dog? He loved to chase people. Maybe he would hurry the man across campus. As thoughts of sleep consumed Maggie, this plan began to agree with her conscience, which had at first been insulted. Why not?

But what if the dog jumped up on the man and knocked him down? He could lay there all night singing that horrible, loud song.

Maggie went back into the bedroom and looked at John. She could get him up and send him out. Somehow it made her mad just to see that nothing—absolutely nothing—interfered with his rest!

An hour later the song continued. Still not a beam from a flashlight. Not a watchman knew that anything unusual was happening on the campus. John had been too nice. If she had handled the watchmen, she would have been tougher! But that wasn't women's business!

So there was nothing she could do except endure. Maggie sat down in the rocker and turned to her notebook and Bible. How many nights lately had she spent with them? She decided to add a poem to the notebook, which was bulging with random thoughts and experiences. Putting things on paper seem to help clarify them. Her pencil wrote a new title, "Patience."

She smiled as she thought about what she had learned about that precious commodity. She finished the poem an hour later and the drunk's song faded far into the distance.

The sun came up at 7 A.M., as usual. Maggie stirred, thought of the man on the path last night, and drifted back into mixed-up dreams. Sam began to yell and Maggie fixed his voice to the swaying figure in her dreams.

Karen woke and carried Sam to her parent's king-sized bed. "Mom, Mom, Sam wants something. Can't you hear him?"

Maggie turned her face to the mattress and tried to drift back into semiconsciousness. "Mom, why don't you wake up?"

Sam was dropped onto the mattress and began to climb over Maggie's back. This seemed great fun and Sam crawled up and down Maggie's spine. "Eat. Eat, Mommy!"

"Sam, quit seesawing. You're killing me. Your dad makes waffles on Saturday. Get him up."

Karen went to the other side of the bed and shook John. "Come on Dad. Wake up. We're hungry!"

John refused to comply until Karen played the wake-up game he had taught her years earlier, "When you kiss my nose, my motor goes."

Karen smacked his nose several times before John started to sputter. Several more kisses and he chugged to the edge of the bed. Finally he hummed and sat up.

Karen returned to verbal encouragement as John got to his feet and stumbled the eight steps across the bedroom. Just as he opened the bathroom door, Maggie heard a sound on the carport. She turned over quickly and sat up. "Is Mark outside?"

Karen's head turned toward the sound of steps. "Yes, Mom, he took his pellet gun and went out to shoot."

Reality had come. Maggie found herself wide awake. "I bet he left the back door open!" she said, as shuffling feet came into the living room. A man's voice shouted, "Boss, Boss."

Maggie jumped behind the bedroom door, which led into the living room, and slammed it shut with her foot. At least the man wouldn't get into the bedroom. Humbug! Why did someone always come on Saturday morning—every Saturday?

"Wait small. Wait small," Maggie called with some irritation in her voice. Then she started to add, "Sit down," but thought better of it, remembering the last time she had used those words. They had been mistaken for "Come." Maggie made the most of the instructions she knew would be understood, "Wait small. Wait small."

"Ah, Missy," came from the other side of the door.

Maggie's thoughts turned toward a way to be rid of the voice. Through the bathroom door she whispered, "John, John, there's a man in the living room! Can you see him? Take him into the office while the rest of us dress!"

The bathroom door opened quickly and out came John. He pulled on his trousers and exclaimed, "Did Mark leave that back door open again?" Karen did not have time to reply before John went on, "How many times have we told him an open door is an invitation to enter. Every Saturday—every Saturday—before breakfast!" John continued to mutter as he closed the bedroom door.

Maggie quickly dressed and headed toward the kitchen with a "Change Sam," aimed in Karen's direction.

Karen exploded, "But, Mom," and then after stomping over to the bed jerked up a frolicking Sam and turned toward Sam's bedroom. This was another game to Sam and he rubbed a wet mouth all the way across Karen's face. Karen warmed a little, but then thought of how difficult it was to change Sam's diapers when he was jumping around. She began to caution him, "Now Sam you have to cooperate. Don't get the powder; lay still!"

Maggie was sifting flour and baking powder into the waffle batter when John and the man came through the kitchen.

"How do, Missy," the man said cheerfully. His dark eyes beamed a "mission accomplished" as he stepped out the back door. John called after him, "You get the money and then come."

John came to look over Maggie's shoulder and explained. "Varney wanted me to take a man to the doctor in town. Seems some guy got drunk on palm wine last night and started a fight. He got stabbed in the thigh." John sat down at the kitchen table and watched the waffle iron light blink off. "I told Varney to raise the doctor's fee and then we'd talk about transportation to the hospital."

Maggie looked wide-eyed at John as last night's figure on the path passed before her again. "A drunk? What time?"

"I don't know. Why?"

"I felt like stabbing that man myself," Maggie answered.

"What?" John looked puzzled. "What are you talking about?"

Maggie poured some batter in the waffle iron and said, "Let me tell you about it. Last night about 1 A.M., I heard an iron ore train and then when I was about asleep again there came loud singing. I got up and spotted a man on the path in front of the house. He was stumbling all over the place. Being clever. . . ."

"Ha!" John cleared his throat. "Miss Clever, pour me some coffee."

"Do you want it on your head or in your cup?"

John covered his head with the cup and said, "Here!"

Maggie finished the story in a hurry as Mark came through the back door. "It sounded like the man stopped in the first village."

"That's where he was stabbed," John said.

"Who was stabbed?" Mark asked, excitedly.

"You, young man, if you leave that back door open again on Saturday morning."

"Oh, Dad," Mark exclaimed. "Who got stabbed?"

"Ask your mom. I have to get dressed."

"Somebody tell me. What man?" Mark sat down and without thinking poured a whole plateful of syrup on his waffle.

Maggie stared at the syrup but checked her impulse to correct Mark. After all she told him about syrup every morning, just like she told him about brushing his hair! Instead she quickly recounted what she knew about the stabbing incident.

Mark gulped down the last bite of waffle, left the plate still full of syrup, and headed for the door. He had gotten off easy on the syrup, but Maggie decided to stand firm on the work. "Mark, your Saturday work—remember?"

"Oh, Mom. I wish I was five again," Mark retorted, with a growl.

"Why?"

"So I wouldn't have to work!"

"But life is growing—always growing, Mark!"

Mark thought a moment before he dismissed Maggie's idea. "Even when I get married. I could be just a tall five-year-old!"

Maggie laughed and Mark edged toward the door. "Oh, no," Maggie commanded. "You're funny but you have to work, anyway." She pointed toward the bathroom. "Go, young man."

Mark decided he was trapped. With Prince's help, he could clean the bathrooms in almost no time. He went toward the window to call for Prince, who lived within shouting distance.

Ten minutes later, Maggie decided it was time to check on Mark's performance. She had just started down the hall when a voice in the living room called, "Boss. Boss."

Maggie turned back to the living room and when she got there chose her words carefully. "You frighten me. You can bock and then wait outside. No?"

The expected answer came, "Yah, Missy." Verbal consent—but Maggie knew this man would walk in the next time without knocking. Should she make an issue of it? Village boys picked her oranges and papaya. Students came at all hours. Did she live in a house by the path or a house with the path right through it?

Suddenly the phrase, "House by a path," drew Maggie into the past. It was her high school graduation and she was listening to Virginia sing, "Let me live in a house by the side of the road and be a friend to man."

House by the path. That was the dream. This was the reality! How much easier it was to live with dreams.

This picture faded and Maggie saw Jesus and the crowds. She was beginning to understand how he felt. How would he handle this man? If she wasn't tired—but Jesus hadn't slept well at nights, either, sometimes. Maggie groaned and slowly turned toward John's office. To the waiting man, she said, "I'll call Mr. Blake."

When John appeared, the man held out some change. "Boss, I get the money. See."

John didn't count the change, but he knew it wouldn't be enough for the hospital fee. He hoped he was doing the right thing as he went into the kitchen for the keys to the car. Why had June taken this weekend to be off the campus? She could have handled this in no time.

John gave Maggie a fleeting kiss and said, "This will take all morning."

When John and Varney reached the group of huts, which were only a few yards from the campus, John half-expected to find a singing man. After all that was how Maggie had described him. Instead he found a man in too much pain for that pleasure. John looked at the man's thigh—it was sliced like a big beef roast. John wondered how the man had managed to climb onto the hammock, where he still lay. He went back to the car for his first aid kit and a bandage.

The man groaned as John taped a gauze patch over the carved flesh. Then John turned to the other men. "Put him in the car."

Several village brothers rather roughly helped the man down and then climbed into the back seat of the car with him. Three other men came around to get into the front seat.

"Only two," John cautioned. "This sedan only holds six men."

The men palavered and finally one stepped back and the other two larger men climbed in. John wished he had indicated only one could ride, for he found himself jammed against the door. During the thirty-five minute ride to the hospital he dwelt at length on the stuffed car. Each bump produced a new thought along that line and a groan from the stabbed man.

When the receptionist in the emergency room of the hopsital quoted the fee, the village men quickly turned to John for more cash.

"No. I said I would provide transportation. That's all." John knew that the men had not planned it, but they had an offhanded, professional way of securing more funds. He waited silently while they went aside to talk about the next maneuver.

Soon Varney returned. "We go to his relative. He live in town."

"Where in town?" John weighed the alternative. It would be easier to just pay, but then he would be carrying all the load. He was somewhat relieved when Varney indicated a street, which was only ten blocks away.

John looked at Varney closely and questioned, "Are you certain we can get the money there?"

"Yah. Yah," Varney said, and each village man repeated the words as if to make them convincing enough for John to drive there.

John thought the men were faking certainty and wondered when they would trust him enough to present the facts. He thought about the games people play, as the men climbed back into the car. What about the word, "Boss"? That put one man above another or apart from the rest. John didn't like the distinction. "Boss" could also indicate a "You take care of me" attitude. John knew these men were capable on their own when they had to be.

As the car stopped in front of the house which belonged to the relative, John continued his line of thought. By the time the men reached the front door, which was opened by a houseboy, John was grabbed by the size of the house. Wow—worth $70,000! Well, with two piazzas all the way around, maybe $75,000. John turned to the stabbed man who was too stiff to get out. "What job does your relative have?"

"Government job . . ." and the rest was lost as a knock came at John's half-opened window. John whirled around.

"Boss. Boss. Five cent. Five cent."

John found himself about three inches from a beggar's face, which was as far in the car as the window would allow. It wore the fixed smile that John had seen a hundred times. John ran through all the responses he had tried on beggars and half-grinned as a new angle came. "My friend, I'm not the boss. I'm the chauffeur. That man the boss!" John gestured toward the man in the backseat.

The beggar's face froze. Slowly his mouth dropped to show a row of dirty teeth. Then a more determined smile came and he thrust a dirty hand palm up in the window. "Na, you fun me. You the boss."

"No, no, man. I'm the chauffeur. That's the boss man." John pointed to the steering wheel and insisted. "See I drive for that man. He boss."

Again the smile faded and the beggar withdrew his hand. His head turned toward the man in the backseat. He took a half step toward the back window.

Suddenly from the backseat came a flow of heated words. The first sounds were English and then as that vocabulary was exhausted, a tribal dialect took over. John knew he could translate part of what the man in the back had said, but he decided not to. Instead he thought about how the stabbed man didn't mind asking for a ride to the hospital or for cash from a relative, but deeply resented this beggar. What was justified begging?

The beggar had heard enough. He began to yell and shake his finger, as he backed away from the car. The exchange between the two men continued until the village men reappeared. They held out one dollar. "He help only small."

John sat silently. "I'm the chauffeur," he said to himself.

The men began a lively discussion about what to do next. John heard a part of what they said as his mind hit another thought. Why would this richer relative give only one dollar? John tried several explanations. The stabbed man was probably a three times removed cousin. Or the man had helped a half dozen relatives already that month. Maybe the big house was full of children sent from up-country, who would be educated at this uncle's expense. Yes, all these things did happen and often.

The men interrupted John's search for an answer. "Another relative live close. We go there."

John looked at his watch. Past noon already. "Where to this time?" John quickly ran through all the work that had to be done at school that day and some impatience showed. "Not far, I hope!"

Varney reassured John, "Near place." These words were repeated by each man, "Near place. Near place."

The echo died and there was no more dialogue until the men returned from this relative's house with the rest of the money.

John drove back to the hospital where Varney placed the three dollar

fee on the nurse's desk with some cheer. He had accomplished the task with time and words—commodities that were plentiful to him. The job done, Varney backed from the desk and unconsciously reached in his own pocket where John was certain he was fingering a silver dollar all his own. He had not had to make the final sacrifice!

By the time the doctor came, the stabbed man was showing some apprehension. Hardly had the doctor touched the wound when the man began to howl loudly. When alcohol was poured over the cut, he danced and hollered with real zest. John waited for the doctor to give a shot for the pain, but instead the doctor began to suture. The village men moved in, football huddle-style, to watch and John stepped out of the circle and became a bystander.

On the way back to Gbolupa, the stabbed man's spirits rose. He had endured the treatment and his fourteen stitches were impressive—more than any of the men had ever seen before! He began a monologue in an excited voice. All the way back to campus he stayed in the limelight, even when Varney tried to turn the talk to the events of the night before.

John listened in silence and thought about the village brother system. Well, they did take care of each other. But how would they solve the problem about the stabbing? If it were a village brother, then what?

5

To Run Again

"There's more than one recipe for chocolate cake. Yours isn't the only one, Duncan!" Bill threw out.

Duncan puffed up, rose, and walked around the room. Tom, who was chairman of the committee, seized the floor. "Now, let's not turn this into a discussion about strategy. This is the property committee, remember?"

Everyone else shifted uneasily, hoping that Duncan would go down quickly like a punctured balloon. But this was not to be. Bill wasn't going to get off easy this time. Duncan held out for five minutes and when he was deflated there was not a movement or sound in the room.

The chairman, who had tried several times to stop the heated monologue, seized the floor. "Duncan, for goodness sakes, sit down! Now let's see. How can we handle this?" Tom looked desperately toward the wiser, cooler heads in the room. Dennis didn't look up from where he was painting a series of circles on the carpet with his eyes. June gave a neutral hands-up sign, which meant she wasn't going to make any suggestions.

Silence held and Maggie looked hard at Duncan, trying to make no judgment about this missionary she had scarcely met before the meeting today. His conviction that he had seen it all before and had the answers, made it a little hard to remain neutral. Wow! He could outtalk any auctioneer Maggie had ever heard at a farm sale back home.

Maggie looked from face to face trying to read them for information. Duncan had touched the wrong nerve, but which one? Obviously no one except Maggie was shocked. Maybe they had been down this route before. It was obvious no one wanted to delve any deeper.

For what seemed like yards of space, the silence continued. Then Tom, knowing Duncan's tendency to dictate all policy, decided to rest the case until Duncan cooled down. But if he did, what about poor Bill? Bill had asked the committee for action at least six times. Should he be denied again because Duncan had another system for training leaders and building dormitories for students? Tom looked again at June and Dennis. Why didn't they make a recommendation?

Dennis by this time had covered the floor with circles and now he began to make squares on it. Hopeless! Hopeless! He'd pushed Bill's stalled plan up the hill twice already with June's help, and each time the committee had let it roll back down. He'd push if there were a chance, but there wasn't any right now. Maggie was too new. Duncan was opposed. Corinne wasn't supposed to be on the committee, but there she sat. Delay! Delay!

Tom looked at the long agenda and decided to go to the next item. "Let's consider the second item—a missionary residence up-country." There was a stirring as stiff backs began to relax against metal office chairs.

Bill sighed, wiped his forehead, and tried to hide his disappointment. For an instant he thought of objecting. Duncan had stormed, why shouldn't he? If you shouted people listened, and sometimes they gave in. You got what you wanted. But there was more at stake than getting your own way. There was what the Lord wanted to do with a missionary. That was as important as what the Lord planned to do through a missionary. Duncan—now what did the Lord intend to do to him? Bill thought about his first encounter with Duncan. Duncan had greened somewhat since then—there was some new growth!

But what were Bill's students getting? There was no place in the overcrowded dormitories for them. Cut enrollment? Never. Not after Bill had encouraged the men to come for more training. For their sakes, he couldn't give up.

Bill wiped moisture from his eyes which wasn't perspiration. How could it be so difficult to get anything done here? Years and years of delay. First his wife's medical leave to the United States, that had stretched into six months, then lack of funds, and now Duncan.

Bill looked again at Duncan. Duncan had done a good job with his pastor's training program, but why couldn't he see the two situations were different. His buildings were OK if you built close to the capital city, but up-country they were impractical. Any roof was as good as Bill's men had in their own villages. If Duncan weren't so busy with his own thing, he'd come up and Bill could show him. How many times had he been invited? Bill picked up Duncan's voice.

"You always say that! We'll build a house with what we have!"

Tom, who was on the other end of this argument, countered. "No way. The house would be smaller than one for single women. This evangelist has three children, Man."

June spoke up, "$45,000 is the answer. Now what is the question?"

Dennis looked from the floor where he was now building pyramids and caught June's cue. He sat up straight and planted his feet firmly on one pyramid and took off with enthusiasm. "Right. Right. This family must have every consideration. There's no school there. Electricity stays on half a day if you're lucky! There's no town and no missionary close. There's no church, no buildings for meetings—nothing but bush. All their work at first will be in their home. We've got to give them more space than the families at Gbolupa have."

June backed Dennis up with facts they had discussed many times. "It's hard up there. Really hard. I don't think I could live there."

"Ha," Duncan exploded.

Dennis looked toward him, wondering what he meant. June knew what it was like to tramp to villages with wet feet and push herself to the point of physical exhaustion. What did Duncan know? He'd come to a ready-made situation and never got off the concrete.

Dennis spoke up. "Nobody could live up there in a house we could build for the money we have. We've got to have $15,000 more."

Duncan took issue. "Nobody?" He defended himself. "Ha. I can do anything I have to and I could live in the house and they'll have to!"

Dennis replied, "Now Duncan, we're not talking about surviving. We're talking about ministry!"

Corinne, who had come to the committee with Tom, chimed in. "New missionaries are always soft. They ask for more and more!"

Maggie frowned. What had Corinne said earlier in the evening, when a secretary was chosen for the committee? "Let Maggie do it. All the rest of us have a job. She can do something!"

Maggie had wondered then. Now she was confused. She could remember at least five times that Corinne had made negative comments about new missionaries in her presence. At first she thought Corinne was kidding. Now she wondered.

Tom shot a hard look in Corinne's direction and laughed in an affected way. "Well, some of us are super-heroes and some aren't. I read this new couples' biographical sketch. They've had two cars and a nice house and a good-paying job and a school next door. What a switch—there's nothing where we're asking them to go! Man, oh, man."

Dennis laid on some more facts. "Let's not talk about surviving. Let's talk about making it possible for them to live with some degree of satisfaction and have time for a ministry. If they spend all day, every day on their own kid's lessons, keeping a generator working, and doing laundry by hand, how can they minister?"

Duncan was somewhat pacified. "I agree with that 30 percent!"

Tom shot back, "What's this 30 percent? Did you ever agree 90 percent with anybody?"

Duncan, without the slightest grin, said, "No. We can't get an extra $15,000, anyway!"

"What we need we can get," Tom batted back.

Duncan thought of Tom's need for a new water system at Gbolupa. "Huh. How many days a week do you spend nursing that homemade system, which is supposed to provide water for 500 students?" He sat back and let the question soak in. "Tom, you've asked for a water system for Gbolupa for years. You still don't have it. We didn't get the money . . . . "

Tom broke in, "Wait. . . . "

Duncan countered, "Don't interrupt me! I'm not through!"

Tom had had enough detours for one day. "You're interrupting—not me," he shouted right at Duncan. "You're opinionated. I'll say it to your face—you're biased!"

Backs began to stiffen again and Maggie glanced toward Duncan to see if he'd blow up again. He sat brooding and June came in, "Unforgivable!" Then she added in a light manner. "Unforgivable. One missionary speaking frankly to another's face—unforgivable. Speak behind his back!"

Dennis laughed out loud, Tom smiled broadly, and Corinne snorted. Duncan allowed a slight smile to pass his mouth before he proceeded. "Touché, Tom." Then he veered back to his one-track argument, "How about the money for the water system?"

Tom wouldn't be sidetracked, not even for his own cause. "We have a water system. The campus has grown and that is another issue. Stick to this one. We must build something that is adequate regardless of what else we need. We can get the money."

Duncan came back. "OK, you mentioned need. Let's talk about need. What about the need for an evangelist in this area?"

Dennis sighed, "Duncan, we've been through that. The mission has studied the need. We are now doing something about it!"

Duncan puffed up again, "I didn't discuss the need. I wasn't on this committee two years ago. I think there's a greater need in the county next to me."

Dennis spoke softly. "But Duncan, there are hundreds of obvious needs. Would an evangelist in your city of 1,000 be more needed than an evangelist in an area of scattered population? Yes, if you equate need with number of people. But the final result does not depend on how many people might be evangelized. We count results in how many are actually reached! One man can witness to only a few people each day without mass media, anyway. The end result may be more converts in an area of scattered population. The people in the area we are now considering are responding!

We've prayed this thing through. God knows where the need can be met. Let's depend on him."

The chairman broke in. "Your point is well taken, but the placement of missionaries is a personnel problem and this is the property committee. The family has been placed. Let's build a house!"

Tom turned to Maggie. "What do you have down?"

Maggie looked bewildered. "You told me to record only recommendations. I have nothing!"

"Good grief—two hours of nothing. Come on committee, let's pull ourselves together. What do we want to recommend?"

Tom sat back and looked at the ten other items on the agenda. Why did this committee stall when there was so much to be done? He could make quick decisions. Why couldn't the others? He exhorted them again. "Come on. We've plowed this field before—now let's produce a house!"

Another hour of discussion brought out other problems involved. The land available was not suitable for a house. The committee turned to discussion about renting a house temporarily. June, who always researched ahead of time, reported the only house to rent was a country one with cement floors, shutter windows with no screens, and no wiring.

By this time Maggie's head was spinning. This was not like the committees she had been on before, where some church member brought a report on something like a new piano for the church. That hadn't been too weighty. Beginning the mission across town had taken more time and thought, but even that didn't compare with this. This committee was voting on somebody's life—some family they had never met. A man, a woman, and three small children, who would all be evangelists up-country. Wow! Maggie was humbled. How would a family begin up-country with no help, no church, and people who understood little English? Maggie couldn't even imagine what she'd do. She was drawn back into the group as Tom gestured in her direction.

"Get this recommendation down!"

Maggie picked up her pen. "Delay assignment until proper housing can be provided. Send it to the personnel committee for consideration."

The committee members rose and stretched. Some yawned, ready to go home, but Tom wasn't satisfied. "Come on committee. We've got to push on. Get some coffee and we'll start again in ten minutes!"

Another hour dragged by with no solid recommendations on the items discussed. Finally Tom threw in the towel. "OK. We will meet again next month and be prepared—do your homework!"

On the way home, it was raining hard and the road was muddy so Dennis at first gave full attention to driving. Finally he turned to Maggie,

"What did you think of your first committee meeting?"

Maggie, who couldn't play parts easily, struggled for a good line and found none. "I don't know—I haven't decided anything yet."

Dennis made a suggestion. "You didn't think we acted like missionaries!"

Maggie turned quickly, wondering how Dennis had put her thoughts into words. Dennis continued. "It's called missionary shock—sort of goes along with culture shock!"

Maggie made no comment until the next mud holes were safely behind them. "June. . . ." She picked her way cautiously, glad that June had gone home another way. "June always seemed bold and to the point before, but tonight. . . ."

"June is bold and competent—a competent female."

Maggie wondered why Dennis had said "female"; but she didn't ask. "But in that meeting she was devious and funny."

"Right. You're observant. I noticed you watching her."

So Maggie hadn't been the only one studying people. She hadn't thought that anyone could reach her, though. Suddenly she remembered how many times John had gone to Dennis with questions about students, only to find that Dennis could give a complete background study on each.

He began in the objective way he always had when he considered people. "See, as I said, June is competent. She can handle about anything. Watch her sometimes in village clinics. The people think she can work miracles! Anyway, she works well with almost everybody. But when competence meets insecurity there is a problem. June could have given all the answers which she had spent long hours obtaining and lose the ball game or she could take another course, look silly and propel the group toward its objective. When she said, 'Unforgivable,' you noticed everybody listened, stopped, examined his motives, and finally the group took another course!"

Maggie tried to evaluate what she had been told. This was the first time anyone had trusted her with inside information and she didn't feel quite so much an outsider anymore. No wonder the students at Gbolupa loved Dennis so.

A thought slipped into Maggie's mind which she didn't let stay for long. Duncan. Now Duncan made you feel like you had sinister motives. Maggie wondered if Dennis were describing Duncan as insecure—she'd call him aggressive—but they were pulling onto campus and Maggie didn't ask.

The next morning, Maggie patted the recommendation with satisfaction, folded it, and took it across the road to Tom's house for his signature. She had completed her first mission assignment and felt good.

Tom was on his way to school and stopped only long enough to quickly scan the letter. He handed it back to Maggie and abruptly said, "Fine, except the recommendation goes to the strategy committee."

Maggie thought back. "Tom, I thought you told me last night to send it to the personnel committee."

Tom looked at his watch and then to the road where a big black car was pulling into his drive. He had already had two callers and he wasn't at the office yet. Tom wondered why new missionaries always had to have everything explained twice, as he recognized the parent in the car. Yes, the man was important and behind on his children's school fees. Tom started to plan his strategy. "But Mr. Jacobs, you know how it is. The school has to pay its bills, too."

The man got out of the car, came forward with a wide grin, and grabbed Tom's hand. He shook hard and then snapped his fingers off of Tom's, in the customary handshake.

As the visitor's arm went around Tom's shoulder, he said, "How is your health?"

Tom replied, as was the custom, "Fine. How is your family?"

The other man chuckled. "You should know. All my children are here in school!"

"Yes, yes. I mean how is the rest of the family?"

"Fine."

"Could you give me a ride to the office so we can talk there? I'm late this morning."

Maggie had been forgotten until Tom started to open the car door and discovered he was still holding the letter.

"Oh, oh, Maggie!" Quickly Tom turned to place the letter in her hand. "We'll discuss this later."

Before Maggie could reply the big chauffeur-driven car sped away with two backseat occupants.

When the two men went through the waiting room, Tom quickly counted the people who needed to see him. Automatically, he speculated why each had come. The truck driver wanted the purchase orders so he could go to town. Mr. Oaki wanted another salary advance. The student was back from yesterday. He wanted to palaver some more over book fees he owed. The chief. Now that was a puzzle. Tom hoped he had only come by to say, "Mornin," as he sometimes did. Surely there hadn't been another palaver in one of the villages on the school's property.

Tom sat down behind the large desk which was covered with work. His eyes fell on a letter at the top of one stack. Oh, no, he had forgotten all about that meeting tonight. Just then the plumber opened the office door, saw the man in the expensive suit, and retreated. Tom groaned.

Not the water pump again! He thought back to the meeting last night—he should have asked for a cool $30,000!

Tom knew this day was going to be another one full of storms. How he hated thunder! To relieve the pressure, Tom began with the man seated opposite him in an automatic way, "What is bothering you, Mr. . . . ah . . . Mr." He was snapped out of his rote beginning as the name of this old acquaintance evaded him. Tom concentrated. "Oh, Mr. Jacobs. What can I do for you?"

Having gotten through that swell, Tom settled back and tried to tranquilize himself by thinking ahead to the list of food and building items that had to be purchased that day.

Mr. Jacobs rattled on and finally got rather hot as it became evident that he was being ignored. Finally, he stood and headed toward the door. As he went through the outer office he continued to shout back at Tom, who stood with a steel-like face, in the doorway.

The teacher, who had been sitting quietly, decided it was his turn to relate his woes. He began before the office door was slammed by the departing parent. Suddenly Tom felt like a wastebasket which collected annoyances and gripes. Why was someone always throwing frustration his direction? Tom turned toward the teacher and began to growl. This unexpected move surprised the small man, who slumped down into the chair by Tom's desk.

Tom stood by the door, and the teacher regained his composure. "My pa died. I need small money."

Tom almost choked on that, but finally coughed out, "He died last month. Remember?"

The teacher bristled with apprehension and tried to find a way out of the trap. He sensed defeat. Mr. Wilson had seemed naive before but this morning he was playing a better game.

There was a long silence and Tom finally ended it to gain further advantage. "Two months ago your child died. I gave you an advance. The month before that your auntie died. I gave you an advance. I am sorry about your people, but you have not paid back any of the money."

Tom realized he had talked himself into a conclusion and in his strong-minded way he intended to stand fast, regardless of the pressure of another thunder burst. "There will be no advance!" he stated in a voice so composed that it was a shock even to his own ears.

The teacher jumped up and began in a loud voice.

Maggie stood a long time at the Wilson's house, looking toward the school. Now she turned toward her own house. She placed the letter on the mail rack by the kitchen door. All day as she passed, the letter seemed to say, "Couldn't you do even that?"

During the next weeks, Maggie sent three notes to Tom and went twice to see him but each time he was busy. Finally it came time for another property committee meeting and Maggie asked about the recommendation.

"What recommendation?" Tom asked.

"You know the recommendation from the last committee meeting." Maggie could tell that Tom didn't have the vaguest idea what she was talking about, so she read the recommendation to the group.

When she finished, Tom said, "Fine. Fine, but you should have sent it three weeks ago."

"But, Tom, I couldn't. You said . . ." Maggie stuttered and Tom turned to look at her, wondering why a committee which functioned so poorly had also chosen a secretary who didn't know what to do. Good grief!

Tom controlled his vexation. "I go to the meeting tomorrow. I'll take the recommendation." He stretched out his hand for the letter and went on hurriedly. "Now, what's next? We've got to get someplace this time."

Maggie reluctantly gave the letter to Tom and wondered what she should have done. Sent it without his signature? Why had this seemed so important? She hadn't done anything wrong, had she? Then why did she feel so deflated?

Maggie turned to thoughts about group action as Duncan began a long monologue. A group. This group wasn't a church. It wasn't a family. What was it? And what was Maggie supposed to offer that others didn't contribute?

Maggie looked at each person in the circle. June—capable. Dennis—sensitive. Tom—organized. Then Maggie chuckled to herself and added "too busy" to her description of Tom. Bill—he was concerned. Duncan? He was something else. Far too complicated to fit a simple word. They were all leaders! All leaders! Who ever heard of a group of all leaders? Maggie thought back—there should be followers. Some people not too involved who could be objective. But in this group everybody had a stake—everybody's work was up for question. Everybody's car was assigned. Maggie thought of being assigned to share a car with her father-in-law. That would be a laugh!

Of course, there would be misunderstandings. Why hadn't Maggie anticipated disagreements? As the meeting wore on, Maggie's case of missionary shock subsided slowly and she began to listen, with interest, to what her fellow missionaries said.

During the next weeks Maggie thought about the issues before the committee. There was so much to do but where was the handle? Maggie found no answers and finally said one night to John, "Let's get away from the campus for a while. We haven't been anywhere in months. Twenty-four hours a day of the same thing is too much!"

"That sounds good," John said with a twinkle in his eye. "I'll see if we can have a car tomorrow night."

The next day looked brighter as Maggie got a baby-sitter with no trouble. She was dressed and ready to go when John came from school. Maggie decided to go to the Wilson's for the car, while John showered. As she crossed the road, she stopped for a close look at the shrubs she had recently transplanted. Two looked alive, but the other fell into her hand as she twisted it for a closer look. Termites! Their 6-foot hills were everywhere. They must be a hungry crew. Oh, well, two plants had outdistanced them. Maggie went on singing softly to herself.

When she reached the Wilson's house, Corinne came to the door and began a monologue about the students. Maggie tried three times before she slipped a sentence in, "I came to get the car."

Corinne stopped abruptly and gazed at Maggie. What was this? "The car, as you see, is gone. Tom had a meeting. He just left."

Maggie tried to hide her disappointment, "But he told John we could have the car tonight."

"Oh, did you have a meeting, too?"

"No, we're going out to eat."

The worried look that had come to Corinne's face vanished. Maggie wasn't certain what was stirring inside Corinne when she half-grinned and said, "Out to eat on a school night?"

Maggie was taken aback. "Why not?"

The silly grin came back to Corinne's face. "Well most of us do class work on school nights." Then with a shrug she signaled the conversation was at an end.

As Maggie turned, an idea flashed across her mind—how about the other cars on campus? She started toward June and Don's yard. But Corinne called out loudly, "All the cars on campus are gone. Everyone went to the meeting!"

As Maggie looked from empty carport to empty carport, she realized Corinne was right. How did Corinne always know everything? And what was this meeting that John didn't know about?

Maggie walked back to her own house and closed the door softly. She was still standing by the door, when John came into the kitchen. She cast him an angry look. "Well, guess what?"

John hesitated, studying Maggie's face. "He forgot! Again?"

"Right. He had a meeting and Corinne thought it was silly to go out to eat on a school night, anyway."

John quickly suggested, "Well we have a baby-sitter. Let's do something."

The children hearing voices in the kitchen came to investigate, just as John pushed Maggie out the door. "Good-bye, kids. We're going now," he called over his shoulder and slammed the door. They walked a few steps before Maggie could free her arm. "Why did you do that?" she asked in desperation.

"Because we are going somewhere—anywhere and we're going tonight!"

"Oh?" Maggie flipped back. "Where? In what? Maybe to the palaver hut! Great!"

"That doesn't sound so bad. Yes, to the palaver hut. We'll build a fire, lay in our hammocks, and talk."

John walked the few steps to the palaver hut, leaving Maggie behind feeling like she had been hit with a bucket of cold water. "You're kidding! I haven't been off this campus in two months except to go to meetings and grocery shopping and now this!"

Maggie followed John into the hut, where he was lighting a fire, and continued in self-pity. "He said we could have the car. Why doesn't anything work right? Why did they assign us a car with Tom? He uses it every day and night. Don't we have any rights? Can't we decide anything on our own?"

Maggie thought back to property committee meeting and the new couple coming soon. Didn't they have a right to decide somethings about their new life?

Maggie laid back in the hammock and fell into her own search for explanations. In a few minutes a gentle rain began to fall on the thatch roof and John said, "You're far away. A penny for your thoughts."

Maggie didn't answer and John tried again to get her attention. "Let's make the most of this. I know you wanted to eat out, but we can go inside and get something when the kids are asleep."

Maggie stood up. "That is not the point and you know it!"

"OK," John said with some heat. "Cool down."

Maggie's voice rose. "Don't lecture me. Don't you start making up my mind for me, too!" Maggie turned her back to John and walked to where the rain had began to come over the low palaver hut wall.

Finally she turned with, "Do you have any other word on how to handle this situation?"

John studied her face carefully before he replied. "Maggie, for goodness sakes calm down. You're getting some sort of complex. Everything isn't that bad!"

John was immediately sorry that he had made the last statement for it opened a Pandora's box which refused to be closed. Like a volcano whose inner pressure has reached the boiling point, Maggie began to spill over her grievances against the neighbors, the school, the students, and even the weather.

An hour later John and Maggie ended the argument with an uneasy truce, leaving both with the uncomfortable added frustration of the biggest disagreement of their fifteen-year marriage.

Maggie was still wondering the next morning what was happening to their relationship when Tom came to the door.

"About last night," Tom began, before Maggie could open the door. Tom cleared his throat and brushed aside Maggie's invitation to come in. He stuck to his line. "About last night. Really, I forgot. I hope you'll understand that business comes before pleasure."

Maggie had begun to warm to the idea of Tom's concern when his last line hit hard. She stepped back and blurted out, "No, I don't understand. There are a lot of things I don't seem to know about!"

Tom was taken aback. The tone of Maggie's voice sounded a little like Corinne's when she was about to give him a bad time. Tom didn't intend to get into that with Maggie. He put on his clocklike, unmovable expression and hurried off the carport like a bird fleeing from a hunter.

Maggie slammed the door, turned, and was surprised to find John standing a few feet behind her.

"Why did you say that? Couldn't you see Tom was trying to make up for last night."

"Was he? I thought he was talking about business versus pleasure and his interest versus mine." Maggie sailed past John and threw open the refrigerator door. "No wonder Corinne acts like she does. The man has a ledger for a heart!"

A quick survey of the refrigerator showed that Maggie had forgotten to mix up powdered milk the night before. She barked toward John. "Get the kids up. It's late."

She turned on the water filter and it began to drip slowly. With each drip, Maggie's impatience grew. She dumped in the powdered milk before the pitcher filled with water and began to stir vigorously. Suddenly Maggie noticed brown spots on top of the white swirls of milk. She looked closely—ant corpses. Ten ants had been in the pitcher. Maggie looked where the pitcher had been and saw a line of ants coming up from the floor and another one coming down from the ceiling. Quickly she spooned the floating ants into the sink and poured some of the mixture into Mark's glass.

Mark sat down, rubbed his sleepy eyes and said, "Yuk. I hate this powdered milk. Put chocolate in it. Ice, too."

Maggie shot back. "You do it."

Mark was still doctoring the milk to suit his taste when Prince came through the back door. Prince sat down and watched as Mark took a drink, savoring the flavor, and absentmindedly put the glass down on the edge of his cereal bowl. Prince jumped in time to avoid getting wet and the milk ran off the table and down onto the chair and floor.

Mark looked up sheepishly and defended himself. "Who put that cereal bowl there?"

Prince laughed and grabbed an ice cube off the chair. Deliberately he aimed at the wastebasket in the corner.

Maggie turned in exasperation. "Prince, not in the wastebasket!"

Mark, who had watched Prince's shot with admiration, said, "That's OK, Mom. Two points."

Prince added, "It'll be easy to clean the wastebasket today with all that water in the bottom!"

Mark chuckled and Maggie glared. Without another word, Prince fished out the ice cube and put it in the sink. He sat back down on the same side of the table as Mark, obviously pleased with his good deed.

By this time, Karen had poured milk on her cereal and jumped up. "Look at that. Bugs. Bugs!"

Maggie went for a closer look, thinking there was still an ant in the milk. No such luck. The newly opened box of cereal was full of crawling protein.

Maggie bit her lip to keep anything harsher from coming out and said, "Great. Great! Just great!" She turned back to the refrigerator for eggs and while she was scrambling them began to put frozen sandwiches in the lunch boxes.

As the children boarded their bus, Maggie wished the school day could be at least a month long and sat down to address herself to her knotty problems. What was happening? Why was she so upset and impatient? Was this culture shock? Maggie's explanations made no more sense than the squeaking sounds coming from the rocker she was sitting in.

Why did the problems keep coming so fast? What was the real issue—the rock overhead that seemed about to fall and crush her?

Was it her fellow missionaries who were so involved in her life that she couldn't eat out without their permission? Was it no space? No way to get away? And her everyday life was so much more complicated by bugs and food preparation and clean floors and the rain. The ceaseless rain that only stopped long enough for the heat to come on. Although there were no heat registers in any houses in the country, Maggie suddenly felt like there must be at least three registers in this very room and all were blowing overheated air. Maggie didn't have to feel her arm to know it was damp. She walked over to the bookshelf to read "90 degrees and 90 percent humidity." The thermometer couldn't be wrong and it was only 8 A.M.

How could Maggie do anything in this heat? Oh, how she had expected to do great things on the mission field! And now look at her—splitting headache in the morning, grouchy disposition—just enduring was enough. Why should the Lord ask her for more?

She had been reined in, all right, like a horse in training, with weights on its feet and a tight bridle in its mouth; a horse, whose trainer was trying to produce something that didn't come natural. No, this wasn't natural. Living here was humanly impossible!

Maggie thought of the old song, "Mold me and make me after thy will." Did that song also have something about the Holy Spirit breathing on you? If it did, it should have said hot air! Suddenly Maggie was not certain she wanted any more molding and reshaping. The spiritual diet the Lord had her on was too strict and Spartan.

Maggie turned back to the appointment process. Somehow what she had been told was unrealistic, like a person standing far off and seeing a country through a curtain of optimism. For some reason she had felt the process itself was the high mountain to climb. Once you were over that hurdle of paperwork, examinations, and recommendations your worth was proved. After all, the mold was there, all set, and ready to produce pottery that was complete and beautiful. Maggie thought about the missionaries on campus. They didn't exactly fit any one mold but there was a strong-willed, aggressive streak running through them.

Maggie longed for a friend who was simply easygoing and gentle. A friend like Sally. Yes, good old Sally. Always fun to be with. Could there be a missionary like Sally?

Maggie pondered the question and then answered it herself. Sally wasn't organized enough and single-minded enough to get through all the paperwork. She seldom took a stand on any issue, and doctrine wasn't anything but a word to her.

Take Corinne now. She took a stand on every issue. Boy, was she dedicated! Probably hadn't missed a day of teaching in the seven or so years she'd been on the mission field. Then why did Maggie dislike her? What had Corinne said several times? Something about others have gone home. Only the tough make it.

Maggie had wondered if Corinne were accusing or threatening. No one could threaten another enough to make him stay here. It did take inner steel and a certain flexible strength. Maggie frowned. It took more than that—it took a voice that whispered in 90 percent humidity, "I sent you." And a voice at 2 A.M. in the still of the night saying, "Stay. Hang on."

But what if the voice didn't speak? What if you weren't certain. A quiet panic seized Maggie—what if Corinne were right? "Some don't fit. Some go home. Some don't make it!"

Maggie suddenly realized her self-interrogation was leading to more puzzles. Look to God and others and away from yourself, she counseled, and got up.

Today was Mrs. Ophelia's birthday. Why not make her a cake? Maggie hesitated, got Sam down off the table, and decided Mrs. Ophelia might not like birthday cakes with icing. Alfred didn't like icing. Maybe she should ask somebody what to do? Maggie flipped quickly from indecision to certainty. It might not be usual, but it would show friendship and appreciation. Any matron in a girls' dorm could surely stand some appreciation!

The first thing John noticed when he came from school was the decorated cake. "For me?"

"No, silly. It says 'Happy Birthday.' Can't you read?"

John was pleased that Maggie seemed in a lighter mood than last night and ventured in a good-natured manner. "It's lopsided and a little runny!"

Maggie gazed at the cake. "It looked great to begin with. The flowers looked like real roses before the humidity began on them." Then her tone cheered, "Oh, well I tried." She picked up the cake and started for the back door. "Can you keep Sam out of the sugar and oleo while I'm gone? He's mixed them twice today already, plus dumping the powder in the stool!"

John laughed and turned toward Sam. "So you had a fun day!"

Maggie stopped outside as she passed the bird of paradise. It looked better. The orange color was coming out. The bloom looked like a grown bird. Maggie could imagine it flying right into the sky.

An hour later Maggie returned, whistling as she came up the steps. Loud grunts coming from the living room told her where she could find John and Sam. They were wrestling on the rug and John seemed happy that Maggie had come to relieve him. He tossed Sam at her, "Here, take this kid. He's too much. Every minute into something!"

Maggie smiled. "And you think I don't know that?" She squeezed Sam and asked John, "Do you know what happened?"

"No, but you're going to tell me!"

"Right. I'm running again."

"You're what?"

"Remember what I told you last night. I felt like I was tied or bridled or something. Well I had one successful dash!"

"That makes sense. You took a cake running."

Maggie laughed, "Quit being silly, John, and just listen." John put on a dignified air and pressed his lips together tightly. Maggie continued, "Guess what happened when I got to Mrs. Ophelia's?"

"She thought a cake with runny icing was funny!" John laughed at his own joke and then put back on his serious face. "OK, what happened?"

"Mrs. Ophelia was not only pleased, she was elated! She hugged and kissed me and called everyone in the dormitory. Then she made a speech."

"Oh." Maggie's story had become interesting enough that John no longer had to pretend to listen. "And what else?"

"Mrs. Ophelia said that the cake was the nicest thing that anyone had ever given her for it was a tree of life cake."

"A what?" John tried to figure out where Maggie was leading, but quickly gave up. "Tree of life?"

"Yes, tree of life. That runny looking decoration had gone all over the cake before I could walk to the dorm. I thought it looked awful and almost brought it home. But to Mrs. Ophelia it looked like a tree and meant a wish for a long life—a good life here and hereafter!"

"How about that?" John shook his head in disbelief. "You goofed and it turned out well! You must have had some outside help on that one." Then John quickly changed the subject. "Did you see the mail I brought in?"

"Mail! Goody. This is my day!" Maggie shuffled through the letters and noted each return address. A letter from her mom, one from John's mom, one from her sister, an unknown sender—probably a WMU member—and a letter from the home church. Great!

Maggie began with the letter from her mother and noted that her dad wasn't feeling well; her oldest niece had a boyfriend. Maggie's sister wrote about her horses, cats, and dogs, as usual.

Quickly Maggie read to the home-church letter. It was brief and she was disappoined to find no news about old friends. The last lines were important, though: "The church has voted to designate its foreign mission offering this year for an air-conditioned car for you. We have read your letters and know that you travel a dusty road and share a car. Let us know what amount will be needed."

Before she told John, Maggie wrote a letter in her own mind. "Thanks. We accept."

John was more cautious, though. "I don't know. It would solve our problem, but it wouldn't do anything for anybody else."

Maggie pleaded, "But John, remember all the times we needed a car and didn't have one. And an air-conditioned car—that would be like almost going to heaven!" Maggie ended with an emphatic, "The church wants to do this!"

Maggie thought to herself of the freedom the car would bring. Corinne wouldn't even know when Maggie went out to eat on a school night.

Several weeks later, Maggie was listening to a favorite radio program when the minister said:

Of all my mother's children,
I love me the best.
When I get my stomach full,
I don't care about the rest.

Clever. True. Maggie would have to remember that. She could use it in Sunday School class. Maggie decided to write it down. She hurriedly found her meditation notebook and a pencil and started to write, "Of all my . . . ," but the pencil stopped as her mind did an instant rewrite:

Of all God's children
I love me the best.
When I get the car I want,
I don't care about the rest!

The words drummed on, "When I . . . I . . . I"; no matter how Maggie pronounced "I" the meaning was the same.

Maggie wavered and thought about Jesus' last night on earth. Jesus had washed the disciples' feet! Why should he? Every disciple in that room had known that it was the custom to wash the feet of all the men present. Then why did each wait for the other to do the job? Nobody even offered to wash Jesus' feet. Maggie thought about that a moment, and decided each disciple would gladly have done that part of the task. But to wash everybody else's feet? That was different.

The rock overhead pushed down hard on Maggie. She had the answer—Jesus' solution. He had thrown out "I" and put "love" in his vocabulary. "By love serve one another" (Gal. 5:13).

Humility? Submit to Corinne? Maggie thought back to property committee meeting. Bill? How about Bill? His decision had been harder than Maggie's, for the training of a dozen pastors was at stake, but he had washed Duncan's feet—almost with tears.

Maggie pondered and then began a letter to her home church she knew John would approve. "Thank you, but we can't accept." The heavy rock moved and Maggie suddenly felt free and ready to praise the Lord. She wrote, "God has given us some victories. We feel the interests of his work around the world would better be served if you share your money with others through the Lottie Moon Christmas Offering."

Maggie sighed, leaned back, and relished the joy of moving forward without wheels.

6

The Students

Rose Seahfa had been at Gbolupa Institute only two weeks. She wished she had never come. Oh, how she wanted to go home, where her friends were. This had been her pa's idea. "You got to know book." Every day he had encouraged her and threatened her, as if knowing book was the only important thing in life. Maybe to him it was. After all he hadn't had a chance to go to school and Rose had seen the men who knew how to write their own names shame her pa.

But writing your name wasn't everything. Rose knew how, but her life hadn't taken on instant success. In fact, she was as miserable as when Ada had been sent away to school. Rose could still see Ada, her only sister, walking past the banana trees and away from the village. It didn't matter that Rose's pa had said it was good for Ada to go live with an uncle so she could have a fine education. All Rose remembered was that Ada had never come back again to play with her. That had been ten years earlier and all the family's money had gone at the end of each rice season to keep Ada in a country far away from home. Sometimes Rose wondered if she'd ever see Ada. The picture she held close to her heart was of a seven-year-old, skinny girl. But Ada was seventeen now. Rose's small sister had vanished with the passing years, and Rose couldn't imagine what she had become.

The bells began again and Rose knew she must get up. Breakfast was being served and that would be the last food until lunch at 2 P.M. That is unless you had money like some of the girls for goodies from the market.

Rose swung her feet around and sat on the upper bunk. She shivered as the cool breeze came through the open door. It had rained all night. Rose dressed quickly in her blue uniform and started down the steps leading from the second floor of the dormitory. Suddenly she remembered her umbrella and went back to find it in the trunk under her bed. She was soon on the slippery earth in front of the large building.

There were no cooking fires here to warm you, so Rose shivered again and wondered why the dining hall was so far away. The rain dripped on her umbrella and there were puddles everywhere. Rose slid right into a puddle which she had not even seen. Crossing to the other side she realized both her feet were wet.

Rose scarcely noticed the birds by the path which said, "Coo. Coo." She was tired of their talk, talk. A wheelbarrow met her. It was loaded with bags of cement. Maybe the workers were going to repair the steps today. Squeak. Squeak. A tractor chugged across campus to a work site. Women passed with large fishing nets. Hurry. Hurry. The sun will be hot soon.

"Noise. Noise—always noise!" Rose thought to herself as she walked on hurriedly down the uncertain path. Why was there so much noise and so little talk? Why had she said those dumb things and made the girls in her room vexed? Now they were "withholding speech."

The dining room was already crowded with several hundred students when Rose arrived. Plates clanged on the tables and silverware was dropped in the kitchen. Rose picked up her bowl of oatmeal and cup of tea and sat by herself. No one spoke as she left the dining hall.

Rose went to six classes that morning. She could not have said later what was taught in Bible, biology, algebra, English, social studies, or French for her thoughts were only on the tenth grade girls in her dormitory room.

Rose was vexed when she heard one girl give right answers to questions asked by a Nigerian teacher. Maybe she could have answered, but she couldn't even understand what he asked. The English used by the teacher from France and the teacher from the United States was just as confusing to Rose. Rose remembered the first day when she had tried to answer a question only to find that the teacher was talking about something entirely different. The other students had snickered and stared. It was better to keep quiet and act like you heard.

Then there had been the first test. Rose had never gotten an "F" before. She had always been first in her class. That's why she had gotten a scholarship to Gbolupa from the foreign concession her father worked for.

Tuesday, Wednesday, Thursday, and Friday went much the same for Rose. Her third week on campus was no better than the first two. On Friday night, Rose was alone in the dormitory room. She had watched as the other girls put on their denim pants, T-shirts, and long, gold earrings and gone to the movie in the school auditorium. Some had talked excitedly about boys they would sit with. Chatter! Chatter! Who cared about boys?

Rose thought of her pa's one pair of long trousers and knew he would say, "Lapa for girl; long pants for old man for church." Neither could Rose imagine having money for movies when there was no soup for rice at home.

Rose clicked off the light as a sob came to her throat. She held it back and listened to the birds singing and the frogs croaking. But Rose's tears suddenly spilled over and she threw herself on the bed and cried into the mattress so no one would hear.

Slowly the sobs ceased and Rose blew her nose. She walked to the door and looked out across the campus. The buildings were big and lighted and modern. Rose remembered her friend back home had said, "Gbolupa looks almost like heaven."

Suddenly Rose noticed a light in the missionaries residence a few yards away. That was the new missionaries' house. Mrs. Blake was her Sunday School teacher. Quickly Rose had a plan. She would go to visit at the Blakes.

Rose washed her eyes as she thought about ways to get out of the dormitory without a pass. Maybe she could just leave and go toward the school building. No pass was required to attend the movie. Then when she was out of view of the dorm director, she could turn and go to the Blake house.

Rose got her umbrella and started down the stairs. The dorm director, who was on the downstairs porch, said, "Hear ya. Come soon after the movie," as Rose passed.

Rose walked quickly to where she had decided to turn, but then thoughts of Mrs. Blake scared her. What if Mrs. Blake didn't want to see her? Rose couldn't go back to the dorm. She decided to go to the school building. When she approached there were girls and boys standing outside in pretty, new clothes. Rose looked down at her school uniform. She couldn't go there in a uniform—not on Friday night. Rose turned back before the others saw her and almost ran to the Blake's house.

When she reached the carport, Rose hesitated. What would she say? What if Mrs. Blake asked to see her pass? Rose had decided she couldn't go in when a bark came from the yard. Rose, who was deathly afraid of dogs, knew the Blakes had a big Rhodesian Ridgeback. Rose flew up the three steps and pounded on the door as the bark got closer. Her heart beat wildly until Mark came to the screen door, unlocked it, and said, "Come in."

As Rose passed Mark, he yelled to the dog, "Be quiet, Soin. It's OK." Then Mark turned back to Rose and said, "My dad isn't here. He went to school to run the projector. I wanted to go but my dad said the movie was scary!"

Having the dog outside and being safely inside and Mark's friendly manner, somehow reassured Rose. She was able to say, "I wanted to see your ma."

Mark blinked. "Oh, most students want to see my dad. I'll call Mom. Come on."

Before Rose could get to the living room, Mark returned to say, "Mom says Sam is about asleep. Sit down and wait."

Rose looked around the big room at all the soft cushions and then sat down on a straight chair. Soon Karen came and shyly said, "Hi." The silence quickly grew uncomfortable. Rose was upset again. The girls in her room knew that was the worst punishment—to never have anyone speak to you. Why had they done that to her?

Mark, who had been playing cars before Rose came, suddenly looked up from his vantage point on the floor. "Do you like to play cars?"

Rose's eyes opened wide and Karen snickered, "Oh, Mark, girls don't like to play cars!"

Mark looked slightly downcast for a minute and then began to talk at a rapid pace about the kinds of cars he had. Then he told Rose about his school. With each new topic he moved closer and by the time he found the photo album he was standing right beside Rose. He turned a few pages and then decided it would be easier to handle the album if he were seated. He pulled a straight chair from under the dining table and plopped it down beside Rose's chair. When Mark got to the picture of his grandpa on a horse, Karen joined the conversation. Rose began to feel better. They finished two photo albums and Rose saw her first picture of snow before Mrs. Blake came.

"I see Mark and Karen have given you the whole family story," Maggie said, as she sat down on the sofa.

Rose smiled shyly, "It is too fine."

"Did you want to see me, Rose?" Maggie asked.

Rose was thrilled that Mrs. Blake knew her name, but she stiffened. She couldn't tell Mrs. Blake about her problem. Now that Mrs. Blake was so close Rose again found her frightening.

Mark encouraged, "My mom is good to talk to."

Maggie sensed she had been too quick to get at the cause of Rose's visit and backtracked. "I want to get to know all the girls in my Sunday School class. Maybe you could come next Sunday to see me?"

"Yah," Rose said in a rush, happy to find a way out. "Yah, I come Sunday."

Maggie went to write a pass and Mark picked up the conversation. This time he told his favorite story. "My dog chased a rogue the other night. When my dog came, the watchman had the rogue by the seat of his pants. The rogue got so scared he leaped away and his trousers stayed right in the watchman's hands!"

Mark fell on the floor in laughter and rolled from side to side. Finally he proceeded with the story that he had decided to enjoy even though Rose hadn't responded much to it. Maybe Rose hadn't gotten the full picture. Mark decided to try again. "See the watchman had a hold of the rogue's pants and then my dog came gallopy, gallopy!" Mark hopped across the floor in a poor imitation of a dog at full speed. "Gallopy—like so—and that rogue he turned around and he see my big dog and he plenty fearo! He scream for his life and pull away from the watchman." Rose began to smile, for with Mark's shift to her style of English, she was getting the story. Mark continued. "The man's panto they stay right in the watchman's hand. Then my dog he chase the rogue right into the bush without his pants. The rogue going run—run—run cause he feared for his life and my dog going gallopy, gallopy right after him!"

Again the story was too much for Mark and he broke up in laughter. From that he switched again to galloping around the living room. By this time Rose's smile had taken on more lively proportions and she began to giggle.

Mark continued to bounce around the room imitating the chase. Finally he slowed down and said excitedly, "My dog he come back thirty minute later. That rogue he still be running. He go deep in the bush. He not come again!"

Finally Mark sat still on the floor. He looked serious. "My dog is a real hero, isn't he?"

Karen, who had taken some interest in the story, snorted, "That lazy animal, a hero? All he does is eat and sleep!"

Mark was disappointed, but not to be stopped. He thought about his scaly anteater, who wasn't afraid of fire ants.

"Soin's as brave as my pangolin." Turning to Rose, he added, "Would you be feared if Soin chased you?"

Rose shuddered. "I feared plenty of dogs."

Mark wondered why, but didn't ask. "Are you scared of dogs as much as of snakes?"

Rose sucked in her breath hard. Mark knew that meant yes.

"For true?" Mark asked. "I'm plenty scared of snakes. There was a green mamba in our tree and Mom read in the snake book that its bite could kill you in thirty minutes. I plenty scared of it."

Karen's eyes suddenly got wide and she asked Rose, "Did you ever see anybody hurt by a snake?"

"Plenty of people," Rose said, as she thought about her own cousin who had died in their hut after being bitten by a snake.

Mark shuddered as a quick wave of fear gripped him. "Sometimes I dream about a big snake that gobbles me alive!"

Maggie decided the conversation had gone far enough to result in bad dreams and said, "There aren't snakes on the paths. They stay where there is big grass to hide in."

Mark's apprehension about snakes turned him toward a safer creature—monkeys. Maggie half-listened as her thoughts turned to why Rose had come. She searched but found no clue in anything Rose had said in Sunday School class. Maggie turned back to Mark, "OK, young man it is time for your bath. You've talked Rose to death!"

Mark replied by pointing to the window. "See my pet dragon on the screen. He catches mosquitoes. Once I pulled his tail off but lizards grow new ones right away!"

Rose suddenly realized that it should be time for the movie to be over. She rose quickly, almost surprised to find that she was still on campus. This talk had been so different from any she had had in three weeks. Mark and Karen had actually acted like she was real. Mrs. Blake hadn't sent her away. Rose thought about what the students had said about Mr. Blake, "He's plenty clever. You can't trick him!"

Rose got up with a lighter heart. "I go now. I come Sunday." She went quickly from the carport into the darkness. On the path she thought about Mark and how the girls liked to run their fingers through his wavy hair and call him "Frisky." Rose wished she were so brave. She walked to the path that led to the dorm and sat down. She would have to wait until the girls came from the movie and then she would go back ahead of them so the director wouldn't know where she had gone.

Rose fell deep into her own thoughts and did not realize the rain had begun to come softly until she was suddenly aware of noise coming from the school. She turned to see students scattering in all directions. She quickly got up, raised her umbrella, and pushed the thoughts of her ma into the back of her mind.

Rose was the first into the shower and was already in bed when the other girls reached the room. She knew they had lingered to talk to the dorm director, for they were her favorites. Tonight it didn't matter, for Rose's eyes were heavy with sleep.

Sunday came more quickly than Rose had expected and she walked toward the Blake's house with some apprehension. Mark, Karen, and several friends were in the tree house when Rose passed. Mark, who had been so friendly on Friday night, hardly had time to speak. Rose wished she had stayed in the dormitory. She was thinking of excuses for going back there when Mrs. Blake opened the back door. Rose soon found herself in the office where Sam was playing on the floor.

Maggie tried several leads, but Rose followed with only "Yahs." Maggie checked her watch and realized that company would be coming for supper in less than an hour. Why were students always an hour or two late for conferences? Maggie looked closely at Rose and noticed her hands were tightly clasped in her lap and her face was very serious. She looked scared to death. Maggie softened, but got to the point, "Was there a special reason for your visit Friday?"

Rose still looked at the floor. "Yah."

Maggie was wondering where to go from there when Sam pulled up on her knees and begged to be lifted. Maggie picked him up and began to talk to him. Rose's eyes lifted and Maggie could tell she was interested. Slowly Maggie shifted from Sam to talk about children in general. Without being aware that she was being drawn in, Rose found herself talking about her village sisters, and her ma and pa.

When the conversation shifted back to her problem, Rose was ready to talk. The story unfolded in a few sentences. "A girl in my room sat on my bed. I don't know why, but I scream at her. I said she was spoiling my covers. Then the girl say that I was lying on her name. The other girls in the room are friends of the girl who sat on my bed. They make plenty palaver and they make plenty trouble for me."

Maggie thought about the girls in her Sunday School class. Which ones were these? Not Eliza—she was too kind. Martha was too independent to be pushed along by a group. There were two rooms of tenth grade girls. Maybe these girls were the ones who always came late to class. Maggie decided to clarify. "Were these girls friends before you came?"

"Ah, they stay a long time at Gbolupa. I be here only three weeks." Rose's eyes fell again and she suddenly became aware of how much she had revealed about herself. She was silent.

Maggie pushed for more information. "What happened after this?"

Rose's eyes searched the room and rested on the door. Then she looked back at Sam and he crawled toward her. When he got to her knees, Rose said quietly, "The girl on my bed—she lose her gold *v* ring. She talk that I took it. She talk plentyo!"

"Do you know anything about her ring?" Maggie asked kindly, as she looked at the *v* ring on her own right hand. It had been her first African gift from John, and Maggie knew the girls valued their gold jewelry.

This time Rose answered with certainty. "What my hand touch is still there when I go."

It took Maggie a minute to interpret the expression she had never heard before. Somehow it didn't reassure her as much as Rose's straightforward manner. Still she had been tricked before. Maggie remembered the five students the week earlier who had insisted identical homework papers were coincidental. Maggie had almost decided to question Rose for the details about the ring when Rose went on.

"The girls say I rogue. They plenty vexed with me. Now they withhold speech."

"Withhold speech?" Maggie said with a frown. "Now what is that?"

Rose explained. "People here palaver plenty. But when they very vexed they not talk. They pass and not say, 'Mornin'.' This is bado. It hurt inside."

Maggie studied Rose for a clue to her sincerity. Cheap, white anklets. Shoes that needed polishing. Cheap material in her uniform and she wore it even on Sunday afternoon. Why? Tense hands. Slender figure. Attractive enough, but she wouldn't be noticed much on this campus, among the outgoing, self-confident girls. Rose's speech pattern was also a disadvantage. She was too shy to find friends easily. Maggie sighed, realizing how much effort the girl before her would have to make in order to graduate from Gbolupa. Probably this was her dream or her pa's dream. But that was two years away. What about the immediate problem? Was she a rogue or a misunderstood girl?

Maggie looked carefully at the girl's face for the tenth time and was swayed by compassion. The girl was lonely and needed a friend. Rogues didn't come with this kind of story.

Maggie asked gently, "And now the girls haven't spoken to you for several days? You are new on campus and lonely?"

Rose looked up and her eyes filled. Then she looked down at her own trembling hands. Quickly she regained her composure and whispered, "And the boys don't speak either. Everyone withhold speech. It hurt inside."

Rose's last statement hit Maggie hard. What could she do? Finally Maggie pushed her voice through a tight throat, "I'm sorry, Rose. I'm sorry things aren't going so well for you here. It is very hard to go to a new school, where you don't know people. Mark and Karen had a hard time here at first, too. We all did."

Maggie hesitated as Sam pulled up on Rose's knees again. This time he raised his arms to be picked up. Maggie thought of all the girls who had come to the house and tried to pick up Sam. He had had nothing to do with any of them. This was a switch. Maggie waited, expecting Sam to scream when Rose reached for him. But Sam responded to Rose's hug. He began to feel her curly hair and Rose willingly let him go ahead with his investigation, which finally reached her eyes. At this point she grabbed Sam's hand and he decided he had found a good playmate. He tried her hair again—pushing it down and then squealing as it bounced right back up on top.

Maggie thought of Mark chattering to Rose. She had liked that, too. Warmth, not words, was what Rose needed. Maggie smiled to herself knowing that her children would probably do more for Rose than Maggie herself could do. They were the best missionaries in the family! Suddenly Maggie knew why God sent families to the mission field. She was encouraged and happily said, "Rose, I think you're going to get through to the other girls. You're a fine girl and the other girls will like you in time. Just be patient."

Rose looked up startled. She gasped, "For true?"

"For true. Rose, I heard you say in Sunday School class that you are a Christian. Didn't you say you belonged to a small church in your village?"

"Yah. I be baptized there. Jesus is in my heart."

Maggie's smile brightened. "Good. Then I know you'll get together with the other girls. Jesus will help you."

Rose smiled for the first time that day. "You can pray for me?"

Halfway through the prayer, Sam interrupted with squeals of delight. Maggie quickly said "Amen," realizing the Lord already knew what she was asking for. Besides company would arrive in the next few minutes and there was much to do. Maggie's thoughts quickly turned toward supper plans as Rose got down on the floor and began to play with Sam.

Before Rose left, Maggie asked her if she'd like to baby-sit sometime. Rose exclaimed, "Yah. Yah," and left singing.

The next week Rose came to Maggie with good news. "The girl in my room found her gold ring. It was in her own trunk. Now she speak to me."

After that Rose came every week. On one visit she mentioned her friends on campus and Maggie realized Rose was over the first hurdle. Finally Rose was around so much that Karen's conversations began to carry "Rose says" phrases. It was then that Maggie remarked to John, "I guess Rose was our first student success story. What a family project!"

John, who was in the middle of another student's problem, replied, "I wish Moses' situation was improving as fast. He's going backwards. Failed another test this week; can't sleep; hardly eats. I wish I knew what to do."

John thought about Moses' last visit. It had brought several surprises, but none so hard to explain as the "witching." John recalled Moses' words, "There's a pretty girl on campus. She smiled at me and waited after class. The other boys said I was lucky. Then some of the girls asked this girl why she went with Country Boy. The girl didn't mind for a while, but then some big shot's son wanted to go with her. He began to kid her about Country Boy, too."

That much of the story wasn't so difficult. It sounded like teenagers anywhere. One thing was certain, Moses cared more for the girl than he was admitting. That's why he never identified her by name. John wondered, but knew there were too many pretty girls on campus to pick this one out without more details.

John mulled over the rest of Moses' story: "The girl got sick. She had to go to the clinic. I was too sorry and I bought a Coke for her. When I gave it to her, she pushed me away and yelled, 'You witched me. You witched me. Now you bring a witched Coke!' "

John remembered how strongly Moses had proclaimed his innocence, as if John would join the girl in accusing him. She had accused all right. Even after Moses got another Coke that still had the cap on, the girl screamed and became hysterical. It was clear she believed she was dying and Moses was the cause. After all he was a "Country Boy" from an area where witching was common. It had taken several teachers to bring quiet back to the clinic and even then a shadow fell on Moses. The girl's accusation quickly spread around the campus.

John had first heard the story from one of the students and had dismissed it. Now he realized that Moses actually believed that he had somehow by accident witched the girl.

John thought of others who were victims of this belief. There was one man who had asked John to store a mattress. When John asked why, the man said he couldn't take the mattress to the village, because no one else there had a mattress. "Someone will witch me!"

Then there was the man who had come to the Blake's house last week with a sick child. His eyes had been glassy with fear as he pleaded for a nurse. Over and over he had lamented, "The boy is witched. He will die. He is witched!"

John looked at his watch and knew Moses would be coming soon. What could be done this time to help him? What did John know about witching, anyway? Why couldn't he come up against a student problem he was experienced in handling? Understand. Understand. John remembered Maggie's words on their first morning in Africa, "I wonder what else we won't understand?" John could fill a book with the topics. He sighed, realized Moses was at the door, and went to let him in.

One look at Moses' face convinced John that no solution had been reached. John decided to get right to the point for he had to be back at school in thirty minutes. "Moses, you're still troubled?"

"Yes."

"I've been thinking and thinking," John went on, "and I don't know much about witching." He stopped to study Moses' face. Still serious. Too serious. All of life was a struggle. John had seen too many village men who had Moses' frame of mind. How did a person keep a light heart and an optimistic view when all around him was a daily struggle to have food for the stomach? Fear of hunger. Fear of death. Fear of witching. Fear was powerful. It controlled everything unless God was on the scene. John decided to test Moses.

"Moses, do you think you could actually witch somebody?"

Moses didn't look up and his hands continued to fold and unfold in his lap. "I would not want to witch anyone. I don't like witching."

John realized he hadn't gotten what he wanted. "You could but you wouldn't, is that right?"

Moses looked up, studied John a moment, and then looked down again. John pushed, "How would you witch someone?"

Moses shrugged his shoulders as if the question were too much. Maybe he didn't know what took place. Even if he suspected some human hand put a little poison in somebody's food, he probably wouldn't say so. John quickly dismissed that idea as his own. Moses likely had seen only the results of witching. He had been afraid to ask, "How?"

"Moses, have you seen people die from witching?"

"Plenty people."

John, who hadn't seen plenty of people die of anything, suddenly felt sympathy. He could see Moses as a small boy listening to the whispers of adults, "He die. He witched." And there was the proof—another dead body. What a person saw he began to believe. John relived the day when he saw a sasswood trial. The cutlass blade had been heated red hot in a fire of sasswood. Three men were on trial. The first one willingly allowed the hot blade to touch his leg. Nothing happened. The player shouted, "Innocent." But when the man holding the cutlass approached the second accused man, he broke and ran. The third man submitted to the blade, but was badly burned. How? John couldn't guess. He hadn't believed his own eyes. That was the point—he didn't believe in sasswood trials and spirits in the wood and fire.

John ventured out. "Moses, I just don't believe in the kind of witching you talk about."

Moses looked up startled. "For true?" Moses had never seen a man who wasn't afraid of evil spirits. He had never heard a man who doubted witching. He was frightened for the professor. Mr. Blake best not say these things where certain people could hear.

John went on. "Moses, if I were you, though, and I believed in witching, I would have one hope."

"For true?"

"Yes, I believe that God is the strongest spirit of all. I would call on him to free me and protect me from the spirits that might hurt me. God could do that!"

John had no idea whether Moses understood or not for there was no reply except a quick lifting of his eyes. John laid on more hope. "You know Moses, God knows all about you and what you've seen and where you've been. He even knows the number of hairs on your head!" Moses almost with a reflex motion reached for his hair. Then he stopped and his hand remained a moment in midair. John laughed. "Do you know how many hairs are on your head? Have you counted lately?"

Moses's hand flew back to his lap. A wavering smile came. "Nah."

"God knows. He cares. He saw you when you were a small boy in a distant village and he decided to send you to the best school in the country."

Moses seemed to like this idea. "Yes, God helped me. The church people paid my tuition even when my grades were bad. They have done more for me than my own pa."

John returned to the immediate situation. "You may not see now how God can lead you through this situation, but he can. Sometimes when we think things are bad, it's only because we haven't turned the situation over to God. And sometimes there are no good things in our lives until we learn to trust without them. Then God gives us good things for true!"

Moses by this time was listening with interest, but John glanced at his watch and realized he was already late for lab.

Some weeks later when John checked semester test scores, he found Moses had failed two. John waited outside the classroom ready to suggest another conference. But when Moses came past, he scarcely looked up. Either he did not see John or he wasn't ready to talk.

Just then Joseph came by, stopped and said, "I'm coming over tonight. Is that OK?"

"Fine," John replied. "I always like to talk with you."

On the way home, John thought about the semester break. There was a lot of work to do for next semester. It wouldn't be much of a break. Then Annual Mission Meeting took up the only other free time until school was out. When you were locked into a classroom schedule, you were chained for certain. But John admitted he liked the classroom and the students. Take Joseph, he was the first with the answers and was generally correct. John thought back through his teaching career for the names of "best students." No, there hadn't been any better than Joseph.

Besides academic excellence, Joseph had other things going for him—family background, good looks, personality, and musical talent. Joseph would spend his semester break in the city having fun and Moses would go back to the village and try to raise enough money to get through the next semester. What a contrast.

Even harder than raising money would be Moses' attempt to prove himself to his fellow villagers. They would be suspicious because he knew book. The old men would wonder if that alone would mean a challenge to their authority. The witchings Moses mentioned so often were evidence of how far some would go to hold power. John wished Moses was up spiritually, but he knew he was down.

John thought about students in the United States. There was always pressure from some group or another to conform. Conform. Some had had no more parental help than Moses had. But the responsibility of the teacher was certainly different. In the United States John's students usually didn't see him after school hours and on weekends. Here he lived with the students seven days a week, twenty-four hours a day. Involvement in depth was the joy and the challenge. And then John thought again about Moses, of the frustration and strain.

John was grading papers that night when Joseph came. "You're later than I thought," John joked. "What senior prefect wrote your pass?"

For a moment Joseph took the professor seriously. "I don't need a pass. I'm a prefect!"

"I know. I know," John kidded. "I see you read all the university catalogs," he added, as he noticed the books in Joseph's hand.

Joseph spoke to Maggie and then sat down on the sofa. "Yes, Professor. I read them all. I wanted to ask about a couple of colleges in the United States."

Maggie excused herself to wash dishes and from the kitchen heard a long conversation which covered world news, education in Africa, and universities in the United States which had good science departments.

When Maggie came back into the living room, Karen was there. "I thought you were in bed," Maggie whispered.

Karen smiled shyly, and looked at the floor. John continued to Joseph. "I found the physics book you wanted, and we're through with this stack of magazines. You can take them to the dorm and pass them around." John thought about the four or five senior boys who devoured all reading materials placed within reach.

Joseph rose to go. "Thanks a lot, Professor. I'll think about those colleges. I'd like to go two years here and then on to the United States." With a chuckle, he added, "If I get a scholarship."

John went to the door with Joseph and said, "Your pa can afford to send you even if you don't get a scholarship. Of course, you no doubt will. See you in class."

As the sound of Joseph's steps were lost, John turned to Karen. "Why do you always show up when Joseph comes to see me?"

Karen blushed and looked at the floor again.

"Ah, ha," John laughed. "He's too old for you. He's a senior."

"Oh, Dad," Karen said, and looked uninterested. "I don't like him. He's just nice."

"Yes, I know," John said with a smile. "And he's good-looking. I heard you MK girls talking about him one day and how neat he is."

The thought of her dad hearing a private conversation was too much for Karen. "I don't like him," she repeated in defense and retreated toward her room.

John picked up the newspaper, rolled it quickly, and tossed it at Karen's disappearing form, "Here, read this. Then you can talk to Joseph, too, when he comes."

Karen caught the paper and tossed it back. Then her head reappeared in the doorway. Shyly she said, "Dad, did you have a girlfriend when you were my age?"

John laughed, "Why do you ask?"

"Oh, Dad, did you?"

John noticed Karen's serious face and replied slowly, "Yes. I did."

"Really?"

"Yes." John's mind leaped back twenty years. "She was pretty. She played baseball better than the boys, like you do. But she didn't know I liked her because I was too bashful to even speak."

"Oh, Dad!" Karen's eyes opened wide. "Your're not bashful. You talk all the time!"

John laughed as he thought about how many times Maggie had waited on him while he finished some long conversation. "Yeah, I talk now. I didn't then. Around girls I was shy, sort of like a girl I know, who ought to be in bed now!"

Karen was satisfied and left with, "Good night, Mom, Dad."

There was silence for some time as John graded papers. Maggie decided to check the fans in the kid's rooms and go to bed early.

John stopped her with, "Listen to these test scores—98, 97, 94, 88, 87, 85, 82, 70, and then the bottom falls out. There are as many 50s as 90s. Either a student here is like Joseph—very good—or he is terrible."

Maggie asked for another verification of the conclusion she had reached weeks earlier while grading many sets of papers. "Are the poor grades mostly girls' grades?"

John shuffled through the test sheets. "Right. Same old story."

"I wish I could figure that out. Every senior class I ever had in the United States had good girl students. The last year I taught eight of the top ten were girls."

"That puzzles me, too. I talked to a couple of principals in town about it the other day. You know what they said?"

Maggie shook her head and waited for the answer. John gave it. "They said the girls at Gbolupa want a big-shot's son for a husband more than they want an education."

Maggie ran the thought around in her mind. "That can't be all the answer. Maybe it's the male-dominated society."

Returning to Joseph, John thought out loud, "Boys like Joseph are in the majority here. Their dad's have government jobs. They have a technical background—that helps." John smiled as he thought about Alfred, the houseboy, and the lawn mower incident of sometime back. Alfred probably couldn't figure out how to put gas in the tank of the big car that Joseph drove when he was home, much less drive it.

Maggie quickly lost John's train of thought for upon the mention of husband hunting her mind settled on Rose, a subject she had tried all week to push aside. Rose had made so many adjustments. That was one reason Maggie wasn't prepared for what had happened. What had the girls in Sunday School class said?

"Rose is gone."

"The old chief came to get Rose, but she wouldn't go."

Another girl had chimed in, "I wouldn't have gone either. The chief strutted like so." The girl got up to demonstrate. She held her head high and gathered a make-believe long robe around a fat body. "He was like so. Fine. Fine in his fine robe."

Another girl broke in, "He was rich, though. He had five wives."

By this time Maggie was completely confused. "What are you saying? What does the chief have to do with Rose?"

"Rose's pa to marry her with the chief!"

"What?" Maggie asked in disbelief, trying to comprehend what this would mean to Rose. "Are you certain?"

"For true. For true," one girl stated. "Rose wouldn't go with the chief, but her pa came to get her. All of us were in class, but the dorm director talked to her pa."

It took Maggie the rest of the week to learn the full story of Rose's departure. The African principal finally supplied the last details. Yes, Rose's educational background was poor. She was failing. Her pa thought she would lose her scholarship. A better offer for help had come. Marriage to a chief represented lifelong benefits to the family.

Maggie finally got to her main question. The principal looked away when she asked, "Is marriage to the chief good for Rose?"

The principal looked out the window. Then he shifted papers on his desk. Maggie decided he thought her question was foolish. Maybe she shouldn't have asked. Some of the girls on campus said Rose was lucky to marry a chief. Others said they would choose their own husbands. Some thought the chief would be OK if he weren't so old and ugly. Obviously a campus vote on the issue of arranged marriages would be split, for the old traditions held firm in some areas of the country.

The short, stocky principal finally looked at Maggie. She noticed again how immaculately dressed he was, as usual. He said, "My pa picked my sister's husband. They got divorced." Maggie realized the principal hadn't thought her question foolish. Perhaps he himself had been worried. But his sister wasn't Rose. His sister could get a divorce; Rose couldn't in her tribal situation.

The principal fingered his gold cuff links and looked uneasy, but he went on. "I picked my own wife . . . and we're separated."

Maggie knew this to be true, but she'd never heard the principal mention it before. Arranged marriage—personal choice—neither held a guarantee. Maggie searched for an answer. When it came, she shared it in part with the man across the desk from her.

"Maybe God should have a hand in mate-picking. I guess that's how I got John. I really wasn't looking for a husband when he came along. I was nineteen, in college, and enjoying myself. What did I need with a husband?"

The principal smiled and Maggie felt encouraged. "Well, God sort of took a hand and John asked one day if I thought I could be a missionary's wife. I was really shocked until romantic love entered the picture and God worked out the details."

Maggie ended abruptly when the office door was opened by an overly eager student.

The principal rose to shake Maggie's hand and she left, wondering if he thought God had anything to do with marriage. Where did that put Rose, though? Maggie remembered the words of one of Rose's friends, "Rose's pa knew the chief was the richest man up-country." Being rich didn't rule out being good, but God wouldn't choose for Rose to be the sixth wife of even a good man. Maggie's doubts soared to 100 percent.

Rose had no choice. She had been placed in a bad situation. Could God do anything now?

Maggie thought about ways to contact Rose. Maybe something could be done.

Maggie was drawn back to the present situation when John said, "These students are good, but how can you teach science without lab equipment?"

Maggie responded lightheartedly, "Well, you can use the pulleys off my living room drapes and the plastic cover off my phonograph and the motors out of my appliances." Maggie stopped, trying to remember what else had gone to school for science demonstrations.

John was half-listening, though. "Maybe next year I'll have equipment." He stopped to calculate. "No, if I order the equipment this semester break, it won't be here until next year at this time. That's too long!" John frowned as he thought about another year with no equipment. Improvising could be as effective as having the best equipment, but it took five times as long and time was limited. John decided he had had enough problem-solving for one day. He looked toward Maggie. "What did you say?"

"I didn't think you were listening? So you won't know!"

John patted the sofa cushion next to the one he was on. "Sit here, and I'll listen."

"No way," Maggie teased. "You never told me about your early romances at age ten. How come?" John started to answer, but Maggie didn't allow it. "You're bashful, remember?"

John finally answered with a raise of his eyebrows and a sly wink. "That was a long time ago. Now I can talk. I even use cologne with sex appeal. Like the advertisement says, I pat it behind my ears, slop it on my neck, and splash it on my chest. For you, I'd even pour it on my feet!"

7
Beggars and Money

John bent over the school's ancient projector and watched as the grumbling machine began to chew on the film. Quickly he turned off the motor. Drat! What to do now? Perspiration ran down his back as he thought about science lab that afternoon. How could he explain without the film? He loosened a screw just as a loud bock, bock sounded at the front door. He glanced up briefly, but clung to the faint hope that the caller would become discouraged and return the way he had come.

It hadn't happened before and it didn't this time. The caller moved to each window, and when he reached the one nearest John, called in a loud voice, "Howdo, Boss."

John knew he was trapped when a face was pressed to the rogue bars. "Wait small," John called over his shoulder, and turned the screw to the left several turns. It came loose from the rusty metal and slid through his open fingers. Shoot! He ran his hand across the tile but his searching pats produced nothing.

The face at the window couldn't be denied. The man began loud, urgent pleas. "I beg you. I beg you." John ignored them and ran his hand under the projector. His fingers closed on the treasure he sought. He picked up the screw and turned to the window.

The man gave the appearance of being in jail as he pressed his face between the bars on the window. When he saw John approaching, he raised his foot. John blinked and wondered what the man was doing. Then John saw that the heel of the foot was all right, but the toes were gnarled stumps. The man lowered this foot and raised the other. It, too, was deformed. As John drew closer his eyes shifted to the man's hands which were holding to the bars. There were knots where fingers had once been. Suddenly, John knew what was wrong. The man had leprosy.

The same interest that caused John to pamper growling projectors went out to this man. He was jailed—not by the bars he looked through, but in an unworkable body. What a house for a man's spirit!

The voice that pleaded was not a man's. It was a whimpering child. "Help me. Help me. I beg you. I beg you."

John opened the front door and stepped onto the concrete porch. The man fell to his knees and grabbed for John's foot, which was instantly drawn from reach. The beggar's forward lunge stopped when his face touched the floor. He cried again, "I beg you. I beg you."

The man's act of submission repelled John and he stepped to the beggar's side, put a strong arm under his arm and half-lifted the man from the floor. "Get up. Stand up. I'm a man. You're a man."

The surprised beggar stumbled onto his stubby feet and grabbed John's hand. "Help me. Help me." As tears came into the beggar's eyes, he rubbed them on John's arm. With a gentle shove, John pushed the man onto his own legs and said, "We will talk. Come."

John turned before the man could grab him again and hurried down the steps that led off the porch. The beggar stood watching for an instant and then followed John as if he might suddenly disappear. John went around the house, across the carport and to the round, open-sided palaver hut in the backyard.

"Sit down," John insisted, and pushed a country chair in the direction of the man, who stumbled forward on his heels and then fell back onto the chair.

Before John could inquire, the man began, "I beg you. Twenty-five dollar. Twenty-five dollar for hospital."

"What hospital? Where?"

The beggar ignored the questions and repeated his request for twenty-five dollars. John's mind turned to other beggars who had come to his house during the week—one for bread, one for money, and now this one. He looked at his watch and thought about the projector that had to work in less than an hour. Suddenly he was tired of intrusions. "My man, speak true," he said sharply, and then glared until he was certain he had the man's attention. "You waste my time. You answer now."

The beggar's mouth hung open where it had stopped in the middle of another plea. He hesitated, looked at John, closed his mouth, and stood in silence.

"OK," John began. "What's your name and where's the hospital?"

"Far place."

"My man, I know the big towns in this country. What town is near the hospital?"

"Boobalu."

John quickly calculated that was one hundred miles away and then suddenly he brightened, "Ah, I know the place. We have a missionary close."

John decided he was getting somewhere and started to continue the questioning. The beggar read his hesitation as uncertainty and began a long monologue. "See, Boss. I there, but the doctor say I go because I not pay." The beggar leaped to his feet with a swiftness that surprised John and whipped a letter out of his shirt pocket. "See. This letter from doctor. He say I pay. I beg you. I beg you."

John took the letter and noticed it was well-worn and dirty. He began to read. The beggar seemed not to notice John was reading, for he continued to babble in John's ear from a distance of a few inches. The letter had no date and the words were written uphill and down. "To whom it may consirn." The next line was less legible and had three misspelled words. No doctor would have used such a vocabulary. The writer couldn't have had more than a third grade education. Maybe he was a fraud claiming miraculous cures for fantastic fees. John folded the letter quickly, as he decided the truth would be hard to learn.

"My man," John began, seriously.

"Yah," the beggar replied, and put his fingerless hands carefully across his chest.

John shifted his gaze uneasily to the man's face and went on. "I know lepers at the hospital where you were. They not pay. They go free! Who wrote this letter?"

John drew a blank as the man's face changed expressions. Suddenly the beggar's face contorted and his eyes grew wide. Then they rolled back and around in their sockets. For an instant John was afraid the man was losing consciousness, and then he remembered another beggar who had done the same thing. The earlier beggar had wanted everyone to think he was crazy and therefore dangerous. His maneuver had worked, for money had rapidly exchanged pockets.

John decided to play another game this time. "You like to roll your eyes? I roll mine, too."

As John's eyes began to rotate, the beggar's eyes stopped. For a minute he enjoyed the show. Then he remembered his own mission. Tears came to his eyes and he fell at John's feet, where his cries for mercy began to lacerate the air.

John let the man stay on the floor this time. Why should he get involved? He'd just give the man some small change and be finished with him. He had other work to do. John's conscience began to take over, though, as he thought about what he had been reading about Jesus and the needy. What would Jesus do?

Only twice had Jesus given food when the crowd asked for it and on both occasions ordinary methods of getting bread were not available. On the other hand, sometimes Jesus just disappeared in order to be alone and pray and seek the will of the Father.

Jesus was good at asking questions which uncovered hidden needs. People had lots of ways to say, "I hurt." Here the most common way seemed to be to ask for money. How did you unscramble five-cent requests that came daily? John remembered the well-to-do landlord who had asked for five cents before he realized he had met John before under other circumstances. A landowner couldn't need five cents. Then there was the shoe repair man, with a good business, who asked for "Boss's car when he return to the United States." What did he really mean? What was his reasoning? Was he lonely, frustrated, restless? Maybe he had no goals and no God to take requests to.

John looked again at the beggar, who still knelt in a prone position. This man couldn't support himself and he had to eat. He was repulsive to look at. Who would want him around? Maybe he presented his case poorly because no one cared about his true story.

Several plans for help went through John's mind and then one stuck, just as if it had been inspired. John smiled as he remembered that Jesus was more concerned with this beggar than he was, and Jesus knew his need. Maybe God had sent him here.

John headed for the house. "You wait. I help you."

John returned ten minutes later to find the beggar sitting calmly in a chair. "I will pay the $25 for you to return to the leprosy hospital."

The beggar jumped to his stumpy feet and pressed his palms in front of his chest. His head nodded up and down and his words were gentle, "God bless you. God will bless you."

"I know. God has already blessed," John began, but saw the man was too involved in his own performance to listen.

When the beggar stopped being thankful, John held up a letter. "This is what I do. I write a check—see." John held the check up, but out of the man's reach. "See it says $25. Then I write a letter to the missionary close to Boobalu. I say to the missionary that he must take the check and go to the hospital. He must ask about you. If he finds you owe the hospital, he will pay for you."

The man's reaction left no doubt that this was not what he wanted. He let it all out—head shaking, eyes glazed, arms loose and swinging, shoulders heaving. Before the tantrum was finished, John looked away unwilling to see more of a personality which was more crippled than a body. So the man was a fraud—an actor who had played the same scene for years. John wished the beggar had come with the truth. Then he might have helped. Now he couldn't. Maybe this man was not yet at the state of perfection where he believed his own lies. Maybe if this method didn't work he'd try a more honest one.

The beggar finally controlled his movements and his voice began with a whiny, "I beg you. Fifty cents for a taxi to town."

As John moved away, the voice became high and scratchy. "Twenty-five cent for bread. I hungry. I hungry."

John realized the man was getting closer to the truth but he stood firm in his decision not to help. John remembered beggars of every size who had come to his door, but he had never heard anything like this. In fact, there had been pleasure in meeting some of the requests. Ice cubes on a hot day sounded reasonable. A tire pump to put air in a soccer ball so the team could play. John would never forget the village boy who had received his first real toy truck. It had round wheels rather than square ones carved from pieces of wood. When the boy realized that a slight push could send the truck sailing across the dirt, he had left the truck and hollered, "Whoo . . . Whoo . . . oo." Then he had come to shake John's hand and John had lost count after the boy's tenth, "Thank you."

John remembered one of the men on campus who waited an hour on his doorstep to pay back fifty cents. He was more than honest in a culture where credit usually meant give.

John looked toward the house and remembered the student who had come to the back door to ask for $20 for shoes because he had none and the other boys kidded him. John smiled as he thought about how long it had taken to convince the boy $5 tennis shoes would do. John hadn't felt so good when he found out the same student had collected another $5 from another missionary for the same pair of shoes.

The boy that John most liked to remember was the one who hadn't asked, but had taken a need to God. John could still see the boy's expression when the needed money had been placed in his hand with this explanation, "A church in the United States sent this. I have a feeling you can use it!"

That boy had praised the Lord. Faith, as well as money, had been involved.

John's attention came back to the beggar who was rapidly becoming exhausted. "I cannot help you, my man. I not come here to be your pa. I come to be brother. I come to tell what Jesus can do. Jesus one fine friend."

A bored look crossed the beggar's face. He had heard about Jesus before, but that talk never brought him money. He got up, whirled around, and sat down with such force that the chair almost turned over. "I not leave. I stay." Then he raised one foot and put his hands out.

John looked beyond them to the man's eyes. "I sorry you not have good hands and feet. Is bad, but you can get help. The people at the hospital help you free. But they not give you money. They expect you to work while you stay there. They not pay you for talk, talk."

The beggar grunted as John left the palaver hut.

"What's going on?" Maggie inquired, when John came in and locked the back door.

"A determined beggar. Keep the door locked or he'll be inside and never leave."

John returned to his projector. Where had he put that screw? Several minutes of searching produced it and John worked rapidly to finish before time for lab. He had almost forgotten the beggar when his face appeared again at the front window. The face was all smiles, as if the man were meeting John for the first time. In a quiet voice, the beggar said, "Five cent. Five cent, boss."

When John ignored him, the man became less controlled. John turned his back to the window and plugged in the projector. To his surprise the film began to roll through. John unplugged it and looked at his watch—ten minutes late. He grabbed the projector and hurried out the door, locking it behind him. A few steps off the porch he realized the beggar was at his heels. John quickened his pace, hoping the beggar wouldn't return to the house to humbug Maggie.

For a dozen steps the beggar stayed with John. Then he spotted a house he hadn't visited that day. He turned toward it and the missionary who answered pushed one dollar through the door. Soon the other houses on campus were canvassed and the beggar went through the gate a happy man. He had more money than the workmen on campus earned in two days of hard labor.

Later, when John walked home from lab, he saw Dennis in his yard and waved.

Dennis turned off the lawn mower and motioned to John. As he drew close, Dennis asked about how the lab had gone and then offered him a cool drink.

John sat, waiting, and soon Dennis returned with two glasses of Fanta. He handed one to John and remarked, "This 90 percent humidity makes me feel dry as a desert!"

John reported on the lab and drank half his Fanta before his mind returned to the beggar. "Hey, did a leper come to your house today?"

"Did he? He held my foot for ten minutes."

"What did you do?"

"Gave him a dollar."

"Really," John was somewhat surprised, but tried not to show it. Dennis was experienced here. Maybe John had done the wrong thing. "I spent an hour with that guy trying to unravel his story. I still don't know whether he had a legitimate need or not."

Dennis's interest grew. "I've tried all day to place that man. Finally it's getting through. Did that guy have an old letter?"

"Yes, crumpled, and poorly written."

"Ah, ha, now I have it. That man was on campus six months ago with that same letter and story."

It was John's turn to be puzzled. "He was?"

"I'm certain now. He didn't show me the letter this time. It's open season on missionaries, as you know, and the stories all begin to sound the same after awhile. But that was the same man. Well, I've probably been taken again."

"That's the problem," John said with gravity. "How can you sort the needs? I could give away a hundred dollars every day."

"And you don't have it, and neither does the Mission."

"Right. And besides, who wants to be a rich uncle? I'm spending so much time with beggars I have little time for anything else. It's getting to me."

"I know. I know what you're talking about," Dennis said, with a frown. "When I became a missionary, giving away money was the least of my reasons and now I run into money palaver everywhere. We all do. Money for churches. Money for schools. Money for cars and houses and shoes. Money! Money!"

John leaned forward, "And sometimes it takes a congressional investigation to get any facts. Then you begin to feel sneaky as a lizard!"

Dennis laughed. "That may be OK. It's biblical—'Wise as serpents!' " (Matt. 10:16).

John looked toward his modern house. "There's another problem, too. Every missionary speaker I ever heard said I would feel guilty about having so much when others have so little. Well, the people's needs here are more obvious than any I have seen before, but I don't feel guilty."

Dennis laughed. "Man, if you don't have a problem, don't make one." Dennis studied John for a moment for a reaction, and then regretted his remark. John was really struggling. Dennis knew the feeling. He had spent his first two years in West Africa deep under the problem of how to relate to the people.

John didn't notice Dennis was scrutinizing him as he went on to justify his remark. "If I had spent my time trying to make money, I might feel guilty. But I came to the big job-success-money decision when the last good job was offered me. I decided then doing what God wanted was more important." John sat back and finished his drink. "What I have came from God. It's enough, but not plenty. Why should I feel guilty about what God has given me? Should a doctor or lawyer feel guilty because they have skills others don't have?"

Dennis thought for a while. "It all depends on how they use the skill. Blessed in order to bless is an idea as old as Abraham. Blessed sometimes is taken, though, as an excuse to keep. A boy in my Sunday School class said something about that a few Sundays ago. He said at first he thought missionaries had too much, and he was jealous. Then a missionary bought him some new shoes. Then he realized that if the missionary had been as poor as he was, the missionary could not have shared."

Dennis stopped to reflect on Mary, a girl his eight-year-old Peggy had wanted to help. What had Peggy said? Oh, yes, "But, Daddy, Mary wears ugly clothes to church." That didn't sound like a good enough reason. Dennis remembered that was exactly what he had told his inquisitive eight-year-old. Then why had he finally gotten the new dress? A wide grin crossed Dennis' face as he decided to tell John the rest of the story. "One time Peggy asked me to buy a dress for a girl at church. You know the reason Peggy finally gave?"

John looked up and shook his head. "No telling."

"Peggy told me that God had told her that Mary would look nice in a new dress!"

John's serious face turned to a smile. "Really?"

"That's exactly what she said. And I thought about it and it figured. God dressed the trees in beauty and the sky in many colors. Why wouldn't he like a girl in a pretty dress? When Mary wore that dress along with her big smile I said right out loud, 'God you're right. She does look nice. Black is beautiful and so is white and red and yellow!' "

Dennis was looking into space now savoring the joys of that experience. John looked at him a moment and then his eyes fell to the ground. Dennis had it—that gentle nature, the other part of the verse that he had just quoted. He was wise as a serpent and also harmless as a dove. That was what John wanted. It wasn't enough to be called a missionary. You had to feel like one. Mind and emotion had to agree. John sighed as he started toward home. All he could do was ask for the right attitude. God knew what he wanted to be. Maybe.

8

First to See Jesus

While the new missionaries were battling with personal adjustment, the most severe test came in a crisis which shook everyone on campus. The first indication of trouble came when the stillness of dawn was shattered by a dozen screams. Maggie stirred and, as the shrill wails came closer, sat up startled, ears registering a sound she had never heard before. What was this? Maggie's four months in Africa brought no answer.

The shrieks came closer and Maggie was frightened. In the half-light she found her housecoat, and tiptoed to the back door. She opened it softly, so as not to wake her sleeping household, and went down the two steps and onto the carport. Then she saw the dim outlines of people gathered around Ruth's house. What were they doing? Maggie controlled her impulse to get John and hurried past the bird of paradise, across the road, and into Dennis and Ruth's yard.

A form stepped out from the crowd and as it approached Maggie recognized Tom Wilson. She stopped and watched his brisk approach. When he was within a few feet, Maggie flinched as she glimpsed his wide eyes and ashen skin. Tom's clocklike face was gone. The plastic veneer that it usually wore had melted and a heartbeat throbbed at the temple.

"O God!" Maggie cried within, as her own heart began to pound in her ears.

Through tight lips Tom whispered, "Dennis was killed last night!"

Maggie gasped and found she could hardly breathe. She couldn't believe it. How? How? She glanced past Tom to where the Baker car was usually parked. It wasn't there.

Tom answered the question that was in Maggie's gaze. "There was a head-on collision." The words said, Tom looked down, rubbed a hand across his eyes and struggled to continue. "Dennis died instantly. Ruth and the children weren't in the car. They were visiting a missionary in town and they're still there."

Maggie began to tremble as Tom took a handkerchief from his trousers pocket, blew his nose, and tried to regain his composure. "The students heard the news on the radio at 6 A.M."

"Oh," Maggie managed, as she looked toward the teenagers, who ran hysterically around the mission house next to hers. Further words would not pass the knot in her throat. She wanted to flee the tight trap of grief which now held her. A far-away voice finally came. "I must tell John."

Maggie turned and tears flooded her eyes. By the time she reached her own back door, she could not see anything. She fumbled for the handle and John opened the door. The look on Maggie's face told him what the wailing was about.

"Who is it?"

"Dennis." Maggie tried to control her sobs, and finally in one sudden burst whispered, "Car wreck—others OK." Then she motioned toward Ruth's house. "The students. They're frantic."

John pulled Maggie close and unconsciously patted her shoulder as he tried to absorb the rapid-fire information Maggie had just given him. Quickly reaching a decision, he pulled away. "I must go to the students."

As the door closed after John, Maggie crossed the waxed floor, came to the living room, and sat down in the rocker that had been her grandpa's. Suddenly, the chair became a time tunnel back. Maggie was at her grandpa's feet and he had finished reading a child's book and for the fifth time that noon said, "Now that's the last book today!"

Funny how Maggie should remember him now. She held on to this picture for several minutes. It was the only one she had for her grandfather had died soon after that, when she was only three. The picture evaporated as quickly as it had come and sobering thoughts of Dennis' death took its place.

Death? Death? What was its picture? Was it bright or dark, beautiful or sad? Right now Maggie was not quite certain for she was looking at an overexposed negative. She half-saw and she was half-blind. She knew Dennis was OK, but God, how she hurt all over.

Her mind tossed out questions like a defective engine tosses oil. Drip. Splatter. Blop. A smoking engine could be turned off, but Maggie's troubled mind ran on and on. Seven years at Gbolupa ended, finished in a split second. Maggie's tears had been dripping and now they came in uncontrollable sobs and wet her face and housecoat. She tried to control them as a stirring came from Karen's bedroom. Please God don't let the children get up yet. Give me time. What will I tell them?

Maggie listened for a long minute. Karen became quiet again. Maggie touched the arm of the chair where her sister had carved her name years before. Maggie's finger unconsciously followed the letters as she thought about Dennis and Ruth leaving the campus yesterday. They were just on their way to town to shop. Mark had chased the car as it drove by and Karen had shouted, "Hurry back," to her best friend, Peggy.

As Maggie rocked, the gravity of their situation rolled over her. What about the children? Dennis' parents? Gbolupa? Muddied questions sloshed around and around in her brain until Maggie with exteme effort pushed them back. She did not know how long she had rocked, but she knew there was a hard day ahead. One step at a time, she cautioned herself, and rose to begin breakfast.

Somehow the hours passed and night came. The whole day blurred. Maggie tried not to think as she got into bed. At least Ruth was doing well. The one-year-old was too young to understand. He had played in the Blake's yard part of the afternoon. Everytime Maggie looked at him her tears began. A one-year-old needed a father. Peggy had walked around all afternoon like a robot. Finally Karen had come in. "I don't know what to say to Peggy."

The muddy images that Maggie had shoved aside that morning, now ran over in her mind like a river at flood level. Maggie got out of bed and didn't wake John as she slipped into the living room.

The night was cool. The moon bright. Maggie paced and ached deep inside. How could she help Ruth? Ruth had been so good to bring food the first week the Blakes had been in Africa. Ruth had shared practical information that had seemed crucial at the time—how to mix dried milk so the kids would drink it, where to shop, how to treat beggars.

John and Dennis had quickly understood that their relationship would become close as they shared bits of information about how God had brought each family to Gbolupa. Maggie remembered Dennis talking for hours about the students and their needs.

Thoughts of yesterday only made her sadder. How could Maggie handle this death? Why had the missionary closest to the students been taken? Tears surfaced as Maggie began to address her questions to God. Slowly a new idea took shape. God hadn't planned for funerals! In the Garden of Eden there was only harmony between man, animals, and nature. That was God's original life of joy and satisfaction. Then man sinned and the animals revolted and nature turned to earthquakes. What a mess the perfect plan became. No wonder Jesus wept at Lazarus' death. He had planned that life would be so much better than that! So different from this! God had brought Lazarus back to life and God was still working. Death to life, like a seed becoming a flower.

With these thoughts rushing through her mind, Maggie slept the two hours that remained before another day.

The funeral was two days later. Maggie and John drove in the procession from the capital city to Gbolupa. Behind John's car came missionaries from various groups, European friends, students, and teachers. As the cars left the city, sirens made a way, and people stopped to stare. As the first village was passed, Maggie noticed men and women standing silently by the roadside. At the second village there was another solemn crowd, dressed in dark lapas. Finally, when the third village came into view, Maggie realized that something unusual was happening. She turned to Prince's mother, who was riding in the back seat. "The people? At each village there are people. Why are they standing by the road?"

"Respect for the dead."

"But lots of people die here and I've never seen crowds along the road."

The African teacher considered a few moments and replied, "The people knew Mr. Baker. He had been at Gbolupa a long time."

"No doubt, the people saw him drive by. They know all the missionary's cars," John said.

"Missionaries are special to these villagers, particularly Mr. Baker." Prince's mother waved at a woman she knew as the car slowly passed another village. "You know Mr. Baker stopped to give these people rides and carry zinc for them. Many came for help with their children's school fees. Of course, some of the men work on campus."

John carefully considered the extent of the acquaintance. "Yes, there was personal contact. The path that goes through Gbolupa is always full of people from dawn to dusk."

Maggie's admiration for Dennis increased as her thoughts took another turn. This road was just a dusty, inconvenient way to go to town for weekly shopping. The faster she passed the villages, the quicker she got home. Perhaps this road was for purposes other than travel. Make the path straight—make the path straight. What did that mean? Maggie decided to find that reference when she got home.

The car slowly passed more serious faces. Maggie looked at the motionless hands and the sad eyes which followed the hearse on its journey to Gbolupa. Maggie looked ahead, too, for the procession was almost to the campus.

The cars went through the gate and stopped thirty yards up the road. As Maggie got out of the car, she noticed the sun was low. The drive from town had taken much longer than was expected. Still a crowd waited at the grave site, as the casket was carried by. When the people had crowded as close as possible to the grave lined with concrete blocks, the campus pastor indicated the choir should begin.

The first lines they sung touched the crowd and quiet weeping began. "Beloved, [beloved,] how are we the sons of God, And it does not appear what we shall be: But we know when he shall appear, We shall be like

him; [We shall be like him.] For we shall see him as he is" (1 John 3:2).

Guide me, O thou great Jehovah,
Pilgrim through this barren land,
I am weak, but thou art mighty.
Hold me with thy powerful hand.

Maggie marveled as the students sang the next two stanzas of the hymn in strong, clear voices. Only when they sat down did she notice handkerchiefs, that had been held in tight hands, wiping at blurred eyes. Several missionaries gave testimonies about eternal life and Scripture was read. The entire service had lasted a mere fifteen minutes.

Then the missionary kids came with flowers they had picked hours earlier and held for this moment. The wind murmured through the two palm trees above the grave site as the children placed their wilted gifts on the casket. There was no sound until the children turned and then as they passed, Lois whispered, "Uncle Dennis was the first of us to see Jesus!"

Maggie placed that sentence beside all the beautiful ones she had ever heard. A hasty review of the best poetry she knew found no comparison. Lois had found a joyful answer.

Maggie turned to walk the two hundred yards to her own house. She wanted to be at home when the missionaries from up-country, who would stay that night on campus, arrived. As she hurried, her eyes caught the first pinking of sunset. The flowering shrubs were hanging to the ground with yellow blooms. Cotton balls blew across the ground. In the background Maggie heard the shovels begin their work. A beautiful day—a bad day? Maggie swung between frustration and hope. She was walking in another of life's sad-glads. Suddenly the glad words caught her spirit and lifted it. "We shall be like him; for we shall see him." Dennis was looking at Jesus now!

John got up very early the day after the funeral. School would be in session again. The principal had found no replacement for Dennis, so his classes were divided among the other missionaries. Two hours into the day showed John that no one really knew all that Dennis had done. Several times John stopped during that morning and almost unconsciously headed for Dennis' classroom to ask for help.

At two o'clock John came home for lunch and to relax, only to find a houseful of people. In private Maggie asked, "Did you forget the preachers from the United States on the evangelistic tour of West Africa?"

John's mind flew back and dimly he remembered a letter months earlier.

Maggie read his doubtful expression and continued, "I had forgotten, too, in the rush of the last days. It was good the missionary in town sent a radio message this morning!"

"Are they staying for lunch?" John asked with a quick glance toward the stove.

"Yes, luckily I found two meat loaves and a cake in the freezer, so we're all set!"

John gave Maggie a smile of appreciation. "You always come through in the emergencies. I'll go meet everybody while you finish lunch."

After lunch John went back to school to go over Dennis' class rolls and lesson plans for the week. The day quickly passed and John still had his own lessons for the next day. He turned on the lights in the laboratory and worked until Maggie came to knock at the door.

"I was worried. We had supper and I finally got the kids to sleep. They're upset. Mark is seeing tigers again and Karen is concerned about Peggy."

John looked past Maggie and at the work left to do. Maggie's gaze caught the pile of papers, too. "You can't work all night. You're only one man. You can't do all of Dennis' work."

"I know. I know. This was some day. The students were far away. Oh boy!" John hit the palm of his hand with his fist. "I'm beat. Did the preachers leave?"

Maggie studied John's face for the calm that was usually there. He turned to the desk and she knew answering his question would be like throwing leaves into a strong wind. "John, please let's go home. The children may wake up and they'll be even more frightened if I'm not there."

John picked up one book, pushed the others to the back of the desk, and turned off the lights. On the way home they avoided Ruth's yard as if walking by the house would only increase their anxiety.

A bird that often sat in the road flew up as they approached and drifted into the cool night. John was too preoccupied to notice when Maggie took his arm. Maggie could not remember when her touch had failed to bring some response. First the children, now John. How could Maggie handle her own loss and comfort the whole family, too?

The joy that she had felt after Dennis' funeral slowly faded as students and teachers brought their gloom to the Blake's house. Maggie swung back to frustration as she helped Ruth sell part of her household goods and pack the rest for shipment to the United States.

Three weeks passed and the day for Ruth's departure found everyone on campus still numbed by the sudden events. Not only had the students lost a favorite teacher and friend, now they were losing "their boy." When the Bakers had first come to the campus, there had been only Peggy. It was unbelievable to the students that the Bakers should not have a son. They began to pray. For five years students kept this petition before the Lord, even when Ruth laughed and said, "But we can't have another baby." Finally, to everyone's amazement except the students, the Bakers not only found they were expecting, but the newborn was the much-prayed-for son. He had been teased, pampered, and enjoyed since birth. He reminded the students of their brothers and sisters at home and became part of their family away from home.

Now the students gathered around the car which would carry Ruth and the children to the airport. Hands reached to pat the small boy as the car began its halting drive around campus. Clusters of students and teachers stood at each corner and Ruth touched the outstretched hands. Then to the next corner and more hands. Ruth's smile and kind words continued. When the car was in front of the Blake's house, Ruth called, "You have been such good friends. I'll see you when you come on furlough."

The final group of missionaries was soon behind and the car pulled through the cotton balls falling from the huge tree and went out the Gbolupa gate. Oh, how it hurt to see them go!

Maggie hugged Mark's shoulder as he began to cry, and turned toward the house. Karen asked, "Will Peggy ever come back to Gbolupa?"

John blew his nose and put Sam on his shoulders. "Nobody knows. There's a lot we don't understand."

The full impact of Ruth's departure did not come until night when Maggie looked anxiously out the window to see if the lights in the laboratory were still on. Yes, John was still working. Maggie's eyes came closer to home and suddenly she realized there were no lights at the Baker's house. Never before had the house been dark at night. During Maggie's first week on campus, she had learned she could read her fellow missionaries activities by watching the lights. Outside lights only meant the family was gone. Living room lights meant someone was up. Dim lights inside and a few lights outside indicated sleep. It was months before Maggie could look at the dark house next door without feeling waves of pain and sorrow. Gradually their intensity lessened, but many questions still flooded her mind. Maggie knew she must find the faith to quit asking God, "Why?"

Maggie, who had thought her days could hold no more, soon found a more constant line of students at the door. They had turned to John for counsel. Increasingly John became aware of how extensive Dennis' influence had been. Finally James, a vocal Muslim student, asked the question that seemed to be on many minds, but had not been voiced.

"I do not understand," James began. "I did not know a missionary could die like that!"

"What?" John was startled by a question he had not anticipated.

"I never see anything bad happen to a missionary."

John reflected on that. It puzzled him. Did this student know so little about missionaries? "You mean a missionary never told you about the bad times he faced?"

"Missionaries always seem happy. They have cars and houses and food and clothes."

John knew the deprived background of this student well enough to understand why the necessities of life seemed important to him. "Yes, we have these things. But my pa is sick now and in the hospital."

"Your pa living?"

Again John was surprised. "Yes, he lives. Does yours?"

"Nah. He not stay."

"How about the rest of your family?"

"My ma go when I small boy. My ma have ten children. Three of us stay."

John could see the student had a point. He had experienced much loss during his lifetime, while John had known little. How could he help James handle his doubts? John grabbed for some way to indicate all men suffered and died. "My friend, we're all men. We all put our pants on the same way!"

James was dismayed. This earthy comment opened a door. He'd never thought about missionaries putting on their trousers. Much less the same way he did!

John continued quietly, "James, are you questioning man or God?" This thought hung for a minute. "Do you think God makes special rules for some people?"

James gave a hands-up sign. He didn't know. "The students are upset. I'm confused."

John leaned back in the chair and sighed. He deliberately turned his mind toward God in search of help. A minute later, he tipped the chair forward, eager to share. "James, I have a story for you.

"One day Mark and I were on the beach when way down the shoreline people began to run and yell. Mark and I decided to go see what was wrong. People were pointing out to sea by this time. I looked, but saw nothing except a coconut shell bobbing up and down. Obviously the excitement wasn't over that, so I asked a man what was wrong.

"The man was so excited he could hardly tell me. He just continued to point. Finally I pieced his few words together and knew that someone had just drowned. The man was watching the spot where he had last seen his friend, hoping that he would come up again.

"Mark and I walked on to where the crowd was gathered and heard the same story again and again. How they had seen a man go down and come up several times and then go down for the last time.

"I asked if anyone had tried to save the man and the people pointed to a man who was pulling trousers over a wet swimsuit. The man had been too far out and the best of swimmers could not reach him.

"Mark and I waited for maybe fifteen minutes and still the people stood pointing to where they had last seen the man. Finally, Mark asked me if I would save him if he were drowning.

"I told him I would if I could. And then Mark asked a tougher question. 'Would I drown to save him?' "

"I turned that one back to him and asked what he thought. Mark was silent as we walked toward home, but when we got there he said, 'You love me too much to let me drown!' "

John paused and looked carefully at James. "Now Mark had hit on the key—love doesn't let a person die."

James looked up with a puzzled frown. "That's what I say. God says he loves Mr. Baker and he let him die!"

"No, James," John answered. "God loved Mr. Baker and he didn't let him die!"

"How's that?"

James's frown grew deeper and John knew he had no inkling where he was leading him. "For God so loved Mr. Baker that he sent his only son, Jesus, so that Mr. Baker believed in Jesus and did not die, but lives forever!" John sat back in his chair to see what response came.

Slowly James's countenance brightened. His lips began to move. "For God so loved the word, that he . . ." (John 3:16). James's voice dropped as he began to examine the words he had heard since his first week at Gbolupa. Suddenly it was important to know if they were true. He compared them to his own Muslim belief that death was Allah's will. But the professor had said God loved. Love? Could it be?

As James continued to reflect, John pushed. "James, did God let Mr. Baker die?"

James looked beyond John and then to the floor. Finally he shrugged. John, who knew it required faith to answer that question said, "I want to believe that Dennis laughs, talks, and lives now with God."

John would have preferred to use his own phrase which showed more certainty—I do believe—but instead chose the phrase he had often heard from the students. "Yes, I want to believe that going from earth to heaven is the most exciting trip we'll ever take."

John could tell James wasn't following this line of thought for he came back with, "But, Professor, God not love me. God just makes trees."

John had heard this so often that he answered with more force than he intended. "You can't have a God who makes only trees!"

James's eyes opened wide. He had offended the professor—something he would never have intentionally done. Why? His mind grasped for some reason as John supplied an explanation in a calmer tone. "There is only one God! The God who made the trees is the same God who sent Jesus and he's the God who lives in my life through the Holy Spirit."

James was still bewildered and John tried again. "You can't take God apart and hand him out to every religion under the sun. He's too big to handle in one bite. If you want him, let him be God. Don't try to make him Allah, the creator, and then the animistic God of spirits, and then another God of Christianity. There is one God and only one!"

"Really? You mean everybody worships the same God?"

"No, there are many imitations and some people worship these false gods. There is only one true God and few people worship him."

John could tell that James was lost again and so he pointed him toward Jesus. "If you want to know God, James, come to Jesus. Jesus is the way!"

James was not listening and so John leaned back. Well, at least James was searching. John sent a request to God. "From Dennis' death bring new life to James."

9
The Path

As Maggie walked across the road her thoughts turned to June, whose house lay right on the path. Maggie suddenly realized she hardly knew her neighbor, who was only two doors away. When she knocked on the Pearce's door, June answered with a smile.

"Hi, I'm glad you came. We haven't had much time to visit in the few months you've been on campus." June led the way to her attractive living room.

Maggie found June to be a good listener and soon confided, "I'm homesick or something."

June nodded in sympathy and said, "I've been upset myself since Dennis' death."

"Well, I guess that's it," Maggie said. But deep down she knew it was more. She felt inadequate and unable to do what she thought a missionary should do. Everybody else on campus seemed to be doing so much.

June sensed Maggie's uneasiness but didn't know how to respond. Misreading Maggie's feelings, June attempted comfort. "It's fine to speculate about life after death until you lose someone very dear. Then you want to know for certain life goes on. That's the joy I have—thinking about Dennis still alive and with God."

Maggie was touched and her own sorrow almost came to the surface. Yet a strained, "Yes," was all she managed. She excused herself with, "Sam will be awake soon. I have to go."

June watched as Maggie crossed into her own yard and thought about how John had first introduced Maggie. "She's my country girl. Always walks like she's crossing the furrows of a plowed field." June had read behind that a certain pride, for Maggie was attractive enough to be noticed, with the figure of a fifteen-year-old. Probably at fifteen she'd been just tall and skinny, but now at twice that age, June, like all women who had weight problems, couldn't help envying a woman who could eat anything and never gain a pound. Maggie had a pretty face, too, but it was hard to read.

June's mind leaped back seven years to when she was a new missionary.

The church members at home had pushed the idea that missionaries walk on paths so grand that they are lifted out of the ordinary and practical side of life.

But real experience? June smiled to herself. No heavenly chariot had ever carried her over the muddy paths in the middle of the night to meet medical emergencies. There had been no dead men raised. In fact, she'd lost 80 percent of the very ill babies brought to her that first year. She flinched as she remembered how it had been to see so much dying. She had never tried to even put into words how defeated she had felt. Sometimes she had felt only anger—surely the Foreign Mission Board had goofed again! She didn't fit; this was too much! How long had it taken her to learn to trust the Lord when the results all seemed bad, even disastrous? Two years? No, it was more like three or four. Even now she was often walking down what seemed like blind pathways. Like when Dennis died. That had shook her more than any experience of the last few years. And that had been Maggie's introduction to the Mission!

With that kind of introduction to God's course, the rest of the curriculum was bound to be deep. June looked toward Maggie's house and a new thought came. Maggie was going to go beyond usual understanding. God had big plans for her!

June stopped, puzzled. Was she to play a part? What? June remembered that a personnel man had said Maggie's file was filled with glowing recommendations about her teaching career. Maggie liked children. Her yard was always full of them. An idea slowly took shape and in two weeks June went to Maggie with it. "I've been thinking you need to get out more."

Maggie quickly agreed. "You're right." Then thoughts of the difficulties of getting a baby-sitter came. "I don't have anybody to keep Sam since Rose has gone."

June had anticipated this problem in advance. "I have a good houseboy and he makes a good baby-sitter." Getting to the other issue, June said, "Then you can help me on Tuesday mornings with the clinic."

Maggie looked startled and managed, "You do have plans!" She hesitated not quite knowing where to go from there. "I don't know anything about a clinic."

"You'll learn. Two Tuesdays each month and every Thursday I see village patients. On the other two Tuesdays I go to seven villages for well-baby clinics. The other days are for students."

Maggie was still puzzled. "Me, a nurse? No way."

"I don't need a nurse. I am a nurse! I need somebody to keep records, but mainly I need a teacher. I need demonstrations and charts on baby care and you could do them," June continued.

"Well, that's different. Now you're talking about something I feel comfortable with." Then a doubt entered her mind. "But I don't know how to teach village women. I can't even talk to them."

June said in her most convincing tone, "My dear, you can learn. The needs are obvious and you'll find a way."

Later when Maggie approached John with the idea he thought it was great and said, "Do it!"

In September when Karen and Mark went back to school, Maggie deposited a crying Sam with June's houseboy and went to her first well-baby clinic.

At the first village June began with a short meditation and song. The women continued to move to the rhythm of the hymn long after the singing stopped. How they loved music!

While June weighed babies and gave DPT, polio, and smallpox immunizations, the women chattered at a rapid pace. They made a group, rather than a line and Maggie could never tell who was next. In fact, nobody seemed to care if the cards had to be sorted over and over again because someone from the back decided to move to the front of the line. This confusion, the makeshift table and Maggie's inability to understand the slurred way names were given soon got to Maggie. As they left the village, Maggie wiped her forehead and exclaimed, "I can't understand a thing they say!"

June laughed. "They read you and you'll learn to read them."

The reception at the second village was cold. The women gave information sparingly and in muffled tones. There were children everywhere, playing in the dirt, but few of them were brought to June. Maggie whispered to June, "What's wrong here?"

Out of the side of her mouth June whispered, "The Old Lady. She doesn't trust clinics—particularly Christian ones. She's Muslim."

Maggie tried to piece together the information she had heard about "Old Ladies." Yes, each village had one. They were old and respected. Yes, they told the younger mothers how to take care of their children. No, they didn't always deliver the babies.

The following Tuesday outpatients came to the clinic. Maggie was again in charge of the card file. All morning long she found herself calling for "Ma," the clinic assistant, who could understand all the tribal dialects and knew half the people. Ma would listen to the patient and instantly repeat a name in sounds that Maggie understood. Under her breath, Maggie tried to repeat what the patient had said, but eventually gave up. English with a tribal accent was too much for her.

Half-way through the morning, June called for Maggie to come into the examining room. On the table lay the skinniest, most pathetic baby Maggie had ever seen. Maggie looked at him only a minute and then gazed away to escape the sight.

June's tone was filled with both clinical knowledge and compassion as she explained, "This is one of the babies from the Old Lady's village, where we were last week. None of those children had their measles immunizations. Measles have now gone through the entire village." June turned to get her stethoscope. "This child had measles two weeks ago. His temperature went unchecked for days. Now he's weak and dehydrated. He can't suck."

June put the stethoscope to the baby's chest and he let out a moan as soft as one from a newborn kitten. June went on, "Black babies don't break out with measles very well. I can hardly touch him anywhere."

Maggie watched as the infant flinched each time June examined a sore. June finished and turned to the baby's mother and the three other women with her, "Mommie, this baby cannot live without liquids. He can't take tittie because he too weak to suck. He need to go to the hospital now."

The young mother turned to the older women and they talked together in tribal dialect. Then the mother turned back, "Missy, he not go to hospital. You help him!"

June looked around the small clinic. It was OK for simple lab work, shots, bandaging, and giving some medicines. She tried to persuade the mother. "I not have right medicine. I not hospital." Then as she looked at the baby, who was to weak to even cry out loud, her voice deepened. "The baby can't live. He need strong medicine." Then she lifted the charm tied with a piece of cloth around the baby's waist. "Stronger medicine than this!"

Ma, who had been standing by the table, to make certain the baby didn't roll off, turned to the women, "Aa ya, hear what Missy say." Then she shook her finger in order to emphasize each point about the baby's care that she made to the women in their own dialect.

The women listened and then turned in a circle to talk with each other.

June guessed what was wrong. "The Old Lady not let you take this baby to the hospital." There was a sharp rise to her voice indicating they should answer honestly.

The women looked at the floor. June raised the mother's chin and said pointedly, "Mommie, the Old Lady not let you take this baby to the hospital?"

Slowly the mother's head nodded, "Yes."

June, who was well-acquainted with the yes-no process of village communication, knew that yes actually meant, "The Old Lady says no."

June turned away to hide her frustration. On her way to her desk, she passed Maggie and whispered, "No way. No way."

She got a bottle out of the drawer and motioned for the mother. "I can help only small. I give you boiled water with sugar. Here is dropper. You must feed the baby drip-drip-drip." June approached the child and cradled its head. As she demonstrated she repeated the instructions. "Drip-drip. Every hour give small water. You can do?"

The mother nodded her head. She would try.

June picked up the baby and he gave another kitten-like moan. Ma patted the limp form and tears filled her eyes. Maggie stood like a stone, unable to do or say anything as the women tied the infant on his mother's back and left.

June turned to Maggie. "His heart is weak. He'll die. He'll die like all the others!" She sighed and then continued, "I'll go to the village tomorrow." Then almost to herself, she added, "I'm going to see the Old Lady, too."

The last patient that morning was another seriously ill baby. This time both the ma and pa brought it. June looked toward Maggie and said optimistically, "These people mean business. We'll save this baby even though he has measles!"

The pa somehow raised the hospital admission fee and was on June's doorstep with the child that afternoon when she came out of the house to leave for her weekly shopping trip. And as she had promised, she provided transportation to the hospital.

The next morning Maggie had misgivings about leaving Sam two days in a row, but he seemed happy with June's houseboy when they left for the village. Maggie's attention was quickly drawn to the path which led to the sick child's village. Maggie smiled to herself as she remembered it was almost October. But the cool crispness in the air was lacking. She breathed deeply, but felt drugged by a dose of heat. This was like the steamy Great Smoky Mountains in July. The seasons here weren't locked to temperatures. There were only two seasons and they were measured in inches of rain. One to four inches of rain per month in the dry season and thirty or more per month in the rainy season.

Maggie's steps began to slow and even her feet got hot as hot steam boiled up from the wet, sandy soil. No topsoil here. Maggie remembered the black dirt on her dad's farm. You couldn't even get stuck in this soil unless you got into a hole. You couldn't farm like they did at home, either. Here the nutrition needed to grow citrus fruit or pineapple was locked in the vegetation, rather than in the soil. The nutritiments were constantly circulated and recycled to produce the greatest variety of plants and animals on earth.

Maggie responded to the tall, oversized plants and trees. Vines way up high reached from tree to tree and held even the decaying trees upright. On the ground lived most of the animals and insects which were either camouflaged or too small to be seen without a microscope.

As they passed an almond tree, Maggie's spirits soared as they always did when she saw something beautiful or different in nature. This tree with horizontal branches was like nothing she had seen before.

June was also inspired, "These footpaths fascinate me. The villages are strung on them like beads placed irregularly on a necklace."

Maggie replied. "I guess I hadn't thought so much about the beauty of the paths as about the function of them. So many people pass this way. The huge headloads never cease to amaze me. One day I saw a man with a cutlass on his head. When he got to our grapefruit tree, he picked a grapefruit and with his cutlass cut it into. One half of the fruit he placed on his head, juicy side down, and the other half he peeled and ate."

June laughed as the picture brought to her mind the family she had seen pass the day before. "I don't see many families together on the paths, but yesterday I saw one. First came pa with a black umbrella over his head as a shade from the hot sun. Then came mommy and she carried a baby on her back and 100 pounds of rice on her head. . . ."

"One-hundred pounds? Are you certain?"

"I even went outside to see. It was the usual big bag and it was full of rice. After mommy came the small boy with a small headload and lastly came small sister with a suitcase on her head."

"The old system," Maggie exclaimed. "A wife here is certainly worth the forty dollars invested for her. She plants the rice, cuts it, feeds her husband, and takes care of the kids."

Ma, who had not had a happy marriage, had remained silent during the walk. Now she spoke up, "That's why men have several wives. My man wanted another wife, too. When she came, I left."

When they reached the first village, June said, "This path is a good communication line, too. Who needs a telephone? Watch!"

June stopped at a hut where a woman with a friendly smile stood by the door. "Mornin."

"Mornin."

"You know the plenty sick baby," June began. "The baby that came yesterday to the clinic. Is he still there?" She pointed toward his village.

The village woman looked down the path and quickly replied, "Yah,

Missy, he not pass this mornin. He there."

"Thank you, Mommie," the nurse said, as the trio proceeded down the path. A few steps out of the village, two men stepped from the path to let the nurse pass. This was a courtesy they would extend to few women, but they liked the nurse. One took a sack of cement off his head and held out his hand. June accepted the hand, shook it, and snapped her fingers off of his. Ma came alongside June, and spoke to the man in his own dialect. Then she turned to June with a translation.

"The man say he build new house. You come see when finish?"

June replied slowly, so the man would understand, "Fine. Fine house. I come. . . ." She pointed to her eye indicating she would come see it with her own eyes.

The man understood and smiled. Then he turned to the man with him, who had zinc on his head, and repeated June's message. The two men continued to talk as the women went on.

Ma began to feel more talkative. "Many people on the path. Man with gun and possum. Child with books. Man with lapa cloth to sell. Man embroidering on hat. Sunrise to sunset—always people."

Ten more minutes of rapid walking brought the women into sight of the village they wanted. Maggie, who was dragging behind, wondered if a village man could actually walk fifty miles a day. Some said they could, but did they know how far that was? Well, anyway Maggie knew the four miles she had just come were enough for her. She wondered if she'd manage those same miles on the way home.

The sick child's village was smaller than most, with only seven huts. Maggie guessed forty people probably lived there, but it was early in the day and the men were away. There were a few girls eight to ten years old. They were washing clothes in a bucket. Evidently they weren't the lucky 10 percent who got to go to school. "No boys here," Maggie remarked. "They're all in my yard on campus!"

It didn't take long for Maggie's eyes to scan the whole village for beyond the banana trees the village quickly ran out. Maggie searched for a palaver hut, where she expected to find the women who weren't in the field. But there was no palaver hut. Instead several women sat under an open sided, thatch shelter. Maggie suddenly remembered Ma had said, "That village no good. The men there can't stay."

June approached the women and spoke.

"Mornin," they replied, and some extended their hands.

June shook each hand and then turned her attention to the sick child. "Mommie, has the baby eaten?"

"He not eat." The mother looked toward the ground and stirred some palm nuts that lay there with her toes. "He not eat."

June reached for the child. "Let me see."

The attractive mother handed the half-conscious, one-year-old to June who remembered the first time she had met this mother. She had been a young girl—a beauty with even teeth and an instant smile. This must be her second or third child. The first had died. June thought the father had left the village and taken the second with him. This baby belonged to a man who worked up-country at the mine. He was home some weekends, but he hadn't come last weekend when this young woman needed him. June turned to the mother.

"You have the dropper I gave you yesterday?"

The mother nodded and brought the dropper and jar of water. June opened the jar and tiny black ants crawled from it. "Ants! Ants!" June brushed wildly as the ants started up her hands and arms.

Ma came quickly, took the ant-filled jar and set it down at a safe distance on the ground. From her pocket came another jar of liquid and she asked a small girl for a pan of water.

When the child returned, Ma put the jar in the water. "The ants can't get through the water," she explained and chuckled.

Maggie grinned and said, "Sam's bed was full of those ants the other day and so was my dresser drawer. Ants conquer the world? Living in the tropics, I believe it!"

"Not the huge ants of science fiction," June added. "Just these tiny nuisances." June chased an ant up her arm, brushed it off, and picked up the dropper.

She began to drip-drip the sugar-water mixture onto the dozing child's lips. The child stirred and choked as the first liquids went into his mouth.

"It's almost as hard to get this liquid down the baby as it was to get an intravenous feeding to working in the hospital," June commented. "Could you guess what the problem was with the IV?"

Maggie let an absurd idea run through her mind, but decided on a "No, what was the problem?"

"You don't get off that easy? Guess!"

Maggie expressed the ridiculous idea, "Ants!"

"Right on. Ants were in the bottle of fluid and it wouldn't run. When I was visiting the hospital the other day, I saw two nurses and a doctor spend several minutes figuring that one out. It was pretty humorous to hear the comments!" said June.

"I bet the patient wasn't laughing. I thought ants only liked real food!" Maggie chuckled.

By this time June had fed the child about one-third cup of the liquid.

She broke the silence which hung around the watching women. "See the baby can eat. You must feed him a drop at a time. Baby must have liquids. You must go slowly."

Then she handed the baby to the young mother and repeated the instructions.

Ma turned to the other women and repeated in their dialect. The women said nothing.

The nurse rose from the low stool and said, "We go now." Then she patted the mother on the shoulder and shook hands with the other women.

As she passed the first hut, June turned to Maggie and said, "That's the Old Lady's hut. Did you see her leave through the bush when we came?"

"No, I didn't see," Maggie replied, as she looked deeply into the heavy, 20-foot tall bush—jungle indeed! "What is she called?"

"Old Lady Williams," June replied. "She's from Williamtown so she's called Williams like everyone else here."

Maggie halted, "You mean all those people who come to the clinic who are called Lincoln aren't of the same family?"

June laughed, "No, that's their village name. Some are blood relatives and some aren't!"

"How about that?" Maggie said in wonder.

"Missy, Missy," a voice called from the last hut in the village as the trio passed. "Missy, come." The nurse stopped and saw an old woman in the door.

"Missy, you know my daughter?" the old woman inquired.

June shook her head, "No, who your daughter?"

"My daughter die last week. You know her. She MoMo wife."

June quickly ran through the card file that she carried in her mind and grabbed out a MoMo's wife. "Yes, I think I know her. She come to clinic?"

"Yah, Missy," the old woman continued. "She go last week. She go quickly."

June turned to Maggie and explained, "The daughter died in childbirth in her village. The baby didn't live, either."

The old woman went on. "She my last daughter. I have no grandchildren now." Then the tears started to roll and she touched her heart, "My heart hurts. It hurts too much."

By this time some of the women of the village had gathered. They listened and nodded. The children also came. No one was insulated from the grief.

"Mommy, I too sorry," June said, as she patted the wrinkled hand.

"I too sorry. But you know your daughter still living. Your daughter in heaven with God. I know she trust Jesus. She lives still."

These words did not comfort the old woman, though. She continued to touch her heart and weep and say, "I only one left. My heart hurt. I have no grandchildren now."

Finally June freed the old woman's hand and said, "I go. I come again." As she turned, Maggie saw June had tears in her eyes.

The trio walked for several minutes in contemplation before Maggie asked, "And what about the other baby?"

June slowly replied, "The child is never alert. The mother is tired. She can't keep up the hourly feedings. She has no husband to help and the other women think there is no hope. They won't encourage or assist. There's no way."

When Maggie went to the clinic the following week, she recognized some of the women from the sick child's village. When she inquired, the women answered, "Baby not stay."

Before the clinic day was finished word of the death of two other children, who had been treated during the last weeks was also brought by women. The simple explanation always came with lowered eyes and quiet words, "Baby not stay."

Maggie thought about a letter she had recently received from a friend at home. "I couldn't stand all those sick children that come to the clinic."

Another writer had said, "I couldn't stand by and let them die. I'd take the children into my home."

Maggie struggled with these options as she watched the children that day at the clinic. It took a few weeks to come to a decision. The important issue wasn't what had happened last week, but what could be done today. No, she couldn't take these women's place as mother to their own children. All she could do was try to teach them. Maggie began to work on demonstrations. How to teach about germs? The word didn't exist in village thought, much less the concept. Charts began to take shape. Maggie drew some of them about dirt and soap and toilets and wearing shoes and showed them to the missionary kids.

With her captive audience she began, "Kids, today I want to teach you about bare feet and how worms can enter the body through your feet."

All the MK's, except Mark, laughed, "Oh, Aunt Maggie, we know all about that stuff. That's simple."

Mark said, "Really, Mom. In your feet?" He looked at his dirty tennis shoes.

"Yes, Mark. Threadworm and hookworm larvae drill right through bare feet!"

"Wow," said Prince, as Mark sat stunned.

Soon even small Sam would tell people who came to the Blake door, "You barefoot. You get worm."

"Well," Maggie thought, "If the MK's can get this, the village women can, too."

The next Tuesday Maggie took her first chart confidently to the villages. She was a few lines into the explanation about bare feet and worms when a woman said, "But Missy, we have no shoes!"

Not to be stopped, Maggie said, "Then pottie in a latrine. If you not pottie everywhere, you not walk in it and get worms."

"But, Missy, we have no la . . . , lat . . . ," and then there were embarassed giggles as the word wouldn't come.

It was a funny word, but the idea was even funnier. The rest of the demonstration was a complete flop. Finally June stepped in, "That is not a new word. I have talked and talked to you about a latrine for this village." Pointing down a path, she continued, "The villages there, VooVee Town and Lincoln Town. They have latrine. You know this."

The older Missy had a reputation and the women got serious. June continued, "I go today to tell the chief. I tell chief I not buy anymore medicine for this village unless a latrine is built. The money is finish."

"No more piperazine. No more mintezol. The money finish." June turned her hands down indicating they were empty. She turned abruptly with, "I go now to see the chief."

The women watched in silence as June walked the few yards to the chief's house. Maggie collected her materials and was ready to leave unnoticed. But then she thought better of it. June was well-known. She could leave without the customary farewell, but the women would misunderstand if the new missionary left in a hurry. So Maggie walked around the palaver hut and shook hands with the women who were seated on the three-foot wall. Maggie sensed as she completed the circle that the women were more friendly to her than they were to her ideas.

When June arrived, the chief was in front of his four-room concrete house. Behind his house she recognized one of his wives coming out of her own house and waved. After handshakes and ten minutes of the customary asking about the family, June got to business.

"Chief," she began. "You good man. You good chief. You speak and the people hear. Remember I talk many time to you about a latrine."

The chief stopped shaking his head in agreement when June got to that last statement. He said, thoughtfully, "But Mrs. Pearce, we not have anything to build latrine."

Not taken back by the usual excuse, the nurse continued. "Chief, you can build with sticks and palm thatch. Palm thatch is everywhere. Part of the huts in this village are roofed with it."

"But, Mrs. Pearce, the men busy."

June came back quickly with, "That's what you said three months ago and three months before that and last year. The men not in field. They sleep by hut. See." And she pointed to several men resting in hammocks.

"They must save themselves," the chief began.

June knew the local theory that a man who worked too hard could not father many children. She sidestepped and came to her main bargaining position.

"Chief, I buy no more worm medicine for this village. My money is finished. I buy too much medicine for you. People take medicine this week and worms go. Next week they have worm again. I buy no more medicine even if people's belly hurt plenty. The money finished!" And then the nurse added, "If people want treatment they can bring fifty cents each time to clinic."

"A ya," the chief began, and this speech lasted ten minutes. It lauded the nurse for her help and finally promised the building of a latrine if more medicine were available.

June rose from the country chair, straightened her white uniform, and said, "I go now."

The chief grasped her outstretched hand and gave it a shake which ended with a loud click.

As June left, the chief thought about what she had said. He knew the nurse was a friend. She had come for years when there was an emergency. She had delivered live babies from dying mothers. She had brought babies back that the women thought were dead. No, she would not ignore his plea for help for his people. She would palaver and he liked that. He liked a missionary who could talk long. He didn't understand the silent ones.

Weeks later Maggie was working on the records at the clinic when the chief's prettiest wife came. Her black beauty was accented by a blue lapa and long, gold earrings. The waiting patients looked as she passed. When she reached the desk, she stretched out her hand to Maggie and said, "Mornin."

"Good morning, Mazu," Maggie said, as she shook the hand. With her other hand Maggie pushed back her long hair thinking she hadn't been to a beauty parlor in six months.

"How you?" Maggie questioned.

The chief's wife touched her stomach and frowned. Maggie guessed the problem was either a runny stomach or Mazu was "with belly."

"You with belly? You expect baby?" Maggie asked.

"Naa, my stomach runny," was the immediate reply.

When Mazu's turn came, Maggie showed her to the examining room, handed her card to June and said, "Runny stomach."

June stood up, pleased to see an old friend. She hugged Mazu's shoulder and inquired about the chief.

Then June was quiet. Maggie knew she had come to a hard decision.

Cautiously June began, "You bring fifty cents?"

"Naa, Mrs. Pearce. I never pay except for card when first come. You always see me," Mazu said, with a pout.

"But, Mazu, you know what I tell women and chief. No latrine, no medicine. Chief not start latrine. I go through village yesterday—no latrine. I cannot get lab man to look for worm if I not pay him and I not have more money for your village." June showed her empty hands, "Money finished." Mentally she calculated what remained in her small budget for medicine. She knew that to buy more medicine for Mazu's village would be to rob others of help and so she repeated, "Money for your village finished. No way. No way."

June went to the next patient while the chief's wife waited. Mazu thought her persistence would change June's mind so she waited through the next three patients. The nurse returned to her, "Mazu, you dear friend and I sorry, but I not treat you. Go tell chief what I say. Ask him today to send the men to cut poles and thatch for a latrine. Then I treat you."

The next day the chief brought Mazu and with a big smile entered the clinic door. When June appeared, he said, "The poles cut."

"For true? For true?" June asked with some excitement.

Looking straight at the nurse with hurt eyes, the chief said, "Mrs. Pearce, we friends. I always speak true to you."

"OK Chief. This is not village day. It is day for students, but I treat Mazu, anyway."

The lab technician began his work and soon returned with a report, "Hookworm."

June turned to her closet of medicines and unlocked the door. This was harder to cure than round or pin or whipworms, which were more common. All came from fecal contamination of the soil. She chose a medicine that should work and gave it to Mazu with verbal instructions. Then she did a replay of the instructions and asked Mazu to repeat what she had said. This was standard procedure for patients who could not read. Sometimes June had difficulty switching to written instructions when she treated the students. It always delighted her when she found a third grader who could read instructions with no difficulty.

Mazu turned to leave and June had an afterthought. "I best check your blood." When she drew a drop from Mazu's finger, she didn't have to compare it to the chart in order to diagnose, "You have no blood! It's light orange." She knew it wouldn't do any good to talk about hemoglobin count and iron.

Instead she looked at Mazu's eyes. "How long you with runny stomach?" she asked with some apprehension.

Mazu hesitated and finally answered, "Many days."

June went back to the medicine closet for vitamins and iron and gave these to Mazu with full instructions. Their business completed, the chief shook the nurse's hand and the hands of the people in the waiting room and left.

A month later when Maggie and June went back to the chief's village for another well-baby clinic, June noticed that the poles were still sitting and the thatch was there, but it hadn't been used for a roof. She kicked a hard almond nut from the path and said, "See no progress. The latrine will wait until someone gets very ill and needs medicine badly."

Several weeks later, the chief's oldest son came to the clinic with Mazu. He produced fifty cents from his pocket as soon as Maggie looked at him. When the boy's mother helped him to a chair, Maggie put his card in front and took him immediately to where June was. "He looks pretty sick. He brought fifty cents." Quietly she added, "The chief must be partially convinced you meant what you said."

Soon the lab technician diagnosed amebic dysentery. June groaned when she read the report. Turning to Maggie, she said, "Amoeba—more feces contamination of food or water. This is a tough one. I hope he came in time. I've seen too much organ damage from amoeba."

Then turning to Mazu, the nurse explained the disease and its source and ended with, "I would like the doctor to see this boy. The doctor is due late this afternoon. You take the boy home and I will send someone to get you when the doctor comes. If the doctor doesn't come, I'll bring medicine before dark."

When all the waiting patients had been seen, Maggie counted thirty-three cards. There had been seven pregnant women, three cases of headaches and chills resulting from malaria, ten runny stomachs, five with infected sores from mango fly or other insect bites, two with venereal diseases, one man "jooked" by a poisonous thorn, a man with a badly burned hand, which looked like a puffed-up plastic glove. The remaining patients were very young mothers who wanted advice about babies who wouldn't eat or couldn't pottie. The babies were usually OK, but the mothers needed reassurance and the nurse was the "expert."

While Maggie was filing the cards, June talked. "When I first came here, I was introduced to village nursing by the missionary who preceded me in the clinic. I had come from a large hospital nursing situation where I followed the doctor's orders. At first I thought the missionary-nurse must be crazy. I kept telling her, 'You can't assume so much responsibility. You'll get sued or something.' "

"Finally she went on furlough and I was on my own. I carefully decided what diseases I would treat and what diseases I would refer. But as you have seen, patients referred never went to the doctor. They went back to the village and the Old Lady treated them. That man's hand you saw today—the Old Lady used hot sand on it. She meant to cauterize a bleeding hand, but she got the sand too hot. Now I have a dirty, burned, and cut hand to treat!"

"Someplace along the line, you began to treat those who had diseases which you had classified as 'referrals,' didn't you?" Maggie asked.

"Yes, the turning point came when a baby was brought with sores on his head. I thought the case was too difficult for me. I didn't treat the baby. The mother put country medicine on the sores and the green herb mixture ate clear through the baby's skull in two weeks time. She brought the child back to me right before he died." June paused a long time before she continued.

"I was shocked. Then I began to think. Surely I could have done better than that. I got out all my medical books and I started to read and study. When a difficult case came, I investigated and researched it. Gradually I became more competent in tropical medicine. I don't like the arrangement. I would prefer to have a doctor, but I don't like to stand by and see people die when there is some possibility for a cure!" June concluded, as she locked the clinic door.

A week later when June and Maggie walked to the chief's village for a well-baby clinic, June mentioned, "We'll see the chief's boy before we leave the village. He isn't doing so well."

Maggie thought about what June had said at the clinic the week before and asked, "Did the doctor see the boy?"

"Nope. The government doctor never came. I'm on my own again! I figured and figured on this dosage. The trick is to poison the amoeba, but not the person."

June was interrupted as a boy walking on one leg with a stick supporting his withered leg met them on the path. "Morning, Kamo," June said.

"Mornin," the teenager answered.

When the young man was out of hearing range, the nurse remarked, "Polio. A lot of it here."

The lesson that day on bathing a baby seemed to go well. When it was finished and June and Maggie were on the way to the chief's house, Maggie commented, "Did they get it?"

"I hope so," June replied. "I hope it stops some of the women from bathing the baby in a dishpan and then giving him the bath water to drink! I wonder how many women I have seen forcing dirty bath water into a baby's unwilling mouth!"

"The next thing I'm going to try to teach is giving the baby mashed fruit and crushed fish rather than rice water! That rice water doesn't do much for a kid, either. It's slightly better than bath water!" Maggie added, with a laugh.

When the women arrived, the chief greeted them and they went quickly to where his son lay on the only mattress in the house. After a thorough examination, the women and the chief went outside to talk.

June looked worried as she said, "Chief, the boy is still very ill. Many boys die of amoeba. Without medicine your boy would be gone already."

June's voice halted and she lapsed into thoughts about other cases of amoeba. She hadn't thought for a long time about the agricultural missionary on campus who had returned to the United States following a hard bout with amoeba. The liver damage was permanent. Now she remembered how badly that family had been needed. Medicine and agriculture were closely tied. More live babies demanded more food.

June returned to the present. "Chief, you must do something. You must finish the latrine." Determination crept into her voice, "You must talk to the Old Lady in the next village. The babies must have their polio shots."

"Na, Mrs. Pearce," the chief said quickly. "The Old Lady give me plenty hard time. Palaver. Palaver."

"I know chief, but you the boss. You responsible. The people must get their cholera and smallpox shots. I don't want to see any more cases like we had last year. Too many people die. Too many babies d . . ." Here June's voice caught.

The chief, who had been looking into nowhere, quickly gazed at June's face. His eyes stayed there until the frustration and discouragement which were deep inside June spilled. A single tear ran all the way down her face. The chief looked away quickly.

Maggie wanted to say something to lift the burden but no words came. She looked at the chief. It was his turn. He was definitely upset. But he said nothing. In his discomfort he looked down at his own feet, which were bare.

June looked suddenly at them, too, and anger came to her voice. "You get sick, too. Why do the people have to die?" And then June rose abruptly and without the customary handshake walked hurriedly from the village.

The chief's eyes followed her white uniform, and he thought long. "Was what she said really true? Could a latrine actually stop some of the dying?"

There was no conversation on the way back to campus. Even the singing birds didn't delight Maggie. She hardly noticed the flowers which usually pleased her. Through her mind kept running. "No way. No way. No way."

No way for long life here and no way for eternal life. It was as hard to tell the people about Christ as it was to get them to wear shoes. Both decisions meant a change in life-style. Having just experienced a change, Maggie could appreciate the complexities of adjustment. Yes, it had been hard to get used to sharing a car after having owned two cars. From home ownership to calling for a vote of the Mission in order to paint her living room hadn't been done so gracefully, either. It was hard to change life-styles, but Maggie knew it wasn't impossible.

God had taken care of some of the changes in life. Maggie could picture the small children who had so recently left Africa, in heaven sitting at the feet of Jesus, who was giving them love and care. That picture brought comfort, but what about the adults—Muslims and spirit worshipers?

Maggie could see no picture of them at the feet of a man they never knew. Their gods certainly had no power to give new life—then where did that leave them? Picture after picture of adults who had just been buried flashed on Maggie's mind. Flash. Flash. Another face. Another. The pictures faded and the "No way" sign came back. Its flashing dominated Maggie's thoughts.

Even when Maggie tried to sleep that night the lights continued to flash, "No way. No way." Finally Maggie cried out, "Oh, God. Help." The light quickly began to flash a different message, "One way. One way. Christ. Christ. The way. The way."

Maggie outlined in her mind a new poster—her next lesson for the village—and it showed a path leading to God and life.

After clinic the following week Maggie commented to June, "I'm getting excited about the village work. You know what I think?" and then, clicking her fingernails in nervous expectation, Maggie hastened on. "I think there will be a completed latrine when we reach Careytown next time."

June stopped, turned and stared at Maggie. "You think what?"

Maggie repeated, "The latrine will be finished!"

June started to laugh, but then looked again at Maggie's serious face. "Do you think so—really?"

When the two missionaries approached Careytown again, Maggie closed her eyes for a brief second and said, "God, let it be there."

Then she quickened her pace. The buildings in the village took shape as her eyes made a quick survey—the chief's house, the chief's wives' houses, the palaver hut, six other houses, and several lean-tos for cooking. And then Maggie's eyes stopped. They rested on a new building. There it was—a completed latrine. It was the most beautiful building she had ever seen!

Maggie could hardly contain her joy, but she kept silent until June came to her side. Then June, too, stopped and her eyes feasted on the new building. "Praise the Lord," was all she could say, "Praise the Lord!"

Together they walked happily to where the chief stood. He was dressed up for their arrival and for this big occasion. He beamed as he shook June's hand and then he pointed to the latrine, "See. See. It is fineo. It is fineo! No?"

"Chief, I'm so happy. I could kiss you," June said, and she lingered to talk.

Maggie's mind had already shifted to the poster which she held under her arm. She walked quickly to where the women waited in the palaver hut. As she greeted them she decided on the first line of her path to God meditation. When the women were quiet she began, "There is a way."

10
A Happy Song

It was almost dawn—still very quiet. Maggie could see the snow and miles into the distance. A redbird was scratching in the ice for a half-covered seed. The family was coming to the door and they'd say, "Christmas greetings," and hug each other and laugh and bring in boxes of gifts in shiny paper and baskets of turkey and dressing and cranberry salad and applesauce cake with black walnuts on caramel icing. But that was at home.

Maggie turned back to the heat and went to the window. Outside the palm trees stood in silence. A bird that had been singing on the roof of the house for some time finally caught Maggie's full attention. She wondered if he were attracting a mate or just gossiping with the night. Maggie listened closely. The song was clear and short, but who ever heard of a bird's song coming in an open window on Christmas Eve? Santa was supposed to be traveling across a snow-draped world.

Maggie turned to the felt stockings. Each member of the family had his own. Maggie's was a bell. John's and Mark's were boot-shaped and Karen and Sam's were high-heeled shoe designs. All were covered with sequins which reflected the Christmas tree lights.

Maggie put gum in the children's stockings and then selected a red apple, small candy, and the right color of toothbrush for all the stockings. Then she smiled to herself—gum and apples; candy and toothbrushes—wouldn't the dentist love those combinations?

Maggie drew closer to the tree to get enough light to read the name tags on the small gifts which were also for the stockings. She was caught up immediately in the magic of the miniature, twinkling lights. Christmas trees were of a fairy world where children danced and played and laughed. This tree, though, looked homemade—a family kind of tree. The star on top looked like it might slide down at any minute. A felt Santa was perched on the bottom limb and obviously children's hands had placed the loop chains which hung in a haphazard way on the artificial evergreen branches. Two gold balls, the only stylish ornaments on the tree, were all that remained of Maggie and John's first Christmas decorations. Maggie smiled as she remembered how it had been then.

She thought about several other Christmases before the bird on the roof became more insistent in its song. Maggie tried various chirps and Tweedledees before she came up with, "Wick." No, the sound was, "Quick." Maggie repeated the word along with the bird, "Quick, quick." It sounded just right, but what was the other sound? "Quick-Da." "Quick-da-te." Maggie tried a faster combination in harmony with the bird and it came out, "Quick, Doctor, quick." She tried again. Yes, that was right. It was "Quick, Doctor, quick." Maggie laughed—no doubt the dentist was being paged!

Maggie ran through the words several more times before she picked up another bird call. Maybe a prospective mate had been summoned. "To dle, to dle." Maggie was fascinated and finally decided this must be a bird, which was commonly called "Pepperbird." He usually sang at dawn from a high perch. Maggie addressed the bird she couldn't see, "This time I'll find out what you're really called." She picked up *Birds of West African Town and Garden,* a nature book, which was well-worn and began to flip through the colored drawings.

Small birds . . . drab colored in neutral colors. There were dozens of them. Finally Maggie's eyes rested on the right picture. There was the bird who liked to eat peppers. "Common bulbul." Common bulbul—what a disappointing name. Drab bird—drab name. Maggie decided she'd go back to the nickname, "Pepperbird." At least it had a ring. She closed the book before she realized she hadn't read about the bird's song.

Maggie quickly found the right page again and read, "Alighting it sings, 'Toodlee, Toodlee.' While perching the song is often represented as, 'Quick, Doctor, quick.' "

Maggie pointed her finger in reproach, "You did call the dentist, you rascal!"

Maggie slowly finished stuffing the stockings, thinking about how the children would react to the gifts in just a few hours. Sam would dance up and down, Mark would shout and chatter, and Karen would wear a big grin all morning.

John, who was usually an eager Santa, finally came into the living room. "Can't wake up. What's going on out here?"

Maggie gestured toward the tree and didn't answer. John quickly surveyed the stockings and then read the note that the children had left for Santa. As he began to eat the peanut butter cookies that the children had made for Santa's snack, he said, "I wonder how the kids knew these are Santa's favorite kind of cookies?"

John and Maggie sat for a long time in silence looking at the tree, while John finished the milk that was also a part of the snack for the long-anticipated Christmas Eve visitor. Then he wrote a thank-you note and signed it "Santa."

When the early risers came the next morning yelling, "Get up. Come see what Santa left!" John felt like he'd hardly slept.

Thirty minutes later when a caller came to the door, John was half-dozing in his favorite chair. Maggie opened the door and the teacher bolted in and headed straight for John. "You must help me. My wife to deliver today. This is her first baby."

John's eyes opened wide and he tried to decide what the teacher wanted. Good grief! He didn't expect John to deliver a baby!

For the tenth time John wondered why June had picked this week to leave the campus. The first time he had wondered was when June came to his back door with her hands behind her back and a big grin on her face. Her opening sentence had been, "Guess what I brought you?"

After five minutes of "You can't be serious," and another five of heavy persuasion, John had found himself practicing shot techniques on Mark's teddy bear. The practice ended two days later when the real patient arrived. Mark, who was all the way across the campus at the agricultural farm, came home to witness his dad's debut as a doctor. When John couldn't get the needle through the drawn skin of the TB patient, Mark had assured the patient, "Don't worry. Dad gave my bear shots and now he never gets sick!"

Although the second round of shots went better than the first, John still wasn't ready for anything else in the medical line. He finally found his voice, "What help do you mean?"

John waited apprehensively as the teacher blurted out, "I have no car. My wife must go to the hospital."

John sighed in relief and Maggie frowned. A trip to the hospital on Christmas Day? Mentally she calculated with the drive and then the waiting it would take three or four hours. Dinner was planned for noon. John couldn't possibly make it. Maggie looked toward John and he looked at her. Each read the other.

John got up to dress and Maggie went into the kitchen to hide her disappointment and check on the turkey in the oven. By the time John passed through the kitchen with the teacher, Maggie had consoled herself. After all it would be best for the woman. Having a baby wasn't routine.

John gave Maggie a quick good-bye kiss and whispered in her ear. "I won't wait for them. He can get a taxi home. I'll be back at one."

Maggie replied, "The first qualification for a missionary should be a chauffeur's license. And don't be late today!"

John got the car keys and laughed. "Me—late? Never!"

Maggie threatened him in a good-natured way with the spatula she had in her hand, "Yes, you! You are always late! But not today!"

By twelve the dressing was in the oven along with the sweet potatoes and hot rolls. In the refrigerator was cranberry salad with real apples and walnuts, both treats in West Africa. Maggie went over the menu—date cake, iced tea, celery—everything was ready. It would have been cheaper to have had roasting ears, watermelon, and pineapple—all of which were plentiful now. But they didn't seem right on Christmas. Maggie was pleased with the meal prospects and decided to take a quick shower before the company came. As she took off her blouse, Maggie noticed how damp it was. In fact, she couldn't remember a hotter day. The shower felt good and Maggie decided on impulse to wash her hair.

After she dried, Maggie turned to the closet. Quickly, she passed a long dress that had been made the month before for this occasion. It was too hot. Instead, Maggie got out the coolest skirt and blouse she could find. Then looking at her hair, she decided to leave it wet. It felt cool.

No new dress. No hairdo. Maggie couldn't remember a Christmas Day without these.

Maggie looked out the bedroom window to where the birds sat with their heads under their wings. Even under the palm trees they found no shade. Poor things. Maggie thought about the white heron or cowbird or cattle egret or whatever you wanted to call it. The one who had lingered after dry season ended and after his friends had gone. That bird's feathers knew he should go to the Sahara Desert for they had turned brown like the sand there. Then why hadn't he gone? Why had he continued to walk around the yard on those crazy stilt-like legs with his migratory senses three months behind time?

At the moment, Maggie felt like the bird. Why had they stayed on campus for Christmas—their first out of the United States? The students had all gone home. The missionaries were gone. It had sounded OK when June suggested somebody had to stay in order to handle the emergencies. Duty? Well, it must have been duty for it wasn't natural instinct. Maggie's reason would have led her where the rest of the family was.

Maggie headed toward the living room where she heard the voice of the wife of one of the teachers. Yes, she had to stay on campus, also, because her husband had gone out of the country to see his people and there had been no money for her air fare.

In the living room, Karen was showing Mrs. Boala the photo album. This could always be counted on for a conversation opener. "That's my grandma and her cats. And this is Grandpa and his tractor, and that's my other grandma and grandpa beside their yard swing. And these are all my cousins."

Karen's voice drummed on and Maggie was instantly sorry she hadn't hidden the photo album, for she was being consumed by the worse wave of homesickness she had ever felt. Why did Karen have to talk about the family back home today? Maggie walked around the room straightening chairs and books. That done, she looked for another job. See about the food? No, it was overwatched already. Read a book? Not with company. Play with Sam? He was asleep—thank goodness. Mark? No, he was playing checkers in his bedroom with the only student who was left on campus.

"Well, that's another first," Maggie thought to herself. "Nothing to do on Christmas Day." She walked to the door and looked down the road. It was two. Where was John?

Maggie sat down in the living room and looked at her watch every five minutes. It said almost three P.M. when John's car passed. Maggie watched as he sped by on his way to the teacher's house.

When John returned in ten minutes, the dinner was on the table and the candle centerpiece flickered.

John ran up the steps, flung the door open and said, "It's a Chris."

Karen came running and then stopped abruptly, "A what?"

"A Chris."

Karen got the message and grinned, "Yeh, but is that a boy or girl?"

"The most important baby born at this time of year was a boy, but this one is a girl! A sweet one—like my first girl!"

Karen tucked her head and murmured, "Oh, Daddy."

Quickly the family, along with their two guests, began to eat. Mark was on his third plate of dressing when he remarked, "I like this. Christmas is the best time of all." Then he turned to the student who sat next to him. "You like Christmas?"

The boy looked up surprised by the question. Actually he'd never thought about Christmas being much different than any other day. For him it had never been. He looked around the table and was suddenly moved and in a frank way found it possible to express his deep feelings. "I never got a Christmas present before today. This is the first time I haven't been by myself at Christmas."

Maggie looked up shocked and thought about all the "firsts" this day had held. The boy's gaze met hers and his eyes dropped. "Thanks for asking me." Then the student looked at Mark and his black eyes danced above a toothy smile, "This is the best Christmas I ever know."

John answered for the family, "We're glad you came, Sando."

Maggie got up to serve the dessert and for the first time that day thought deeply about Christ. Yes, he had come to serve; not to celebrate.

Before they finished dessert, a big gust of wind blew the dining room curtains straight out. Maggie looked at the sky and John said, "Rain? In the middle of dry season?"

Sando grinned. "For true. The rain coming."

When the next gust of wind blew the napkins to the floor, Maggie felt better. This wasn't snow, but Christmas Day was beginning to seem right.

"Let's sing Christmas carols, when we finish here," Maggie suggested. "Christmas is a joyous day all around the world!"

The picture of the bird on the roof came back. "You know that a little bird told me Christmas was a time to sing a happy song!"

Karen snickered, "Oh, Mom, birds don't talk to people."

"You think they don't. Well let me tell you about last night before Santa came." Maggie looked toward John and winked, "Before Santa came in yawning, this little bird on the roof sang a happy song."

Mark, who was caught up in the story said, "Yeah, I heard a bird talk once."

Karen laughed, "Oh, Mark, you can't talk to birds either."

"I can to. Parrots do talk, don't they Mom?"

Maggie smiled and said, "I don't know about all birds, Mark. But this little bird at dawn liked to talk—he couldn't keep a secret at all."

Mark was well-pleased and John laughed. Mrs. Boala, who hadn't managed eight words during the entire meal, began to smile and without hesitation joined the song Maggie had just begun:

> Joy to the world! the Lord is come;
> Let earth receive her king:
> . . . .
> And heav'n and nature sing,
> And Heav'n and nature sing.

11

Gbolupa Institute

Lightning zigzagged across the sky and lit the night. John checked the last of the ten classroom doors, all of which opened to the outdoor patio rather than onto a hall, and started down the steps, wondering if there weren't a more secure way to build a school and still have rooms that would catch the breeze.

This had been some week, but usually the first weeks of school were hectic. Uniforms, books, registration fees, placement—what a scramble! John reviewed the vacation with some satisfaction. He had gotten the science equipment ordered at last, and his experience in the classroom the year before had been a good springboard for planning this year's work.

John walked off the steps and onto the damp ground and speculated about the rain. March was too early for the rainy season. This must be an in-between season storm. That meant a lot of lightning and some wind. The rain began coming softly before John's flashlight picked up an umbrella on the path to the senior girls' dormitory.

The students should have been home from study hall ten minutes ago. John crossed the road and started down the path just as another flash of lightning came. Four legs! Four legs under one umbrella? Was it two girls? John quickly discarded this idea and his light shone on the surprised faces of a boy and a girl.

John decided to skip the usual lecture on "No two people under one umbrella," for with the next bolt of lightning a different idea rolled across John's mind.

"I'm sure glad you're here," John said to the boy. "Since you've already gone out of your way, you won't mind sharing your umbrella with me! Funny thing—I didn't even think about rain tonight."

The two students stood motionless trying to figure out if they were in trouble. John continued, looking at the girl, "You have your own umbrella, don't you?"

The girl stammered, "Ya, Professor," and jumped from her shelter into the rain which was now coming down hard. She was two steps down the path before she realized the umbrella was still hanging at her side.

John stepped under the boy's umbrella, which was already held at the right height for him, and said, "Let's go."

As the new twosome headed for the Blake's house, John smiled inside and waited for the boy to open the conversation. The youth finally began, "I like your physics class, Professor."

"Oh," said John, "I know you're in physics this year but I haven't gotten all the names straight."

The boy sighed in relief as he dwelt on the possibility of using someone else's name in case Mr. Blake asked. Then he said, "I didn't quite understand about wave motion. Could you explain it to me?"

In his mind, John ran through the list of names he had typed at registration. Two Samuels, an Israel, three Benjamins, five Davids, six Josephs, two Abrahams, six Johns, two Solomons, one Aaron, three Moses, two Joshuas, and then he started on the girls' names—eight Marys, and then Naomis, Ruths, Hannahs, Lydias, Marthas, and Rebeccas galore. On the famous man side, there were Rockefellers, MacArthurs, Caesars, Aristotles, Lafayettes, and Washingtons.

But there was only one Roland. The boy under the umbrella had to be Roland Minor. He was as much discussed on campus as Mazu, who insisted on straightening her hair and cooking food on the new electric irons in the dormitory.

John almost used Roland's name, but then decided to play a less obvious game as he answered the question that had been put to him several yards back. "The wave motion business—oh, yes, the general principle is . . ."

This intellectual conversation proceeded as the two came to the Blake's carport. Here Roland stopped abruptly and said, "Thanks for explaining that." Then he hurried toward his own dormitory. Two more flashes of lightning revealed that he was on a straight course this time.

As John dried, he thought, "Score one for the teachers."

The next week while John was finishing the bookstore statement, Roland appeared. His first words were, "Hello, Professor. If you're busy, I can come back later. I know you teachers are overworked."

John reflected on this game and wondered where it would lead. Then he said, "I was finishing the bookstore statement. Most of the students have their books now and 85 percent are paid for. That's some kind of record. We have done about that well in the uniform store, too. We've made a good beginning."

John knew Roland provided a good avenue for spreading news and quickly decided to tell him all the impressive facts. "Yes, we've started well. The water system didn't break down like it usually does. There are enough mattresses in each dormitory. All the books came and the work and dining crews are staffed. This is the principal's second year and he seems to have a grasp on things and the teachers are doing OK."

John would have continued, but he noticed Roland's half attention had turned to no attention. John returned to the long rows of figures.

Roland after a few seconds realized that there was silence. He quickly got to his point. "I'm running for president of the student body and I thought you'd like to know since you'll be working with me."

John looked up sharply and thought about the former year's senior class. They had been tremendous. Joseph had come by during registration to report that he had made the top score on the university entrance exams. The other graduates had also done well but this group of seniors was different. It was activity rather than academically oriented. Being activities director was going to be hard this year.

John looked up at Roland. "Do you have a platform or are you running on your standing as a senior?"

"I'm working on my speech."

Although John often read student speeches ahead of time, he knew this year he wouldn't be asked to. Roland would want more activities, more food, more money, and more trips. He'd want to inform the students and then let the teachers work through the resulting programs.

A week later, John went to the auditorium for the campaign speeches. As the seniors' candidate, Roland spoke first. "Honored administration, faculty, staff, and beloved students, I come today as your candidate for student senate president." Cheers began in the senior section and slowly filtered through the other upper class groups.

Roland raised his hands and continued. "Upon this auspicious occasion I congratulate you on your fine senate in the years past." More cheers came from the senior section.

"We are now entering a new day—a day of progress—a day of activities. This year's senate under my leadership will promote bigger and better activities." The seniors did not have to begin the cheers this time.

Roland was warming to his speech, which was full of big words and vague promises. By the time he finished twenty minutes later the whole student body was on its feet. The cheering continued until the principal called for order three times.

The next candidate rose and began, "I rise to nominate myself, Thelma Morris, for student senate leader." A few juniors cheered, but they were answered by seniors mumbling. There was no more applause as the girl rapidly concluded her logical but undramatic presentation.

John whispered to a co-teacher, "Good try. But no drama and backing." The other teacher shook her head and replied, "Roland is a born politician—he can't be beat. Good luck with the student activities this year!"

John thought about what moved people and then remembered Roland's recent answer to the old senior question, "What is your ambition?" Others had said doctor, lawyer, engineer, diplomat, businessman, but Roland's answer was a clarion call, "I'll be President someday!"

At the time John had smiled. Now he thought seriously about the possibilities. Other Gbolupa graduates held high government positions. Roland's father belonged to the group which held economic and political power. Roland might just see his dream come true.

For the hundredth time since coming to Gbolupa, John weighed the responsibility of teaching in Africa. There were only seven good high schools in the whole country and they were all heavily subsidized by Christian groups around the world. That meant the future leaders were being influenced by Christian missionaries.

How to be God's force rather than just another student activities director entered John's mind time and again as the weeks flew by—particularly whenever Roland came for a conference. That was three or four times a week and always at supper time.

One of the early encounters was over a trip to Cape Hill, a town fifty miles up the coast. Roland had the students fired up a long time before he approached John. John sent Roland back to his group to plan a way to raise money for the trip.

After the Friday night movie money was collected, Roland's committee, still desperate for finances, decided to sell sandwiches at an all-school party. The total result was ten dollars and John's investigation produced evidence that most of the sandwiches had disappeared during the preparation process.

The proposed trip was only two days away when Roland tried what John would later catalog as the "jammed method." "See, Professor, I promised the students. I always keep my word to them. They're counting on the trip and you can't cancel it now!"

His speech finished, each of the four boys who had come along for support added their, "That's for true."

John studied Roland's handsome face and thought about his future ambitions. "Roland, a good leader keeps his feet on the ground. He doesn't promise what has to be bought with somebody else's time and money when the people with the time or money aren't willing!"

Roland raised his eyebrows and looked puzzled. "Professor, the students will be vexed if we don't go. . . ."

As Roland continued, John planned his counterargument. John knew where he stood—he was the channel through which children and women on Social Security and wage earners in the United States gave to foreign missions. More than that, the money was a love gift to God. How did you balance student desires with Christian ideals for the school? How could he make Roland understand that all trips weren't educational? Some were too expensive, even if students needed regular breaks from the campus routine.

John thought about Roland's dad bringing Roland to registration in his big chauffeur-driven Mercedes. Roland was rich, even by United States standards, and he actually believed that United States Baptists were even richer. What were his words? "Huh, Baptists in the United States have plenty of money."

John sensed Roland was coming to the end of his often repeated argument. John began, "Roland, how about the other students on campus who can't afford this trip? Sure you and your friends could chip in a few dollars, but we don't plan activities here that only a few of the students can afford."

Roland turned to his friends for support for his latest money-making venture and one by one they backed out with, "I don't have that much money."

Roland came back, "But we shouldn't have to pay for the bus. It belongs to the school."

John went into his office and came back with the student activity budget and the recent bills for bus trips. He handed them to Roland. "You figure out how much this trip will cost!"

When Roland didn't reach for the papers, one of his friends took over. John, who knew this boy was good at math, waited only a minute. "Wow! Does it cost that much?"

John smiled. "You figured it. What do you say?"

Roland wasn't about to get caught in an argument which involved facts and figures. He returned to his original position. "The students expect this. You can't cancel it now." Thirty more minutes of his most persuasive palaver resulted in John standing firm. Roland finally left and John speculated that he was on his way to see the principal. It was clear the palaver would get more heated during the next two days.

John was face-to-face with the demands of institutional missions. There was student discipline and curriculum and social activities. And, if you asked the business manager, there was also money palaver, and advances and where to buy the cheapest rice, and how to manage the men and the water system. If all the missionaries were polled, there would be a list of nitty-gritty choices a mile long. Most were in the grayed areas—neither right or wrong; moral or immoral—just problems that had to be settled one by one. How did you get through all this into areas of spiritual renewal and awakening? John thought of the afternoons that week. Four out of four had been spent on student activities. Was that good use of missionary time? Was he getting through to Roland?

John decided to look carefully at all the student activities. The next afternoon, he began with the Life Service Band. A senior, Bestman Varney, was their leader. He explained the program this way. "Some of us teach Sunday School on campus. Some of us go to villages every week for services. All of us have committed our lives to Christ and want to serve him."

When John asked to see the work first-hand, Bestman invited him to a special service which was to be held in Bestman's own village.

When the appointed Saturday came, John and Maggie drove through the bush with part of the Life Service Band. Another station wagon, driven by the journeygirl on campus, followed.

Maggie saw villages she had not seen before, during the one hour drive over roads which were not much more than footpaths. All along the way villagers waved and smiled and Bestman spoke to people he knew. "See that boy. He came to know the Lord one Saturday when we preached in his village."

As Bestman continued to produce name after name of those who had been reached by the Life Service Band, John tried to nail down the figures. "How many people have you brought to the Lord this year? Last year?"

Bestman thought a minute. "We don't write this down. It's just in my heart. When I see a boy or a man or woman I just remember when I talked to him and I remember what he thinks inside."

Maggie was pleased with Bestman's response and said so. "You must teach me how to talk with these people. No?"

Bestman grinned in a shy way. "I not teach you, Mrs. Blake. You're a missionary."

Maggie wavered a minute and decided to speak on a person-to-person level. "I don't know this. Some things I can teach you. Some things you can teach me. God says we should help each other."

As they went through another village, Maggie elaborated. "See. There's a stack of palm nuts and a whole yard full of coffee beans. Do you think I see these where I come from?"

Bestman shrugged and realized he didn't know exactly where this missionary came from.

Maggie continued. "And see those trees with bananas and papaya and grapefruit? I don't see any plantain or lime right now, but there are trees with them someplace close, no doubt. Where I come from, we have none of these. I can't know about them like you do. So you must teach me many things."

John got into the conversation. "Do people here realize how good God has been to them? Nobody planted those trees. They just grew. Nobody has to starve here."

Bestman, who had come to a concept of the world which was bigger than most village students had, said, "I doubt it. They don't know other people don't have the same things. They think the world is all like their village."

John frowned and thought about what it would be like to never read a book or travel anywhere. "I guess so. One woman here asked me if I walked from the United States to Africa, and a student asked if the ocean were bigger than a river."

Bestman replied, "A village man thinks the world is as big as his feet can carry him. Most haven't been to the capital city."

"These oranges are spoiling on the tree," Maggie commented, as a branch full of brown, soft oranges brushed across the windshield. "Why aren't they being picked?"

"That's the way of agriculture here," Bestman replied. "There's no truck in the village to take the fruit to market. The people can eat just so much fruit and only a few sacks can be carried on their heads to nearby markets. A taxi costs more than the fruit will sell for. So the fruit stays."

Maggie thought about the high cost of canned and frozen fruits at the supermarket. Of course, they were all imported. She suggested, "But can't they can or something?"

Bestman liked this topic and he began a lengthy monologue on the need for processing plants in the country. Then he discussed marketing techniques.

John was impressed. "What about you, Bestman? When you graduate, do you think you'll get a chance to put your ideas into working plans?"

Bestman looked doubtful. "I have no financial backing. I'm a village boy. I learned a little about agriculture from the missionary on campus, but he's gone now. I miss Mr. Hasson. When he left, the people wept and brought him gifts. Do you think we'll get another agricultural missionary?"

"I don't know, Bestman. The job may be up to you and other students who have some background." John rubbed his forehead and thought about the medical and agricultural needs around the world.

Just then a voice from the back seat called, "There's your village, Bestman."

As the car stopped, Maggie noticed the neat, painted houses. Maybe ten altogether. Bestman opened the car door and stepped forward to shake the outstretched hands of his village brothers who had seen the cars on the road a long time before they reached the village. John and Maggie met the same friendly response.

The other car carrying students parked as Bestman pointed the way to a small building which was obviously a church. Maggie was surprised for she had seen few villages with an actual church building. Usually the people met in a palaver hut where other meetings were also held.

Bestman walked the few steps to where an empty butane bottle hung on a wooden support. He picked up a metal rod and began to hit the bottle. Dull, regular sounds went throughout the village and even to other villages. Church was about to begin.

Maggie watched in amazement as people began to appear from nowhere. Within ten minutes time the church was full. The visitors entered last and were led to special seats in the front. John, as was the tradition, was placed in the biggest chair on the platform. Maggie, the journeygirl, and the teacher who was sponsor of the Life Service Band, sat on the only chairs in the church which had backs. Everyone else positioned himself on wooden benches.

The people became quiet as a village elder rose to welcome the visitors and begin the service. He beamed and smiled so that Maggie began to feel this was indeed a special occasion.

When Bestman rose to lead some songs, the expectancy of the crowd could be felt. On the first note, voices were loud and husky. Bodies began to sway in rhythm. Women began to clap and old men smiled. A gourd and a tamborine made sharp sounds from a row directly behind Maggie. This was like being caught in the middle of an avalanche of sound. Maggie was involved whether she wanted to be or not.

The singing went on and on until Bestman reluctantly finished and was seated again.

A Gbolupa student came to the platform and gave her testimony. It was greeted by "Amens."

Three students sang a spiritual. Before they finished, the congregation was clapping and the boys sang three extra verses.

As the elder prayed again, the congregation began to murmur and someone shouted, "Jesus." The prayer was long and intense.

Then the elder introduced the speaker to the visitors. Maggie knew this was the man Bestman had talked about earlier. He was going to talk about "Forbidden River," a story that the people of the village knew well. As the old man rose, tension mounted. He began, "When I was a small boy. . . ."

Maggie was pleased by the man's good English and sat back to enjoy her chair and the story.

The bent head lifted and the storyteller went on. "A missionary came to this village. To this very spot. He stood here and he preached Jesus."

A voice from the back of the church murmured, "Ya. Ya."

The speaker didn't hesitate. "The white man—he say Jesus was great spirit. He say Jesus was only God. As he speak something moved in here." The old man pointed to his chest. "Yes, it moved. I cried out 'Oh Jesus' and Jesus he come right through my body and deep down in me. I feel him. Oh, yes, I feel him inside."

"Amen, amen," some voices agreed.

The old man looked around. "My three friends feel Jesus, too. He come right into their heart, too. They all gone now to be with him." The old man wiped both eyes and then picked up the story. "Brothers, Sisters, I come right up here and I took that preacher's hand and I say I want to follow Jesus. That preacher pray and I fell on my knees. That preacher stay two weeks and he talk every day about Jesus, but no one else feel him—just me and my three friends!"

The old man paused and breathed hard. "Well, that preacher say we must be baptized. We say this be fine. The preacher say we be baptized in the creek there." The old man pointed a shaking finger in the direction of a creek that the visitors had crossed on their way to the village.

The congregation sat spellbound and the old man with trembling lips went on. "Me and my friends we say 'No.' We can't go near that water. That Forbidden River. All village know it forbidden. My Ma she say every day that water nege [Bassa word for *witch in the water]* get you. You die if you go there. Whole village say bad spirits are there. But that preacher he say Jesus more powerful spirit."

"Me and my friends we talk. We talk plenty. We talk two nights. Then voice inside say to go to be baptized."

A man sitting behind Maggie took a deep breath. Maggie found herself moved and anxious. How would the story end?

The old man's voice became strong and loud. "I say to my ma I go to Forbidden River. She wail. She scream. All village wail. But me and my friends and the preacher we walk out there." The storyteller pointed toward the thirty-foot wide creek. "When we walk the death wails get louder and louder. My ma throw herself on the ground and roll. Inside I was feared. I shake plenty. I want to run back to village, but preacher just keep walking. My feet just keep walking, too, but my legs hardly know it. My friends keep walking, too. The death wails get louder and louder. I say to self, 'if I die, I die with Jesus.'

"That preacher walked right into water. My feet keep walking right on to the water. Then one foot stop and next foot stop. The preacher turn and say, 'Come. Come on with Jesus.'

"My feet start walking and they go right into water. Nothing happen. I think I see water nege but eyes not really see nothing. Those spirits were nowhere.

"Joy broke like the morning when I went down into that water. The preacher say 'I baptize you in name of God Jesus and the Holy Spirit.' I come out of that water and I shout, 'Jesus. Jesus.' I shout all the way back to the village. My feet run. They not shake anymore. I shout to people, 'Jesus is life.' "

The congregation began to relax. Maggie suddenly found a tear was rolling down her cheek. The young two-year mission appointee beside her blew her nose loudly.

The old man stretched to his fullest height and said, "I tell my ma. See fear spirit is nowhere—is nothing. Jesus—he everywhere!"

"My ma she quit wailing. She get off ground. She go right down to that creek and right into Forbidden River. She be baptized, too. Other people go. Many people begin life with Jesus that day. The next day the people start to fish in Forbidden River. There was no fear and no more hungry time. Jesus good for the heart and send fish for the belly. Jesus make life good."

With that the old man turned, wiped his forehead with a clean handkerchief, and sat down.

For a moment no one moved. Then a sister began softly to sing, "Jesus, O how sweet the name!" Other voices joined and repeated, "O, how sweet the name. Jesus. Jesus."

Slowly the worship and adoration dissipated. Finally Bestman rose and thanked the congregation for coming. The elder dismissed the group and the building was slowly emptied.

Outside all the women shook Maggie's hand and the elder brought her a bag of pink grapefruit. Maggie looked to John, and he replied for both of them. "Thank you. Thank you. We like the grapefruit, but best we like the message. It has cooled my heart."

John touched his heart and the elder smiled. He was obviously pleased that John had picked up the common expression for showing pleasure, "cooled." In the tropics, no one ever spoke of a "warmed heart."

On the way home, the students began to ask about one of their favorite subjects—America. Each question revealed a lack of information about the size of the country and the variety of the occupations of the people there. America to most of the students was a huge, beautiful city with many office buildings and four-lane highways.

The students were still asking questions when Maggie realized they were approaching Hollah Camp. With the first view of campus, Maggie gasped in surprise. Was this a mirage? It must be, for nowhere else in the bush was there large buildings and yards with grass that was mowed by lawn mowers and flowering shrubs that grew in hedges. Maggie realized she had never seen the campus before from the viewpoint of a villager who lived every day in an unmodern village on a footpath.

John's thoughts were running in the same lines. He verbalized them. "After hours of driving through villages, this place is . . . unique." He groped for words and thought about the contrast between the castles he had seen in Germany and the surrounding area. "Like a fine castle on the Rhine."

John stopped in front of the bachelor quarters to let the sponsor of the Life Service Band out. "Big Do . . ." John corrected himself, "Uh, Mr. Gaere, you're doing a fine job. The Life Service Band is doing great."

Mr. Gaere's face turned into a big smile. "Thanks. You can call me Big Dominic. I don't mind. Everybody calls me that."

John looked up at the man who was a head taller than himself and a head and shoulders taller than the men in the village and replied. "Well, you Sudanese warriors do make an obvious contrast standing beside these short West African farmers! Thanks again for taking us today."

As John drove away his mind returned to the castle idea. The Lord of the castle—he was the important factor. The castle was only a structure without the Lord who commanded protection and sent provision for the people. It was God who had taken Forbidden River. He was the most powerful Lord of the area. Yet, he worked through people—like Bestman; like the storyteller. He was Lord but he hadn't come yet in full force. He had limited himself but he was adequate. John marveled, "God in me. God in me, the hope. . . ."

John's thoughts came to a sudden halt as he noticed three students crossing into his yard. He pointed them out to Maggie. "Guess who?"

Maggie laughed. "Roland, of course." Then in mock seriousness she added, "The Lord no doubt sent him to perfect some virtue in you!"

John frowned. He'd never thought about it that way. He'd always supposed God sent Roland in order that Roland would learn something. John extended his hand to Roland with more respect than he had felt before and wondered what God was producing in Roland and in himself.

12
Capital City

John stopped beside the paved road to wipe the mud off the side view mirror and wondered if this weekly shopping trip would be like the other ones he had made recently—hurried and hectic. He turned toward Maggie, who was wrestling to keep Sam away from the open car window, and asked in a tired voice, "What's on the list today?"

Maggie frowned. "A whole lot more than we can possibly get in one trip!" As she thought about the possibility of having to drive over the muddy road again that week, her determination to somehow get it all done in one afternoon increased. She looked at John. "I've got it in order. First stop—Waterfront for a kerosene burner."

John thought about his last trip there. Out loud he said, "If I could only figure out what store has what, shopping wouldn't be so tough."

Maggie half-grinned. "Yes, I know what you mean. You can find everything or anything if you have the time to look."

John went back to the shopping list. "What after Waterfront?"

"It's get the kids off the missionary kid bus, take them swimming at the hotel, while I shop for some things for Sam. After that it's grocery shopping for me."

"And to get some electrical and plumbing supplies for me." John had a sudden impulse to try the government office again. Quickly he decided to put that off until next week.

John pulled onto the two-lane bridge which was the one route into the city from the Gbolupa campus side, only to be delayed by a car which was in the middle of the bridge with a flat tire. Tires squalled, cars swerved, and heated words were blown back and forth as traffic came together in one lane at the stalled car. John wiped his forehead as he waited his turn and wondered if he'd ever been hotter.

Ten minutes later John pulled off the other side of the bridge and was immediately stopped by a policeman directing traffic. A line of cars coming from the left passed and the policeman waved John on. He accelerated only to go a few yards and slam on the brakes to avoid hitting two women with babies on their backs as they ran into the street. When the other pedestrians noticed that John had stopped, they joined the two women in the street. Horns behind John began to honk and the policeman came to John's open window. "I say go. You go now!"

"But . . . ," John stammered with an eye on the people "I can't go through all that."

"You can't stop here," the policeman insisted, and John eased forward and honked his horn. The people saw that the car was moving and scurried to the safety of the sidewalk.

Maggie watched a man with an overloaded wheelbarrow who had barely gotten across the street in time and now could not get the wheelbarrow over the six-inch high curb. Finally she exclaimed, "Traffic in Africa is ten times more dangerous than elephants and snakes!"

John would have agreed with her but didn't have time before a taxi in front of him pulled out without a backward glance. John slammed on the brakes. The taxi pulled through a group of pedestrians, sending them into the other lane of traffic where an oncoming car stopped quickly to avoid hitting them. John pulled up and quickly backed into the parking place vacated by the taxi. When he was a foot from the car behind him, a couple of men on the sidewalk motioned for him to stop. John ignored their instructions and backed another six inches. When the parking was successfully completed, the two men smiled, waved, and went on their way, happy to have performed a good deed.

As John locked the car, Maggie started down the narrow sidewalk. She had been here so often she no longer had a strong reaction to the street which was dirty and crowded with portable merchandising centers. One type of sales stand was a two- by three-foot table which actually looked like a wooden suitcase with legs. When a "Charlie" wanted to move to a new location, he closed a hinged lid over his merchandise, put the table, legs up, on his head, and walked off.

Another type of portable merchandising center had no legs, but a glass front that locked. Inside might be small items, like watches or sunglasses, which could be easily stolen.

One Charlie blocked Maggie's route by holding a wooden statue in her face. "Missy, Missy, this ebony plenty fineo. You never see anything like this!"

While houseboys and watchmen were men who worked at menial tasks for low pay, successful Charlies were another breed of men. They were actors, who learned their lines to educate, persuade, and entertain unsuspecting customers. Since there was no set price for the things they sold, a Charlie knew profits depended on his ability to talk and convince.

This Charlie eyed Maggie's purse and wondered how much to ask for the statue he held in his hand. Eager for a sale, he said again, "Missy, you never see anything so fine. This be fine in your house. Everybody see and like."

From a distance the statue didn't look so bad. Maggie decided to look closer. She turned the statue over and scraped her fingernail across the bottom. "What's this wood?"

"Ebony."

Maggie looked up into the Charlie's straight face and saw not the slightest hint of falsehood. She scratched another time on the bottom of the statue before the Charlie pulled it away. "See," Maggie declared, knowing she had won this contest. "It's not ebony. The wood has shoe polish on it—it's not black underneath!"

Another approach was in order. The Charlie said, "I give you plenty good price."

"How much?"

The man's face became all smiles. When a Missy asked the price he knew he was halfway to a sale. "Twenty-five dollar, Missy. That be good price."

"What?" Maggie exploded. "You're kidding!"

The Charlie let a small grin wrinkle one corner of his large mouth before he put his serious face back on. "That be good price, Missy."

Maggie laughed and divided the Charlie's price by one third. "So, it's worth eight dollars, no?"

The Charlie hesitated a moment and brought his price down to twenty dollars. Maggie, who was aware there was a first price, a second price, and sometimes a third price before a selling price was reached, decided to cut the process short. "I don't want the statue. It isn't ebony. Now let me pass."

The Charlie stood with his feet planted wide apart so Maggie couldn't get away. He beamed, certain that the next words would fully convince this Missy to buy. "Twelve dollar. That be my last price."

Maggie's slight inerest in the statue began to melt as perspiration poured down her back. "I don't have time to talk-talk today. You don't want to sell bad enough to give me a good price. I go now."

The Charlie held the statue up again at some distance so Maggie could admire its better features without noticing the flaws made by a careless carver. "What your last price?"

Maggie replied quickly. "Five dollars."

"Missy, I have more than five dollar inside this statue."

"OK. Finish," Maggie said sternly, and looked hard at the Charlie.

He read the look; his eyes dropped; he grinned and slowly stepped aside. "Next time you buy from me, Missy." His eyes traveled down the street where he saw the next customer approaching.

Maggie walked on down the street thinking about the day she had bought a similar statue for four dollars. Of course, that had been at 6 P.M. and the Charlie hadn't made a good sale all day. He had to have enough money to buy rice and fish for the evening meal. Only the Charlies who sold ivory and expensive artifacts made enough for some of the luxuries of life—a refrigerator, gold jewelry for their wives, and transportation by car, rather than on foot.

Maggie tried five stores which all looked alike and had similar low-priced merchandise without finding a kerosene burner. The sixth store Maggie entered was also a fifteen- by fifteen-foot box which had no openings except the glass windows and doors in front. Inside it was stifling hot and smelled of mildew. A clerk slept on a low stool in one corner. As Maggie walked down the center aisle in the crowded store, she studied the tennis shoes, which were stacked to the twenty-foot high ceiling. Next were pans and glasses. She was getting close. A smiling clerk came from the back room, passed the sleeping clerk without any indication he saw him, and asked, "What today, Missy?"

"Kerosene burner. You have one?"

The man looked puzzled and Maggie tried again. "My electric lights go plenty. I need burner to cook chop."

On the word *chop,* the clerk's face changed. "Ah, chop. Missy, you want to cook chop."

"Yah, you have burner that use kerosene?"

The clerk looked toward the expatriate who owned this and several other stores on the waterfront. The owner came forward and answered, "No. We had some, but they're finished now."

Maggie thought about going to the other one hundred or so stores on the street and looked pleadingly at the owner. "Maybe you can help me. Do you know which store has a burner?"

The owner, who had spent a monotonous morning sorting bolts of material in the back room, brightened and a smile crossed his handsome face. "I'll show you." He took Maggie's arm in a way that was a little too friendly to suit her and walked her to the door. Then with his other hand he gestured toward a shop across the street which belonged to his brother. "I think you'll find what you want across the street—there."

Maggie thanked the owner and crossed to find John had been directed to the same store. While John was paying for the burner, Maggie investigated the merchandise in this store. Sandals from Red China. Shoes from Taiwan. Material from Hong Kong, France, and Britain. Tools from Poland.

Producing? Manufacturing? No. That wasn't the way of life here. Of course, there were those who made silver and gold jewelry, tie-dyed cloth, and woven baskets. But the majority didn't produce anything. They simply sold what was imported. Selling on the streets was the way of life. It was all purchased in a store owned by some expatriate shop-keeper and often sold a few steps from his shop door.

Maggie thought about the woman she had passed last week on the street. She was one of hundreds of market women who sold greens, palm oil, fruit, candy, and ground nuts. For a while Maggie had counted as the woman filled a jar lid with ground nuts and emptied it into a paper funnel, which she had rolled from old newspaper. Then Maggie had noticed the baby asleep under the woman's table. As Maggie paid for the roasted nuts she inquired, "The baby for you?"

The woman, who had seemed plain, smiled, and Maggie realized how pretty she would be if she weren't so tired looking. "Yah, Missy. The baby for me."

Maggie's eyes took in the pink panties, the plaited hair, and the round body. "The baby fine. You take good care of her."

The proud mother looked for a long time at the child. "Yah, the baby fine."

Maggie turned away somehow brought back to a sense of what is important in life. Maggie wondered how many children this mother had raised underneath her work table? How many were now old enough to sell on their own? Even an eight-year-old could carry toothbrushes, buttons, zippers, Vaseline, T-shirts, fruit, hose, shirts, and pencils. If he were strong enough to carry it, he could learn to sell it.

Maggie and John walked out of the store and came to a shoe shine boy John had set up in business months earlier. The boy greeted John with a big, "Boss, I do fine, No?"

John patted the boy's head and smiled. "You do fine. You make small money, no?"

"Small, small," the boy replied, with a toothy grin.

John looked at the boy's tattered shirt and holey cutoffs and noticed there were several deep sores in the top of his bare feet. John pushed some words past the lump in his throat. "You keep trying my man. You not beg, anymore. You work like man with dignity. Someday you get better job. OK?"

The boy turned away with a twisted grin on his face and John new he had no comprehension of how hard he would have to try if he ever got a good job. He'd never been to school a day in his life and would never go.

John suddenly knew it wasn't the dirt and the inconvenience that really bothered him in the capital city. It was the living conditions of the people. There was no hope, no way up. There seemed no answer to the economic situation of most of the people. The solutions within their reach meant work one day; make enough to eat. Would it be the same for the next generation?

John picked up his own children and drove to the hotel for the long-promised swim in the pool. Mark was enthusiastic and jumped into the water first. Karen soon followed and John got into the cool pool on the shallow end with Sam. Maggie took a lingering look at the ships in port, which were a part of the panoramic view from this hotel which set on the highest hill in the city. She looked down at her long shopping list. She had to get these things today.

Maggie drove down Embassy Drive, a street which belonged with the cosmopolitan atmosphere of the hotel. Here were big houses with piazzas and yards with six-foot high walls and night and day watchmen. Here were country clubs and fine restaurants. On the next street were shops which sold Italian shoes and French suits and gold bracelets that cost $500. This was the world of diplomats and politicians and rich men.

Maggie admired the ocean view and the flambeau trees with millions of bloodred blooms. She watched the sails of the ships at sea give with the wind and for a moment felt like a rich woman, too.

Then the shoreline drive ended abruptly at the modern supermarket and Maggie hurried inside to fill her cart with canned goods from Europe and the United States. She looked at a couple of prices and computed them to be twice the United States price and then decided to forget price. She had already learned she couldn't live off of fish and rice and greens and stay well. Doctor bills could be more expensive than grocery bills. So, Maggie picked up hot dogs and bologna from the United States, beef from Australia, canned soup from Switzerland, dried milk from Holland and an array of other groceries which made a supply enough for two weeks in case next week's shopping trip had to be postponed because the road had washed out again.

Then Maggie bought pineapple, bananas, avocados, and oranges from the market women in front of the store and cassava fish at forty cents a pound from the fish market. On the way to the hotel she delivered a message to a friend, thinking all the time about how great it would be to have a telephone at Gbolupa.

On the way home, Mark spotted a soccer game in progress on a field beside the road. "Look at that! Whammy!" Mark's body moved an inch in a miniature duplication of the foot high jump and Maggie knew Mark would gather a group of boys for practice as soon as he got home.

Karen's thoughts were on something else. "Hey, bamboo goal posts! Mark, did you know that bamboo can grow four feet in one day?"

Mark, who wasn't impressed with Karen's newfound knowledge, replied, "So? Who cares." With one quick motion Mark's foot flew up in another imitation of the play taking place on the field. Unfortunately he connected with Sam's arm and he began to yell. Mark stopped only a minute to comfort him and see if his dad were going to punish him. Then he said, "Wow! Did you see that ball? It took off like a jet. Bang! Pow! Like a rocket! Just like when I kick the ball."

Karen saw a chance to get even with Mark. "The last time you did that, the ball hit you between the eyes, Stupid!"

"Peace, Bartie," Mark yelled, and shoved Karen away from the window. "Look out your own window."

Maggie looked at John in desperation. John gave her a pained expression and turned toward the backseat, "Only three more mud holes and we'll be home, so for now kids let's. . . ."

13

Politicians and Preachers

As the bus left campus, John thought back to the afternoon he had gone with the Life Service Band to Bestman's village. That had been the day Roland first suggested the Gbolupa choir sing at his father's church.

John decided to follow the bus and turned to Roland, who was in the backseat of the mission car. "I thought you'd go on the bus."

"No, Professor, I like cars better." John thought about the difference between a Peugeot and a Mercedes and asked Roland about his father.

Yes, he was pastor of the church. No, he didn't preach every Sunday. He was too busy with government travel and responsibilities as a senator. Yes, he had a home in the capital city, but his home place was thirty miles up-country. There he had a residence and land close to the church.

Roland's background information on his father flowed readily and John listened with interest as they drove past a field of sugar cane. Its white tassels waved eight feet from the ground and John thought again about what a lovely day it was. In fact, it was hard to believe that this was the middle of rainy season.

John intended to enjoy this day for he and Maggie hadn't been off campus on a Sunday since school started. John turned to look at Maggie, who was so caught up with the sunshine and tropical view, that she did not notice. Several cassava patches and a lot of villages were passed before John turned off the main highway and onto a new road.

John inquired, "How come the new pavement?"

Roland answered with a hint of pride. "They paved it all the way to Kapita, my dad's town."

John was aware that paved roads led to important men's houses and decided not to pursue the subject. Instead he turned to the church. "What position does your dad have in the church convention?"

"He's vice-president."

"For how long?"

Roland laughed, "Ever since."

"Does he spend a lot of time on convention business?"

"Yes, he travels to other countries on convention business and he has meetings in the capital city all the time." Roland considered this explanation enough, for he really was not certain what his father did at all the meetings he attended. After all, schoolboys were never invited when important decisions were being made.

During the remainder of the trip Roland elaborated on extensive plans he had for student activities. John half-listened and marveled at Roland's nimble intellect and big ideas.

When Roland saw his dad's house, he pointed it out to Maggie. She looked carefully as the car sped past. Beautiful gardens and flowers. The three-story house looked like an old country home. It wasn't as large and modern as Roland's home in the capital. Maybe twenty air conditioners were mounted in the exterior walls all around the house. There was a circular drive and a covered walk over several steps up to the large doors, which opened out to make a grand entrance way.

The church set nearby on a hill and was neat, but small, according to United States standards. The low educational wing looked like it had about eight classrooms and the auditorium was tall and narrow and topped by a steeple. A large bell hung in a bell house to the right of the church and Maggie counted the steps up to the auditorium as they went up them. There were twelve in all.

At the door on the left stood a well-dressed usher who smiled warmly and told Roland where the choir should sit. Roland wore a sweet, church-door expression as the choir members passed through the door, two-by-two and took their places close to the front of the church.

John was directed to a large high-backed chair on the platform where some other deacons and reverends were already seated. Each of them greeted John with a firm handshake.

Maggie sat with the women in the center seats of the chandelier lit auditorium. Other guests and church members came and were seated—the women in the center, the men on the left, the children on the right with the choir.

At ten minutes past the hour, Roland's father and mother entered the auditorium from the back, center aisle. Reverend Minor came first and shook only a few hands as he made his way to the front. Behind him came Mrs. Minor, tall and wide in a white gown which flowed around her ankles. The gown and matching headdress were elaborately decorated with white, African embroidery, which complemented the gold and ivory necklaces, earrings, and bracelets she wore.

Suddenly, Maggie was aware of the tension that had come to the crowd. Some of the women on the far aisle pushed toward the center aisle to greet Mrs. Minor with the usual welcome, a kiss on each cheek. Mrs.

Minor's warm smile and handclasp left none out, and each returned to her seat beaming because of the recognition she had received.

Maggie stood uncomfortable on her side of the culture gap, not knowing what to do. She had never seen a minister and his wife enter a church like this. When Mrs. Minor reached the pew where Maggie stood, she stopped and motioned. For an instant Maggie thought Mrs. Minor was calling for someone else. When she motioned again, Maggie excused herself and stepped in front of several women to reach Mrs. Minor in the center aisle. Mrs. Minor greeted Maggie by name, folded her close to her large bosom, and kissed her on each cheek. The warm welcome extended, Mrs. Minor hurried on to her place on the front pew. Maggie started toward the seat where she had been earlier and found the women who had scarcely noticed her before were now friendly.

On the platform, Reverend Minor greeted each deacon and pastor with a hearty handclasp, his fingers snapping off of theirs. When he got to John, Reverend Minor clasped John's hand with his right hand and squeezed John's shoulder with his left hand. Then, he sat down beside John and the service began.

The opening prayer was long and intense and then the congregation sang a familiar hymn at full volume. When the Gbolupa choir rose, Maggie looked with pride down the rows of handsome students. They had never looked better. Every white dress was neatly pressed and the girls must have spent most of the early morning hours on their fancy hairdos. To Maggie's amazement, the black ties, which the boys usually wore carelessly knotted, were all pushed up in a firm knot at the collar of their white shirts, where they belonged. Maggie wondered how the young American choir director had achieved this neat look. Her respect for him grew even more as the choir finished the first line of a moving spiritual.

Immediately, the congregation was caught up in the rhythm and several of the sisters began to clap and sigh, "Oh, yes. Oh, yes." Mrs. Minor's foot began to tap and Reverend Minor wore a proud smile all during Roland's solo part. Two numbers were soon finished and the congregation wanted more. This time the choir did a modern hymn and the women beside Maggie had difficulty understanding the words.

When the song was finished, Reverend Minor rose to preach, and John was reminded of Roland's student senate speech. This message was not meat for the brain or strength for the spirit, but wine for the emotion. Reverend Minor's voice rose to a high, rhythmic pitch and the listeners "amened" and called, "Preach it, Brother." One woman swooned and fell across the seat in front of her. The sermon stirred and bubbled on for forty minutes and no one was ready for it to end. When Reverend

Minor stepped down from the elevated podium, John found he had been strangely moved. His emotions had opened wide and he had been lifted. Still he could not have cataloged the message except to say it was about Jesus.

Now it was time to lift the offering and to John's surprise Reverend Minor announced there would be a special offering for the Gbolupa choir. Two well-dressed deacons and two stout sisters came to sit behind the offering table. Each encouraged the congregation to give generously by placing their own roll of greenbacks in the offering plate. Soon the aisles were full of people coming to the front to make their contributions. When the church choir, which wore black robes and mortar board hats, finished the fourth stanza of a hymn, Reverend Minor asked the lifters to count the offering. Soon a figure was read, which seemed large to John, but was evidently less than Reverend Minor expected. Reverend Minor came to the offering table, pulled out a twenty-dollar bill, and addressed the crowd. "Brothers and Sisters, these are our children. The students at Gbolupa need our help. . . ."

As the exhortation continued, John looked toward Roland and quickly decided by the look on his face, that this offering was his idea. He had found a way to pay for some student activities. Even when John continued to stare at Roland throughout the plea for a large offering, Roland kept his eyes on a nonexistent spot high above the elevated podium.

As soon as Reverend Minor finished, one of the sisters picked up an offering plate and began to sing a lively spiritual. She shuffled down the center aisle and to the back pew. The other sister at the front table picked up another offering plate and said, "Dig deeper. Dig deeper." Her long, shiny blue lappa dress danced around her legs and reflected the overhead lights as she half-waltzed, half-walked down another aisle. Soon the whole congregation was happy and searching for the change at the bottom of their pockets and purses. When the sisters quick-stepped back to the table in front, the plates were full. A quick count showed more had been given than Reverend Minor had asked for. The sisters thanked the congregation, and a deacon held the full offering plates above his head as he prayed.

The announcements were quickly read by another deacon and John was called to pronounce the benediction. As John turned from the lower podium, Reverend Minor drew him close and walked hand in hand with him down the center aisle and out of the church. Outside several photographers from the local paper took pictures of Reverend Minor with the Gbolupa choir. Then John was ushered to Reverend Minor's big black car for the five minute drive to the Reverend's residence.

John, who had not anticipated this move, tossed the car keys to Maggie,

and she stood alone, wondering what was expected of her. Roland came to her rescue, "I'll ride with you."

When Maggie got to the Minor's residence, she realized that the entire congregation had been invited for dinner. Mrs. Minor, who had disappeared quickly from the church, soon reappeared in the gardens, where she graciously showed people to chairs and saw that waiters, dressed in white jackets, served everyone with cold, citrus juice.

From a seat in the rose garden, Maggie watched as other waiters brought food from the house to long tables which were inside two long, outdoor dining halls. These buildings had tile roofs and concrete floors and a gentle breeze blew through the open sides, ruffling the white tablecloths on enough tables to seat two-hundred fifty guests.

When the serving tables would hold no more huge platters of food, Reverend Minor found Maggie and John and asked them and the Gbolupa choir to serve themselves first. Maggie passed up the usual rice and soup dishes in favor of potato and lettuce salad and sugar-cured ham and Swiss steak. Fantas were soon served at the head table where Maggie was seated beside Reverend Minor. She turned to him, "The ham tastes like the smokehouse, sugar-cured ham my grandma used to serve. Where did it come from?"

Maggie waited, half-believing the senator would answer, "Hatton, Missouri, United States of America." Instead, he laughed and said, "You like it?"

"Very good—excellent."

Then the senator drew attention to the steak. "How about the beef? It's from my farm."

Maggie had not tried the steak and now took a small bite. For local beef it was excellent, but Maggie knew it wasn't prime by United States standards, so she answered, "It's good. I come from the best beef growing area in the United States—the Midwest. My dad has Angus cattle."

The senator turned to Maggie with awakening interest and a long conversation began about agriculture. Maggie tried several times to end the conversation as she noticed the men across the table were trying to get the senator's attention. But once the senator found a topic he liked, he pursued it and he definitely liked United States agriculture.

One of the men finally became a little heated in his remarks, and the senator looked toward him. The man immediately asked for a favor and Maggie could tell by Senator Minor's cold response that he either didn't intend to grant the favor or the man had chosen the wrong time and place to ask for it. The man did not give up easily, even when the senator turned to John and began to talk about Gbolupa, which was also one of his favorite subjects. As the students passed with filled plates, the senator called many by name. "She's Sister Bertha's girl; he's Brother Joe's son," and on and on. Finally John began to piece family trees together and realized that many of the Gbolupa students were actually cousins, nephews, or nieces of the Minors.

Before the meal was finished, Mrs. Minor brought a large platter of ham to the head table and insisted Maggie have more. Then she called for waiters to serve more soft drinks and spiced pound cake. At the students' tables, she placed huge trays of grapes and apples and served them with many hugs. Maggie had to look twice at the grapes to believe they were real, for she couldn't remember having had white grapes at all in Africa. Apples were an expensive treat, also. Mrs. Minor's simple, often repeated explanation as the trays got lighter and lighter was, "Nothing's too good for my precious children."

Later when Reverend Minor bade John farewell, Maggie couldn't help noticing that John towered above this squat man. Even then, Reverend Minor was impressive in appearance. Maggie wasn't certain whether it was the cheerful, open way he greeted and listened to everyone or because he was surrounded by those who seemed to have no purpose other than to hang onto his every word and motion.

On the way home, Roland slept with such a pleasant expression on his face that Maggie imagined he was dreaming of ways to spend the money the church had collected. Maggie ran through the day's experiences in her mind. She slid over toward John and took his hand. "This was one special day—like hearing a great symphony orchestra in person or seeing the Grand Canyon for the first time."

Maggie's comparisons triggered John's memory and he thought about opening a package containing an expensive tape deck, which Maggie had encouraged him to buy, even though it was way beyond his missionary salary. "It was luxury. Few missionaries get that kind of red carpet treatment." John thought about the other people at church. "Everybody wanted to walk on the carpet, didn't they? The men at the table tried hard to get Reverend Minor to take off his preacher's hat and put on his politician's hat."

Maggie realized John had hit on the problem that had puzzled her all day. "I never saw the same man try to wear both hats before. I felt Reverend Minor seemed most at home in the church. He was relaxed and comfortable, like he was in his own living room with his shoes off."

"It was family all right, but they willingly included us." John continued to think about Rev. Minor while Maggie turned to the letter she would write John's mom, "You'd never guess what we did today."

14

Tarzan for Jesus

A few months back John had come to a firm conclusion—every church member and pastor in the United States wanted to visit Africa. This morning, though, his mind was on other things, as Maggie rolled over in bed and threw her arm across his chest. She kissed him on the nose playing the old family game, "Kiss my nose, my motor goes." John kissed Maggie a couple of times before he realized she was clicking her fingernails like she always did when she was planning something important. She'd mark off each job on her fingers and then give decided clicks as jobs were properly disposed of in her mind.

John tried to get Maggie's attention. "So that last kiss was cool. What are you planning?"

Maggie answered sheepishly, "How did you know I was planning something?"

John moved a few inches away from Maggie to look in her face. "Remember I've been married a long time—a hundred years or so—your fingernails—you're clicking them."

"Oh!" Maggie exclaimed and quickly stopped clicking. Beyond that she didn't answer, so John repeated his question.

"So you're still a million miles away. What are you thinking about?"

This time Maggie answered. "The big tour group from the United States and dinner tonight."

John started to ask what tour group and then remembred a radio message from several weeks back about a group which would pass through West Africa on their way to an evangelistic crusade in East Africa. He tried to recall the details. "I'd forgotten. What are the arrangements?"

"You've forgotten?" Maggie asked in unbelief, as if forgetting were the unpardonable sin. After all, she'd spent days making arrangements. "The pastors and musicians—remember—you're supposed to get them at the airport this afternoon!"

John knew that a plane was the only way any group came to Africa, but still he couldn't remember volunteering to get anyone. He knew Maggie would remember who, what, when, why, and how. So, he asked. "Did I volunteer to do that?"

Maggie hesitated. "Well, you sort of volunteered."

John turned over and sat on the edge of the bed. "That means you volunteered and I'm supposed to help, right?"

"Not exactly."

John thought about Maggie's early morning kiss before she'd thought about the visitors and wished this weren't going to be another hurried day. Why was there always a schedule to keep?

John sighed and decided to concentrate on the day's plans. "OK, Miss Efficient, fill me in on the details."

Twenty minutes later John was on his way to school with his mind doing time-juggling stunts. If he skipped the bookwork, he could grade the tests. No, that wouldn't leave time for lunch. He'd have to delay a meeting. Even then he'd be late starting for the airport and Maggie would grumble.

When John got home for lunch at two, Maggie met him at the door with bad news. "The Pearces can't go to the airport to get the overflow."

John looked at Maggie in astonishment. "The overflow? You said this morning four people."

Maggie suddenly realized John was not aware of all the changes in plans that had come since he left home at seven-thirty. She wasn't certain she could explain, even if she had time. "You know how it goes—the latest schedule hasn't happened yet! We got an early morning radio message. Then we got another message at ten. We've had two changes of plans since then. And I'm still working on the last plan."

John looked at Maggie's furrowed brow and a feeling of warmth went out to her. Why didn't plans ever work here? John knew Maggie had typed out three sets of plans several days back and thought she had covered all the possibilities. He was proud that Maggie could handle the shifting and booking, but somehow her efficiency also irritated him. He tried in between the details Maggie gave rapidly to decide why. He gave up before his search went far and caught Maggie's, "The plan now is for all ten people in the group to spend the night on campus."

John exploded. "Ten?"

Maggie looked at John with some irritation, as she had already gotten the same reaction earlier in the day from several missionaries. Surely this wasn't her fifth time to smooth out frustrations. Maggie's voice came out too loud. "I said ten!"

John read the irritation in her voice and responded, "So why are you getting angry with me?"

Maggie looked at her watch and realized they would be late to the airport if they didn't leave in ten minutes and ignored the question. "John, you haven't eaten. Sit down and eat while I try to tell you."

John, who was happy for a cold drink, complied and finished three glasses of cold water before he looked up again. "OK. Who is going to the airport then?"

"Us—only us!"

"I thought you said . . ."

"I did say that."

"Well, then how do you get ten people in one car plus we three?"

"That's the problem. You finally got it!"

"So you have a solution?"

"Yes, two of them."

"What?"

"Either we each drive a car or we take the bus."

John thought only a minute and replied with some heat. "You and I go together. You can't drive a car the fifty miles to the airport over these roads and handle Sam, too. I haven't seen you for weeks except in between big activities, anyway. We go together to the airport in one vehicle."

Maggie looked at John's stern face and realized the decision was made. She turned toward the door. "OK, I'll go get the bus keys from Tom." Then another thought came, "And what if he says we can't have the bus?"

"Then he can go to the airport!"

Maggie left and returned with the bus keys before John finished his sandwich. John looked up and Maggie began, "Corinne said it was unnecessary to take a bus all the way to the airport and then Tom gave her a dirty look and said since there wasn't anyone else to drive, that seemed like a good idea. Then he said you'd have to get gas and gave me a gas ticket and we're ready as soon as I get Sam up."

John finished his sandwich hurridly and wondered again why the mission didn't just hire three or four chauffeurs.

That evening around the mahogany Ping-Pong tables, which had become cloth covered dining tables for the occasion, the conversation was lively. Maggie glanced again at the clean living room, happy that the houseboy had done a good job while she was at the airport. Of course, he usually performed superbly when he knew company was coming. Tourists often gave him a dash and Alfred had stayed around long enough to decide which tourist's pocket was the heaviest with cash. Karen had put the silverware on the table correctly for a change and there was nothing left for Maggie to do except finish the meal when she got home at six. All had gone well and it was time to serve the papaya pie.

Reverend Green, the visitor who seemed most verbal, took one bite of the pie and smiled. "Great. That's terrific pumpkin pie."

Maggie decided to reveal her secret. "It isn't pumpkin. It's papaya."

Several of the men loosened their neckties and questioned Maggie about this and the plantain chips they had eaten. Maggie began a lengthy discourse on African foods and one of the men asked, "Do you entertain people often?"

Mark broke in, "Every week, and it costs two dollars to sleep in my bed."

Everyone laughed good-naturedly and John began to talk about Maggie's ability at juggling schedules. When he realized some of the men were looking at Maggie as if she were the most ingenious woman they had encountered lately, he decided to change the subject. After all, he didn't want visitors carrying "Superhero" stories back to the United States about missionaries. John liked the idea better that missionaries were just Christians who had been called to settings that were different than the United States. He decided to talk about the setting and got immediate help from Mark, who began his favorite story.

"See, Uncle Ken—he's a missionary up-country—well, Uncle Ken was driving down a narrow road and he saw a tree trunk in the road. He slammed on the brakes and got out to move the log, which was big as a man and reached all the way across the road. When he got close the log suddenly wiggled from one end to the other."

One of the tourists caught the bait. "What was it?"

Mark giggled, pleased with the effect the story was having, "A boa constrictor. Uncle Ken, was plenty scaredo. He'd never seen such a big snake. He thought about driving over it but decided the car might turn over."

One of the men at the table took off his tie and pulled his perspiration soaked shirt away from his body. "Really? The snake was that big?"

"Yeh. So Uncle Ken backed down the road to a village and found a man with a gun. Then he came back and shot the snake."

"Why didn't the snake get out of the way while the missionary was gone?" the only woman in the evangelistic group asked.

"When the men in the village skinned the snake, they found it had just swallowed a small deer whole. It couldn't travel with a deer in its middle."

"Oh!" the woman replied, as a shiver ran down her spine. She decided to change the conversation to more comfortable topics. She gazed around the living room in appreciation. "You have a nice house."

"Yes," John answered. "Everybody likes it. We're very pleased with it. We have all the modern conveniences."

"Your electricity blinked during supper. Does it go off often?"

"It's pretty reliable," Maggie replied, quickly deciding not to share the time the electricity and water were both off for eighteen hours when they had an important woman as a visitor. She had been the only guest Maggie could remember who had brought only discontent and left feeling the same way. Maggie could still hear the woman's question, which had come as Mark and Prince walked through the living room arm in arm. "Aren't you worried about your children playing with blacks?" Thinking of it now, Maggie remembred she had not understood the question at first. Finally she had mentally removed Prince from the "boy" group and reclassified him, "black."

Maggie still remembered how she had answered the woman. "There has been no problem with our children. In fact, color has been mentioned only a couple of times since we came. The only time Prince and Mark seemed to be concerned was one morning when both sat eating cookies at the kitchen table and Prince said, 'I'm a black American and Mark is a white American.' "

Maggie remembered she had been puzzled and then as she looked from boy to boy, she had answered, "Prince, you can be any kind of boy you want to call yourself, but Mark there—he is—let's see." And then Maggie had noticed a bruise on Mark's face. "Mark's a blue-green boy. See!"

Prince turned in astonishment to look closely at Mark's face and he, too, saw the big bruise which held plenty of color. Maggie continued. "In fact, Mark is really a blue-green monster!"

Then Mark had laughed, "Oh, Mom," and poked Prince in the ribs. Soon Prince began to laugh, too. He realized it didn't matter to the Blakes what color a boy was.

Maggie could still see the visitor, listening openmouthed to the explanation and then she had drawn back into a shell where she stayed for the rest of the visit. Maggie had wondered later if it would have helped if she had said that every citizen of the country, all five-hundred students at Gbolupa, and all the neighbors, except the American missionaries, were black. Thinking about the situation again, Maggie decided this would have upset the woman even more.

Maggie came back to the guests at the dining table and suggested they move to the living room. On the way the last suit coat came off and one man stopped in front of the fan and raised his arms. Maggie knew what the next question would be, and she was right. "Is it always this hot here?"

John stopped to talk about the weather with this man and Mark began another of his favorite stories before the other guests were comfortably seated in the living room. "Do you know driver ants?"

"Are they like the ants I saw in the kitchen?" the woman asked.

Mark laughed, proud to display his superior knowledge. "No, they're big flesh-eating ants with pinchers. They grab on to your skin and hang on!"

The woman's eyes grew larger and several of the men turned their attention toward Mark. Mark went on, "Well, once the carnivorous ants, called drivers, came on our carport and got all over my dog, Soin. He began to bark and bark because he couldn't get away. He was chained. My mom woke up and went outside and stepped right in the ants. They started to bite her feet before she knew they were there. She started to stomp her feet and ran back to the house but then she realized my dog couldn't get away and she ran right back through the ants and unchained him."

Maggie, who had overheard the last part of the story, from the kitchen door, came to the living room door and scolded Mark. "No more snake stories. No more ant stories. It's to bed with you. Now!"

Before he left to take his bath, Mark had time for one more comment—the one he hoped would be a clincher. "You know what? If my mom hadn't unchained the dog, we would have had a barking skeleton the next morning!"

The woman smiled at Mark's humor for only a second and then she began to wonder if driver ants ate people. She looked at the floor. Did drivers come into the house? Although she'd been exhausted earlier from not sleeping the night before on the plane, she doubted she could go to sleep tonight.

Reverend Green, who had been the chief entertainer at the dining table, took over when Mark left and John sat back in his recliner and looked at the guests in the living room. One was important; another, he had been told, was rich; one was sleepy; one looked bored; several he couldn't read; and the rest were comsumed by the heat. They fanned themselves with magazines, while John tuned Reverend Green in.

"Do you know what the WMU women asked me to do?" Everyone shook their head, not knowing whether the women had been interested in food, people, scenery or missions. The storyteller went on. "They nicknamed me 'Tarzan for Jesus' and asked me to return with films of myself swinging down a bush path!"

Several of the other ministers laughed and thought about what their congregations expected. One said, "You're kidding."

"No, I'm not," the handsome, graying minister said, in all seriousness. "And that only starts the list. After that I'm supposed to go to the White House, or whatever it's called here, and take films while shaking hands with the President. Then I am to tour several villages, speak there, and appear on national television."

The rest of the visitors joined in the laughter and all began to shake their heads. Maggie looked toward John, who was now thinking about the various people who had come recently to West Africa. They'd been interesting, a lively bunch, talkative. They'd soaked up a lot of information in a hurry and returned home with the stories their Sunday School classes would want to hear. There had been two or three visitors every week in the last month, but these were the first this month. John looked toward the storyteller and decided to give him a big shock.

"Reverend Green," he began in a loud voice to get his attention above the uproar in the room. "Reverend Green, what your WMU asked for, we can probably produce!"

Reverend Green stopped in the middle of a long sentence and his mouth hung open in disbelief. Was this missionary playing some sort of trick? He didn't know how to reply and neither did the others.

John went on. "Movies in the bush, at the executive mansion, appearances on TV—they can all be arranged!"

Reverend Green looked at John with new appreciation, but still didn't believe what he had been told. He thought about the mission tours he had been on before. They had been exciting, but hadn't provided these things. He wondered if John had some special prestige as a missionary. Still he didn't ask.

Everyone in the room waited for further explanation and John proceeded. "The problem is time—you have only four days. You also have a schedule that has already been sent to us."

"Oh, well, we can change the schedule," Reverend Green replied, suddenly hoping that it might actually be possible to do everything the church expected him to do.

Maggie looked crossly at John and thought about another week of schedules that changed every day. How could she know who to cook for and which person went to what place. These problems she kept to herself and wondered why John was making such an offer. By the end of the week he'd be two weeks rather than one week behind. She looked at John's tired face, and tried to quiet her own doubts. After all, John like herself, wanted the visitors to get to do what they had planned and dreamed of doing. But how could it be done with the things that had to be done on campus? All visitors were like caring for Sam. They might be grown men at home, but here they didn't know how to buy artifacts, how to talk, what to wear, how to escape malaria, and what foods to avoid. Maggie thought about what she had planned for the next day and decided to throw away that schedule. She deliberately turned her mind in another direction, for she realized she was living on an emotional level again, where frustration could easily trap her. She'd enjoy this group. They seemed pleasant and sincere. It would be a good four days.

John outlined a broad plan for getting the group to the most places in the shortest time. Then he looked at Maggie and knew she would handle the details. John got up to show part of the group to the homes where they would stay for the night—two at the Pearces; two in an empty apartment; the man-wife team at his house. When the first four were settled, John came back to confer with Maggie about plans for the remaining four men.

"They'll stay in the guest house on the ocean."

John looked up startled, "But you said earlier they'd be on campus! The guest house is thirty minutes from here."

"I know. I know," Maggie said, with a discouraged look on her face. "Didn't you see Corinne come right after we got back from the airport?"

"No," John said, trying to figure out what that had to do with the present situation. Maggie supplied the information without further encouragement. "Corinne at first said she'd keep the four. Then she said she wasn't ready for guests. I went to June. She could keep two more men but not four, unless they slept in double beds and we figured they'd keep each other awake. So June came to the rescue and went over to the unoccupied mission house to put sheets on the beds. Don offered to drive the men there and get them in the morning."

John looked at Maggie with relief on his face. "Thank the Lord for June and Don." John would have gone further in his praise but realized Maggie already appreciated them. Instead, John went across the road again—this time to tell Don the guests were ready to go. His only instruction to Don was, "Now tell them to leave a light on in that upstairs bedroom."

At first Don looked puzzled. Then a broad grin crossed his face. "So you've stayed there too. You mean to keep those inquisitive creatures from coming down?"

John laughed. "Right on, man. The last night I was there I spent most of the time throwing my shoes in the air, trying to get those stupid bats to stay up in that high-gabled roof. They insisted on flying straight for my chin and then doing a steep climb at the last minute."

Don slapped his leg as a serious thought came. "Do you think the bats are dangerous?"

"I doubt it," John replied. "They're just a nuisance. But the light trick will keep them away."

John turned toward home. A few steps away, he turned back, "But don't tell the people why. Mark has already tried to scare them to death with snakes and ants. The bat business may be too much."

When Maggie greeted John at the back door, he had a big grin on his face. Maggie looked twice and the grin got bigger. "So what's the joke? You left here disgruntled."

John winked at Maggie. "The best joke hasn't happened yet! The bats. . . ." John Spread his wings and did a pretend lift-off which included a sharp climb toward the ceiling. "Remember the bats in the guest house?"

"Oh, no," Maggie exclaimed, as her heart fell. "In the hurry to get everybody situated, I forgot. I forgot about the bats. What do we do now?"

John took Maggie's arm and smiled down at her. "We go to bed. They go to bed. They can worry about the bats tonight! I will sleep. Remember, we've had monkeys in the attic, as well as birds and kittens, and we endured." John chuckled as he thought about a definition he had just read for endurance. He decided to try it on Maggie. "Endured—that's the ability to sleep under!"

"What?" Maggie looked at John's face, trying to decide if he was still kidding or serious. "to sleep under?"

John made a slight correction in order to clarify. "You know James 1 says trials produce endurance and endurance carries you off to sleep!"

Maggie looked up in a doubtful way and John knew she was working on a better solution. Suddenly he realized what had been irritating him about her efficiency. She never gave up. A good plan had to be improved even when she wore herself out and made everybody else uncomfortable with her overconcern. John looked seriously at Maggie and said, "I want to tell you something important about yourself."

Maggie turned away, knowing the conversation would take a long time. "Not now. I don't want to think about anything else today."

John held on to Maggie's arm. "Tonight. Now. Because tonight you'll understand what I'm talking about. Come on to bed. Let's talk."

Maggie started to make a final check on the children and on the guests, but John wouldn't give in. "They're OK, Maggie. You've done twice what you need to do. Let's talk. It's husband-wife time."

In the morning, when the couple who had spent the night helped with the breakfast dishes, Maggie's spirits soared. Gene and Clara were OK. They had even helped get the children off to school. Even though Maggie knew they had spent a restless night, they were cheerful. She liked guests with that attitude.

Maggie's thoughts went back to the long talk she and John had had the night before. John had been perceptive, as usual. Maggie hadn't liked the way he had torn into what she thought was her strong point—efficiency. But she knew John was right. When she had decided she could handle anything, she had wound up in a circle of activity which led nowhere. John had hit another bulls-eye, too, when he said the devil attacks at the point of strength rather than at the point of weakness. The devil promotes pride, and no one takes pride in his weak traits. It is in the areas of obvious talent and ability where a person is trapped by pride. Maggie wondered what the Scripture actually said that John had half-quoted the night before. She picked up the Bible that she kept on the kitchen counter and turned to James 1:2–4. "Dear brothers, is your life full of difficulties and temptations? Then be happy, for when the way is rough, your patience has a chance to grow. So let it grow, and don't try to squirm out of your problems. For when your patience is finally in full bloom, then you will be ready for anything, strong in character, full and complete" (TLB).

Maggie read the passage again and was amazed at it. Messed-up schedules should make her happy? Why? Tribulation-patience-endurance-maturity were steps put in a sequence. Once you started through the steps you would inevitably get to the end, completeness, unless you decided to run ahead of God or turn around and end up with frustration. Maggie tabled her thoughts along this line, as Clara came into the kitchen.

Clara's big smile brought a ready response from Maggie. "I'm so happy you stayed with us. I hope you didn't have too bad a night. I heard you up several times."

Clara replied, "I don't usually sleep well the first night in a new place. There was so much to see and do yesterday, I had trouble unwinding. But actually this morning I'm eager to go."

Maggie smiled. "Good. Because there's a lot to see. I want you to know, though, how happy we are you came our way. It's strange how the Lord often works out arrangements in spite of us that result in putting people together who can learn from each other. June came over this morning and said what a great time they had last night with their guests. They talked until 2 A.M."

On the way to town that morning, Maggie listened with interest to Gene and John and marveled at how quickly Gene had evaluated the campus situation. This man didn't act like God's nephew, with a special position. He just seemed like a good listener. Maggie began to look forward to the special service that had been planned for that evening at the church on campus. She'd already decided Gene's testimony would be worth listening to.

The most pleasant surprise that night, though, was not the testimonies, but the song Clara sang. Maggie's heart skipped a beat as soon as she heard Clara's clear, soprano voice. Maggie was lifted right out of the school auditorium and gently put down back home. Around her were church members she had known for years. For a few seconds Maggie's mind stayed in America. Then she came back to Africa, wondering why the song had so easily moved her. Was it Clara's voice? Maggie would have recognized the peculiar American quality anywhere. No African woman sounded like this. Maybe it was the words:

> There is never a day so dreary,
> There is never a night so long,
> But the soul that is trusting Jesus
> Will somehow find a song.

Maggie reached for Sam, who had climbed under the seat and realized his shirt was wet with perspiration. Then her thoughts turned back to the chorus of the old familiar hymn:

> Wonderful, wonderful Jesus.
> In the heart he implanteth a song!
> A song of deliverance, of courage, of strength;
> In the heart he implanteth a song.

As Clara took her chair on the platform, Maggie looked at the motionless rows of students. The song had touched them, too. The Holy Spirit had translated from heart to heart to meet needs. Suddenly Maggie realized she had seen a living example of what John had tried to explain. Clara had a highly developed talent, but the song had been sung with such warmth and calmness that only the message had been obvious. The physical pressure of the heat, the lack of sleep, the emotional pressure of an unfamiliar situation, and a piano that was out of tune were not important.

Gene rose to speak and again the students were motionless, listening intently. None of them, Maggie knew, would ever have guessed how deprived Gene's early years had been, had he not shared the facts. Gene had been an orphan like many of them. He had been poor like many of them. Maggie looked at the students who sat in the row with her. She could tell they were puzzled, for it was very unusual here for a poor boy to become the successful man that Gene appeared to be.

Gene's testimony took another unexpected turn. "I got through college by washing dishes and then something unusual happened. I got a good job and in a few years I bought part interest in a store. The store prospered in an unusual way. I bought another store and it was successful. Then I bought a factory. It made money. I got a construction company and it was successful. Soon I was the richest man in town. Everybody thought I had everything, but I was frantic and miserable. One day I was so angry at what I thought was a deliberate put-down by a competitor, I got in my car and speeded up to eighty-five miles per hour on a narrow highway. Suddenly, I came to a curve and realized too late I couldn't make it. As my car flew through the air and off the road, I prayed my first prayer in twenty years. It was, 'Help, Jesus. Help me.' "

One of the students beside Maggie moaned and Gene went on. "My car hit and crumpled in around me. I thought I was probably dying, but I wasn't. In fact, when I finally got out of the car, I found I was hardly scratched. A policeman came and looked at my car and shook his head. Your getting out of that was a miracle, he said.

"Then I remembered the prayer, 'Help, Jesus.' *Could Jesus have heard me?* I wondered. I looked at the policeman and for some reason, unknown to me at that time, I asked, 'Do you know anything about Jesus?'

"The officer looked at me in surprise, put his arm around my shoulder and said, 'Friend, I know Jesus. Do you want to know him?'

"I fell on my knees right beside that demolished car and asked Jesus into my heart. He's been there ever since and my life has never been like it was before. Although I never knew my human father, I have a real father and a family. For I was born right then into the family of God.

"Everywhere I go people say that here comes a rich man, but I say, 'No, this man is a man born again who goes all over the world to share what he has with his brothers and sisters in Christ."

As they walked home, Mark continued to question Gene, who by now had become Uncle Gene, about his car wreck. When Mark was finally satisifed and he, Karen, and Sam were asleep, John, Maggie, Clara, and Gene talked until midnight about news from the States. When Clara brought some books and cassettes out of her suitcases and gave them to Maggie as gifts, Maggie was pleased beyond words. She read a couple of book titles and exclaimed, "I've been wanting to read these." Then she looked through the stacks of cassettes and turned with moist eyes to Gene, "How did you know this was just what we wanted and needed? Karen will learn to play these songs on her guitar and John will listen through his earphones and shut the world out for a few hours."

John joined in, "Yes, of all the things our visitors bring, the best is the feeling of sharing with American Christians. Then we want the news from home. After that the latest music and books is the thing that helps us most spiritually. They're like a fresh breeze in the desert."

Karen added some other things to the lists of blessings from visitors as Uncle Gene and Aunt Clara's plane pulled off the runway two days later. "I didn't want them to go. They were like having Grandma and Grandpa come."

"Yeah," Mark agreed, as he rubbed tears from his eyes. "They were nice. But visitors never stay long enough."

Maggie watched without a word as the light on top of the plane spun round and round lighting the dark sky. Reverend Green had gotten to the Mansion and been on television. The others had their suitcases full of ivory rings, ebony statues, and tie-dye tablecloths. Everybody was happy. Then the lights of the plane were lost in the night and Maggie turned to the children.

"Yes, it was nice—exciting—a break in the routine, but now kids, Uncle Gene has to go to East Africa. He's got a whole week there to tell about how God took a ninety pound weakling and turned him into a 'Tarzan for Jesus.' "

Karen laughed and suddenly her melancholy over the farewells was gone. "Oh, Mom, Uncle Gene wasn't a weakling."

Maggie straightened Karen's long, black hair and thought about how pretty Karen had become—almost a young lady. "Sure he was a weakling—spiritually, but God turns weakness into strength and small girls into beautiful big girls."

Karen grinned shyly as the family walked toward the car to go home.

15
Lean Hard

The unfamiliar, past-midnight sound of slap, smack, drifted into Maggie's consciousness. She half-awoke to see John standing on the bed gazing intently upward. With the flyswatter he slapped repeatedly at the ceiling. Maggie stared as John tiptoed to the foot of the king-sized bed and with a venegance smacked the ceiling again. Maggie's eyes scanned the ceiling and saw nothing. Then they rested on John's favorite sleepwear—a pair of gym shorts with a lightning design embroidered on the side.

Taking a cue from the design, Maggie ventured, "Hey, Flash, are you practicing your tennis swing or doing a superman?"

John jumped at the sound of a voice in the still night and looked down for a second. Then his attention was grabbed by a flying form to his left. He lunged toward it, but his step was poorly calculated and he came down in midair a foot beyond the bed. Luckily the wall was close and John threw up his hand and bounced from wall to floor.

"Are you hurt?" Maggie jumped out of bed on the other side, and started toward John.

John hesitated only a moment, for the target was still in range. He pursued it to the screen and landed a hard blow, looked closely, and exclaimed, "Ah, ha, you rascal! I got you!"

Maggie sighed, got back in bed, and pulled the sheet over her head. Last night John had sprayed a putrid insecticide all over the screens. The night before he had fanned the air half the night. Now this! The irritation that Maggie felt surfaced. "John, for heaven's sake, give up and admit the mosquitoes are a match for you. Just let them bite and let's sleep tonight!"

"I hate mosquitoes. Who can sleep? Buzz, buzz around and around my head all night. There must be some way to get rid of them and I'll find it!"

Maggie knew there was no use arguing, so she slunk deeper under the sheet. Long ago she had learned John had a mind bent toward problem-solving. No mechanical, electrical, or natural problem was uninteresting. He would pursue and try a dozen things until something worked. When it came to fixing the washer his determination was great, but washers weren't repaired in the middle of the night. Why couldn't mosquitoes be eradicated by daylight, too?

Maggie tried again. "But can't you do something tomorrow?"

John started to reply, but was interrupted by another mosquito. He pursued it around the room and finally into the bathroom. "Good grief! This bathroom is full of mosquitoes," he yelled. And then Maggie heard the old familiar "sss" of the aerosol can. Not that again!

The next morning Maggie counted five bites on Sam's face and his bed sheets had spots of blood. She moved the antimalaria pills to the center of the kitchen table so they'd all remember their Sunday to Sunday pills. As she went toward the range she spied a line of ants going up the wall and across the ceiling. Curses on mosquitoes, ants, and cockroaches. As she reached for the spray can she wondered if the King James Version of the Bible forbade swearing at insects.

Soon Karen and Mark were at the kitchen table and Karen began in an impatient way, "Hurry, Mom. The bus will be here soon."

Mark's head drooped over and rested on the small table. Karen began on him. "Come on Mark. You're so slow. Get your socks on—you know the bus waits every morning on you!"

Mark responded by hurling his sock at Karen. Then the fight was on. The fifth time Mark hit Karen, Maggie knew this was going to be a day like all the others recently. Living at the Blake's house had gone from the excitement of arrival to grouchiness and now there was continual war. Maggie would have cried if she had been the weeping type. Since she wasn't, she wheeled and shouted. "Mark, sit down. Eat your breakfast. Don't hit your sister again. Karen, be quiet!"

Mark batted back a hot statement as wheels stopped on the road outside. A horn honked. Maggie clicked her fingernails indecisively and leaned close to the window to see if it were the MK's bus.

Karen began. "It's the bus! The bus! Our lunches aren't ready. See what you did, Mark!"

Mark gulped down the last of his cereal, grabbed his half-filled lunch box and fled with Karen at his heels. As Karen approached the bus she yelled, "Ah, yah. Quit honking. We're coming! We're coming!"

Another day had turned its back on Maggie. She whined in self-pity as her thoughts turned to the book she was reading about victorious Christian living. What had it said about problems under your feet, defeated? Ha! Problems over your head and to each side and in front was more accurate. Maggie knew her faith was at the two-inch level and that was not enough to overcome the thunderstorms that kept rolling in. What was wrong? Was it the inability to do things the African way? Was it Dennis's death? Separation from the family in the United States? The climate? Sam being sick, or just the housewife blues? The list of possibilities seemed endless and Maggie didn't want to go through it again.

The thought that had swept through her mind the day after Dennis's death had taken roots. Now it reached the surface. "Oh, Lord, let me go home. Don't make me stay here where everything goes wrong."

Her request quickly turned to an accusation. Hadn't she dared walk through God's open door. Now what did God want? Maggie's mind wandered through many answers and finally came back to one that she had been hearing of late. "Sit still and learn. Be patient!"

Wait. Wait! Wait on what? No, she wanted to run and be useful and be busy. She wanted to absorb everything in a hurry. Still there was no reward for impatience and selfishness. Waiting produced patience and patience brought faith. Maggie trembled, still uncertain. When would her new life begin to take shape?

Sam's cry shattered Maggie's contemplation and she realized John's oatmeal was boiling over on the stove.

John came into the kitchen. "Maggie, can't your hear Sam? He's sick again!"

Maggie dropped the spoon and hurried to Sam's bed. The floor and the bed were covered with vomit. Sam sat with his head against the bed rails whining. "Oh, Sam. Sam, you're sick again! Six weeks of this is too much! If only the doctor could find out what's wrong."

Maggie carefully lifted Sam from the bed and checked her impulse to hold him close. Holding him at arm's length, she hurried toward the bathtub. John began on the bed. When Maggie and Sam came back, John said, "We've got to take him back to the doctor. This is enough. The doctor has to find out what is wrong or admit Sam to the hospital."

As Maggie put on Sam's diaper, she winced at his skinny form. "He looks awful but we've been to the doctor twice this week already!" Then she pleaded with God. "Please, let the doctor find out what is wrong."

That afternoon Maggie's prayer was answered when the doctor said, "Amoebic dysentery." Maggie thought immediately of all the bare feet which went through her living room in a week's time. Her house was on the path and she couldn't lock the door. Neither could she keep a toddler off the floor. Curses! To live with the people meant to even share their amoeba.

Maggie gulped and a chill ran down John's spine. "I was afraid it was amoeba." John's thoughts turned to the medical book he had read that morning. "Without treatment most patients die. A healthy person can overcome amoeba with proper medication."

John looked at the doctor, who was calculating the amount of medicine. "For a baby this is hard to figure. It's potent stuff!" The doctor tore up one prescription and figured some more before he wrote final instructions and handed the slip to John. "Let's try this a week. Then we'll need another check and possibly a stronger dosage."

John asked a few questions before he and Maggie slowly got up to leave. No milk, no cheese, no ice cream—the innards were already churning in rebellion. Yes, plenty of rest.

The next days were more sleepless than ever, though, for the medicine made Sam hyperactive. He screamed, walked, and fell. Then he would pound his head on the bed and cry some more.

After two weeks of this, Maggie found herself completely spent. The houseboy was doing OK with the housework, but there were still three meals a day to cook. Why couldn't there be a cheap hamburger place handy? And a telephone, instead of those long trips over muddy roads to the doctor? Maggie knew John would pay $10 for a strawberry malt for he, too, was exhausted.

The medical reports hadn't been good either. "Seems worse. Needs stronger medication. Another complete dose."

Now as Maggie sat with her head against Sam's crib, he began to scream again. She steeled herself and patted his shoulder. "Sam. Sam. Please lay down. Mom will sing a song."

Maggie began the words of a song John had made up especially for Sam as he sat by his bed during the nights when Sam needed constant changes and attention.

O' Buddy Boy, O' Buddy Boy
You are my darlin,' my Buddy Boy

'Tis time for you to go to sleep
Now close your eyes and don't you weep

O' Buddy Boy, O' Buddy Boy
You are my darlin, Buddy Boy.

Maggie guessed she had sung the song at least a hundred times and it was 2 A.M. Sam finally slept fretfully. Maggie felt like her head was full of cement, which had partially set, as she went back to the time before Sam was born. The doctor was saying, "RH complications—we'll induce labor early—expect a blood change."

Sam had been delivered and the doctor had almost shouted. "I'm relieved. He's healthy!" And Sam had been healthy. A miracle! How many miracles would God work for one small boy?

Maggie knew she had been on the fringe of prayer for many days, but was not willing to submit to the Lord. Through hot tears, she finally completed the prayer she had often started. "You know what I want Lord, but he's in your hands."

The cement, which had made it impossible for Maggie to think clearly, set. She had done all she could do and fell into a deep sleep.

Two more weeks dragged on and this time the doctor said, "I think we've killed the amoeba. Now, feed the baby."

But Sam still didn't eat well and woke several times each night to cry for hours.

One morning, John awoke to find Maggie's bed had not been slept in. He hurried to find Maggie beside Sam's bed. "Didn't he sleep?"

"He's doing better, but I can't sleep. I keep hearing him cry out and when I check he's actually asleep, but restless."

"You look worse than Sam, Maggie," John said, with apprehension in his voice. "Are you sick?"

"No," Maggie replied in a far-off way. "I'll get your breakfast."

"I can do that. You go back to bed." John helped Maggie from the chair, and gently pushed her toward their bedroom.

"I don't feel like sleeping now. Besides you have classes all day and then a television program tonight. You're too busy to cook. Get dressed. I'll get breakfast."

John studied Maggie's face. It was dark. Her step was slow without its usual bounce. He was worried. What if she were sick, too?

That night when John came home from his weekly TV program, his voice was flat as he said, "It was awful. Did you see it?"

"No, I turned on the set and Sam got sick and screamed until you were off the air. Was it that bad?"

John patted Maggie's shoulder. "It was bad. The cameraman got on most scenes a good ten seconds late. Then he took only long shots. One camera wasn't working at all. The mike was humming—sounded like grease frying all through the program. It was awful!"

"I'm sorry," Maggie said and touched John's broad shoulders, which were wet with perspiration. "I'm sorry and you wrote such a good program this time. Did they practice at 5:30 as planned?"

"Sure, but the cameraman didn't. The sound man played tapes in the studio all the while. Local broadcasting is not quite what you would expect!"

John suddenly realized that his words were upsetting Maggie and he abruptly changed the subject. "Anyway, I'm home and you're here." John gave Maggie a lingering kiss and held her close, but she didn't respond.

He pulled away and studied her face before he headed for the shower. Still there was no response.

Maggie watched as John retreated, sorry that she had not given much comfort, but was too exhausted to think what she should have said. She wondered how a man who liked to do a professional job could adjust to amateur performances. Regardless of the time and effort somehow the program always came off amateurish. How did John stay so cheerful and calm? She remembered a remark one of the cameramen had made one time when Maggie had been at the studio with John. "John's a gentlemen. He never yells—no matter what happens!" Maggie knew she had a lot to be thankful for with a husband like John. She was glad he was working for God rather than for success or a name.

Another month passed and Sam began to improve, but Maggie's uneasiness continued. She still woke every two hours at night to listen for the cry that didn't come. Sometimes she got up to rock for a while and think. The more she concentrated on her feeling of emptiness and discouragement the less she was able to focus her life. Why weren't the answers coming?

Tonight the air was cool as Maggie rocked and the curtain blew out revealing a caterpillar on the wall. It had been making progress when all of a sudden its black and yellow body flipped over backwards and fell almost to the floor. What had happened? The wall wasn't wet—no crack. Quite a feat actually. Climbing inch by inch straight up a smooth wall. The caterpillar couldn't see the top where he wanted to go. There might be a predator. Maggie smiled as the picture caught her fancy.

She was like a caterpillar. A caterpillar climbing Mount Rushmore. How impossible! How dangerous! There was no elevator lift to the top, either. It was one step at a time. Maggie played with the idea for a while, but it didn't quite suit her. Mount Rushmore was also beautiful—there should be joy in the climb. Why had her home church always sung, "Lord, plant my feet on higher ground" rather than "I just want to praise the Lord?"

There had been happiness back home, but most of it had been in the family. Maggie's mind drifted and in the next fifteen minutes she talked to her sisters and brother and walked through a wheat field and smelled red clover and sat by her mother's fireplace. She small talked with her dad and hiked in the Rocky Mountains with John. The air was chilly there, and a squirrel rustled through yellow leaves. There was the sun shining through a pine forest on a fall day.

Having looked at her favorite things, Maggie shifted back to the present with more ease. The caterpillar on the wall was making steady progress again. If he actually reached the ceiling, Maggie wondered what he would see that he couldn't see from his halfway up position.

Several days later, Maggie went through the living room and stopped at the spot where the caterpillar had been. John, who had been sleeping in his recliner, opened his eyes and Maggie went quietly to the kitchen to put away the dishes.

It didn't register for a while, until John cleared his throat, that he was standing at the kitchen door.

Maggie spun around. "What are you doing?"

John didn't answer and Maggie found herself getting vexed over his lack of activity. "Why don't you help?"

Still John stood in silence.

Maggie pushed a drawer shut with a little too much force and approached John. "OK. Why are you staring at me?"

"I'm tending my oasis."

"What? You're doing nothing!"

John tried to get the most out of his statement. "I'm tending my oasis."

"And what does that mean?"

"When you have time to stop, I'll tell you," John said, and left.

Maggie's resolve of several nights back to enjoy what she was doing quickly deserted her. She wiped the counter for the second time and went into the living room where John was reading. She sat a minute and then got up and turned the taped music down. Then she noticed a cookie crumb on the rug and picked it up. On her way back from the wastebasket, she realized John was watching her again. His anxious voice began, "Are you going to keep going until you drop?"

"I may!" Maggie found John's question disconcerting. She could usually read him, but this time she was puzzled. She tried to concentrate on the music. Five minutes of violins brought her to a calmer state. She turned to John.

"What did you want me to hear?"

"Are you ready to listen?" John asked, with raised eyebrows.

Maggie got slightly angry. Why did John have to ask that? Why didn't he just say what he wanted to say? How did she know if she wanted to hear what she hadn't heard? Maggie cautioned herself and spoke with more calm than she felt. "I'm trying small!"

"Good." John began slowly with dialogue that he obviously had given much thought to. "You're my oasis." Maggie's interest grew.

"I was thinking about how I come to you for a cool drink in many scorched and unpleasant deserts and I feel refreshed. I love you and delight in you in every way a man can adore a woman. To me, you're beautiful physically and as a person."

John paused and rested back in his chair. His next words came with difficulty. "But my oasis is turning brown. The sand is covering the green vegetation. The water is low. I want to feel close to you, but you're not listening and understanding half of the time. I've never felt more abandoned. This has been the worst one and a half years of our entire marriage."

Maggie felt suddenly humble and hurt. Tears came. She knew John was trying to be honest. He hadn't meant to hurt her, but why had he picked the moment when she felt so low?

John read her thoughts. "I'm trying to help you, Maggie. I need you—you're more than a half of my world! The kids need you. Everybody needs you, but you're holding too many people and too many problems in your heart. Maggie you're not going to make it if you continue this way!"

Now Maggie was shocked. She had thought her relationship with John was the one constant in a changing and new life. Why hadn't she noticed when he cleaned off his desk and straightened his dresser drawers—jobs he always did when he was troubled.

She had assumed. She had leaned on him when Sam was sick. He had supported her. Funny how her needs could be met while John felt stranded. She hadn't had time to check out John's feelings.

John tried to read Maggie's face, but couldn't. Why didn't she offer something? "Maggie, I'm not criticizing. I know it's been tough lately. Sure you're strong and capable but you can't carry the whole load. Maggie, you need my love, but you've been too preoccupied lately to accept love from your husband." John's voice dropped and he hesitated a moment. "And love from God makes the oasis green again. Accept me—accept God."

Maggie couldn't handle what John was saying anymore than she had handled the knotty adjustment problems that continued to stalk her daily. Finally she wiped away her tears and crossed the room to sit down on John's lap. She began slowly. "I know you're trying to help. But I can't get out of this current I'm in. God isn't answering like he used to. I have a few clues, but the pictures get fuzzy again. My sense of security and safety is gone. You feel like I've abandoned you and I feel like God has deserted me!"

John held Maggie close. "Don't try so hard. You don't have to prove yourself. God loves you like you are—you don't have to feel right to know he's around. Maggie, I love you—I've never seen a woman I'd rather have—I may keep you for thirty or more years!"

John laughed and Maggie began to soften to his attention. Sam chose this moment to wake up from his nap. He began to yell and Maggie squirmed in John's arms. "Maggie!" John said, with some alarm in his voice, "Quit worrying. Sam is OK. Quit responding every time somebody asks for help!"

Maggie pulled away and jumped up, leaving John with more frustration than when he had begun the conversation.

For three months the uneasy stalemate continued. Then one day Maggie burst through the kitchen door with Sam in her arms. "Good news. Good news!" John looked up and Mark and Karen came running from their rooms.

"What, Mom?"

Maggie wasted no time. "The doctor found no more amoeba and ole Sam is actually gaining weight!"

"Hurrah! Hurrah!" Mark shouted, and threw his tennis shoe in the air.

"He's really well?" Karen asked in half-belief. She grabbed Sam from Maggie's arms and spun him around. "You're well. You're your old funny self. Good ole Sam."

"Six months is long enough. Sam actually weighs what he did when he got sick." Maggie collapsed on John's lap and gave him a big kiss. "I'm so relieved!"

John grinned. "Try that kiss business again!" Maggie laughed and hugged his neck before he continued. "Hey, everybody. Silence! I have good news, too."

Mark, who had been dancing around the living room, came to a slow stop. "What, Dad?"

John added to the suspense. "It is actually going to happen."

"Oh, Dad! What? What?"

"Well," John said, and stopped again. Maggie punched him in the ribs and Karen came to kiss him on the nose, as she had learned years ago to do when she wanted him to hurry. "Well, we are going to leave campus for five whole days!"

"Really?" Maggie thought of the four-day trip up-country, which had been their first local leave. It had been fun, but it had taken one day to drive there and one day to drive back. "Not another of those long drives over bad roads with only two days at the end?"

"It won't be like that!"

"Then it will be like that other night where we had two hotel rooms on separate floors and paid $50."

"Pessimist!" John laughed. "This will be different! This time we have a car, complete house with sheets and towels furnished, quiet, and it's cheap and pretty!"

Maggie looked away dreamily, "A real vacation!"

Karen dropped Sam onto Maggie's lap, who was still sitting on John's lap, and joined Mark, who by this time was running around and around the bamboo partition which separated the living from the dining area.

John wrapped both arms around Maggie and Sam and went on. "It's all worked out. I have no school Friday and Monday and nothing on Tuesday until five o'clock and Mark and Karen can go to school from where we will be and . . . ," John's voice rose, "Hear this!" Mark and Karen peeked around the divider. "We leave this afternoon!"

"What?" Maggie exploded. "You're kidding. I can't be ready!" She sat up and looked at John's face. "You are kidding?"

"No, I am not," John said and planted a firm kiss. "I didn't say anything earlier for fear something would come up and you'd be disappointed. Knowing you, I realized that in your highly organized fashion you could get ready to go anywhere on just a few hours notice! You'll probably have five minutes to spare!"

The last remark was lost on Maggie, for she was already clicking off on her fingernails what to take. John broke in, "Only two suitcases. We need only swimsuits and school clothes for the kids. You and I aren't going anywhere and no one is visiting."

Maggie retreated into the bedroom and began to count out under-clothes and stack them in piles on the bed. Soon the two suitcases were full and Sam's diaper pail had been emptied into the washer. The staples were in a box by the kitchen door and there were ten minutes to spare. But Mark couldn't be located. It took a complete tour of the campus to locate him at the agricultural farm.

At his dad's insistence he reluctantly put down the rabbit he had been holding and came to the car. Maggie held her breath as the car sped past the dormitory, faculty housing, and the cotton tree. When they went through the gate, she almost yelled. "Free. We made it. A whole five days of vacation. Wonderful!"

As they bumped over the road, John unfurled the holiday plan. "It's a house on the ocean!"

"Wow! By the ocean?" Mark added.

"Yes, and it's air-conditioned."

"Air-conditioning!" Mark licked his finger and held it to the breeze. "Real cool, Man."

"We'll stop in town for the groceries your mom needs and then we'll do nothing except relax," John said.

During the next couple of days Mark and Karen were so occupied with the ocean and the toys that belonged to the children whose rooms they occupied that Maggie hardly saw them. Maggie read a couple of books and at the end of the third day suddenly realized she had not answered the door or met a single request. She came out of the air-conditioned bedroom to ask, "John, hasn't anyone come to our door?"

"A couple of people, but I didn't answer."

Campus and responsibility seemed a long way off and Maggie decided to walk on the beach. The waves came with the sound of a windstorm. Maggie closed her eyes to check out the vibrations. Right—she was back in Olathe, Kansas, and a Kansas twister was coming. It was close. She'd best run to the basement. The vision faded and Maggie stood unmoving and fascinated. Why didn't this force twist? Maggie looked into the water. Ah, down there was the undertow—the pull out to sea. Many a good swimmer had found that hidden power as deadly as a Kansas storm.

Soon John appeared and stretched out on the beach. He looked from coconut palms to ocean. "I like this. I like you. All we've done lately is rush. It's good to do nothing." John lapsed into silence as his attention was drawn to a small canoe out at sea.

For a long time they watched the fishermen. "The Midwest has nothing like this," Maggie speculated. "The ocean is beautiful! It's so big and . . . ," Maggie groped for words, but at that moment found none.

John studied her face. "You're frowning."

"It's the sunlight on the water. Wow! A million green jewels. Could I have an emerald as big as one of those drops of water?"

John laughed and knew no answer was necessary. As Maggie stared, the glistening drops of water took form. They became waves thirty feet wide and six feet tall. After several had crashed on the shore, Maggie closed her eyes to listen. She was caught in the beat. Crash. Silence. Crash. Silence. This was the ocean, which had always been on the other side of the world! Amazing!

Maggie's eyes opened just as a bigger than usual wave flipped into an arch and then crashed forward with an impact that sounded like a gunshot. Maggie waited. Another wave rose, flipped back, and then pounded forward. The water changed from blue-green to a rusty brown as the wave arched. Then as the wave sprang forward the color became white and foamy. Maggie waited five seconds and another wave rose. Presto. Zippo. It, too, changed colors. Now green, now rust, now white.

This time Maggie followed the water's forward motion until bubbles dissipated on the sandy beach. Maggie looked back out to sea and blinked. She was too late to see the next wave rise—it had come almost to the shore where it slowed down, turned, picked up a few grains of sand, and then ran back out to sea. Now Maggie saw the pattern and began to marvel. In-up-over-crash-dissipate and then return to the sea. The eternal surf, with its ebb and flow.

Life had its ebb and flow, too. Yesterday's worries were emptying. The days of pressure were slipping away like the waves which rose and swirled where Maggie didn't want to follow.

What had she read in the Psalms? "Let every breaker on every shore, Praise the Lord!" Wow—a flood of praise that was never silent. Regardless of the sun, the day, the spectators, the ocean kept drawing attention to an eternal God.

Maggie was ashamed. Ask so much—praise so small. She had brought wilted bouquets rather than fresh blooms. Maggie wondered what other secrets the ocean knew. This was the time to learn.

Soon the sun became a red ball which rested lightly on the horizon. For a second it was suspended between sky and ocean and then it made a slow dive. One for the money; two for the show; three to get ready; and four—it was gone! Splash!

John, who had been taking pictures, came back from his vantage point a few yards away. "I hardly had time to roll the film between shutter clicks on that sunset."

"I know. I was afraid to blink for fear I'd miss something. What a show!"

As John sat down beside Maggie, the only evidence left of the sun was a pink sky which shaded out to gray. Slowly it wrapped the palm trees in pink celophane. Maggie watched, almost hypnotized, as the top-knots of the palms swayed in the breeze. Soft reed-like music came from their long leaves as the wind plucked them like the strings of a harp. Maggie remembered her first morning in Africa when she had thought the palm trees clapped. Now they sounded like a pine forest. The rustling sound was comforting. Slowly the trees became black silhouettes against an all-gray sky.

Maggie looked beyond the trees and saw that the sky and ocean had become one. Her eyes traveled upward and she realized she had missed the coming of three stars. They shone as brightly as the lights from a ship, which suddenly came into view several miles out. It took only ten minutes for the sky to be filled with stars which were so bright that the gray horizon was lost.

John drew Maggie back. "Above you are stars never seen in the northern hemisphere. Millions and trillions of them."

"Yes, and some old familiars, too. The big dipper is upside down."

"Right and it's spilling stars."

Conversation died as the ocean calmed enough for land noises to be apparent. Maggie listened and felt the earth draw near. For a time the palm fronds whispered softly and responded to the solo of the crickets.

This stalemate like the others that night lasted only a few minutes. These sounds became background as the visual part of the show took center stage again. The last player came as a silver beam. It, like the sun, which had set an hour earlier, was huge and round. The moon promenaded and made a glistening path on the rolling waves. The wind grew stronger and the palms grew noisy as if in applause of the moon's performance. The waves rose doubly high and crashed like blasts of dynamite on the sand.

The moon marched on, making the waves silver foam on the beach. Maggie had no idea what happened to the next thirty minutes for she was a part of what she saw and heard. The earth, the sky, the sea rolled close, and brought a message of encouragement. As always, she instantly responded to the beauty of nature.

There were no words to choir a proper praise as Maggie began to feel God. Discouragement was crowded out by joy as Maggie felt God's arms and his quiet whisper. "I am here. I am."

Maggie knew the caterpillar had reached a plateau. There might be something higher and better and yet there was no hunger and no desire to move. She was content for the first time in months.

The moon would not wait. It moved over and John stirred. Maggie reached for his hand and held it tight. John responded as love and joy moved to him. The oasis was suddenly greening again.

Several minutes passed before John sighed. "That was the best two-hour show I've ever seen. I'd rather stay here, but maybe we'd better check on the kids."

"First, I want to tell you I'm sorry about how I've been neglecting you. I want you to know you're God's best gift to me and like all his other gifts—sea, sand, sunset—you're beautiful and perfect. Just what I need," Maggie said.

"Oh," John said, with a silly grin on his face. "Tell me more!"

"OK, I've got a lot more surprises for you," Maggie replied, as she reluctantly rose to walk arm in arm with John toward the borrowed house.

The five-day local leave ended quickly and the Blakes were back on campus. Teachers and students waved as they passed. MK's ran over with excited stories. It was the same, but to Maggie everything looked brighter. Her ocean experience had lasted only a few minutes and yet its impact lingered throughout the rest of Maggie's days at Gbolupa.

As they pulled into the carport, Maggie realized how close she had come to a physical and emotional breakdown. She hadn't been what she should have been in all her relationships. There was something she had to do.

When Maggie reached the Wilson's house, Tom answered the door as Maggie had expected he would. She began while her courage was still strong. "I've been worried about how I treated you the morning a long time ago when we disagreed about the use of the car. I want to tell you I wasn't very nice and I'm sorry. I should have recognized that you cared enough to come."

With this rush of words out, Maggie stood speechless. She hadn't planned what would come next. She looked to Tom for a lead. He shifted his feet and looked intently at Maggie.

"I wanted to tell you something else," Maggie said with determination. "You're doing a good job of a very difficult task."

Tom flinched. He looked shocked as he said, "Really?"

Maggie backed off. She hadn't realized what an impact that statement might have. Tom was obviously very uncomfortable. He stammered, "That's the first time—the first—in years that anyone has said that!" As he gained composure his expression become somber. "When you collect people's money and repair their buildings all you get are complaints." Then Tom paused, as if Maggie were gone, and finally whispered, "Since Dennis is gone it has seemed . . . ."

Tom looked far away and an emotion crossed his face which Maggie couldn't quite read. Then Tom blinked, realizing Maggie was staring at him, and said in a businesslike tone, "Yes, the job can be demanding."

Maggie responded to the look that she thought she had seen on Tom's face, rather than his words. "I'm glad I knew almost nothing about Dennis's job or how he did it. That way I can just appreciate him as a person." Maggie wanted to add, "Let's be people rather than job-oriented," but she knew not to push the point. How she wished Tom trusted her enough to verbalize the deep feelings that he had almost loosed, and then hid. If he could only say he was hurting and quit wearing an administrator's mask.

Tom took one step backwards indicating he had nothing more to say and Maggie turned with an "I'll see you," and was gone.

When Maggie returned home, John knew by the expression on her face that her mission had been accomplished and so he dared, "OK, Florence Nightingale. Now it will be interesting to see what you and God do with Corinne's disagreement with you!"

Maggie groaned. "Don't mention that. I only have a small indication on that one."

The day ran on with a wave of students and villagers coming for help. "Missy, do you have a pill? Could you help with my English? I need twenty-five cent. My son won't stay in school." The people were like the ocean waves. They rolled on and on—now troublesome; now pleasant.

Then night quieted the campus and the Blakes slept. Maggie could hardly bring herself away from a dream about the ocean when screams began. They got louder and louder and Maggie turned over and tried to pinpoint their source. Girls' shouts. The dorm. Yes, the dormitory.

Maggie rolled back toward John and shook him. "Wake up. Wake up! Something's wrong!"

John sat up and listened long enough to determine that there was an urgency to the screams. Quickly he pulled on his trousers, grabbed a flashlight and cutlass and ran to the carport. He decided to take the car in case the emergency was a rogue. The cutlass was for a snake. That covered the usual problems. He spun out of the drive and the car hit two bumps as it crossed the road. John turned onto the footpath which led to the dorm. In front of the building he saw girls running back and forth.

John steeled himself and leaped from the car before the engine died. "What is it? What's wrong?"

The first girl was too excited to answer—she just pointed to the building. The next girl screamed, "Snake! Big snake!"

John entered the room the girls had pointed out and cautiously with his cutlass moved the trunk which was under the first bunk bed. "Nothing there," he said to the girls who stood in the hallway. "I'll check under the other beds."

An hour's investigation of all the first floor rooms produced no snake, so John went out onto the sandy ground where the girls sat in huddled groups. "Girls, the snake is gone. You scared it plento with all that screaming!"

None of the girls moved. June, who had come late on the scene, looked toward John in a helpless manner. John gave a hands-up sign indicating he had no idea either about how to get the girls back into bed.

Finally, June sat down on the ground where the largest group of girls was. "Come close." She motioned with both hands. "Come on. We will talk."

John leaned against the porch column as June began in a soft mother-like voice. Soon one of the girls who had been most frightened came from the back of the semicircle to sit close to June. The girl's shoulder shifted until it was against June's and June drew the girl's head into her lap and stroked her forehead. Soothing words continued, and slowly the other girls drifted back into their rooms. John headed for home where Maggie met him at the door.

"It was a snake?"

"Right."

"I thought so. Welcome back to campus! Your night for being a spectator has passed. You're back in the storm again!" Maggie said and patted John's shoulder. She locked the door for the second time that night and said to no one in particular, "Catch it. Catch it if you can. Life never stops—it grows!"

"What?" John asked, in a puzzled voice.

"Nothing, just philosophizing," Maggie said, with a certainty she hadn't felt in over a year. "We might make it here—God and us!"

As Maggie headed toward bed the voice on the beach came again. "I'm here. I'm here. Lean hard!"

16

Missionary Gift

Maggie and June had just come from the well-baby clinic. June placed her fishing tackle box, which contained medical supplies, on the utility shelf and crossed to the sink to wash her hands, as she always did after a village trip. Three steps from the sink she suddenly stopped and gasped in horror, "Maggie! Come! Come!"

Maggie, who had started toward the bedroom to get Sam, who was being baby-sat by George, the houseboy, read the alarm in June's voice, spun around, and grabbed the broom which was by the kitchen door.

June had not moved when Maggie dashed back into the kitchen, broom held high ready to attack whatever enemy was near. Maggie stopped abruptly when she came to where June still stood. The name of the invader that hadn't come to June, escaped Maggie's lips. "Good grief! A huge snake!"

A second look showed Maggie that she was wrong. The thing in the sink looked like the picture of a miniature, primitive dinosaur she had seen in a book. Maggie imagined this one couldn't bring loud huffs from its scaly throat, which hung nonchalantly over the edge of the sink, but it looked wicked.

June's eyes stayed glued to the reptile to catch its slightest movement. She had recovered enough to yell again, "George, George, come quick!"

At this moment, a breeze caught the kitchen curtains and blew them across the scaly body. It was then that June first received the long-dead smell. Two gusts of air later, she grabbed her nose to keep her stomach from further rebellion. Putting one and one together, she quickly came up with, "George, George, where are you? You get in this kitchen and mighty fast!"

George was standing behind June before she could turn around. "What, Missy? What wrong?" he asked with a look of shock in his eyes. He had never seen Missy so upset.

"What wrong? You ask what's wrong? What have you brought into my kitchen?" June flung her hand toward the sink with its contents and raised her voice even higher. "What is that?"

George looked toward the sink and his tension eased. He almost clucked, but suddenly realizing the seriousness with which Mrs. Pearce was approaching the subject, caught himself. "Missy, that one iguana. It dead. Many hours dead in my trap." He poked the head of the reptile which still hung at a funny angle as if its neck were broken. "See—it dead!"

What should have reassured June only made her more upset. "That's the point. It is dead and it stinks and why is it in my sink?"

"But, Missy, the meat plenty sweet! It taste sweeto. Vanetta to cook it here."

Maggie edged into the two way conversation with a quick, "And what is an igu . . . or whatever you said?"

"One large lizard, Missy. It plenty sweet!"

This was too much for June and she shook her finger in George's face. "You not say that overgrown reptile is sweet again. It stinks and you get it out. Out! Out of here! Now!"

George took only an instant to go into action. "I sorry. I sorry, Missy. I go." He edged between Maggie and June who stood three steps from the sink, blocking the way to it. George grabbed the striped iguana by the tail and raised it to its full four and one-half foot length as June gasped. The two women parted quickly to make a pathway for the iguana as George turned. He fled out the back door with the reptile swinging back and forth.

June's voice followed him. "You not cook here anymore. You cook at your house. My kitchen will never smell right again."

Sam, who had come only in time to see the iguana disappear out the door, took the chance to say, "Pretty. Pretty snake."

June's face softened as she patted Sam's head. "Pretty? Well, it did have nice brown and black stripes, but it didn't look good with my blue and gold curtains." She started toward the sink to finish the hand washing job she had begun minutes earlier. A foot away she stopped and shuddered as she looked closely at the place where the iguana had been. "I'll probably see that thing every time I come to this sink. It scared me to death."

"I saw some lovely olive green coloring, too," Maggie said, with some mockery in her voice.

June glared at her. "I bet you did—that was me!" She decided to wash her hands elsewhere and turned around, "And I'll send George to your sink with his next wildlife specimen!"

Maggie laughed and mimicked Sam, "But it was so pretty, Aunt June." Then she, too, fled out the back door with Sam under one arm squealing for another look at the "pretty snake."

As Maggie opened her own kitchen door, she speculated that George or Vanetta would be cooking again soon on June's range in spite of June's harsh warning. And Maggie was right. It was the day of George and Vanetta's hut raising.

Hallah Camp had a festive air that day which Maggie had never noticed there before. Why not? As Maggie was to learn, raising a hut meant a lot of work and a lot of fun. That is, if you like slinging mud.

Maggie was within a few yards of the village when she realized she had made a mistake. Why had she brought Sam to this? She turned to June with her accusation, "Why didn't you tell me all this mud was involved? I'll never keep Sam out of it."

June, who hadn't quite forgotten Maggie's amusement over the iguana, chuckled, "Well, that's the way it goes. Some of us like slinging mud and . . . ." She brightened and looked right at Maggie. "Some of us like iguana with olive green stripes!"

Maggie countered, "OK, I will never again laugh at your inconveniences or anything in your sink. Do you forgive me?"

"Now that I've gotten even, yes." June intended to enjoy this day, like she used to enjoy county fairs in the United States.

Maggie grabbed Sam, who had caught his first view of the activity and was eager to join the fun. Mark was too far ahead for Maggie to control him except by her voice and Mark pretended not to hear her shout. After all he already had his shoes and socks off and why wouldn't a mother love for him to jump right into a tub of sand and dirt along with the other villagers? And that is exactly what he did.

Mud splashed everywhere and a few spots landed on Mark's face and hair. He brushed at a dab close to one eye with a muddy finger and the spot grew larger. Maggie groaned and knew there was no use complaining. Mark was already dirty, he might as well enjoy himself. She dared not caution, "Don't throw the stuff," for fear Mark hadn't thought of the idea and would like it.

As June and Maggie approached, several women took buckets of water from their heads and hurried into a hut to get chairs for the visitors. June moved hers to a safe distance and Maggie sat beside her with Sam locked in a leg hold that wasn't too uncomfortable, but restraining. Sam howled as the merriment continued which he was not a part of.

The chant that had been interrupted when "How do's" were said to the missionaries, picked up again and the women sang at the top of their voices as they carried sand and water to huge tubs where other women added termite hill dirt which would make the mixture harden. Mixing was done with the feet, which danced up and down in the tubs to the five-word song.

A little testing for consistency by squeezing the mud through the toes showed when the mixture was ready for the men to use as plaster on the inside of the new hut. George, who had put up the tree trunk studs by himself the week before, stationed himself inside to do most of the work. When a tub of sand-dirt plaster reached the hut, many hands dipped in and slung the mud at what was becoming a wall. Patting and rubbing with the hands and arms completed the job of securing the mud to the tree trunks and cords which made the framework for the hut. Palm thatch had been cut earlier and was already layered and securely tied to make a rainproof roof for the square, two-room hut, which George and his family would probably occupy for four or five rainy seasons. Then extensive repairs would be needed, or a new hut would be built.

Maggie, who had become accustomed to Sam's pleas to be freed, suddenly realized that he had gotten quiet. She turned her head in the direction he was looking to see what had caught his attention. A small girl dressed only in red nylon panties was edging toward June. When the child was within reach, she raised one finger and cautiously touched June's long, light hair. For a moment the child's finger caressed the straight, soft hair. A look of amazement came over the child's face before June, without looking back, slapped at the touch, which she thought was a mango fly.

The child's curiosity was not satisfied and her eyes held the wonder of hair so different from her own for a moment longer. Then with one, quick, sharp cry the girl drew back, spun around, and dashed away, with her pigtails bouncing on each step. June saw the child's black, kinky head disappear. She raised one hand to touch the spot where the child's hand had been, then rose to go and explain her mistake. The child, who was peeking around one corner of George's half-completed hut, saw June coming, screamed, and fled deep into the bush.

June returned to Maggie. "That child reminds me of another experience I had." June's face lit with a sparkling grin, which remained there during the entire story.

"Don and I were on a bush trip and decided to spend the night in one of the villages about five miles from Gbolupa. We walked in late in the afternoon and found a huge tub, like the ones the women are using today, in the hut where we were to spend the night. I didn't know what the tub was for but soon learned.

One woman came to say the bathwater was ready and then several women filled the tub from huge kettles of warm water. This was luxury indeed for I knew the women had carried all the water a long distance from the creek and had heated it over open fires. So I undressed and got in even though I didn't feel like bathing at that moment. I was trying to draw up enough to get my foundation and both my legs in the tub, which didn't seem so large once I got in, when a woman walked into the hut unannounced. I did a submersion act, which was quite silly since the woman was already right beside me when I saw her. I looked up just in time to see a bucket of water come my direction. The woman whirled around and left without a word. I adjusted my legs to a better position just before another woman came in with more water. She dumped it in the tub in a hurry and fled, but not soon enough to keep me from hearing her giggle. Outside she continued to snicker. Now I wasn't accustomed to running around in the nude, so I didn't know if this was the reaction I'd get every time or not."

Maggie threw her head back and laughed. June always had a zest for life and sparkle, but this experience was even better than some of the others she related.

June continued. "I decided to get out of the tub and was halfway up when another woman came in. I flopped back under my water concealment. The woman emptied her bucket in such a hurry that she almost missed the tub. It didn't matter anyway for the tub was already overflowing. This woman covered her mouth to hide a snicker and ran out of the hut to join the others laughing outside.

"A steady procession followed and I decided to give up. I forgot all about the bath and stared at each spectator.

"Finally no one else came and I jumped out of the tub and threw on some clothes. It was getting dark inside or I would have stayed there, because I was rather embarrassed to venture out, not knowing what else was planned. When I approached the women, they gave me the busy-silent treatment. Not an eye looked in my direction. The women finished cooking. We ate and still no one looked my way.

"Finally, late at night an old lady passed the hut where Don and I were relaxing listening to the night sounds. I called to her and she came sheepishly. I asked, 'Why did the women come to my hut with plenty of water and then laugh?'

"My shy informer covered her mouth for a moment as if she didn't dare answer and then with a twinkle in her eyes blurted out, 'Oh, Missy, we just want to know if you white all over. White women never stayed the night in our village before.'

"That explanation broke Don up and he laughed harder than I've ever seen him. This upset the old lady and she fled just like the child did a few minutes ago. I never saw her again while we were in the village and few of the other women got close enough again to say much more than 'Mornin.' "

Mark realized he was missing something and came quickly from his tub of mud. "What's so funny, Mom?"

Maggie controlled her laugher and said, "You, my friend. Your hair has mud balls dripping down. Your hands are monster ones and your feet will never be clean!"

"Oh, Mom, that's not it," Mark said in disgust. "What was June saying?"

"That we have to go home and cook rice for all this hut-raising crew. Where is Vanetta?"

"I'll find her," Maggie declared, as she released her leg hold on Sam. "I thought hut-raising would be great sport, but not with Sam." Maggie rose stiffly and flexed her knees. "Sam's getting too strong."

June winked, "But Mom, life would be more fun if Sam participated!"

"Well, if I wasn't afraid he'd eat dirt and get amoeba again, I'd let him." Maggie lifted Sam and gave him a hug. "Let's go play at home, Sam."

With Vanetta, George's wife, and her two friends in tow, the missionaries walked to June's modern kitchen. Having a new hut was not as exciting to Vanetta as the other things she had planned for her village sisters. The first act was to turn on the front burner of June's gas range. As the flame leaped up, Vanetta's friends jumped back and took a deep intake of air. This was not like coaxing wood. Instant fire, produced by a twist of the wrist, was exciting and frightening. This would mean no chopping and carrying of wood.

June turned cheerfully to one of Vanetta's friends. "You want to turn the knob?"

The woman jumped back two feet as if the knob would reach for her. She put one finger in her mouth and whispered, "No, Missy. I too feared."

The palm butter for the meal had been prepared ahead of time, so Vanetta could be free to show her friends the miraculous things in the rest of June's house. As the rice bubbled, they made their tour. When the toilet was flushed, the women were again frightened and Vanetta assured them. "It OK. Water come by self."

One woman raised a hand as if to push the handle herself. Two inches from the water chamber she stopped. Her hand stayed in midair a moment and then flew back to her side. She giggled and hurried out the bathroom door.

When Vanetta explained the box that made ice, the women felt the cold and "Ah'ed." Vanetta's prestige grew with each new piece of information.

Finally the two women sat on the sofa and poked it to feel its softness.

This wasn't like hard, palm mats. Vanetta was used to the sofa and so didn't go there. Instead she poured her body like water on the floor. June's eyes widened at this unexpected turn on a day when Vanetta was trying so hard to be sophisticated and modern.

Vanetta realized too late she had goofed and decided to take it in her stride. "I hunting the cool." Slowly she pulled herself away from the terrazzo tile, which had a damp chill all year long, and went to get a catalog. This was part of the official treatment and she showed the other women how to turn the pages of the wonder book to see items she had studied all during the past year. A long dress with plenty of lace caught her fancy. Vanetta imagined she was wearing it, and in a spontaneous manner strutted to the door and back again pretending she was a fine, rich lady. The women watched a moment and then figured out what she was doing. They laughed with complete abandonment. They were beginning to feel at home in June's house and June shared the moment by correcting a hand movement Vanetta had made.

"This way, Vanetta. Grand lady can't hold her hand so."

Vanetta copied the movement as best she could but somehow she couldn't curve her last three fingers the way June did. Her poor imitation ended in more laughter and she again flung herself to the floor. "I not fine lady; I village woman!"

The two women on the sofa turned their attention to the pictures in the catalog. They "Ah'ed" and touched the things they liked as if they could by a magic stroke turn the pictures into real objects that could be admired even if they couldn't figure how to use them.

June sat in her rocking chair and appeared not to watch. As she worked on a macrame wall hanging she dwelt on the differences between Vanetta's life and her own. Vanetta could tie knots, but they were for something useful, like the seats of chairs or the springs of a bed or to hold a house together. Tying knots to beautify a house was something June could not even explain to Vanetta. Struggling for firewood, food, and a dry bed didn't leave much time or thought for the nonessentials of life.

Today, though, it would be different. June would share her organ and Vanetta would please the women with her palm butter which contained plenty of meat. Palm butter was a favorite and a real West African dish—the only original of the area. It was made from palm nuts, which had been crushed and boiled, strained and recooked. June guessed it was called "butter" because it had the consistency of peanut butter, and was somewhat the same color.

As June waited for the others to come to lunch, she contemplated the merits of the palm tree. Beautiful. Functional beyond any other here.

Mats, baskets, chair seats, beds, roofs came from its leaves. The trunk made fuel for cooking. The bristles of the leaves made brooms. Salt came from the residue of the nut. Rings and carvings were sculptured from the seed or nut. In the core of the tree was palm cabbage. The sap made instant palm wine. The list seemed endless.

Cooking oil. That was the main thing. June looked toward Vanetta. "How many bunches of palm nuts can you carry on your head?"

Vanetta giggled and pulled herself up on muscular arms. "Can't say."

June had expected "many" or "plenty" and was surprised when Vanetta didn't answer. Oh, well, this was her day to think about fine lady things, not about carrying seven clusters of palm nuts on her head, which was the number June usually saw there. Sometime back June had calculated that each cluster had 200 red nuts the size of a date. That meant Vanetta usually carried 1,400 nuts at a time. That was plenty of palm oil and a heavy load in anybody's vocabulary.

After Vanetta had served rice to her entire village in June's palaver hut, all the people came into the living room for June's promised concert. Every chair was occupied and Vanetta took the best. She was a "fine lady" again! The other women sat on the floor and June guessed some nonworkers had come for the food and show. Don found the only space left was in the doorway, so he stood there.

June turned on the electric organ and began a fast, loud number. The first chords were greeted with sighs and some of the women began to sway. Heads shifted in order to see the keyboard.

During the fifteen minutes of music there was no talking. Lips moved as soft musical sounds accompanied the organ. Finally bodies stopped swaying as June rose. "I finished."

There was no applause, but June realized she had never had a more attentive audience. She groped for words to express what she felt, but none came as she looked from face to face. A glance in Don's direction told her he wasn't going to say anything. June finally said, "I'm thankful for you, my friends. I'm also thankful for Jesus. I played many songs about him for you. He is so good!"

George rose first and came to shake the missionary's hand. "Thank you. Thank you." Each person shook June's hand and then Don's as they headed back toward the village. Chatter began as they neared their own territory. The place was without electricity, running water, refrigerators, and organs but it offered the security of friends, who would help; palm trees, that always grew and produced; and cooking fires.

When the last villager had departed, Don turned to June, gave her a quick kiss on the cheek and said, "Very fine. I wondered how George got all that help. Now I know. Food, a house tour, and a concert will do it every time!"

"George is clever, isn't he?" June said, as she thought about how hard she had worked that day. "He schemed, but I enjoyed it."

George's next scheme almost ended in disaster. For six months, June had been taking care of Vanetta who was pregnant. Her good medical attention resulted in Vanetta's carrying the baby to full term—a first for her. Vanetta could scarcely remember how many babies she had previously lost by miscarriage. It had been agreed that Vanetta would deliver at the maternity center in town, but when the time came she wouldn't go.

At 4:30 one morning frantic knocks came at June's bedroom window. She sprang up to look into George's anxious face. "Mrs. Pearce, come quick. The baby come!"

"What? Vanetta to deliver in town!" June's voice rose and emphasized the last statement.

"Nah, Missy, she not want to go. She say you deliver baby!"

"Oh, George, you know I not want to do this. I not like those village dirt floor maternity centers!"

"Yah, Missy, but the baby begin to come already and can't born."

"What? I not understand."

George gave up in desperation. "I beg you. I beg you. I feared for Vanetta. Please come."

June turned to Don, who had also gotten up. "I wish you could come, but the women won't let any man close to their delivery hut."

June turned back to George and quickly decided what to do. "George, go get Mrs. Blake, while I collect my things. Tell her I need help."

George disappeared in the darkness and June turned toward the closet for her nurse's uniform. On her way through the utility room she grabbed her nonprofessional-looking nurse's bag. Nothing was ready. June grabbed a few items that might be needed and threw them hurriedly in the top shelf of the box. She slammed the box shut and dashed out the back door.

Safari lamps! Where were they? June returned to grab them and rushed back outside. She drove across the road and into the Blake's circular driveway. She saw lights inside and soon Maggie came. She and George got in the car. "What's wrong?" Maggie blurted out.

"Vanetta's baby. She didn't go to the maternity center."

"Oh," Maggie whispered, as her thoughts raced ahead to the village. The car sped across campus and hit the two bumps in the road. George flew forward. Maggie held tight as the car came to a quick halt beside Hollah Camp.

From the backseat, George explained, "Vanetta not here. The women take her to Careysburg."

June groaned for the third time that night. "Great. They always wait until everything has been tried and then they call me!" June grasped her hursing kit as if it were a weapon, and bolted forward. Maggie picked up the lights and followed. George was left in the car as both doors slammed.

The moon made some light and June half saw the familiar path she was racing over. She didn't mind the path but the bamboo bridge at night was a different story. June turned, "Turn on the light. We have enough battery, I hope."

June climbed up on the bridge. The light raced ahead of her. Maggie switched the other light to the hand holding the first light and grabbed the rail with her free hand. She followed June's form. Suddenly one of Maggie's feet slipped through a piece of rotten bamboo flooring. Maggie almost dropped a light, but held on and quickly pulled her foot out of the hole. June felt the sway of the bridge as Maggie's body shifted. She turned and started back.

"I'm OK." Maggie shouted. "Go on."

June turned carefully and slowed her pace, missing several rotten places on the way. Maggie left the light on as both women jumped off the bridge and hurried on toward the chief's village. In the darkness behind them, George stumbled off the bridge and followed. The last fifty yards were covered with amazing speed and the missionaries halted by the door of a hut, which was surrounded by women. Maggie heard Vanetta's screams and a voice called, "Here."

June entered the hut and the safari light quickly showed Vanetta on a mat on the dirt floor. June placed the other light and went to Vanetta. A moment later she turned back to the women. "How long the baby's head showing?" she asked in a strained voice.

June got the nonspecific answer she expected. "Long time, Missy. George say get you."

A muffled sound escaped June's lips and Maggie suspected it was a one word prayer for help. "I need a razor blade. Two razor blades in wrappers," June commanded. The women didn't move. They had not figured what June would do and so stood spellbound. June hurried to the hut door. "George. George! Come!"

Quickly June explained what she needed and George came back with the items in record time.

June knelt and looked at the women and Maggie who were also kneeling on the floor. "Hold her."

Maggie grabbed a hand and found it was so powerful that her own hand was being crushed. Vanetta held on desperately and screamed. Maggie remembered what June had said several months back "Village women don't get enough protein during childhood. Their bones aren't well-developed. Whoever said they deliver easily has never been there!"

This wasn't a prayer meeting with all the women on their knees, but Maggie began to pray. Finally Vanetta's hand relaxed somewhat and Maggie braved a look toward June.

In June's hands was a very wet infant. He lay still. June snapped her fingers time and again against the baby's feet. No response. June's anxious mind rolled back to hut-raising day, "I'm a village woman." A village woman didn't go to the hospital. A village woman lost most of her children.

In desperation, June lifted the baby high and let him drop almost to the floor. A small whimper came. June smacked the baby's rear and he began to gasp. Finally a cry came. Vanetta rose on one elbow and looked toward the baby. The women who had said nothing during the five minute delivery, began to cluck.

The men had heard the cry and a shout came from the hut where they waited. Maggie wiped Vanetta's face with the wet cloth she had been handed earlier and articulated a joyful, "Thank you, Jesus."

June motioned to the woman who had been in charge of the delivery before she had been called. "Come. Get the string in my nurse's bag. You cut the cord."

The woman came forward eagerly. She had lost face earlier, but now June was restoring her to her place with the women. She worked quickly, for this was a job she had done many times. "Good. Good," June encouraged.

June lifted the baby toward the women. "Keep him off the floor. We want no tetanus here. Who wash this baby?"

An old woman took the infant and began to talk to him. June turned toward the woman who had tied the cord. "You deliver the afterbirth."

"Yah."

June rose and shook her numb legs. What a delivery table! She came to Vanetta's side and felt her pulse. "Fine. You have big boy. You fine lady today. You fine enough to wear fancy dress and look pretty."

Vanetta understood the jest and smiled weakly.

June massaged Vanetta's abdomen. "You bravo! I never delivered a stronger lady than you."

The women began the cleanup without any suggestion from June. They cleaned the wet floor with dirt. June watched and shortly said, "I want Vanetta off this floor." Several women came as soon as June had placed three stitches. The job was complete.

The women helped the new mother and soon she was walking toward a neatly made bed on the other side of the one-room hut.

Then the women surprised June by reaching under the palm mat where Vanetta had been and taking out rings. "What this?" June asked.

"Wedding rings, Missy." June was left to speculate about the ritual, which she had not seen before, but guessed was a product of their animistic religion. The trouble was, their god never answered. This was the first time June had been able to bring to life a baby that had such a slim chance for life. June remembred Vanetta's remark a few weeks back, "I love Jesus." Jesus. Jesus. He was greater . . . .

June joined Maggie, who had been outside the door for some time. She glanced at Maggie's face. "How are you? One time in there you looked sick!"

"I'm still sick. Why are you always getting me involved?"

"You're one fine nurse's aide," June laughed, and patted Maggie's shoulder. Maggie glanced up, sighed, and watched as the pink rays of day battled with the gray sky, which was heavy with heat and rain. Steam drifted down to where a few fires had been relit in preparation for the day's cooking. Morning had come to the village before night ended but the people didn't seem to mind. There was loud talk as the events of the birth spread from one hut to the next.

The women, who had been inside all night, came to the door where June stood. The old woman who had washed the baby shoved the newborn toward June for verification that her job had been well-done.

June grinned and held the shiny, clean child to her heart. "Fine. Fine. You do fine. God very good last night. I plenty thankful for this fine boy." Then June started toward George. She sensed that was the wrong move and handed the baby back to the women. "I finished."

A happy magic invaded the hut. The women knew what to do. They made a line of a sort behind the old woman who held the blanket-clad infant. Maggie had never seen village women who could walk, plant, or stand in a straight line. This time was no exception. The women began to move forward to a rhythm Maggie hadn't heard. Clap. Shuffle. Sway. Chant. A four note movement. The women went toward the men's hut.

"What ritual is this?" Maggie strained to see the dance which was becoming visible with the new day.

"I don't know," said June thoughtfully. "I've never seen it before. I haven't delivered many babies out here. By the time I get called there's no birth march just death wailing. I guess it was good we came last night—this morning—or whenever it was!"

"Morning was on its way," Maggie clarified. "And you did very well, indeed. I wouldn't have given you one chance in a hundred. That's why I prayed so hard!"

Maggie's attention quickly returned to the women who had almost completed their march from hut to hut around the village. As they passed George again, the line paused to give him a closer look at his new son.

June was thinking about what Maggie had said and replied, "I wouldn't have given even the one chance, but we weren't working with chance this morning."

Maggie turned with a puzzled look not quite knowing where June was leading. June continued. "As soon as I saw Vanetta, I prayed. Suddenly I had full assurance that the baby would live."

"You did?"

"I doubted only for a moment, when I couldn't get the baby to breathe. Then I reminded God he'd made a promise—foolish, wasn't it?"

Maggie looked more intently at June and had no idea what to say. She hated to admit she'd wavered all the way. That was the problem. It had been the problem ever since she came here. She didn't know what God could do in this culture. She wanted to understand before she believed. That wasn't possible or at least it never had been before. Yet she couldn't climb the wall of doubt.

The women came toward the missionaries. They had not missed a beat in the rhythm. Clap. Shuffle. Sway. Chant. Their swaying line brushed past June and into the hut. The women placed the baby in his mother's outstretched arms and she grasped him eagerly. Pure joy was written on her countenance as she held her first live born.

June picked up her things and floated out of the hut. Alive. No death wails today. Only joy. June was in the high, clear world of inspiration. She stepped to the rhythm that had moved the village women. She was two steps into a poor imitation when the women discovered what she was doing.

"Ah, Missy. Ah, Missy," they shouted, and began to clap again. Laughter followed June as she shuffled toward George. He, too, was caught up with the humor of June's antics. A big grin crossed his face, vanished, and then returned. Joy was contagious—except for Maggie, who trailed along behind.

She didn't feel quite a part of it all. When the village was behind them, June returned to her usual pace. "That was great. Fantastic!" And with a second thought she added, "Don't tell Don I danced in the village."

When the bamboo bridge was reached, it was illuminated this time. The sun had been fifteen minutes in the sky. "This is better," remarked

Maggie. "No hurry. No dark holes." Maggie stopped in the middle of the bridge and her eyes traveled ahead where the agricultural farm's herd of cattle grazed. The small, brown cows were surrounded by white herons, the large birds which always fascinated Maggie. This she understood.

The birds suddenly lifted and Maggie said, "They take off sort of like a plane—only faster. Wings out, engine roar, and they're airborne. Notice how the wheels come up right after takeoff."

"Those are wheels?" June laughed.

"Use your imagination," Maggie said. "Now watch the birds glide in. Engine cut. Flaps down. And then right before they hit, the wheels are lowered. All very graceful and in two feet of space. Good brakes, no? They fly to a rhythm just like the women's. Flap-glide-lower-stop. See!"

"It's good to be alive," June said. "What a morning!"

Each woman withdrew into her own thoughts. Soon the rubber tree grove came into view. Maggie noticed, as she always did, that the trees, which had shallow roots, all leaned in one direction. The direction of the prevailing wind. The trees looked to her like a band marching in step to the music of the wind. What a cool place for a house, but it did get noisy in the dry season when the thick husks over the seeds began to explode and throw seeds a hundred yards in all directions. The effect was like that of a large corn popper.

Maggie began to click the fingernails of her free hand as thoughts dashed through her head. She turned to June. "You know I was on campus one year before I knew that there was such a thing as the missionary gift. Then I had to read about it in Peter Wagner's book, *Frontiers in Mission Strategy.* Do you know what he says?"

"No," answered June, wondering how this tied to the other experiences of the morning. "I was supposed to read the book, but got too busy."

"Well, he says God gives everyone he calls as a foreign missionary a special gift—the ability to work in a cross-cultural situation."

June turned the thought over a couple of times. "I guess so. That's the ability to do things in the African way."

"More than that, I think. To feel at home here. To feel safe here and to be a sister to the women."

June's face changed. She was beginning to see Maggie's line of thought. Maggie went on. "This morning, while you were holding the new baby before he cried, you were compassion personified! I threw out the word *work* and rephrased Wagner's statement—the missionary gift is to love and respect the people of another culture. That's rather ordinary, isn't it? Anybody could say it, but few people are it!"

June searched for the right words. "God's instructions often skip the ears and vibrate the soul. They're soul music!"

"Yes, and soul music shows on the outside. You've heard it. You've got it!"

Something about the way Maggie finished the last phrase, surprised June. What was Maggie really trying to say? Once she'd talked about her difficulty in living up to the perfect missionary expectation. Was that it? Was she beating herself again? June decided not to dig deeper unless Maggie continued and Maggie turned elsewhere.

Beside the path, Maggie suddenly saw hundreds of dew-laden spider webs. The sun was turning each dewdrop into a diamond. Maggie ran forward excitedly and knelt in the grass by the path. Thousands of dewdrops hung on the circles which made each web. They reminded Maggie of the jewels she had seen in the ocean waves. Those were emeralds. These were diamonds. Those were part of something big and these part of something so minute they could almost be missed. "I saw these once before," Maggie said. "I read about them and now I want a picture. One hour's work each night for a spider! That's all these take. Could you believe that? I'm going to get my camera."

As June watched Maggie hurry toward the car, which had been abandoned hours earlier, she was reminded of how John had introduced Maggie—a country girl, who walks like she's crossing a plowed field. June smiled as another comparison came. Maggie walked like a village woman—purposeful; like she had work to do and places to go. If Maggie could only see herself as June saw her, Maggie would realize she was making giant strides toward being a seasoned missionary.

As the car pulled away, June came back to the intricate art work. She had never seen hundreds and hundreds of spider webs in one small area and yet they had probably been here before. She would have missed them again if the sun and dew had not turned them into a sea of diamonds—a necklace for the path.

June knelt to look closely at one web. There was a center and then threads extended out an inch in all directions like the spokes of a wheel. The spokes were evenly placed and held securely by a coil of thread which went around and around in progressively larger circles. June followed a couple of circles all the way around the web and then got lost. What artist's brush could paint circles so perfect and delicate? June tried again to follow the thread around, but quickly gave up and focused at the center of the symmetrical design. There June glimpsed a minute, eight-legged object—only an insect and yet, what a craftsman!

Wonder flooded June as it had when the baby in her hands that morning first breathed. June rested back on her heels a moment. "I see." And then she leaned close to the grass. "Now I see you, you tiny weaver, and I want to whisper a secret." June's voice dropped lower. "You didn't do it on your own!"

17

Crier By the Path

"Fire! Fire!" Mark yelled as he slammed the door and dashed through the kitchen. "Where's Dad?"

"In his office," Maggie exclaimed, and rushed outside to see what Mark meant. She had smelled smoke all week as villagers burned off the ground to make gardens. Was this something out of the ordinary? Maggie's breath caught in her throat when she saw flames leaping high close to the campus gate. Smoke was rising in huge clouds and floating in her direction.

Maggie turned as the door behind her slammed again. Mark and Prince had John in tow and were encouraging him with, "Hurry, hurry. A big fire! See!"

John took one look and dashed to the laundry room. He returned quickly with a shovel. "The flames are coming this way. Maybe we can turn the fire by digging a ditch."

"In dry season?" Maggie questioned. "You can't dig in that hard dirt."

"I'll try," John yelled over his shoulder. "Get out the hose and buckets. We can keep the fire away from the house with water if it comes this way."

John ran toward the gate just as a group of students came through the carport almost running over Maggie. They laughed politely and said, "Excuse us, Mrs. Blake," and hurried on. Soon Karen and her friends and the workmen on campus, also passed.

Maggie watched for a while and then thought of Mark and Karen. They'd probably get right in front of the fire. What if the wind swept it right into some of the children? Maggie shuddered and ran inside to get Sam. She grabbed him and hurried toward the fire. Maggie ran halfway across campus and still Mark was not in sight. Maggie retreated from the smoke and hurried to where the workmen stood watching the fire. Why didn't they do something? "Where's Mark? Have you seen him?"

"Yeh. Yeh. He here."

"Where?"

"Not know. He here."

Maggie, knowing no more information would come, went toward the missionary residences, which were almost hidden by smoke. Before she saw him, she heard Mark's laugh. There he was in front of one of the houses with a hose. He was spraying water twenty yards out from the house and calling, "I'm a fireman! Turn the pressure up, Prince!"

Karen, who had reached an age where she was easily embarrassed, was standing nearby watching. When she saw Maggie, she came to her and said, "Does Mark always have to shame us? He's always clowning!"

Maggie did not have time to answer before the main force of the fire was picked up by the wind and ran fifty yards wide toward the girls' dormitory. The workmen and students ran in that direction. Maggie could see John already at the dorm. With his shovel he was tossing the sandy soil from in front of the dormitory to the side where there was grass. The workmen joined in the fight to save the building by chopping at the grass with their cutlasses. Soon there was a four-foot strip of cleared earth out from the dormitory. Behind that was a row of sand. As the fire approached, the wind caught it again and the flames leaped high. A moan went up from the watching men, as each realized a sudden gust of wind could blow the fire right over the bare ground and onto the building. John held his breath expecting the worst and having no plan about how to put out the fire if it reached the building. There was no water faucet close enough and he had only a short hose. The water tower was almost empty as it always was on Saturday morning after student laundry. There was nothing to do but wait.

The fire was within a foot of the bare ground when the wind died. The flames inched up to the bare spot and sizzled for a minute. Some ran halfway across the ground and then turned to sparks. Only a few sparks leaped to the sand, where they also burned out. A cheer went up from the workmen and they began to talk in loud voices, as if this were a festive occasion.

Mark was the first to venture out on the scorched ground. He took two high steps across it before Prince followed. The men cheered and Mark raised his arms, "We beat you, fire. We beat you!" The students cheered and Karen hid her face. Mark was having the time of his life when John saw him.

"Get off that hot ground! Mark, come here!" John shouted. The students got quiet and the workmen giggled as Mark made a slow retreat to where his father was. "You want to ruin your shoes, young man? Your mom will have a fit. Now you stay off that ground even after it cools. You'll track all that burnt grass into the house."

"Oh, Dad, I was just having fun." With that Mark whirled and started for the gate, where the fire had started. Prince caught up when Mark slowed down in front of the students for another performance. "One, two, three, step. One, two, three, step," Mark shouted as he and Prince paraded for the benefit of the appreciative spectators. When the students cheered, Mark stepped even higher in imitation of a band major. Deciding this was too slow, though, he quickly broke into a fast run.

John, too, walked past the missionary residences and toward the gate to see if the fire were completely out. Here and there he could see red sparks, but everything seemed under control. When John came to Dennis's gravesite, he noticed James, the Muslim boy, who had come after Dennis's death with many questions. James had come often in the two years since then to talk and John had expected each time that James would make some sort of decision about Christ, but still James debated. John didn't feel like a long talk today so he decided to change courses and pass without being noticed. This didn't work, for James suddenly turned and saw John. He yelled, "It's a sign. A sign."

John knew he couldn't escape and turned around. "A what?" John checked his inclination to smile when he saw that James's eyes were wild with fear.

"See! See!" James pointed toward the grave.

John came to James's side and looked. It struck John that something was wrong. But what? The headstone, the flowers, and the palm trees looked fine. Then John gazed beyond the gravesite. Everything was brown and burned. John was still not too impressed and said, "The grass here is still green."

"That's it! That's it! It's a sign!" James grasped John's arm. "God not let the fire touch Mr. Baker's grave. See! God can't let the fire come close to the missionary's grave!"

John looked in all directions and then back to the rectangle, twenty feet by fifteen feet around the grave, which was still green. That was strange. Then John remembered Maggie had cleared the area the week before. That must be the explanation for why this area didn't burn. Then John looked toward the missionary residences. All the yards were cleared and mowed and yet they had burned. The only green places were where Mark had sprayed water. John stepped back from the grave and walked to the edge of the green grass. He turned and walked around all four sides of the grave on the imaginary line which separated green grass from burned grass. It was almost like a fireproof box had been built around the grave. On the outside of the box everything burned. On the inside nothing was touched. Why? How could it be?

John would have gone on searching for an explanation, but he realized James was walking right behind him. James spoke. "Professor, you say Mr. Baker lives with God!"

John turned. "Yes, he lives."

James whispered, "I want to live, too."

By this time, Mark had come close and he said, "If you want to live forever, just trust Jesus!"

There was no response and John said, "James, are you afraid of death or do you want Jesus? There's a difference."

James stared at John for a minute and then his face melted and huge tears spilled from his black eyes and ran all over his cheeks.

John reached for James's shoulders just as his knees buckled. James fell face down across the grave. Mark and Prince stepped back as James began to moan. They stood completely still as James began to call out in what they thought was his own tribal dialect. John had seen this type of emotion many times in church services in West Africa and he knelt beside James.

James began to shout. "Jesus. Jesus." Then he flung his arms as if he were battling some unseen force and yelled in an even louder voice, "Oh, Jesus, Jesus."

James continued to moan for at least a minute and then he jumped to his feet and yelled, "Jesus turned me inside out." Then he hesitated only a moment before he ran in the direction of the boys' dormitory, yelling at the top of his voice, "Jesus. Jesus."

John stayed on his knees several minutes praying for James and then slowly rose as Mark asked, "What happened? Was James saved?"

John answered with confidence, "Yes, Son, I think he was."

"Wow!" exclaimed Prince.

Mark burst out, "That was something! When I became a Christian last year, I just talked to Jesus in the bathtub and Jesus told me to be a Christian."

John smiled and patted Mark's curly, auburn hair. "That's the way it goes, Son. Some of us are quiet when Jesus comes into our lives and some of us are excited."

"Wow!" Prince said, as he glanced again after James' retreating figure. "Double wow!"

"See, Son," John said, as they started toward home. "People here have a different religious background than you do. Images and masks and signs are very important in some religions. Then when we missionaries talk about Christ some people think they have to have signs. So, sometimes . . ." John hesitated, not quite certain how to finish. As a physics teacher how could he explain the green grass? John went through all the laws of the physical world and quickly eliminated each. There was no scientific explanation for what he had seen. John reached a conclusion and continued his conversation with Mark and Prince. "So sometimes God gives those people who need a sign, a sign. God makes it favorable for each person to come to faith!"

Mark thought about this a minute. "But, Dad, when I talked to Prince about Jesus, he didn't wait for any sign. He just decided right there to follow Jesus, and Prince and I were baptized together. Isn't that right?" Mark turned to Prince for assurance.

"Sure thing. We're buddies. Jesus is our buddy, too." Prince's black arm found its way around Mark's neck and Mark's arm went around Prince's waist. The two boys took two giant steps forward before they burst into laughter. "Let's race," Mark called over his shoulder as he broke into a run that would assure him a good lead.

That night John and Maggie walked back over the burned area and stopped where the grass was green. Maggie had wanted to see for herself what had happened. First Mark had come with news of a sign. Then two workmen had stopped by to talk about God's power. Then a student had come. Finally John and Karen had come with the news. "You've got to see what happened. Uncle Dennis's gravesite didn't burn."

Maggie had wondered all day if everyone wasn't just imagining the unusual phenomenon. But even from a distance Maggie was aware there was a contrast between the areas which were brown and the one area on campus, where the fire had been, which was green. As she drew closer the contrast became more dramatic. "Unbelievable!" Maggie said, and turned to John. "That's something."

Several other missionaries came along to talk and John would have lingered except for the fact there was something on the radio that he wanted Maggie to hear. They hurried home and John switched on the radio just in time to pick up the African news. John listened quietly with a smile on his face and wondered when Maggie would catch onto his big secret. Maggie listened for a while only to the information and then slowly she began to listen with interest to the voice. This was a new announcer. His voice was good. His pronunciation was accurate. He was more pleasant to listen to than the old announcer. Suddenly, it began to register that she had heard the voice before. Who was he? Maggie looked at John's smiling face and began to perceive that John's interest had been in the voice and not in the news. What did he know that Maggie didn't? Maggie questioned him, "So, who is it?"

John looked up. "Oh, you finally caught on. Who do you think it is?"

Maggie listened carefully. "I've heard him. Must have been a student here. We don't know anybody else very well. Which student?"

John offered no help, but continued to listen. Maggie asked, "Do I know him?"

"Very well."

About that time, Karen came through the back door. She stopped a minute, listened to the radio and said, "Hey, that's Moses!"

Maggie still wondered. It couldn't be Moses. But he had left campus early. Maggie could see him going—head down, shoulders slumped, a twenty-one-year-old failure. He'd failed two of the five senior examinations. Maggie remembered the first time he had come to the house. That had been when he was having the disappointing romance. He'd suffered a year over that. Moses' way had always been hard. Maggie checked out the voice again. Karen was right. It was Moses.

Maggie looked toward John. "How did Moses get a job?"

John shrugged and put his hands out. "Who can tell. You remember the day Moses left campus after he failed the tests. Well, I picked him up down at the corner and gave him a ride to town. He was so low I thought he'd never cheer up again. I tried to encourage him, but he didn't hear a thing I said until I asked him what he actually wanted to do. Then Moses came to and sat up. For a minute I thought he wasn't going to trust me with the answer. Then he said he wanted to be on the radio. He thought he would like to work for a Christian broadcasting company. Well, I knew only one Christian station here so I suggested that Moses go see them. I took him out there, in fact, that very day, and I gave him a verbal recommendation. Then I left. I really didn't expect much, but yesterday Moses was back on campus. You wouldn't have known him. He was in the clouds. He told me to listen tonight. Said he'd be on and now he could tell people all over the country about what Jesus had done for him. Moses was so high that I wasn't too certain that the job was as good as he thought it was. But, there you are. He is on and who knows. . . ." John was suddenly choked by emotion and ended without completing his sentence.

Maggie sat in silence as Moses signed off. She thought about the week behind them. It had been one of the strangest weeks they had spent in Africa. It had started badly when June came with her big announcement. "Don and I won't be coming back to Africa after furlough."

Maggie had been shocked. Then she had been puzzled. Then she'd been frightened. Her voice caught as she asked, "Is something wrong? Are you ill? Is Don OK? Your mom, your daughter?" Maggie's mind would have run on to all the serious problems that June might be having, except June stopped her with, "No, no, not those things. It's not the usual reasons people don't return. It's just that God has called us back to the United States. Don has said for sometime that his work here is finished."

Maggie's mouth had hung open. Her brain had been stuck in neutral with no functioning power at all. "But, but you're so great here. Everybody loves you and your work is so good . . . ." Suddenly Maggie's mind began to function in overtime and she ran through many explanations, none of which fit. Finally she came to where she hurt, "But you can't go. I need you." Maggie's eyes filled with tears and June looked away and blew her nose. It was a minute or so before June could answer and then she found it hard to say what she wanted to communicate.

"Maggie, I do love you. We've been so close, but you don't really need me anymore. You don't need a prop now!"

Maggie looked up in unbelief, unable to comprehend what June was saying. June didn't understand. She didn't know how weak Maggie actually was. June went on. "God did give us a natural bond. There was never any problem. We always understood each other and it's wonderful to have a friend like that but . . . ." June's voice trailed off as her emotions took over.

June blew her nose before she continued. "We're sort of a Peter-John thing. I'm the activist; you're the thinker." June's thoughts turned to the village women that she and Maggie had cared for, and again she was consumed with grief. How could she leave them? They still needed her. There was no other nurse. But she couldn't resist God, either. She had tried, even when Don had been so certain. Don had delayed decision until June had agreed with him. It was fact. June knew that. God was sending them home. June wanted to ask why, but she knew that was the wrong course. Faith was acting before the evidence was presented—before the proof came. God knew. She didn't have to know yet.

June looked up and realized Maggie was studying her carefully. June had learned to read Maggie well enough to know that she was hurting. June tried to encourage her. "Like I said, you don't need a prop anymore, Maggie." And then thinking of a phrase which Maggie would probably have used, June said, "You're God's special agent. You've got your commission. You've earned your stripes. You can stand. I know you'll stand."

Maggie looked down at her own hands both pleased and humbled by June's evaluation. That night Maggie couldn't sleep. She had gone through June's entire career at Gbolupa. She had remembered the first trip she had made to a village with June and when she had begun to think of June as if she were a blood sister. She was, of course, a sister by Christ's blood. Then June's words, "You've been commissioned," ran back and forth in her mind. Maggie wasn't certain what June had meant. She thought about the commission given to John the Baptist, "Make straight the way of the Lord" (John 1:23). Those words had troubled Maggie since the time her car had traveled down the Gbolupa road in Dennis's funeral procession. If she could only understand that Scripture, she'd know more about what God expected of her.

Maggie came back to the present to find herself still sitting at the kitchen table with John, who was also in deep thought. She ventured, "Moses' job is terrific. I'm pleased. What are you thinking about?"

John looked up, suddenly aware that Maggie was talking to him. "What?"

"I said what are you thinking about?"

"About Moses. About James. It was more than two years ago that we met them. I had been rather discouraged with both. The number of hours I'd spent with each didn't seem to bear much fruit. Then all of a sudden. . . ." John got up without finishing his sentence as a knock came on the door. When Roland appeared, John groaned. "I was supposed to go check the palm branch arches. I forgot."

Roland's first words were, "Professor, we've been waiting on you. The painters have all the tree trunks painted white. The big rocks are all white. The statue of the first president of the country is clean. The road grader got all the chuck holes filled in on campus and now we're braiding the palm leaf arches."

John remembered the water line that the grader had broken, "Did the plumber get that water line fixed?"

"Yes, Yes," Roland said with some impatience. After all that wasn't his problem. His problem was the decorations. He returned to them. "We're waiting for you to hang that wire."

John smiled as he decided to tease Roland. "You mean with all your intelligence, you cannot figure out how to hang one wire from a forty-foot ceiling?"

Roland frowned and checked his impulse to fire back. He knew he needed the professor's help. His words came slowly and carefully, "Probably nobody on campus knows as much about the laws of physics as you know, Professor. That's why we asked you." Roland stepped back and crossed his arms as if he knew these were the right words to say.

John smiled. "Flattery. You're very good at flattery. But I'm not helping you for that reason. Whatever my reason is, though, I am helping. Wait a minute and I'll be ready."

John went to get his tools and then quickly disappeared with Roland, leaving Maggie to visualize how the auditorium would look the next day when the president of the country made his special visit to Gbolupa.

Maggie checked her own assignments. One hundred tea sandwiches. She'd finish them in the morning. Red punch. Maggie wondered how long it would take to squeeze a half-bushel of oranges. Well, at least she had three assistants. June was doing the table settings. Corinne had the cakes in her freezer and the kitchen crew in the dining hall was doing the rice dishes. Maggie had never planned anything for the president of any country, but she supposed it would come off all right. At least everybody on campus said it would. Feelings had run high all week.

Maggie rose early the next morning to find John already dressed. She couldn't remember any day that he had ever gotten out of bed before she did. Then Maggie remembered this was the grand day—the day that the president would visit. She looked out the window. Sunshine was on its way. It looked like it would be clear.

That afternoon all the people from the villages and the students lined the roads. All eyes looked expectantly down the road. Was that dust? Finally in the distance sirens could be heard. They drew closer and became louder. Two police cars appeared. A truckload of soldiers followed them and men with guns quickly stationed themselves beside the Gbolupa gate. Other soldiers had come earlier and were now carefully located all over the campus. Then the big, black cars came into view and sped to Gbolupa gate where they stopped. Everyone watched the car with flags on the front fenders, for it carried the president. Maggie held Sam, but she could not keep Mark and Karen from running forward for a closer view. The first man to step out of the flag decorated car was Senator Minor. Then two more men came out the door. But which was the president? A student beside Maggie pointed and supplied the information. "There he is. The man in the white suit. That's the president."

Maggie watched as the representatives of the school and the band led the president and his group down the road to where most of the students waited in the auditorium. Maggie left Sam at the house with George, June's houseboy, and hurried quickly past the auditorium and to the dining hall where there was plenty of work to be done. The time from then until the president entered the dining hall and shook Maggie's hand went by as if it had been minutes rather than hours. Then a sea of whirling faces, probably about five-hundred, came through the serving line and Maggie was certain the food wouldn't last. When the dining hall was finally cleared, Maggie and the other women realized they had not even had time to sample the foods they had spent a week preparing and decorating. Maggie's thoughts turned toward home and her family which probably hadn't eaten either. She wished she had thought far enough ahead to save some sandwiches. Maggie walked out the dining hall door and realized the sun was setting. Its red rays wrapped the palm trees in a brilliant blanket.

Maggie speculated that it was only two-hundred yards from the dining hall to her house, but her tired feet felt like it was at least a mile. As she walked Maggie thought about the day; about the week. How unusual it had been. It was then that the Lord put the last piece in the puzzle that had bothered Maggie for more than two years. Now she saw. She understood more fully what June had meant by commissioning; what it meant to "Make the path straight."

Maggie was a crier; a herald. She had been stationed in the house by an African path not to be a friend to man. That was good, but not enough. Maggie was there to put out the palm fronds and point to Jesus, like the students this afternoon had identified the president in a way so that no other man could be mistaken for him. Maggie was there to smooth out the rough roads, like the road grader had done on campus days before. She was to call out like Mark had when the fire reached campus. She was to testify to those who passed on the path, "That's him. He's the Son of God. He's the Savior. Come meet him."

The Great Commission was the design for witnessing. It was the ultimatum; the imperative. The wonder of it all—"Ye shall be witnessess" (Acts 1:8). A witness must testify here and now and even beyond death through all eternity. Only the redeemed—Dennis, Don, June, John, Maggie, Moses, the MK's, and now James—could tell salvation's story. Only the redeemed knew firsthand the excitement of meeting and entertaining Jesus, King of kings and Lord of lords.

Maggie looked up in reverence and whispered, "Come. The path is smooth. The palms are out. The people are waiting. Stop here, gentle Jesus!"

18

Tender Inventory

Maggie and John watched June and Don's airplane taxi down the runway. Even though Maggie had had six months to prepare for this farewell, she was not ready when it actually came. Mark, who was standing nearby, shook his head. "Since Uncle Don is gone, who will jog every night with me?"

Karen was too choked up for any words and John took his handkerchief out and blew his nose.

The journeygirl, who had been at Gbolupa when the Blakes came, had gone to the United States months earlier. Now there were no missionaries left except Tom and Corinne, who had taken a short furlough in order to be back before the Pearces left.

There were two bright spots on the horizon. First a new family was in orientation and would be at Gbolupa soon. Then Maggie and John would be due for furlough. Six months wasn't long. Maggie remembered how the personnel committee of the mission had put it, "And what do you want to do when you return?"

John had looked at Maggie and given the answer that they'd spent months agreeing on. "We aren't certain. We've still got a lot of things to sort out in our own minds."

If Maggie had been able, she would have given another thought, "I think the Lord wants us to come back but I don't want to come." She hadn't been able to say that out loud, though. After all there was no reason besides her own feelings why she shouldn't return. God had not withdrawn orders. And yet there had been no clear trumpet call to proceed in the same direction. Maggie knew her faith had grown tremendously. She had new insights, but most of them had come in such hard ways. Maggie wasn't certain she could live with another term like her first one. There had been scarcely a minute to do anything that was fun or just entertaining. It was always as if she was gearing up for the next set of experiences before the last crisis subsided. Maggie was reminded of the time she and John had gone camping in the Great Smoky Mountains. They had had to move every night because the water rose. Then their groceries had gotten soaked, along with the bedrolls. Finally, the tent had mildewed. That was the way it had been in Africa—constant changes, struggles, farewells, and uncertainties.

Sure, camping in the Smokies those weeks had provided a few lovely hikes in the woods, but they hadn't been enough to offset the discomforts and frustrations. There had been the beautiful experiences in Africa, too—the ocean sunset, the spider web at dawn, the warmth of Christian love, the few students whose lives were changed—but for every victory Maggie could name ten defeats. Was she ready for that?

Somehow Maggie just didn't have the strength to decide. She was tired. She needed a furlough. What had June said right before she left? "A furlough will give you time away from the scene to put everything in perspective." Maggie hoped so.

Suddenly the time that had seemed to drag evaporated in puffs a month at a time. As Maggie began to pack for furlough she found the list of house repairs John had made the first week they were in Africa. She laughed as she saw half the repairs still weren't done. Poor John! He'd been too busy at school. Oh, well, maybe next term! Packing was the important thing now and reentry visas and travel arrangements.

Maggie was on her knees packing African artifacts when she began to give serious consideration to what the past three years had meant to the children. Karen had gone from a child to a young girl, who carried notes from boys around in her blue jean pockets. Mark had probably changed least. He was still all fun and activity. Sam had been a few months old and now he could talk, run, and put on his own shirt, sometimes.

People—so many people. Some so dear. Maggie stopped, deep in sweet memories. For a while she did not realize that someone was at the door. When the voices became louder than the background singing of the birds, Maggie went to the front windows. On the porch were several campus workmen and a girl Maggie had never seen before.

When Maggie opened the door, the girl turned to the workmen, smiled, and politely said, "Thanks for showing me the house."

The men did not move or answer. Their eyes stayed on the girl in obvious admiration. They were enjoying themselves as much as when they chased a lone snake across campus or caught a rogue.

Maggie turned toward the center of all the attention. The girl was pretty with fine features, a slender figure, nice open smile. She was attractive all right, but she seemed to not notice the stir she was causing. As this thought of the girl's modesty came to Maggie's mind, she grew somewhat embarrassed by the men's openmouthed stares and quickly ushered her inside, and closed the door.

Immediately, the girl began in easy-flowing English, "I'm Ada Seahfa, Rose's sister. Rose asked me to come see you on my way back to school."

It took a moment for Maggie to put it all together. Then she could not hide her surprise and pleasure, "Rose's sister! How about that!"

Ada smiled from her perch on the sofa. "Rose said to tell you she didn't write much because no one goes to town to carry letters."

"Oh," Maggie replied, eager to learn more about Ada. "Rose told me about you several times. She said you were in school in another country."

"Yes, I've been away twelve years. Rose and I are the only children of our pa." Maggie studied Ada as she talked—nice voice, natural-looking short hairdo, winning smile—not at all shy, like Rose. "I graduated from high school and I came to see Ma and Pa and Rose."

"Did they recognize you after twelve years?" Maggie asked, not really comprehending that long a separation.

"No, they did not know me. I had to ask, too, who they were." There was no self-pity in Rose's voice as she continued, "My ma is proud of me."

Maggie turned this thought over several times in her mind. The more she studied Ada the less she could see that reminded her of a village woman. Ada's Ma was an uneducated, country woman, and Ada's Pa was also uneducated. Proud? Proud of a daughter so different than herself. But she had wanted something different. A different life for Ada.

"You must like the school," Maggie said.

"I love it. It is fine. I always wanted to go to school. I like books. Rose always liked home, but I wanted to go places. I am happy there. Now I go back for two years of business school. Then I return to work for the company where my Pa works."

"Let me get you a fanta." As Maggie got up to go into the kitchen, she speculated, "You must be thirsty. Did you come today from up-country?"

"Yes, by taxi."

When Maggie came back, Ada was talking to Alfred, the houseboy. Actually she was talking in a friendly way and Alfred was staring open-eyed with mop and pail in hand. When he saw Maggie, he looked to the floor and left hurriedly, running over a chair on the way. Maggie tried to hide a smile as she thought about the power of beauty.

"And now, Ada," Maggie began, as her thoughts turned toward Rose. "Tell me all about Rose. She was one of my favorite students. She baby-sat Sam."

Ada laughed. "Rose talks about Sam all the time. She liked him too much!"

Maggie remembered and smiled. "Rose likes all children. I wrote her several times."

"It is hard to get mail in her village," Ada said, thinking of the long walk she had made to visit Rose when her baby was born.

"And did Rose have her baby?" Maggie asked. "I knew she was expecting."

For the first time during the conversation, Ada's eyes fell to the floor and her smile vanished. She sighed, "Yes, but the baby not stay."

Maggie was jolted by the words she had heard so often since she came to Africa. Their meaning was all too clear. Maggie's eyes filled with tears and she pushed the African term of comfort past a lump in her throat. "Never mind. Never mind."

For a minute there was silence as Maggie thought about Rose's love for babies. There had been the unwelcome marriage arrangment with the old chief, Rose's move to an unknown, distant village, and now this. Everything had gone against Rose. Maggie was not certain what to ask Ada. She decided not to ask about the chief. "Is Rose OK? Does she like the village now?"

Ada still looked unhappy. "Rose used to the village now."

So Rose was still having a hard time. The baby might have made a difference had it lived. Maggie thought of the many village women she knew who gave their main affection to their children. Their children, carried on their backs, were constant companions for years, while a husband wasn't usually around. With several wives a man had to divide his time equally between them. Maggie thought about the village woman who had wanted a ride to town. On the way she had waved and shouted when a black Mercedes came up behind the mission car. She had asked John to stop, and when he did the woman flagged down the Mercedes and went to talk with the man who sat in the backseat. One of the other women in the car with John answered John's questions about what was going on. Yes, the woman had been married to a chief. He had died. The family had arranged marriage to the man in the big, black car. The dowry had been paid, but the man lived in a small town nearby with his first wife, a city woman. There had been no children born in the second marriage and now the village woman wanted a baby. She was talking with the man about this.

It had taken Maggie a long time to realize that several types of marriage were possible here. There were those which gave the family prestige and economic security, but provided almost nothing for the husband and wife involved. That was the way this woman's marriage was. Rose was in the same situation. The only way Rose would have any standing on her own was through her children and now. . . . Maggie's heart cried out, "Oh, Rose, Rose! I'm so sorry."

Maggie came back to the moment, as Alfred made his third trip through the living room. "And what about you, Ada? Will your pa choose a husband for you?"

"No," Ada answered quickly. "He says I am too educated to marry with a village man. He says I can choose a big shot!" And then Ada's eyes twinkled, "But I say, Papa, I marry with young man."

"Did your pa agree to that?"

"He said we will see and that I was a clever girl. Then he said if I find a fine, young man he may agree."

"Good," Maggie said. "Then you will find plenty of fine, young men. You are pretty and clever!"

Ada laughed shyly, and added a thought. "I will find a good man, too."

"Ah, that's even better," Maggie agreed, thinking about John. "It is best to ask God for one good man!"

Ada rose. "I must go. I cannot find a taxi if it gets late."

Maggie extended her hand. "I'm so glad you came. I'm glad to know about Rose. Take care."

As Maggie opened the front door she noticed the workmen were still standing by the porch. She chuckled, "Oh, you not work today? It be three o'clock all day long?"

The men looked up sheepishly. "No, Missy, we wait to call taxi for the girl."

"Oh," Maggie kidded. "You get taxi for everyone? There goes old man who needs taxi!" She pointed toward a man on the path with a suitcase on his head. "That suitcase plenty heavy. You can carry it?"

The men looked nervously at the ground, but were not ashamed enough to help the old man. Ada stepped off the porch, waved, and walked away with an easy, graceful stride. The men followed two steps behind.

Maggie watched as Ada stopped for a moment to look at the huge tree which was a landmark on the campus. It had pitchfork-like props, which supported the tree at the bottom of the trunk. Maggie had read that this type of prop was a phenomenon only seen in the tropics. Ada turned to wave again and the tree's kapok fluff came down like feathers all around her. Maggie thought about "Camelot" where the princess rode through the forest in a snowstorm. That sight had been beautiful, too. Maggie wondered what the end of Ada's story would be. Would she live happily ever after, or be like Rose?

Ada wasn't the sister Maggie had expected Rose to have. Neither was she the usual girl who left home at the age of six to go to another country to school. Ada was so confident and friendly. Ada reminded Maggie of Caesar, who had been at Gbolupa, since the third grade. He was capable and outgoing. He had said, "My teachers are more like parents to me than my own parents."

That was the joy of living on campus. Producing beautiful people—that was it. Maggie had never known before how the students of Gbolupa might look to an outsider. Did some of them look like Ada had looked to her? Maggie began to pat herself on the back, but then she realized Caesar and Ada might have been the way they were regardless of where they went to school. Why did some people bloom and some wilt like Rose? Was it attitude or intelligence or matching the school to the pupil or the teachers? Maggie gave up her answer search and decided to be happy with what she had seen. Students were a promise, a possibility, and how wonderful to see a result like Ada.

Maggie turned her attention back to packing, eager to get the living room in some order before John and the MK's came from school. Maggie was almost through with one bookshelf when she came to a book of poems written by the students in a creative writing course she had taught several semesters back. She'd been too busy for that course, but it had been interesting.

"The Day Mama Died," was the first poem in the student-produced book, whose pages weren't quite cut evenly. Maggie remembered when that poem had been read in class. She hadn't dared ask then, but she had later and knew the poem was a real happening; a real experience of Moo Moo's. "Rain in the Bush"; "Devil Dancers"; "The Cooking Fire." These were the lives of some of the students too. Now that she was actually packing to leave, Maggie wondered how it would feel not to be on campus. Not to hear the bells for every student activity every day of the week. Not have someone at the door all day long.

James, Rose, Roland, the women. Maggie began to take tender inventory of her friends. The chief. Now how would you describe the chief to the people back home. Maggie thought of the day he had waited by the path to tell June the latrine was finished. He had a natural dignity. He wore no short trousers like the other men in the village. His were always long and topped by a country shirt with embroidery at the collar and the sleeves. His customary black hat was made in the shape of a short cylinder and embroidered in orange. He wore plastic sandals like everybody else, but always walked fast and with purpose.

The chief was even shorter than most of the men who were very short by any United States standard. Short—yes, but somehow head and shoulders above the rest in understanding. The day he had come to John about the stabbing had proved that. After John had taken the man to the hospital for stitches, the other men had palavered and been puzzled. But the chief knew all about it. He even knew who did it. He had said that much only a few days later. "Nah, he not stabbed at Hallah Camp. He stabbed in Lincolntown but a man there take him back to Hallah Camp to protect his village brothers."

John had asked about the source of that information and the chief had detoured. "These things come out by themselves. I not say this until the trial. By then everybody can know. Everybody can be happy."

John had continued the questioning. "You mean you know who did it, but you won't say? You'll wait until people talk it and then the truth will finally come out and then you'll have a trial."

The chief had smiled. "Yah, that the way. Then no more palaver. It finisho!" The chief had brushed his hands together indicating his hands would be clear.

When John's face had lit in a grin, the chief had smiled, too. John proceeded on a more personal basis. "Chief, you OK. How many cases of palaver you cut?"

The chief threw his head back. He laughed softly. Something John had never seen him do before. "I chief twenty years." He hesitated as the years of settling marital and civil cases rolled through his mind. He could remember only a few cases each year—the important or different ones. The others ran together. "I cut plenty, plenty palaver."

As John continued to study the chief, he grew uncomfortable, and rose to leave. John took his extended hand and felt how hard and rough it was. Five-cent pieces and a cutlass had filled that hand for many years. He owned nothing else except a mud-stick house and four wives. The first wife he seemed to have affection for. The others he tolerated. His children, though, were different—particularly his two older boys. John asked about them.

"How is Homolu?"

"I send him to Muslim school in other country soon."

"Oh, I miss him too much. Every day he plays in my yard with Mark."

The chief looked sad, too. "I miss him, too. My oldest boy he be Muslim. He go to Muslim school. My second boy he be Christian. He stay at Gbolupa."

It had taken John several days to figure that one out. Finally he had told Maggie. "It's concensous agreement, the group rather than the individual. See, some of the chief's people are Muslim. Some are Christian. If he sends one boy to each type of school, he pleases everybody. That's the village way."

The village way. It was the African way. Maggie continued all that week to think about how to describe the village way to those she would meet on furlough. She, also, worried about Rose. The more she thought about her, the more discouraged she became. What about Rose? Again and again Maggie had asked the Lord. But always there remained an unanswered question. Late one night when Maggie couldn't sleep, she went to the living room and opened her notebook. How many random thoughts it contained about Rose. Then a simple message came, "Consider Hannah."

Maggie quickly opened the Bible, which had been laying in her lap. She found the Hannah story in 1 Samuel. Maggie read rapidly. Almost immediately she began to see the similarity between Rose's and Hannah's situations—outdoor cooking pots, mud houses, polygomy, divided homes; husbands of small faith; living with people who worshiped many gods; and no children. Imagine that! Three thousand years separated the two women and yet human problems remained the same. Maggie rocked for several minutes thinking and considering.

The Hannah story wasn't very encouraging in the beginning. But what a climax! For true, for true! Maggie began to summarize. Hannah's desires and needs were not met at first. Her circumstances were used by God to produce a disciplined, godly woman. God finally knew Hannah was ready for the son she had prayed for. What a mother she was! What a man her son became! The greatest prophet of his day!

In it all Maggie read God's promise. There was a possibility, a possibility even for Rose. What could God do with a Christian preacher in the Muslim-animistic area where Rose lived?

Maggie closed her Bible and the next day began a letter to Rose. Her hopes soared as she wrote. "I have just read about Hannah and her prayers. What deliverance God brought to people through her!"

19
Furlough

"Funny how everyone comes when you're leaving and have a suitcase to pack," John commented from his position on top of the overflowing suitcase he was trying to close.

"Well, leaving is a prod for people to do what they wanted to all along—say thanks," Maggie replied with a glance in John's direction. "And packing is the prod toward everything that I should have done, but don't have time for now. Some things will soon be out of grasp. Catch it. Catch it."

John didn't take time to figure out what Maggie meant by the last remark. Instead he picked up his new chief's robe. "This is quite a gift. Do you think it will make me look like a chief?"

"No," Maggie laughed, "and it won't make you wise, either!"

John put the robe beside the other gifts in the suitcase. Since none of them were expected, there was not enough room for any of them. "All I need now is wisdom to get these things inside this one bag."

John's packing continued into the night and he only had time for a few hours of sleep before getting up at five to make an early morning flight. The rest of the morning was a blur. The plane was over the Sahara Desert before John moved a sleeping Sam to another seat so he could flop down beside Maggie. "We made it! Would you believe, we really made it?"

Maggie turned sharply to look into John's face. Was he talking about packing, farewells, or the hurried trip to the airport? Maggie sighed and leaned back in her seat. "My mind hasn't quite caught up with my body. I feel like I'm still dragging an overloaded sack of rocks uphill. The rocks keep spilling out and rolling downhill. I can't quite collect everything."

John turned bewildered, "Now what does that mean?"

"I'm not certain. I guess I haven't had time to evaluate the things that happened to us in West Africa, but I know one thing for certain—I'm so glad to be going home!"

Maggie's mind flew ahead to where she wished her body was. She could see her mom and dad at the airport. Her heart leaped—dear Mom and

Dad, always so concerned and expecting so much. But now she was glad they had. God, education, family loyalty, and hard work were the things that counted with them. Maggie smiled as she thought how many times in her childhood her father had said, "Do you think you'll amount to something someday?"

Had he really wondered? Or was he just enjoying dreaming about the future? He had never doubted his children or their future. He had too much confidence in God for that. But times had been hard. He'd lived through the depression and the hard years after that. Maggie was glad now that he was what people at home called "prosperous" and that her mom had the new house she'd always wanted. Her mom's life had been her children and now with them launched Maggie had read a new interest in spiritual things in her mom's letters. How long Maggie had prayed for that! As she thought about them, Maggie got excited. Almost like Mark and Karen, who had finally quit chattering long enough to go to sleep in the seat across the aisle.

"Why the silly grin?"

Maggie, turned, startled by John's question. "Oh, just contemplating the small pleasures of going home."

John was too tired for serious conversation and his mind drifted as the experiences of his first term in Africa caught up with him. He held a few that seemed important and studied them. All the adjustments would make any psychiatrist interested in the results. Still the big question remained—what next? John was certain the Lord wasn't leading him back to Gbolupa. But would the new job he wanted to do open up? Why hadn't God given him the answer yet? John turned to the view out the window. Soon he was absorbed in the miles of sand which stretched in every direction. Even from the plane's height he could see the wind shifting the sand into patterns which swirled and rose, turned, and then lay still.

John watched for twenty minutes and then realized he had seen absolutely nothing but hills of sand—no trees, no people, no huts. Quickly he calculated that the plane had flown over about two-hundred miles in the short time he had studied the landscape. John looked in all directions and still saw nothing except sand. Suddenly he was glad he was passing over the Sahara Desert rather than crash-landing there. Even as his eyes closed, though, he still saw the beauty of the place—the giant sand paintings of God.

John was asleep when the plane flew over Paris and London. By the time Sam woke him, the plane was over the Atlantic and on a course which passed over Greenland and landed in Chicago.

The custom line in Chicago was a long one. Maggie stood with the suitcases and Sam in tow while John talked to the ticket agent. Yes, they had missed their plane. No, there wasn't another.

Karen began to moan, "Grandma won't know where we are."

Both Karen and Mark wiped away tears and the ticket agent picked up a phone. Soon Karen ran toward Maggie with the news, "We won't be but an hour late."

Five hours later the plane was over St. Louis and Karen asked for the hundredth time, "When will we land? Will Grandma know Sam?"

For what seemed like hours they circled the airport. Finally, with an unexpected lunge the plane dropped into a steep decline. In a few minutes the pilot explained to the worried passengers that there had been a lag in the traffic pattern and the tower had said to come down in a hurry.

As the plane door opened, Maggie remembered the statement Mark had made many times in the past years, "Tomorrow let's go to America. It's my best place. Grandma and Grandpa are there!"

Tomorrow had finally come and Mark rushed to be the first off the plane. Everyone else had the same idea and Maggie was trapped by hand luggage. Ahead she could see that John and Sam were making progress. Mark and Karen were already on the bus that was waiting to carry the passengers to the terminal.

Finally Maggie was down the plane steps. She held back tears as her feet raced over United States soil. Home! Home! It was so good to be in the United States of America! She pushed through the bus door and took the last seat. The bus immediately pulled up several hundred yards and the Blakes got off. They hurriedly counted hand luggage, and, being certain that Karen and Mark still had theirs strapped securely on their backs, started down several block-long corridors. Finally they rounded a corner and Karen yelled, "There they are. I see them!"

Mark broke into a run that ended a step shy of his grandpa. Karen was right behind him and with a loud, "Yippee," shot through the air like a cowboy bucked off a bronco, and landed in Grandma's secure arms.

Maggie tucked Sam under one arm and with her oversized purse in the other, she, too, ran forward. There was only a moment's shyness before Sam surrendered to his Grandma's kisses. Maggie held both of them close until Sam began to wiggle. Had it really been more than three years? Maggie was not quite certain until she drew back and looked closely at her mother's face. Then she was shocked. The time lapse film had run through too rapidly. Maggie could scarcely comprehend the change.

Her mother's unsteady voice began, "I can't believe Sam. I'm so glad you sent pictures every few months or we wouldn't know him. This big boy certainly doesn't look like the small baby who left here."

By this time Karen and Mark were making their second round of hugging and Maggie moved with Sam to where her dad stood. He was trying hard to contain his tears and Maggie's composure completely collapsed. They both wept as their arms met.

A curious old man stopped to watch all the hugging and crying and Mark broke the spell with his usual friendly manner. "I haven't seen my grandma for three years. See! Here she is." He held her arm and pushed her forward.

The old man grinned broadly to indicate he understood and went on down the corridor as the Blake family turned their attention to retrieving their suitcases.

As they walked toward the conveyor belt, Maggie noticed a slight limp in her dad's step. Suddenly she realized the letters had not told all. Her parents hadn't wanted to worry her with their health problems. Maggie wondered if parents ever got over trying to protect their children—maybe that's why they had been so apprehensive about West Africa.

Maggie flinched as she realized the time had come when the pattern would be reversed—she would have to protect her parents. This thought left her close to tears again and she focused on the conveyor belt which refused to be slowed down. One suitcase came around for the third time before John grabbed it. Then they all laughed and Grandma hugged Sam again to make certain he was real and not just in the dream she had been holding.

Grandpa began, "Honey, everybody won't be over tonight to see you, but they all said to call when we got in."

Maggie looked at her watch and calculated what time it actually was with the seven hour time difference. "Midnight! But it's midnight here, Dad!"

"But you didn't think anyone would go to sleep, did you?" he said in a pleased tone.

The sack of rocks that had kept spilling over in her mind when Maggie got on the plane in West Africa began to roll again. She tried to understand what it actually meant to have your sisters and brothers waiting by a telephone. Maggie wondered what had happened in their world—what else the letters hadn't told. How many details she had to catch up on. Her tried mind refused to go further. "OK, let's get all this luggage in the car. It will be another two hours before we get to the house."

It was almost dawn before Karen and Mark finally quit asking questions, petting Grandpa's favorite dog, who still remembered them, and eating brownies. The telephone conversations continued until Maggie was completely exhausted emotionally and physically. The voices around her became distant as she realized it had been thirty-six hours since she had slept. She made her way to the bedroom, which was so familiar, gave it a quick once-over to find it unchanged, and went to sleep with the happy warmth of being with the family again.

A week later, the Blakes moved into a furloughing missionary residence in a town close to John's parents. Maggie could hardly believe their good fortune when she stepped into the house that already had chairs and drapes and a sofa and church members with outstretched hands. Maggie had been so long on the giving end she hardly knew how to receive. Karen and Mark's responses were to run from room to room deciding which had been decorated for them. Quickly Mark returned, "Mom, Mom, come, see. They do have a bedroom for a boy here! Come!"

Mark grabbed Maggie and almost dragged her away from the church members, who smiled at Mark's delight. Mark ran down the hall and opened a door and stood aside with a grand gesture. "See! All for me!"

There it was—twin beds, blue bedspreads, and drapes with a racing car design. There was also a chest, pictures, and even a racing car holding a floral arrangement. "Wow!" Maggie exclaimed. "It's neat, Mark. Do you like it?"

"It's super and I can have a friend stay all night in the top bunk." Mark bounced up on the end of the bed and patted the mattress.

Maggie countered, "But you don't know anyone yet!"

"I will soon, though," Mark dashed out of his room and headed for the back door. As he cruised through the kitchen the sight of the refrigerator stopped him. He swung the door open, peered inside and exclaimed, "Karen, Karen, real Pepsi!"

He grabbed a bottle and found the opener which someone had placed in the proper kitchen drawer, just as Karen burst into the room. "Pepsi? Real Pepsi?"

She looked at the bottle in Mark's hand and then checked the refrigerator to see if there was more where that bottle had been. "Oh, boy! I've waited three years for a taste of Pepsi and to watch television. Did you see that neat TV set?"

Maggie watched as half of Mark's drink disappeared before she went back to the dining room. Table, chairs, buffet, and what was this? A close look revealed it was an original oil painting and Maggie wondered if one of the women in the living room had been the artist. Lovely. Very nice.

Before she got back to the living room, where the women waited, Maggie's mind traveled over the part of the house she had seen. Three bedrooms with all the beds made, a dining room, and a living room. Maggie could hardly believe this "Alice in Wonderland House." She was moved as she looked at the women who sat on the living room sofa.

"It's too wonderful to walk into a house which is all ready for living. I can't believe it. The children are thrilled and I don't know how we can thank you. We are grateful to you and to the Lord for this house and for the car which has been loaned to us and for the thrill of being in the United States of America again."

Maggie didn't know how to continue and looked toward John, who finished the thank you's.

One of the women rose and Maggie quickly surmised that she was the official spokesman for the women's group who had served as a welcoming committee. The woman opened her mouth, looked carefully at Maggie who was wiping her eyes, and hesitated. Instead of speaking, she blew her own nose and the other women looked at the floor. Finally she began, "I really don't know what to say. You are the first missionaries to live in our house and we were afraid you wouldn't like it." The other women nodded their heads. "Really you seem so pleased with it that we are quite overcome. It's a real pleasure for the church to have you here." She paused for a minute and no words came. She looked a little embarrassed for she had never been speechless before. John rushed to shake her hand.

"We're thrilled. You can be certain we love the house. Having a place to move into is something else. Just wonderful."

The other women rose and John shook several other extended hands. Seeing that the women were still caught up with an emotion he could not quite explain, John offered a light touch. "What I really like is strawberry malts and, do you know, I saw a place to buy one only two blocks from this house. Now that, ladies, is real planning. A strawberry never, ever grew in West Africa and I like them too much. A malt will be like a drink of water to a thirsty traveler in the middle of the Sahara. I'm gonna be real happy here."

The women smiled. Many of them said, "We're so glad you're here," and then left.

Maggie and John toured the house and then turned toward the kitchen. Maggie said, "Let's see what they brought for lunch."

"Not until I have a strawberry malt!"

"But lunch is ready the women said!"

"But I need a strawberry malt just like Karen needed a Pepsi—right now."

Maggie laughed. "OK, Flash," she said, using the name she preferred when she wanted to remind John of his foolishness.

John, with a half-grin that indicated he got the message, grabbed the car keys and fled out the door with Sam right behind him. Maggie was left alone to make careful note of what the women had put in each room. Great. The kitchen had a mixer, toaster, dishes, pans, and everything else Maggie could think of that was necessary. As her house inventory continued, Maggie's spirits soared. The women hadn't missed anything. Maggie had to think real hard and along the personal lines to find anything else she could possibly use. By the time John returned, though, Maggie was ready with a short shopping list. She had not missed seeing the large shopping center a couple of blocks away when they came by it on the way to the house. Maggie sat down to lunch, anticipating her first adventure in a real big shopping center. How she hated shopping in West Africa, but here she would make up for lost time.

Within a week the Blakes were at home in their missionary residence and Maggie had learned culture shock could work in reverse. First there had been the phone at her mom's house the night they arrived. Maggie had picked it up only to realize she had forgotten how to dial. She was too embarrassed to say anything as she stumbled through the first numbers. Then there had been the sugar bowl on the table. Maggie had looked at it and seen ants everywhere. She had blinked and on the second look found no ants at all. Then when she got cold one night she automatically dismissed the idea until she suddenly realized she was not in the tropics.

Furloughing missionary conference came next. "How was your first term?" was the question most often discussed as Maggie greeted friends she had not seen since orientation. It took only a day to group the answers. There were those who said, "Ours was great. I used talents I never knew I had." "The work is growing. People came to know the Lord." "The mountains are beautiful. It's a great place to live."

Maggie was stunned. So all first terms weren't like hers. Her mouth opened during several conversations but those who were more enthusiastic gave answers before she could speak. After all what could she say? "Our mission was at a transition stage," or "Well, the tropics are harsh." She didn't dare say, "I was defeated most of the time!"

Maybe she just had a rotten attitude. By bedtime, Maggie had decided that couldn't be all of the answer. After all, the tropics weren't Switzerland. Why couldn't she live somewhere beautiful and cool? Someplace where there was fall? Why couldn't West Africa have a great revival? Maggie fell asleep with a smile on her face as she envisioned the Blakes next term in a wonderful, wonderful place of no discouragements.

The days flew and soon Karen and Mark were enrolled in school. John and Maggie found themselves scheduled to speak almost every Sunday, and often during the week, at churches and civic meetings. Before Maggie could decide what she wanted to say, she was on stage.

Her first talk had come the week after she got home. It was at a Vacation Bible School where she showed the artifacts that had been squeezed into the overloaded suitcases. The children immediately sprang to life with questions. Is that a real boa constrictor skin? Do elephants really have wire-like things inside their tails which can be made into bracelets? Do people beat drums all the time? Do they wear long dresses with fancy embroidery like you have on? Maggie was surprised by all the enthusiasm and found herself giving out information that before had seemed irrelevant and unimportant.

By the time she got through her fifth speech she found she was sharing on a deeper level. She was amazed at how the puzzles in her own life were beginning to take form. As Maggie listened to John's sermons she realized something was happening to him also. There was a new confidence in God and a certainty that hadn't been there before. He warmed to West Africa with each speech.

No one was more surprised than Maggie and John when insights came in words that grabbed those who listened and moved them. Everywhere they spoke God brought people to greater faith. Ten GA campers became Christians one night; twenty the next night. One church had a revival. These results were so in contrast to what the past three years had been that Maggie knew they were of the Lord. Suddenly seeing them, though, Maggie realized they were not what was important. Nothing had happened during her third year in Africa and yet Maggie had trusted; she had learned to wait. Now God was ready. His Holy Spirit was leading. Now God had chosen to give tangible and obvious results.

Maggie smiled to herself as she thought about the caterpillar climbing the wall back in her house in West Africa. He hadn't known where he was going, either, until he got there. He didn't see the view until he had time to catch his breath on one of the plateaus. Furlough had given Maggie time to stop and see and hold close. God's gifts were there. They had always been there wrapped in his shining love.

20
Treasure Hunt

Maggie was at the rusty typewriter trying to organize a speech that had to be given that night. Her mind refused to stay put and wandered back to the packing. In one corner of the dining room were thirty pairs of tennis shoes in various sizes. On the sofa in the living room was a case of toothpaste. On the chairs were underclothes that needed to be sorted into sizes, packed, and labeled. The new refrigerator was in the church's parking lot and John was filling it with paper towels. Toys rolled all over the floor as Sam dug to the bottom of a box John had just packed. Maggie jumped up, ushered Sam out into the backyard, and then sat down again.

Back to the speech. But nothing came. John walked into the room, sorted through new sheets and towels and asked, "Where did you get these?"

Maggie didn't answer until Sam let the cat in for the third time. The half-grown Siamese playfully darted to the sofa and began to sharpen his claws on the fringe around the bottom. "Oh, no, the church's sofa!" Maggie groaned and grabbed the cat. "I'm going crazy. All this packing to do and Sam and that cat and a GA meeting this afternoon and a civic club tonight!"

John, who was used to Maggie getting excited and then settling down to get everything done, paid no attention to this outburst. Instead he continued to walk around the room, this time looking at some gifts the church members had brought. Maggie turned to a more cheerful thought. "You know what I'm going to enjoy about going to heaven?" Before John had time to contemplate, Maggie went on, "I won't have to pack!"

John thought of all the packing a missionary wife had to do. From the United States to overseas with enough things for three or four years and then maybe a couple of moves on the field, followed by storing things to come for furlough. Then it was buying, packing, crating, and beginning the process all over again. In between times there were suitcases to pack. John patted Maggie's shoulder. "I see why. It's kind of nice to think about going someplace where somebody else has done all the work!"

John's last statement grabbed Maggie. Yes, somebody else had done the planning even for this trip. Maggie remembered the moment when she had finally been assured she was going back to Africa. She had been on her knees thanking God for the wonderful experiences they'd had on furlough. Then she began to praise God, realizing her words would never really be big enough for that.

Then God dealt with Maggie in a way that was special and different from anything she had experienced in her thirty years as a Christian. There had been no audible voice, but Maggie received and understood the unspoken words that came: "You are doubting! I want you to know I was in control of everything that happened to you in Africa!"

God brought to Maggie's memory her words from that first morning in Africa. "I wonder. I wonder what we've gotten ourselves into?"

That small seed of doubt had grown as the puzzles continued to seem impossible to solve. But now that God had spoken, Maggie recognized this as the answer she had long ago asked for. The three and a half years between question and answer seemed short for the solution was faith's springboard.

"Everything!" The dominant force in every situation.

"Everything!" Maggie heard clearly, and she was amazed. The treasure hunt of life was to find God in all of life's experiences. To focus on nothing smaller than God himself.

God. God! God was the answer. He was the jewel more beautiful than diamonds and emeralds. With that revelation came the ability to praise God for the circumstances and situations which had before seemed only hard.

God was big enough to handle it all and yet, Maggie was astonished by his attention to personal things. God had time to send special letters to all his children. Hadn't his private message to her just been delivered? Yes, God had noted her greatest sin but, instead of feeling rejected, Maggie felt loved.

As God drew Maggie close she got another shock. She could not take her place in God's family and exclude others who were, also, a part of the family. What about Corinne?

Corinne! She was always there. She had been like a barbed wire fence that Maggie had encountered years ago on her dad's farm. No matter how you approached the prickly wire you always got hurt. Maggie's knees carried plenty of scars to prove that.

Finally you learned to stay away from barbed wire. That had been the way Maggie handled Corinne. Now Maggie knew she had not had Corinne's best interest at heart; she had not really loved her.

Maggie confessed her lack of love to God and found instant forgiveness and acceptance. Then an instruction, "I've freed you. Now forgive Corinne, and receive her as a sister."

Maggie felt love flow into her in a measure she had not known the moment before. She realized she could do what God was asking. God's love was certain. It would flow through Maggie and reach Corinne. Maggie thought about the letter she would write to Corinne and she was already assured it would be received.

But there was more. God reached even deeper into Maggie's thoughts and emotions and this probing hurt enough to bring great sobs. Maggie had no idea where God was leading, but she submitted.

God exposed the red, angry sores caused by the illnesses, the deaths, the sorrows, the failures. Like a skillfull surgeon God began to cut away the diseased, unhealthy parts. His great right hand removed sorrow, anxiety, and pain and within the same space of time replaced them with joy and peace.

From probing, to removing, to making new and whole—it was all completed in a few moments. Maggie felt like a person who had been under psychiatric treatment for years and had just been released—completely healthy!

Maggie would learn in the days to come that there would be no relapses. She could talk about her early experiences on the mission field without anxiety or pain and would praise the Lord for each.

How long Maggie stayed on her knees she could not remember. Slowly she came back to her own bedroom, aware that God had dealt in a special and unique way with her and that the victory was completely of him.

A few weeks later, Maggie got down to serious dialogue about the Blake's return to Africa. Jill, her sister, was visiting at the time and she, John, Sam, and Maggie were on their way to a drive-in restaurant for John's favorite treat—a strawberry malt. Months back, John had lost count of the malts he had consumed. However, the bathroom scales indicated it was too many.

"All this," Maggie began, in an attempt to focus John's thoughts on other things besides strawberry malts. She gestured out the window as the car sped past orange and red leaves on the ground. Overhead the sun shone with a warmth that could only be appreciated on a chilly day. Beautiful. How could any season, anywhere look better? Maggie tried to put it into words, but came up only with, "All this, and God, too."

She put her arm through her sister's arm. "Well, little sister, we've had a great furlough. I can't believe all that has happened. It's been so wonderful to be with the family again and to see how your girls have grown beautiful and nice. We have so much to be thankful for."

"But furlough is ending." Maggie's voice was silent as she thought about what that meant. The decision had been made. Now there was the leaving. Her parents; John's parents; the family—how they'd miss them. Maggie expected to feel sad for she had long ago named leavings with the "sad-glad" experiences. But this time she was mostly glad. Somehow this amazed her. She looked up and her heart spoke. "Even this, God. Thank-you. You've even done this for me!"

Maggie wanted Jill to understand. "Mom and Dad are sort of upset. You know that Jill. They're half-hearted about our going again. I guess in a way we don't want to go either. But we're not running away or hunting a better job or wanting to travel. I hope you realize that and know because we love each of you our natural choice would be to stay right here. We're going because we have to go."

Jill looked up in understanding. "Sure, Maggie," she said through her tears. "I understand. We'll miss you, though, but we know God has sent you there and he's with you, just as he is with us here. We want you to go."

Maggie felt better. Jill's words, she was certain were those of most of the family, although the rest would never be able to bring them to the surface.

Maggie thought of the letter she had received that morning. "The chief's son at the Muslim school died." Those were bitter words. Maggie wondered if June knew yet. How many trips had she and June made to Careysburg when that boy had amoeba? The letter had said he'd been sick for a month. He probably could have lived if he had had the right medicine. But he hadn't! The chief would say in his stoic way, "Allah. It's Allah's will."

How Maggie hated those words. How could people call anyone god, except the one true God as revealed in Jesus. That God never condemned and killed. Maggie knew. God showed her that. She could not doubt his goodness and love.

What had James said after he became a Christian? "I never knew that people had a choice. I just thought your ma born you and if you were lucky you lived a few years before you died. Now I know that God frees people to choose the kind of life that will lead to health and happiness."

The women in the village; the students—some still didn't know there was a choice. Maggie prayed: *Dear God, the first time I went out not knowing what was there. Oh, how I wanted to come home. But now I want to go back. It isn't doing things. It's understanding and presenting you that counts. In fact, you've said ability to witness is the greatest gift of the Spirit* (1 Cor. 14:1). *Give me that gift.*

The brown leaves on the road were caught by the wind and blew onto the windshield as John pulled into the drive-in restaurant. That day the fall turned to winter and snow fell. The next month the Blake's crates left from New Orleans and only a few weeks of furlough remained.

The schedule became more crowded and Maggie wondered how they'd get it all done. Finally there was nothing left except the final good-byes, speaking at her home church, and packing the suitcases. Maggie turned her attention to her home church. What should she say? It hadn't actually been her plan to speak that last week, particularly not at her home church, where there would be too many memories. But that was the way it had worked out and Maggie believed God had plans of his own.

The day came, cold and beautiful with a soft cushion of snow on the small, steepled building. Maggie, John, and the children went inside to be greeted by all of Maggie's old Sunday School teachers except the two who had recently gone to heaven. As Maggie looked from familiar face to familiar face she realized there had been a change in the people. Before she had gone to Africa the people had worried and asked about illnesses and snakes and malaria. Now their questions were about the work. The people were optimistic. Why the change?

Was it that Maggie was living proof that God can take care of his own? Had she become their ambassador to the world? their claim to some fame as Sunday School teachers? Maggie had still not decided as she arose to speak, but she was moved. She realized this would be her hardest speech for already all the old people in the church were wiping their eyes.

Maggie hesitated for only a moment and then found the same Spirit which had been so close to her in her own bedroom only a few months earlier. The message came with no more anxiety or hesitation: "I wonder if you ever considered what houseboys, night watchmen, ants, tropical heat, shared mission cars, and beggars have to do with faith. Well, I never had until I went to Africa and then I went through a faith revolution."

When Maggie finished some thirty minutes later, she was amazed that she had shared personal things she would normally have avoided even in one-to-one conversations. She sat down with a grateful heart and watched as the Holy Spirit continued to work. Until the service ended, Maggie thought about how faith produces faith and doubt produces doubt.

Then a small girl came to the platform to ask, "Are you a real live missionary?"

Maggie reached out to pat the blond hair. "I am, sweetheart and did you know you can be a missionary right here?"

The child's curiosity was satisfied and she turned to make way for others who offered words of admiration and encouragement. As old friends passed, Maggie made a mental picture of each. These she tucked carefully in her heart along with the pictures of her sisters and brothers, who that week had also come to say good-bye. Maggie knew in the four-year term that lay ahead she would pull these pictures to the surface many times and they would warm her and drive away discouragement and loneliness.

The day ended so well that Maggie almost forgot that tomorrow they would be on the plane. The next day when the time came to say good-bye to her mom and dad, Maggie again realized life was constant change—beginnings and endings. That was the rhythm. Good-byes were a part of the whole, but there was strength in knowing they were not the most important part.

Maggie took one long look at her folk's new house and turned to them. She kissed her mother's soft cheek and held her again. They both smiled as they parted. Maggie hugged her father. She had never loved him more, but no tears came as she read her dad's nonverbal communication. He was proud. He would not want her to stay.

There would be constant communication through letters and thoughts and prayers would fly back and forth. Distance between people was not written in miles. Maggie's parents were close to her. They'd always be close.

Maggie crossed the yard to the car where her brother waited. Karen, Mark, and Sam seated themselves so they could see out the rear window of the station wagon and they waved until the grandparents turned slowly and went inside.

There was snow on each side of the road, but what Maggie saw was red clover, corn, and soybeans—the green fields of home. And then two children on tractors raced toward an open gate.

Slowly the past faded as the car turned the first corner. Maggie looked beyond the horizon. They were going to where the palm trees and ocean stood. To a new house by another African path. To the job in broadcasting John had hoped for. That would be like charting a new route through the Sahara Desert. There would be many starts and a lot of back tracking and starting over before workable plans and methods came. The results might be poor for years.

But new paths were never clear until . . . Maggie smiled. Yes, until you got the right guide and had a personal interview with him. Then you began to see the possibilities and understand what God could do.

As they approached the airport, some of the words of Psalm 139 that Maggie had read, before dawn that morning came back, "If I ride the morning winds to the fartherest oceans, . . . If I try to hide in the darkness, the night becomes light around me. For even darkness cannot hide from God" (vv. 9–12, TLB).

The Blakes were journeying with God!